LONDON FROG

A TODD GLEASON CRIME NOVEL

LONDON FROG

JOSEPH PITTMAN

FIVE STAR

An imprint of Thomson Gale, a part of The Thomson Corporation

THOMSON

™

GALE

Detroit • New York • San Francisco • New Haven, Conn. • Waterville, Maine • London

This one's for Phil & Liz Mann

"So vast a sum, all in actual cash, seemed next to incredible."

—*The Adventures of Tom Sawyer*

CONTENTS

PROLOGUE 11

PART ONE: LONDON CALLING 19

PART TWO: CAMBRIDGE CIRCUS 131

PART THREE: A NEW YORK MINUTE 249

EPILOGUE 370

PROLOGUE

Not without a sense of irony did he arrive at the very low-brow Sam's Diner in his shiny new Beemer. His name was Donald Birdie and recently he had hit the big time—the lottery. That accounted for the nice wheels, which even today, six months since winning the jackpot, still caught the envious glances of the locals. But that was life in small-town New York State; a celebrity had been born overnight and even the few who didn't know him considered Birdie a friend. A few folks waved to Birdie as he stepped out of the luxury sedan, like the good suck-ups they were. You never knew when you might need a loan without the assistance of that tight-ass who ran the bank. Distracted, Birdie waved back anyway, a politician in training. His wife, Marta, had wanted tinted windows but Birdie, as he was called, remarked that would be a waste of money. Who else in town had tinted glass on their windshield? Everyone would know it was them, so what's the point, he remarked one night after a particularly unsatisfying night of love-making. Not even riches beyond avarice had cured Marta of her inhibitions.

Sam's Diner, a blip of a restaurant located in the center of a blip of a town called Tuckerville, was fairly empty at three o'clock in the afternoon, but Birdie supposed that was the point. The fewer people who were around, the fewer there were to possibly witness the exchange. In fact, two cars were leaving the parking lot as he approached the front door; one of the drivers waved a hand out his window. Birdie failed to acknowledge the man, busy counting the number of cars in the lot. Which would be two, his and, he presumed, that of the man he was to meet.

"What a jerk," was how the driver felt.

Birdie didn't hear him. He wasn't in the best of moods.

But he couldn't worry about that, not now. In a half hour's time the whole crappy affair, uh, business, would be behind him, that much he'd been assured. He grabbed the handle of the door to the diner with his right hand, even though he was left-handed. His left was already preoccupied, grasping a thick metal briefcase.

The diner was narrow, with a collection of single seats against a counter that ran the length of the room and opposite them, booths designed for either two or four people. Decorations were almost nil and the smell of grease pervaded; a no-nonsense atmosphere for no-nonsense food. Sam, the gray-haired owner and cook, was behind the register, greedily counting the lunchtime receipts. Betty, the lone waitress at this hour, sat at the counter reading the newspaper and popping bubbles. She had nothing else to do.

"Hey, Birdie, what brings you here?" Sam asked.

"An appointment—my, uh, financial advisor. Don't like him to come by the plant, you know?"

"Sure. That him?" he asked, indicating the lone man sitting inside the diner.

The man Birdie was meeting had taken a booth and looked very much the part of a big-shot money man. Three-button suit, probably some fancy European designer with an unpronounceable name. All those greedy guys were into fashion. (Except Sam the Diner Owner, dressed in splattered white.) Gotta look the part, that sort of big city bullshit. For Birdie, the small town existence was just fine for him, especially considering his recent windfall. He still paid ten bucks for a haircut at John's Barber Shop, right around the corner, same place he'd been going to since he was a kid. Same style cut, too, though he had much more gray now and John Junior was doing the cutting. As for the guy he was meeting with, he was one modern dude. Black hair slicked-back; the only concession to nonconformity was the two-day stubble gracing his face.

That, of course, was the little clue that something wasn't on the up and up.

"Mr. Birdie, glad you could make it," the man said.

Birdie slid into the booth, wiping away the sweat that had formed on his upper lip. It was only October but outside the air was around twenty degrees; snow covered the ground. Typical upstate weather.

"Like I had a choice."

The man just grinned, showing off deep dimples in his cheeks. "This is supposed to be a friendly meeting, Mr. Birdie, don't get your knickers in a bunch."

"My what in a what?"

Just then gum-snapping Betty popped over, inquiring if the gentlemen wanted anything to drink, eat. Coffee for two, skip the cream and sugar.

"You got a muffin?" the man asked. "I'm in the mood for a muffin with my coffee."

"Blueberry? Corn? Cranberry?"

"Oh, cranberry. And please, make my coffee to go." After Betty left, the man looked to Birdie and said, "You know the cranberry is very good for your heart, no matter what form you eat it in. Juiced or canned, you know like at Thanksgiving, even in a little muffin. Heard that on the news, of all places. You gotta stay healthy, you know. To enjoy life's many pleasures."

"You're a prick," Birdie responded.

The man frowned with obvious disappointment. "There's no reason to be so hostile, Mr. Birdie. This is a clean and clear business deal. No hard feelings."

"Humph. Tell that to my bank account."

"I could tell it to your wife."

Well, the mere mention of Marta sure shut Birdie up, at least until the coffee and cranberry muffin were served. Betty slapped a check down on the table and the man waited patiently for Birdie to claim it. Birdie wasn't pleased to be picking up this tab either, mumbling "bastard" as he looked at the three dollar cost. But as he complained, it gave the man a chance to slide the metal briefcase from Birdie's side of the booth to his, a swift motion that went undetected at first even by Birdie himself. He might be rich, but smart, nope. If he was, there was no way he'd have allowed himself to be put in this oh-so obvious predicament.

"Thanks," the man said.

Birdie noticed then the briefcase was gone from his side.

"You know, this is nothing but blackmail, pure and simple." He was getting flustered and was ten seconds away from exploding, from giving them both away. So the man had to remind Birdie what was at stake.

"There's that hostility again. I don't like that," the man said with a wave of his finger. "See, Birdie, had you kept your little prick—and from what I've heard, little is a generous description—had you kept it to yourself none of this might have happened. You screw the secretary with the big bazooms while the wifey's off at a church social, seems to me you're getting off easy. I'm only taking you for a small amount of your net worth; you can bet wifey'd take more—like everything."

"Okay, shut up about that, people in this town know me."

"So I've noticed. People wave to you like you're the fricking mayor. Hey, that's an idea, you could run for political office—you already know how to sleep around, so that makes you eminently qualified. You'd think there was something more original under the sun, huh?"

"I could kill you," Birdie said.

That certainly made the man laugh. He'd been threatened before, all empty promises. "I don't think so. What you've given me—compared to what you're going to receive every year for the rest of your life—it's not worth killing even a fly. And I'm not going to stay around and buzz in your ear, I'm outta here in moments. Just want to finish my muffin."

To prove his point, the man ripped into that muffin, making sure not to miss a single healthful cranberry. He might not even be thirty—well, soon he would be—but that didn't mean he didn't look after his health. As he chewed, the door to Sam's Diner opened and in walked one of Tuckerville's finest, a fresh-faced cop who didn't have to worry about cranberries or heart problems for decades, much less a razor. Still, the sight of the shiny badge startled the man. He watched carefully the next order of business.

"Hello, Mr. Birdie, how are things?"

"Oh, Officer Carter, just fine."

As harmless as their dialogue was, there was something about the eye contact that had the man worried. Knowing glances, as though this meeting was premeditated. The man felt himself caught in a small-town trap (redundant as that is) as inescapable for him now as some gas-pumping loser from the local high school. For a moment he wished the briefcase was still on Birdie's side of the booth, no transfer, no crime. The cop chose that moment to sit next to Birdie.

"Hi, Ed Carter, Tuckerville Police Department."

"Hi," the man said.

They shook hands like the polite folks they were.

"Don't believe I know your name—or your face, for that matter."

The man tossed Birdie an angry look. Birdie flipped back a smile. A wordless volley. Checking his watch, the man wondered what was keeping her. And just as he thought it, so came true his wish. Because the woman he had conjured in his mind took that opportunity to appear in real-life. She wasn't attractive enough to garner much attention from Sam or Betty, but Birdie certainly looked up.

"Marta!" Birdie exclaimed, silently cursing under his breath.

That was the man's cue.

He stood and excused himself. "Well, I see your wife has arrived. I know you need to discuss my proposals with her, so I'll depart and you can phone me later with your decision. You of course have my number." Birdie had no such thing, but nodded nonetheless. He had no choice, what with Marta, draped in her now customary fur and usual customary frown, having shown up so unexpectedly. On purpose. "Officer, a pleasure. Perhaps one day I might offer you some financial advice."

"Doubt it, what with the force's salary. Thanks, right kind of you." The cop looked as impotent as a Viagra salesman afraid to use his own product.

"Too bad. I have a real knack for making money."

And so with that double-edged remark and a tip of his head to Marta Birdie, the man departed Sam's Diner. He hadn't even left a crumb behind on his plate, and he'd taken his cup of his coffee. Almost as if his presence in town was an illusion. He hopped into his borrowed Jaguar, which was only slightly more ostentatious than Birdie's Beemer, drove to the outskirts of town, where the chewing gum factory was located, the big employer in the area. Birdie was management there, but the man's appointment, to be taken in the parking lot, was with a certain Miss November; swear to God, that was her real last name. Truth was, she looked more like a Miss July, her dyed blonde hair nicely contrasted with the deep tan she'd gotten from a recent trip to Florida. Business, her boss had insisted.

The man tossed her a bundle of greenbacks from the metal

briefcase. He had already budgeted for the necessary expense.

"Wasn't sure you'd live up to your part of the bargain," she said, stuffing the bills into her purse.

"You did your part—and very well, I might add," he said. "So I do mine. I'm an honest businessman, Bert."

Her first name was Bertha, and she insisted on being called Bert. Prettiest Bert you'd ever see, make Ernie go straight.

"Lovely doing business with you," the man said.

"Likewise," Miss November said, who had enjoyed herself so much in Florida she was thinking of returning there; solo this time.

Thirty minutes later the man was far away from stupid little Tuckerville, wherever the fuck that was. Somewhere between Albany and Syracuse, wherever the fuck they were. He was headed back to the city, the Big Apple, the only place that mattered, where he had already begun to plot his next con, his one final caper. He had always hoped to retire from this line of work by the age of thirty. He had that much confidence.

Confidence without caution, though, that led to cockiness, and that of course, led to getting caught. But by whom?

★ ★ ★ ★ ★

PART ONE
LONDON CALLING

★ ★ ★ ★ ★

CHAPTER ONE

Todd Gleason was holding a shiny new penny in his hand and staring at the frog tank when the phone rang. He grabbed at the receiver just before the second ring.

"Gleason."

"Todd, hi, it's Lucille—from Street Help." The Wall Street temp agency that sounded like a Times Square escort service. "I've got a gig for you, probably last at least three weeks. Good money."

Todd hated these calls. Oh, sure, the prospect of making some quick cash was never without its appeal but not when it involved shoving himself behind a desk from nine-to-five and beyond. This temp agency, though, they liked him and the offices he'd worked in liked him too, often asked for him back. They liked that he had more than a working knowledge of the finance industry, his once-upon-a-time imagined career choice. Problem was, Todd had other plans for the foreseeable future and so he was forced to turn down the lucrative offer from Lucille, who looked exactly like you'd imagine, big hair encircled by a fog of cigarette smoke; it was any wonder the only fires she had to put out were for high-paid executives in search of people to order in their lunch.

"Sorry, Lucille, maybe next time. I'll be out of town."

"Humph. Some life you lead, kid. Must be nice."

"All work, as the saying goes."

"Sure, kid, call me when you're done playing."

"Okey-dokey."

"Such a professional, no wonder they love you," she said with a phlegmy laugh.

They said goodbye and Todd hung up the phone and returned his attention to the frog tank. And to the penny, smooth between his finger pads.

"Okay, Toad, here goes, wish me luck," he said to the only other creature who shared the apartment. A three-year-old green frog who liked to splash around in his aquatic home. He'd cleverly been named Toad.

As for his owner, one Todd Gleason, thoughts of temp work faded from his mind as he began scratching away at the rectangular instant lottery card with the penny; tiny silver shavings littered his kitchen table in seconds. When the first square revealed ten thousand dollars, he knew he was a loser again. He shot a helpless look at the frog, who spoke nothing in reply, not even a croak. The second square revealed one dollar, and then the third, again with that teasing ten thousand dollars. Might as well toss it out now, there was no way he'd just won that much cash. Still, he kept going, optimism outweighing history. By the time all the squares were revealed, Todd had come up empty again. He hated these damn things. Most he'd ever won was ten bucks—and that after buying twenty of the damn dollar tickets. Disgusted by his uninterrupted streak of bad luck, he threw the card to the floor. It joined three other losing tickets he'd scratched at before Lucille's call.

"Let's hope those aren't an indication of how the trip's going to go," Todd said, sprinkling some foul-smelling tablets into the tank. Toad gobbled them up quickly.

Just then the buzzer to Todd's apartment sounded. Busy day, first a call for work and now a call . . . for what? It was five o'clock in the afternoon and he hadn't ordered in Chinese, he wasn't expecting company, and there was no way it was the car service, they weren't expected until eight tonight. Cautiously, he moved toward the window of his fifth-floor apartment, tried to look down at the street. In the darkness of a rainy winter's night, he couldn't see who was at the door. The angle was all wrong. The buzzer rang again and he decided he wasn't going to answer it. Hopefully whoever it was would just go away. But then the unexpected happened, he heard the buzzer sound in the apartment below his. Someone was trying to get into the building, to see him, and they'd annoy his neighbors to do it. And while you could reason that having Todd's buzzer go off at the same time as his neighbor's could be counted as coincidence, coincidence wasn't something he necessarily believed in. No, trust your instincts, he'd often told himself. Whoever the intruder was, he meant to intrude on his life. Wasn't that the very definition of intrusion? He needed to get out of here.

Good thing he'd turned down the work from Lucille. Good thing he was already packed. Good thing he'd already fed the frog.

No doubt the unidentified person had seen the lights on—that was the disadvantage of having a front-facing apartment. But he liked that he was on the top floor and that had won out when trying to decide whether to rent the apartment. With a quick wave to Toad and a plea not to run up the phone bill while he was gone, he grabbed his suitcase and his computer case and headed for the door. He opened it slowly, warily, wondering if the person had already gained entry to the building. Running footsteps echoing in the hallway answered that one. And so Todd made a fast escape, closing his door quietly, hearing the click of the lock with satisfaction. He retreated to the rear of the building, where a short staircase led to the building's roof. Up the stairs he went, gingerly so as not to attract attention. As he emerged onto the roof, the cold air swirling around him, he listened one last time.

"Dammit, Gleason, open the door, I know you're in there."

Followed by an angry pounding.

Whoever this stranger was, he knew his name. Did Todd recognize the voice? Only slightly. He certainly couldn't put a face with it, much less a name except for the fact that it began with a capital Trouble.

He closed the door to the roof, virtually locking himself up there. Except of course he had the key. He wouldn't need it, at least not that key. In Manhattan, with the buildings attached to each other, it was a simple step over to the next dwelling, where a similar-looking door awaited him. He slipped into the lock a key he'd made long ago for emergencies such as this and soon he was back indoors. He padded down the steps, the luggage a bit unwieldy but still manageable. When he got down to the building's front door, he hoped the stranger was still banging on his door. Stay all night if you want, Todd thought, give himself plenty of time to get out of town. Which had been the plan anyway, he would just have to be early getting to the airport.

Todd Gleason stepped onto Eighty-Eighth Street and First Avenue and hailed a passing cab. Miracle of miracles, what with this rain. He hated rain, spoiled his mood. For a second he wondered if he'd packed an umbrella.

"JFK," he said after settling into the back of the pine-scented cab. Better that than to smell the cabbie himself, he figured.

"Oh, no, not JFK, the traffic—it is veddy bad."

"License number what?" Todd said, taking out his cell phone. The threat of a complaint to the TLC always worked with these guys.

"It is your money," the cabbie murmured.

"I'm not worried," Todd replied, anticipating that after this trip, money would no longer be a problem and he'd never have to work another day in his life. Sorry, Lucille.

As the cab uselessly sped toward a crawling FDR Drive, Todd

24

wondered, did he have another problem on his hands? Who the hell had that guy been, and how did he track Todd Gleason down at an apartment that wasn't even rented in that name?

Todd smiled at his neighbor when he sat down. Usually he wasn't keen to meet people on airplanes, those close confines tended to prompt too many questions. Todd hated questions, they generally meant answers were expected. Still, he couldn't help himself tonight, the woman sitting by the window was a real looker. Some might have interpreted his smile as one of smug satisfaction, but on Todd it looked good, charming maybe, and the looker looked back with a smile all her own. One of those real flirty-like smiles, complete with a tilt of her blonde head. For a moment Todd worried he didn't look his best, since he'd caught the flight with only minutes to spare, pissing off the airline personnel who insisted that you get there nearly a freaking day before an international flight took off. Actually, he'd been at JFK's Terminal One since seven o'clock—after a two-hour trip through horrendous traffic from the East Side—but he had kept a low profile until the flight was called. He'd been through security, that wasn't the issue, he'd just been watching a game on the TV in the bar. He'd only just gone to the gate when they announced final boarding. But enough about the drama of boarding, back to his looks, which is what he was concentrating on now that the massive Boeing 747 had shot its way into the black sky. Even on a bad day his dark hair fell recklessly into place and his white toothy-smile enlivened those damned dimples that cornered his mouth and made him so easily recognizable; what he thought of as his worst feature the ladies tended to think was his best feature. (Well, maybe second best.) Still he hadn't had a chance to shower or shave—the latter not for two days and the stubble was thick against his chin—and this was an overnight flight. No telling what he'd look like when they landed. Some bearish creature, fresh (or not so) from the woods. He'd worry about that tomorrow, another day in another land. For now, he extended his hand over the empty middle seat.

"Hi, I'm Todd."

"Brandy."

"With two e's?" he asked sarcastically.

"A 'y'."

"Of course, traditional spelling for a traditional girl."

She laughed at that one. "Hardly. My parents' fault. No creativity with names."

Brandy appeared to be a natural blonde, no dark roots visible. Nope, rich honey-blonde hair that curled against soft shoulders. Add to that her form-fitting sweater and it was clear Brandy was as all-American as you get. The swelling curvature of her chest would have impressed any Park Avenue plastic surgeon. Or was that a cosmetic surgeon now, or some other such bullshit twenty-first century label?

During their short exchange, Brandy had been flipping through a copy of *Cosmo* and drinking a glass of white wine. Todd himself had the latest Dennis Lehane book and a mineral water.

"They say you shouldn't drink alcohol when you fly," he told her.

"I thought that was only for pilots," she replied with the utmost seriousness.

Todd took that moment to touch her arm, a friendly gesture. "No, no, Brandy, what I mean is, it tends to dehydrate you. The alcohol, combined with the terrible air that's recirculated in the cabin. Watch, you'll wake up in a few hours feeling parched."

"I need the booze to relax me. I don't like flying."

"Who does?" he said. "You take your life into your hands every time you step onto one of these metal death traps." A passing flight attendant frowned at his comment. "Hey, can I get a beer?" To Brandy, he shrugged. Then once he had popped the top of the can of Heineken he raised it to the air. "To living life on the edge, or better yet, in the sky."

Aluminum can and plastic tumbler connected. Todd drank and Brandy drank and then she giggled. He liked her giggle. He liked how her body reacted to the giggle, all bouncy. What luck, sitting next to Little Miss Model for the long flight across the Atlantic. He'd flown often enough, across the country and to the Bahamas and once to Australia—wow, the woman who sat next to him on that flight was probably bigger than the whole continent. The only benefit he'd seen to flying, other than getting to your destination the fastest way, was the frequent flyer miles, certainly not the people he'd been forced to endure those flights with. Overly large people, overly talkative people, overly populated rows. The only overly he'd liked to see on this flight involved himself and the lovely Brandy with a "y."

"So, Brandy, what brings you to merry ol' England."

"School," she replied. "I'm studying abroad."

He gave her the once over before saying, "Me, too."

That giggle again. "You are a wicked man," she told him. Todd was just glad she got his little joke; he hated to waste wit on the brain-dead. That bon-mot, though, was the ice breaker, and they talked all during the meal and when the flight attendant came schlepping down the aisle trying to pawn off duty-free booze to those who wished to part with their money before they'd even landed at their destination. Todd kept his money right where it was, in his wallet. He hated to part with his somewhat hard-earned cash.

They were flying Virgin Atlantic and so far it had been a smooth flight. The plane was half-empty, but heck, it was headed for London's Heathrow and this was January, so you do the math. Who goes to visit the city with the worst climate in the year's worst month? Well, Todd does, but for him it was pure business. Of course that's not what he told Brandy when she asked. He told her he was writing a movie and was going to London for research. She perked up; Todd reminded himself to keep her perky.

"Have I seen anything you've written?"

He shook his head, improvising on the spot. "First one."

"So then how do you earn a living?" she asked while chewing the tough beef that came with the stir-fry vegetables and rice.

He'd opted for the eggplant lasagna and had switched from beer to red wine. "I do some temp work, mostly for financial corporations." There didn't seem to be any harm in revealing some truth, made him feel better.

"Oh, so are you good with money?"

For a brief moment he thought about the discarded lottery tickets littering his floor. "Good enough," he said, suddenly wanting to change the subject. Too much information led to too many mistakes. "So, what is Brandy studying?"

"Literature," she said.

He pointed to the *Cosmo* magazine she'd placed on the seat between them. "I can just see it, 'Shakespeare's Ten Bitchiest Women—Are You One?' "

She flipped that natural blonde hair at him and then took a drink of her wine. Red lipstick stained the rim of the glass. "You're funny, Todd," she informed him. "If you need to know the truth, *Cosmo* and *Glamour* and all those other rags, they're my release. Usually it is Shakespeare and Chaucer and all the rest, but I'll have my fill of them when I get back to Cambridge."

Todd nearly coughed up his eggplant. "You're studying at Cambridge?" he asked, wishing suddenly he hadn't sounded so, uh, surprised. But come on, potential *Playboy* playmates tend not to study in the hallowed halls of one of the world's great universities.

"My father, Mister Thomas Alexander the Second himself?" she said, her voice mocking academia. "He's an alum of the school and wanted nothing more than to send his son to his alma mater."

"So why didn't he?"

"Because he only had a daughter," she said. "Hey, don't get the wrong idea, Mr. Smarty-Mouth, I had a solid four point zero in college—Yale, no less. I took a couple years off after undergraduate work before I agreed to return to school. We live in Saddle River, New Jersey, so I worked in Manhattan for a while. As a cosmetician—much to Daddy's horror. When the two years were up, he reminded me of our deal. He'd pay for my apartment during those two years and let me do whatever I wanted, so long as I eventually returned to my studies. Hey, if you're in the finance business, maybe you know him? Thomas Alexander—he's some hotshot at Bernstein, Gilbert, and, oh, someone else, Sullivan?"

Actually, it was Bernstein, Gilbert & Young, Todd knew them well enough. But he thought she'd appreciate a laugh at her operatic joke, and then feigned ignorance. "Like I said, I'm just a temp."

"I don't think you're 'just' anything," she said.

Todd absorbed the obvious compliment with zeal when a realization came to him. "Wait a minute, your name is Brandy Alexander?"

She rolled her eyes, as though she got that question—and inflected that way—often. "It's what my mother was drinking when they met. Now I think Daddy regrets the name, especially after not having that revered son he'd always dreamed of."

"You're probably the first Brandy Alexander to attend Cambridge."

Inside the plane's cabin, the flight attendants had dimmed the lights and came around to ask if they wouldn't mind pulling down the shade to the window. It would be light soon, but for everyone on board sleepy-time was in order. They were in the nexus of time zones. In fact, Brandy had started to yawn, blaming the wine, not the company, telling Todd that's why she had the second glass of wine. "I need to catch some winks."

"Oh, yeah, sure."

He offered to move to the center rows of the plane to allow her room to spread out. So he did, stretching himself over the four seats, his head only an aisle away from hers. He said, "Sweet dreams, Brandy," but she was already asleep and said nothing in reply. As for Todd, sleep wouldn't come to him and eventually he gave up and watched *Risky Business* on the tiny screen at his seat.

He had to admire that Tom Cruise, what a scam he pulled. And he has those damned dimples, too, made America fall in love with him. Of course that was back when he wasn't being used as a Hollywood punchline. As for that Rebecca De Mornay, heck, she had nothing on Todd's newfound sleeping beauty, one Brandy Alexander, unlikely Cambridge scholar and complete hottee. It was a shame he was only going as far as London.

The plane hit the ground hard, so much so that Brandy reached over and grabbed hold of Todd's hand. Nice to be trusted, he thought. Nice to be touched. She held him tight while the brakes were applied to the giant machine, bringing it to a near stop at the far edge of the runway. Todd had moved back to his original seat as breakfast had been served over Ireland.

"Ladies and gentlemen, welcome to London's Heathrow Airport. Local time is ten thirty-five. Temperature is zero degrees Celsius—that's thirty-two Fahrenheit," said one of the many flight attendants. Duh. Ten minutes passed before they reached the gate, and then the door was opened and the hurry-up-and-wait escape from the "metal death trap" began. Actually, Todd had to give them credit for a nice flight; he'd been awake the entire time.

Brandy agreed on the smoothness. "Hey, if I was able to get a few hours' sleep, you know I had confidence in the pilot. Or in someone else."

Todd wondered if she meant some higher being, or just her flight companion.

Todd and Brandy made their way down the aisle, emerging onto the jetway. They walked together through what seemed endless corridors of the terminal, following yellow signs that promised "Baggage Reclaim," like a pot of gold at the end of rainbow. As they did, Todd kept looking around him, in front and behind, as though searching for someone in particular.

"Someone catch your interest?" Brandy asked.

"Oh, uh, no. Just curious, I guess, who flies to London this time of year."

"Cheap rates," she said.

Still, he sensed she hadn't believed him.

Before baggage claim came Immigration, and with passports and landing cards in their hands, Todd and Brandy joined the line—queue, he supposed was the term on this side of the pond. It was moving quickly, making Todd realize their wonderful sojourn was soon to end. So he did what any red-blooded American male would do, he asked for her number.

"Oh, Todd—I'll be here the entire semester and . . ."

"I'm here indefinitely—probably a month at least," he said, a slight exaggeration. "Surely you could spare a night away from your studies."

"Tell you what—you can have this." She had a felt tip pen and scribbled on his hand what turned out to be her e-mail address. Ah, modern dating.

"Cute," he said, gazing at her address.

"Bye, Todd," she said, giving him a quick peck on the cheek. "Ooh, scratchy."

As Todd was left touching his stubbly face where her lips had pressed, Brandy was whisked off to a waiting immigration official. Before being ushered to a second line, Todd stole one last look around. Nope, no one familiar caught his eye. He then returned to the task at hand, getting into the country. He hated this part, nosy people with a badge asking nosy questions. As he waited, his fingers dug into his moist palms. And then he retracted them, fearful they'd smear Brandy's address. Like he could forget daddysgirl. The Internet provider was the same as his.

"Next."

Todd stepped forward and handed over his passport to a rather dim-looking gent, who looked as though he'd had as much sleep as Todd.

"How long are you visiting, sir?"

"A week, perhaps more—I suppose," Todd stated.

The immigration official tossed Todd a scowl. "Why?"

Why? Because he wanted to, dammit. "Oh, pleasure. Mostly. Some business." Shit, why did he say that? He hated authority figures and hated even more how flustered they made him.

The man was busy looking at the passport picture, then back at Todd. "Have a pleasant stay, sir," he said, and then stamped his passport.

Todd looked around for Brandy. She'd already been swallowed up in the throngs of people in the airport, possibly never to be seen by him again. Really, what was he thinking, flirting so shamelessly with her, distracting himself from the business at hand. He didn't even like to play the lottery when he was working, what was he thinking inserting romantic fantasy in its place?

And speaking of, in his search for Brandy, his eyes at last locked on whom he'd been searching for earlier. The attractive couple had just themselves cleared immigration and were all smiles, he in his early sixties, she preserved somewhere in her forties. He had seen them at the terminal at JFK, but on the flight they had no doubt been comfortably ensconced in upper class. They could afford it; they were doubly rich.

Henri and Elise Procopio, he the cosmetics king of New York, she the latest lucky winner in New York's lottery, the ideal picture of wealth piled upon wealth. Man, some people had all the luck. And all the money. Which is why Todd thought they should part with some of it—the money that is. Their luck, well, that had just run out.

Todd had followed them to London. On purpose, and with a plan.

Adrenaline fueled his excitement as he realized that, after a couple months of watching and waiting, the game was finally afoot.

Chapter Two

Twenty apartments, twenty possible guilty tenants. It wasn't Todd who had let in the criminal, so that narrowed the list of suspects down to nineteen, and so far none of them had claimed responsibility for buzzing in the stranger who managed to not only get inside the building on East Eighty-Eighth Street but inside apartment 5-A. On Thursday night, as the midnight hour approached, police lights were still flashing as a small crowd gathered in front of the building in question. Two officers stepped out of the building and headed back toward their cruiser. A young woman with a smelly cigarette in one hand, a glass of odorless vodka in the other, and a caustic attitude worse than either of those vices, followed them out, saying, "If I catch the asshole who let them in, I'll give 'em another." Unless she was a good actress, another person had been eliminated from the suspect list.

"Easy, miss, no threats you can't keep," said Officer Dolan, his Irish face young and unspoiled.

"Oh, I can keep it, you can be sure of that." She took a puff on her cigarette, as though that proved her point.

Just then a well-dressed, well-coiffed, well-looking man came running up to the building, unworried about the rain which continued to fall on the city and on his head. He stole a look at the open door, then back at the officers who were busy writing notes in their books. He had thick wavy blond hair and his black coat was unbuttoned, revealing an expensively cut black suit by Hugo Boss. Looking authoritative, he caught Officer Dolan's attention.

"Help you, sir?"

"I'm supposed to be apartment sitting here—what's going on?"

Dolan exchanged looks with his partner, a mustached older man named Chavez. "Break-in. What apartment are you staying in?"

"Five-A."

Again with the looks, making the man grow impatient. "Come with us, Mister . . ."

"Simon. Andy Simon."

Both Dolan and Chavez got out of their car and escorted one Andy Simon into the building, all the while ignoring the inebriated woman who was still spouting off death threats. At last they were rid of her, as they climbed their way upward. Since she smoked, the stairs weren't exactly her best friend, that's why she lived on the first floor. Gradually the three men made their way to the top floor, where yellow crime scene tape was stretched over the entrance to the apartment.

"Oh my God, what happened?"

"Like we said, a break-in. No one was hurt. No one was here, in fact, lucky thing. Whoever the guy was who broke in, he sure was angry, maybe frustrated. As though what—or who—he'd come for wasn't here."

Andy asked if he could go inside, see if anything was missing. Both cops agreed they could use a little insight into this crime and waved him through. They followed as Andy ducked underneath the yellow tape and began to assess the damage, the cops busy asking Andy Simon questions. Like where the owner was, why Andy was checking in on the apartment, any ideas who might have done this, routine stuff, they claimed.

"The owner is out of town for . . . a while. I'm an old friend of his, said I'd look in on things. Feed the frog, you know. And no, I've no idea who would do . . . this."

This proved to be quite a mess. The apartment was, frankly, trashed. Sofa cushions were overturned and torn, desk drawers opened and tossed; a two-drawer metal file cabinet lay open on its side, its numerous contents doing a good imitation of carpeting. Rain came in through the broken window. Andy could only imagine what the bedroom looked like; probably worse.

"Shit, man, what a disaster," he said. "Any clues?"

Dolan shook his head. "Guy found his way to the roof, came down the fire escape and kicked the window in with what we imagine was his foot. No blood, lucky guy. We got the key from the landlord, who'd been called after neighbors complained of a ruckus. Aside from that, don't know anything. Whether our thief found what he was looking for—or who—we couldn't say." He'd already said that, but he repeated it for effect, perhaps for further insight from Andy. He considered his notepad, as though it had formed new questions on it. "So, Mr. Simon—is it? Your friend, Todd Gleason, according to the neighbors, he's where?"

"On a business trip."

"Can we reach him?"

Andy took one further look at the apartment. "What time did this occur?"

"Around five, six."

Todd hadn't been scheduled to leave for the airport until eight, that much Andy knew. Which meant what exactly? Had Todd even made his flight? Had something dreadful happened?

"Mr. Simon—where is Mr. Gleason?"

"Oh, uh, overseas. But unreachable now, I'm sure."

Dolan handed him a card. "Yeah right, thanks for the co-operation. Tell Mr. Gleason if he cares to know what happened here, give us a call. Lots of other crimes to solve, if it's not a priority for the victim, can't be for the police, you know?"

"Of course, officer, I understand," Andy said. "Sorry I couldn't be more helpful, but I'm sure Todd appreciates your checking things out."

They recommended that Andy accompany them outside, where they might have a few more questions, "routine stuff, you understand."

More with the routine, it was beginning to live up to its definition. "Let me check in on Toad, first."

"Toad?"

"Todd's frog."

"His what?" Chavez said.

Andy made his way over to the kitchen table, saw that the redoubtable frog was doing just fine inside his tank, despite the evening's upset. Whoever had trashed the apartment, well, he'd dug up some kind of compassion and spared the tank. Toad was swimming merrily through his murky water, bobbing up to the top in search of food.

"Oh no, I'm sure Todd fed you. No matter how much of a hurry he must have been in. He warned me about overfeeding you."

Toad swam away and Andy walked away, down to the stairs, wondering exactly what had gone so wrong that the police were involved. Todd had never before had police trouble; then again, Todd had never before had *any* trouble. He was *that* careful.

Not for the first time did Andy begin to wonder if Todd's luck had run out.

Then he had no choice, he went to evade more questions. Uh, answer them.

Todd Gleason was suspicious by nature. In grade school he'd always been wary when a pack of boys came up behind him while he waited to get that day's slice of pizza in the cafeteria. With good reason; he was usually stuck eating that same-old peanut butter and jelly sandwich his mother had packed for him, the greasy, dripping, wonderful pepperoni he'd been dreaming about since math class relegated to mere daydreams and other people's digestive tracts. Because those jerks had stolen his money and left him humiliated. Ever since those defining moments in his early life he'd been working on honing his instincts and had come to trust them implicitly. In his business, instinct was often what kept you from being placed behind bars. So when he was racing through a crowd of lollygaggers at Heathrow, headed for the taxicab stand, and a skinny gentleman with thinning hair black as midnight stepped out and said, "Cab, sir?" Todd was immediately cautious.

This mustached man was waiting inside the terminal and the taxi cab sign was pointing outside.

"We're cheaper," he said.

"Who's we?" Todd asked.

"Very Best Services, Limited," the man stated proudly, like an investor who'd made a recent killing in the stock market.

The man slipped him a card—it seemed legit, with a phone number and an e-mail address. Even had that phrase, "We're cheaper." Heck of a sell-line. Still, he was skeptical. Anyone can make these up with a computer and some ingenuity. In the end, Todd decided the man probably had only one of those requirements. So Todd asked how much, knowing the quoted price was indeed much lower than London's taxi service. Forty-eight pounds as opposed to near sixty. No need to spend more than was necessary, at least not yet.

"Okay, let's go."

"I am Habib," the man said. "I am Indian."

"Love that vindaloo, man."

"Brave man, you, very spicy."

Todd followed the man to the parking garage, where a small van awaited them.

During the entire forty-five minute trip to Central London, Todd was convinced the man was going to turn around and suddenly point a gun at him and ask for all he had. Suspicions, whether well-founded, always seemed to ride shotgun alongside paranoia. Nevertheless, the man drove smoothly and professionally through increasing amounts of traffic on the M4 motorway, while outside a surprise showing of snow fell all around them, making the roads that much more difficult to traverse. Once they hit the West Cromwell Road, though, worry over road conditions took a backseat as traffic came to a near standstill. Nearly noon and everyone was busy going somewhere other than where they were.

"Almost there," Habib said, though when five minutes elapsed and they had moved only two blocks, Todd wondered what "almost" meant in cabbie-speak.

To kill time, Todd withdrew from his jacket pocket a newspaper clipping (with accompanying black-and-white photograph showing a smiling, happy couple) from the *New York Post*. Dated just four months ago. Henri and Elise Procopio, he the millionaire founder of Looking Great Cosmetics; she his fourth wife. Turned out, Elise had a passion for playing the lottery—a holdover no doubt from the days she'd been a struggling rich-wife-to-be—and this time her number had come up big time. She was the sole winner of a jackpot that totaled over thirty-five million. Todd had cut out the article at the time, disgusted by the turn of events. His own lottery ticket for that particular payoff lay torn and tattered in the garbage, litter among the rest of his dreams. That week he hadn't even hit one of the drawn numbers, not even that supposed good luck charm, the bonus number. Elise had hit every number, dead-on. Of course his plan was hatched that October night after a smiling Elise accepted the oversize check; it had taken this long to find out what the Page Six–prone Procopios were planning, a bit of investigative work that yielded great results.

"Oh, we're off to London for a romantic getaway, Henri insisted and I'm certainly not going to complain—so long as we're using his money and not mine." That's what Elise told her friend Mimi Ledbetter at Le Cirque one afternoon in late November, while Todd sat at a nearby booth listening to the entire conversation. A germ of an idea had spread to a full viral attack, and so began the great London caper.

"Look, see—South Kensington," Habib said, trying to sound encouraging. Todd had forgotten all about the traffic. He'd been thinking of the subsequent articles and gossip-laden mentions of Elise Procopio, as though her lottery win had dubbed her Society Flavor of the Month. In each picture she smiled and waved like the Queen, her hubby Henri holding her arm and looking less than thrilled, like the Prince who would never be crowned her equal. Still, with Habib's excitement, Todd gazed out the window and saw that South Kensington meant nothing to him. As far as Todd knew, they could be in front of Big Ben.

A month ago Todd had never heard of any of London's neighborhoods, South Kensington among them, certainly not tiny Clareville Street, which is where he had found a flat to rent. In his limited travels—not counting that long journey to Australia for the Olympics—London had never been on his list of wanna-sees. So all this was new to him, the driving on the other side of the road, the double-decker buses, and the two-toned sound of ambulance sirens. Aside from that, his surroundings pretty much reminded him of New York, lots of buildings tightly compacted onto tiny streets, gated parks, and majestic monuments, museums, and most of all, lots and lots of cars and people. In his search for a place to stay he'd gone on-line and found a likeable sounding flat in what he'd hoped was a decent neighborhood. From the looks of it, South Kensington was a fine choice. The price was certainly cheaper than a hotel and as this was the off-season, even cheaper with the agent's proffered discount. After an initial telephone conversation with the affable landlord, Todd had accepted the flat, given his dates required and a deposit by credit card.

"Right, thanks ever so much, Mr. Gleason," the landlord had said, a guy named Timberlake. "We'll see you on the nineteenth."

"Brilliant," Todd replied, feeling like a Londoner already.

Now, with a month of preparations having slipped by so quickly, Todd suddenly found himself standing before the pleasant-looking building on Clareville. Like his own New York walk-up, a bit nicer facade. He paid Habib, retrieved his baggage and computer case, walked up to the door. He'd been told to look for a note on the front door, giving him instructions on locating the keys; if no note, just buzz Flat 3. Flat. Todd liked the word, it was so economical. Unlike apartment, which in New York was a bigger word than most of the places it supposedly described. He put the nonsense out of his mind and concentrated on the task at hand.

There was no note on the door. So he rang the bell. And waited.

There came no reply.

Like the instructions on a shampoo bottle, repeat if necessary.

Still, no result.

That's when he noticed the front door was slightly ajar. Maybe Timberlake had left it open for him? Right, maybe he had high tea waiting and Prince William there to greet him. No, something was wrong, as wrong as the creaking sound the door made as Todd swung it open. The bristles of hair on the back of his neck stood at attention, a clear sign he'd switched into instinct mode. Like those bullies were behind him waiting to steal his pizza money.

Deciding silence was the better part of stealth, Todd quietly entered the building. Hanging on the wall to his left was a mirror, which he avoided looking into; he didn't need to see the fear, feeling it was enough. A small stack of mail sat on a mahogany table, untouched, he wondered for how long. Did anyone else currently live in this building? There were only four flats, each of them with a name taped to the buzzer. They could be old, folks having moved out for more permanent residences. Todd approached the staircase and gazed upward, listened for any sign of noise, of life. Nothing, no noise, no life. Still erring on the side of caution, he began to creep his way up the winding staircase, hoping the carpeted steps would cushion the sound of his feet, hoping too the floorboards underneath the cream-colored rug wouldn't creak. On the first landing he set his two bags down and then continued upward. At last he found his way to Flat 3, his home for the next week or so.

Or maybe less, maybe only minutes.

Because just like at the main entrance, the door to the flat was also ajar. This time he decided he should say something; what if the landlord was just being absentminded, leaving doors open all over the place? Or maybe he was just making it easier on his new tenant, figuring heavy bags would impede his ability to maneuver the keys. Yeah, and Tony Blair wanted to consult him on relations with the EU.

"Mr. Timberlake? Hello?"

No response, just a slight whisper of the wind as it passed through the slim opening in the doorway. Where there's air, there's life, right? So Todd pushed open the door and stepped inside. He was in a small hallway; to his left was a bathroom, to his right a living room. He could see the cushions of the sofa. As he eased himself further into the flat, he could see something else, all the while wishing he didn't.

Shoes, with feet in them.

"Oh, shit."

What he should have done at this precise moment was leave. The flat, the building, check out of town and head back to Heathrow and hop the next flight bound for New York. Or maybe someplace warm, the Caribbean, where he could sun himself on the beach and drink a mai tai and get laid in the waning sunlight. In other words, do not pass Go, do not collect two-hundred pounds. But he moved forward, where he saw that the feet were connected to legs and the legs, well, to an entire body.

The man, dressed in slacks and a sweater, his gray hair long in the back, lay face down on the floor, his arms outstretched as though they'd tried to break his fall. Todd wasn't sure what good that would do, a broken face was only a major injury when it was the only one. The crimson blood that had poured out from underneath the man spoke volumes about the nature of his more serious injury.

"Oh, shit," Todd repeated, he of the clever retorts.

It was obvious the killing was recent. As in, really recent.

Suddenly Todd swung around, thinking maybe the killer was right behind him. Only it was his face that looked back at him, in the glare of a picture frame that hung above the mantel. Todd needed a moment to catch his breath, anyway, surprised by his own appearance, the gaunt expression apparent even in the translucent print of a vase of flowers.

Against his better judgment, he leaned down and checked for a pulse. First the wrist, then the man's neck. Todd had once taken a lifesaving course in college and never before had he needed to use the techniques learned. Turned out, his unused talents would have to remain that way, because the man on the floor who was lying in a puddle of blood was indeed quite and utterly dead. How could he have gone from a lovely encounter with the stunning Brandy high in the harmless sky to this, a clear-cut case of death by violence back here on the brutal Earth? Life could spin out of control at any given moment; death could rear its inevitable end without warning.

Apparently so could the police.

Because that's what Todd heard next, a siren blaring through the quiet afternoon air. It seemed to be growing louder, approaching fast.

"But who called . . . ?"

Todd didn't have time to speculate. The last thing he needed was trouble with the local constabulary, not on his first day in London, first minutes really. Heck, not even on his last day would he want to see them; especially not then, when hopefully his business deal would have been successfully completed. Curiosity took momentary control of his senses as he leaned down and dug through the man's back pocket. He was in search of a wallet. He found it. He pulled out a small leather billfold and proceeded to check the man's name.

Yup, Vance Timberlake.

The landlord he'd spoken to over the phone, who had rented him the flat. He was now lying very dead inside that very flat.

"Nice meeting you," he said, unsure why. Maybe it was good to hear a voice, even his own, it was still the breath of life.

The siren neared, causing Todd to drop the wallet. It splashed in the blood, then lay there as unmoving as its owner. Shame, really, he hadn't checked for cash. Which meant he didn't know if this was a robbery gone bad, or what. Enough dawdling, he told himself, and ran from the flat, down the stairs, where he retrieved his bags and then fled from the scene of the crime. Of course he wasn't familiar with the area, so he didn't know where to run. So around the corner he went, hoping his behavior hadn't attracted anyone's attention.

He came to another small road, Rosary Gardens it was called, and quickly he disappeared down the empty sidewalk. Around the corner he went, until finally he saw stairs that led down to a basement area. Seemed liked a smart choice. So there Todd paused, finally allowing himself to catch his breath, maybe to think too about his next move. Because there was no way he could return to charming old Clareville Street or Rosary Gardens or anywhere in South Kensington. Such nice names, too, he liked roses, or at least he once did; now those beautiful ruby red petals would remind him of Timberlake's glistening, spilt blood.

Chapter Three

"Bloody 'ell, 'oo's 'e?"

The question was asked of the man known only as Bobo, who until this moment had barely looked up from the paperback book in his hands. The Penguin Classics edition of *The Adventures of Tom Sawyer*. He loved reading about America's southern states, the language and the rhythm and the way of life, so civilized with their plantations and their mischievous ways and that ol' grand Mississippi River. There was history there, civility; very unlike the life he'd ever known, where hospitality on any given day meant not being threatened with a knife. Prison sucked; he was glad to be free of it, though at this moment he might just consider himself to be in a different form of prison. Trapped was he, with his friend and associate, who was interrupting his reading with an annoying case of people watching.

"Dija hear me, Bo? I said, 'bloody 'ell, 'oo's 'e?' "

"Yeah, I heard you the first time, like fifteen minutes ago."

"No, I said that the second time, and now this is the third time."

That's what finally got Bobo to look up from his book. "How is it you can say it a second and third time, but not a first?"

"Because the first time I knew 'oo the bloke was, didn't need to ask. 'E was Timberlake, just like we was expecting. It's the second man who come 'round that I didn't know. Sure left in a

46

hurry. And now this third bloke, just walked right into the building."

"Who cares who they are, that's not our assignment," Bobo said, returning then to his book. Our intrepid Tom Sawyer was currently conning his friends into giving the picket fence a much-needed whitewash. The sultry voices of Twain's characters were a welcome return after his friend's near unintelligible accent. His accent was so bad and so thick, not even Henry Higgins could have placed where he'd been raised. "We're to keep our eye on Timberlake. Not a second stranger, or a third. And our first—Timberlake himself—hasn't yet emerged from the building."

Bobo shook his head. Christ, he was starting to talk like Larry.

"Not that yer'd know if he'd haf lef, yer face all buried in that book."

That was dangerous, talking back. Our big Bobo was sometimes as fierce as the man who employed them, and less educated in the subtleties of intimidation. He liked to use his fists.

"Look, Larry, we don't need four eyes to find Timberlake, so you look and I'll drive—when needed. Which right now, we don't need no driving. Just let me know when he shows up again."

Admonished, Larry said, "Right, boss."

Technically, Bobo wasn't Larry's boss, they both worked for someone else, some Clive chap who had sent them on this seemingly innocent stakeout. Though with Clive, things were never innocent. Larry knew Bobo was smart and there were things to learn from him, hadn't he helped keep him alive on the inside? You betcha. So he did as instructed, went back to waiting for the sight of that smarmy Timberlake, scurrying back down the street like a rat.

They were parked across the street from the building on

Clareville, sitting in a taxi. Bobo the driver, Larry the supposed fare, alone in the back. That was their ingenious cover. Bobo was of medium build but was all thick muscle, with dark hair cut close against his scalp. Larry was large, at least six-five, had been since his fourteenth birthday, and still was as clumsy with his size as ever. His brown-thatched head bumped against the roof of the cab, as it often did, which might account for why his head always looked slightly crooked. Like he saw all of life through a *Batman* villain's eyes. They'd been waiting a long time, having followed their target across the neighborhood earlier this morning. To them this all looked routine; to Clive nothing was ever routine. Paranoid bastard, making them wait for hours inside these tight quarters.

When this third man appeared, a youngish looking guy not even six feet, Larry's attention was piqued. Some stakeouts were boring, this one though had its share of activity, so hmm, maybe Clive had been right? The Volvo van had dropped off the third man in front of the building in question, then drove away, leaving the new arrival with his two bags and a funny look on his face, as though he didn't quite know where he was. He stepped into the building; from Larry's point of view, he couldn't tell if he had used a key.

"Something's going down, Bo."

Bobo finally tossed the book onto the dashboard; there was no shutting up Larry today. "Clive just wanted to know what Timberlake was doing, he didn't say anything about other blokes, they could just live there. Clive may think the world is a bad place, but for most people life is a pleasant ride."

Bobo's chirpy outlook on life was shattered by the sound of a siren. One which was suddenly growing closer. Both men exchanged looks of uncertainty. They'd had experience with cops, not the good kind of experience like contributing to the benevolent association or nodding polite hellos.

"That coming this way?" Larry asked.

Bobo gave it a good listen. "Seems like it."

"So much for pleasant rides."

Bobo hated to be proven wrong. As he started the engine and flipped on the "hired" button of the cab, Larry saw the door to the building in question open and someone come running from it. The third man, as he'd been dubbed. The man still had his bags with him as he went darting down the street, disappearing around the corner.

"Follow 'im," Larry said, unusually taking charge.

"Yeah, I think maybe you're right," Bobo said.

The siren was closer, probably just a block or so away. So Bobo shifted the cab into gear and pulled away from the curb. Now just an innocent-looking cabbie taking his fare to his destination, he felt he could relax a bit. Turning to the next street, both he and Larry kept their eyes out for the man, but all four came up empty.

" 'E couldn't have gone far."

Bobo agreed, suggested maybe Larry go out on foot while he circulated the block with the car. That was sound advice, and soon after Larry's bulk emerged from the tight confines of the cab and into the great open sky. He fit better in a world with no ceilings. From the small of his back he withdrew a snub-nosed pistol, tucking it in his sleeve for cover. Just in case, you know?

"Use your mobile if you find the guy—detain him, right?"

"Right," Larry replied.

On foot, Larry began to comb the neighborhood for any sign of a man acting odd. Other than himself. He remembered the bags—one looked like it probably had a computer in it—but what if the guy disposed of them? Would he recognize him then? Black leather jacket, jeans, pretty generic outfit, popular too in the cold of a London winter. He'd have to rely on instinct, sniff out the man's fear. Because that much was certain, he'd been running from something, something real bad.

And even if he hadn't already sensed this, the sight of the police lights flashing before the home on Clareville would have helped him figure it all out. Larry considered that perhaps Clive wouldn't be too happy. He hated any scent of the police.

Just don't blame me, he thought, not without a sense of fear himself. Maybe Clive would leave them alone, take out his anger on Timberlake.

Todd still felt as though he'd left his breath behind in that flat, figuring now if he stayed in one place—however hidden he was—it might catch up to him. Until then, he wiped sweat from his brow, this, despite the freezing temperature in the air the flight attendant had forewarned about. Heck, after what he'd seen—witnessed?—the Arctic would have set him dripping. Dripping—he needed that image like he needed a hole in his head. He silently cursed his bad phrasing. He removed his hand from his brow, as though he'd touched something hot. Suddenly afraid to look down at his palm, thinking blood would have replaced sweat. All that was missing were the tears.

And those weren't that far off, given the circumstances. Just last night he'd been chased from his apartment by—who?—some stranger, and now having arrived in a place as foreign to him as anything, he had the misfortune to stumble upon a dead body. This trip had better be worth it all, and that realization was actually what now sharpened his focus. The Procopios and the promise of a big payoff, enough to end this crazy lifestyle of his. Would it have killed him to have a normal job? To have accepted the offer from Lucille and forget this flight of fancy? Easy thought, not so easy to put into play. This frog knew himself too well, warts and all.

"Just don't let me croak," he said aloud.

The sound of his voice surprised him, made him huddle even

tighter in this basement area. He was hidden beneath a flight of stairs, stashed away behind a shovel and some bagged salt to help melt ice, a bicycle. He had lucked into this place, actually, and had stuffed his luggage as far back out of sight as he could. What next? He no longer heard the siren, but could imagine for himself what was going on nearby. The cops discovering the body, an ambulance, the press, curious onlookers. The circus come to town. Could he blend in, check out what was going on? No, don't risk it, whoever had shot that guy, this had nothing to do with Todd. It was just an unfortunate circumstance, a case of being in the right place at the wrong time, right? A coincidence. (Which, remember, he didn't ever believe in.) What were the odds the landlord he was to meet would be offed within minutes of his arrival at the flat he was to rent?

That's when it hit him, he needed a place to stay.

And the option presented before him was the last one he wanted.

A month ago he'd mentioned to good pal Andy Simon his upcoming trip to London and Andy in turn, good pal that he was, had generously offered to help him with his accommodations. Andy's older sister, Beth, lived in London and would no doubt be happy to house the hunk she'd once hunted. Todd was loathe to take Andy, er Beth, up on his, er, her offer. There was something about the spinsterish Beth that really got his teeth gnashing. Her laugh? Her chatter? Her . . . her everything? No, cross out Beth. He'd go to a hotel, and damn the expense. But where? There were hundreds of choices, none of which was he efficiently versed in. What a predicament. He realized—at least temporarily—he had no choice, Beth Simon it would be.

Leaving his bags behind for now, Todd emerged from the shadows of the open basement and returned to street level. He headed in the opposite direction from where he'd come, along the busy Old Brompton Road. Here he was a faceless stranger, anonymous in a sea of fast-moving people.

As Todd walked innocently enough—he hoped—along the street, he dug into his jacket pocket for his wallet, where he had stored Beth's numbers. Andy had made him jot them down, home and work, and while he'd been reluctant at the time, now he was glad. Next he'd need a phone. That was easy enough, too, coming upon a red-painted phone booth right outside the South Kensington Underground station. Problem was, he had no change, no coins. So that required going into the small shop that was conveniently located right inside the station. He bought a Cherry Coke and a Cadbury chocolate caramel, getting change back from his ten pound currency. Fortunately he had exchanged cash beforehand. At last, he had what was needed and he stepped into the booth, rang the number.

"Hello, this is Beth Simon, how can I help you?" came a loud voice that even had she not identified herself could only have been that of Beth Simon. She barely needed technology to be heard.

"Uh, hey, Beth, it's Todd Gleason, uh . . . Andy's . . ."

"Oh, my God, right, he told me you might be calling. So glad you did, Todd, wow, so you're in London right, that's brilliant, just brilliant. How about we get together? Where are you stay-ing, we could have lunch or just meet for a pint at a nearby pub, oh, I suppose it's too early even for that, even here. Hmm, well, what do you say?"

He wasn't sure there were any words left to say.

"Actually, I've stumbled into . . . well, a bit of a jam, let's say. I may need to crash at your place for a night." Even as he said it he was cringing.

Can you smell the eagerness from the other end of the line?

"Anything, Todd, anything at all, you know that. Why don't you come by my work and I'll give you the keys to my flat. That way you can get settled. You must be tired from the flight, you got in this morning, right? My goodness, yes, sleep is exactly what you need. Silly me, thinking a pint would solve everything, just knock you right off your ass, huh?"

After emitting a braying laugh, she gave him directions to her office. It sounded complicated using the "Tube," as she called the subway. Transfer here, transfer there, should take all of forty minutes.

"Okay, thanks, Beth, I . . . really appreciate it. See you within the hour . . ."

She was still talking as he hung up the phone. He stepped outside and looked at the turnstiles that would allow him entry into London's Underground. He was too tired, though, to figure it out. Piccadilly Line to Victoria Line, go north—don't go south, blah blah blah. So he did what any self-respecting New Yorker did when the city was beginning to piss him off.

"Taxi," Todd called out, and just as fast as he said it, one pulled over. He hopped into the back seat, where the gentleman behind the wheel said, "Where to?"

"The Euston Road and Fitzroy Street."

"Bit of a distance."

But the cabbie didn't drive away from the curb, not yet. Was he objecting to traveling so far in this traffic? Todd was about to speak up when another gentleman grabbed the back door handle and hopped in as well. A big man, who seemed to fill up the entire back of the cab.

Todd was momentarily thrown. New Yorkers did not share cabs. They barely liked to share personal space of any kind and always maintained some distance, even on a crowded subway. And from what he'd learned in his research, neither did Londoners.

"Uh, I just got in, sir. So if you don't mind . . ."

Todd didn't finish his sentence. He had no idea what words he might have used anyway. Because there was a gun pressed against his side.

"Sorry," the cabbie said, "there'll be a slight delay in getting you to your destination."

The driver said nothing more, and neither did the man with the gun.

"As long as you're going to detain me, could we make a quick stop to pick up my bags?"

"Look in the front seat," the man with the gun said.

Todd did, and saw his suitcase and computer case conveniently gathered for him. He fell back against the seat, thoroughly confused. What the hell was going on?

As the cab joined the now fast-moving traffic, the man with the gun spoke again. "Gee, Bo, not even a t'anks for gitting his bags."

"Some folks is just plain ungrateful," said Bobo.

What followed was the cab ride from hell.

Darting through London traffic, weaving along narrow streets that barely left room between cars parked and cars moving, they finally shot onto a larger thoroughfare and crossed a bridge over the River Thames. The sign read Vauxhall Bridge. The three men in a cab at last stopped on a quiet residential-looking street. In the time gone by, Todd had continued to hold his tongue, certain that despite the circumstances, a customary smart remark might slip out of his mouth. As the large man helped Todd out of the cab, Todd found himself saying, "Which of us gets the fare?"

His humor fell on deaf—and possibly dumb—ears. Instead, the big guy pushed him forward, while the other one fiddled with a set of keys. At the front door of a building that housed a pub on the ground floor, he unlocked it and then guided them all up two flights of stairs. Before they entered the flat, the driver turned back to them.

"Just be real quiet as we enter, the boss might not be done."

"Done with what?" Todd asked, not even sure why. He didn't even know who the boss was.

Both men just grinned.

As soon as they stepped into the apartment, Todd realized what they'd been talking about. From a nearby room came the very obvious sounds of a couple in the throes of lovemaking, high-pitched squeals emanating from the woman, eager, near-angry grunts from her male companion. As Todd was led into a sparsely furnished living room, he tried to squeeze the sounds from his mind. That proved impossible, because they grew in intensity.

"Must be ready to blow soon," Todd remarked. He felt like conducting.

Both men shook their heads.

He was shoved to the sofa, told to shut up and wait.

The large man sat opposite him while the other one disappeared into a nearby kitchen. He returned with three narrow cans of Boddingtons Pub Ale, handed them all around. "Might as well have us a drink while we wait."

Todd popped the top on his beer, the contents seeming to explode as he did. He took a sip; it was only slightly cold. Details from the guide book he'd read were slowly returning to him. Warm bitter and good friends, London in a nutshell. Todd took this as a good sign, a slice of normalcy in this pie of insanity he had found himself in. He continued to drink from the can, figuring it was something to do. Both men finished before him, crushing the cans and tossing them into the kitchen. Meanwhile, it appeared the acrobatics in the other room were at last reaching a conclusion. Todd was mid-drink when mutual screams echoed throughout the entire flat. Throughout most of London, he thought.

"Well, now that the pre-show has, uh, climaxed, what do you

say we get onto the main performance," Todd said.

"Just wait."

"And keep your mouth shut of them dumb remarks."

A few minutes later the door to the bedroom opened. A stunning woman with tousled, curly strawberry-blonde hair walked into the room, she quite unabashedly naked. Todd couldn't help but notice a thick reddish bush where her legs met; he was eye-level with her after all. Still, with an easy crane of his neck he got a good look at the rest of her very fit, sweat-slickened body.

"Who's he?" she asked, looking at Todd.

"Unlucky bloke, seems."

"Hmm. Don't envy him. Any beer left for me?"

"In the fridge, get it yourself."

"There's thanks all right."

The woman, who looked no older than twenty, tossed him the finger before heading for the kitchen. As she attended to her newest needs, from the bedroom finally came (so to speak) the man who Todd assumed was his energetic host—the "boss." Thankfully he was dressed, if only in a pair of boxer shorts. He was about Todd's height, solidly if not strongly built, a slight goatee grew out from his chin, matching the thin blond hair on his head. On his chest was an odd smattering of moles, looking like a gameboard for connect the dots.

"Look at this, we have company," the man said. "How do you do, I'm called Clive Remington. You met Fiona, too? Good girl, she is—be a good girl, would you, Fi, wait for me in the bedroom?" The woman left them and closed the door and then Clive returned his attention to Todd. "See, she did just as I asked. She learned fast enough, sweet Fi. I trust Bobo and Larry have introduced themselves as well? Actually, I take that back. Not the most refined gentlemen around. But really, good help is so very difficult to find."

Clive seemed an ever popular name in Britain, Todd had

heard. Some Brit-famous comedian who became the host of the original *Millionaire* game show, he was one. There was a horror writer who people ridiculously thought looked like Paul Mc-Cartney, that's another. So Todd figured he'd meet a Clive eventually—and a Fiona, too, how 'bout that?

"Uh, how do you do," Todd said, put off by the man's eerily polite manner. He merely nodded at the newly introduced duo of Bobo and Larry.

"I trust our boys have made you comfortable—oh good, they served you a drink. Nice going, blokes. Do you think you could fetch me one?"

Both men hopped to attention, unlike when fair Fiona had asked for one. Clearly, this man wielded a large amount of control over these two. No doubt they'd only been doing their duty when they picked up Todd. But none of this explained what the hell Todd was doing here; though he had a sneaking suspicion it had to do with the dead landlord.

"Look, uh, Clive? I think there's been a mistake . . ."

"Please, I need my replenishing nourishment first—then we'll talk."

Still with that disarming, polite demeanor. It was a marked difference from having a gun pressed into his back, but somehow there was a more heightened sense of menace. He knew what to expect from the business end of a gun. This guy might just be more lethal.

When Clive was settled with his beer, taking three long sips to finish it off, he at last got down to the business at hand. Both of the men from the cab were waiting with anticipation. Todd had to admit he was too.

"So," Clive said, "to what do we owe the pleasure of your company?"

"That's a very good question," Todd said.

"Perhaps my associates could fill me in?"

"I'd like to hear their answer too."

Clive raised an eyebrow at Todd. "I think we've heard enough from you for the moment. Gentlemen?"

It was Bobo who spoke. "We were keeping an eye on Timberlake, like you said. Left his home and headed down the Old Brompton Road, we followed, real easy like with the traffic so bad. Goes to check on one of his properties, it looked. So we're waiting and eventually this guy shows up, bags and all, we assumed the new tenant. But he's not there two minutes before he comes fleeing from the flat—and coming up quick is the police. Struck us as a curious turn of events. We hightailed it out of there . . ."

"Tell him about . . ." Larry started to say.

Bobo shushed him. It looked like Clive wanted the details first about Todd.

"Good thinking, we don't need the constabulary detaining you two," Clive said, looking to Todd now. "No fan of the police, are we? I trust neither are you, which accounts for why you ran. But I must ask you, my good friend, whatever caused you to run in the first place?"

"This oughtta be good," Bobo said. "Like Tom Sawyer, let's see him talk his way out of this one."

Todd figured he had nothing to lose. Strange land, strange people, definitely strange circumstances. Maybe it would help get him out of his predicament, hostage in the home of the most civilized criminal he'd ever met. Oh, and of that he was certain, that this gent Clive lived not only on the other side of the Thames but on the other side of the law. And so Todd spilled the beans.

"Timberlake, the landlord. He's dead. Shot. Murdered. And I found him," Todd said.

"Uh-oh," Bobo said.

"He's been . . . what?" Clive said.

"Killed, boss, didn't you hear him?" Larry said. Nothing flew above him, what with him being so tall and all.

Larry's remark went ignored, even from Todd, who had learned fast not to listen to the giant's helpful idiocy.

There was silence in the room as this new piece of info was digested. Todd watched with nervous, wary eyes as Clive stood up from the chair. He began to pace, clenching his fists as he did so, obviously displeased with the news he'd heard. Todd had to wonder, what exactly was Vance Timberlake to Clive Remington?

He didn't get a direct answer, though, at least not to that unasked question.

What happened next, Todd didn't see it coming. Not from Mr. Polite.

Clive raised his hand and lashed out, yelling "Fuck" with an intensity matched only by his own recent fucking. And as though reaching a new climax, his hand swung wide and caught Todd smack on the side of the face, the fury and force behind it knocking him clear to the floor. He might not have seen it coming. But he sure felt it.

That's when Todd knew, Vance Timberlake was the lucky one.

CHAPTER FOUR

"Sorry, with such shocking news, delivered with such, well, how shall we say, precision?—I fear I needed to take out my aggression on someone. You were the obvious choice—don't shoot the messenger? I say why not, if he's standing before you. Eh? My apologies, though, my temper is something my therapist and I have yet to overcome. Considering I slapped him, too, well, so I've still got far to go."

Barely taking in those words, Todd still lay on the floor nursing his stinging cheek. For a guy with the wimpy name of Clive, he sure packed a mean, hard wallop. No doubt there was a big red welt forming, for Todd a nice souvenir of his early days—hours—in London. Take a picture, put it in the photo album. So far, the most appealing thing about the damned trip was the cold, wet, snowy weather. And as thrown by the slap as he was, Todd was further confused by both the apology he heard and the subsequent helping hand from Clive. Todd was back on the sofa almost as fast as he'd left it.

"Get him another pint, myself while you're at it," Clive said to his associates.

They hopped to attention, and seconds later both Todd and Clive had fresh cans in front of them. Todd considered using the beer to nurse his cheek, figured it wasn't cold enough to be much help. He waited, then, for Clive to clear the room.

"Why not return the cab to your uncle, Bobo—no doubt he's

got a living to earn too. Give him my thanks for the use of his vehicle."

"Right, brilliant."

Then, as Bobo turned to leave, Larry leaned in close toward Clive, where some exchange was made. Todd couldn't tell if Larry was on the giving or receiving end of whatever news was being discussed. Instructions? Probably, considering Larry left shortly afterwards, trailing after Bobo.

"They always travel together?" Todd said as they closed the door behind them.

Clive opted not to answer, and instead said, "So, let's get to the matter at hand, shall we? You want to tell me your name? It didn't escape me that you were less than forthcoming with that detail when I generously offered up my name. Can't help upbringing, I suppose. Mum always told me you should know who you're dealing with."

"With a slap like yours, I'm well aware of who I'm dealing with," Todd said.

"It's whom," Clive replied. "And I still don't know your name."

Todd quickly searched his mind and came up only with, "Booker. Richard Booker."

"Well, let's see if you're being truthful," Clive said, and from under his leg he pulled out what Larry had passed him. For Todd it was a familiar-looking leather wallet, notably because it was his. Clive opened it up, shook his head.

"Well Mr. Booker, this says your name is Todd Gleason. An American, I might have figured. Worse yet, a bloody New Yorker. You know, the other thing Mum taught me was to distrust New Yorkers. She got mugged there once, never went back. Me, I've never been, I can get mugged here just the same and not feel any jet lag. So, tell me, are you Mr. Booker who mugged Mr. Gleason, or are you in fact Mr. Gleason?"

"Call me Todd."

"Let's hope that's the last of your lies, if you want to have already seen the last of my, uh, temper," said Clive, not without a hint of malevolence. He tossed the wallet back to Todd, who tucked it into the back pocket of his jeans. "Larry may look dim because of his size, but he has nimble fingers. Comes in handy, his talent. So, let's return to the matter which brought about my sudden strike of violence. Timberlake, what do you know of him?"

"Not much."

"Enough to stumble upon his body—according to you."

There was an implicit threat there that Clive believed Todd wasn't being entirely truthful. Todd recalled the recent warning, and so he quickly added more to his story.

"I never met him, only spoke with him over the phone—twice. A couple e-mails, too, you know, he gave me some details on the apartment—the flat I was renting. He was supposed to hand over keys to the place where I found his body."

Clive nodded, absorbing the info. "Tell me about the body."

"It was a fresh killing from what I could see. I walked in—both the front door to the building and to the flat were open. Timberlake was lying face down on the floor, blood still pooling out from underneath him. It was a gruesome sight."

"If you never met him, how'd you know it was him?"

Todd smiled at this. "Checked his wallet—after I checked his pulse."

"You had time to spare before running out of the flat?"

"I'd just come in a cab and I knew the traffic was snarled, so I figured the police were a few minutes away still. Besides, if it wasn't Timberlake, then perhaps he was still expected. I did have an appointment with him."

"Cheeky of him, not living up to his end."

Todd looked for a hint of amusement on Clive's face, found none.

"Well, Todd, it appears you've gotten yourself mixed up in something rather unpleasant. More so now since you've involved me."

"Coming here wasn't exactly voluntary."

"Hey, Todd?"

"Yes, Clive?"

"Shut the fuck up."

To put a point of exclamation on his request, Clive lashed out once again. He hated smart-asses, that much Todd was getting. Still, the blow came so fast and so unexpected, that Todd was thrown back against the sofa. Had he not already been flat against it, he might have made a permanent dent in the cushion. The force of Clive's blow was that strong, that remarkable. And worst of all, he'd smacked the same cheek.

"Ow," Todd had to admit, while gently rubbing his cheek.

"Tell me what he said."

"Who?"

"Timberlake."

"When?"

"Gleason, you make me want to slap the crap out of you— Timberlake, what the hell did he say before he died?"

Todd admitted to himself that he was confused by the sudden shift in conversation. Clive seemed such a smart guy, what part of "dead" didn't he understand? He kept his thoughts to himself, though, hoping to keep Clive's temper in check. No such luck. Clive's hand slammed down on the table that separated them, knocking over the growing collection of beer cans. Good thing it wasn't glass.

"Stop screwing with me, Todd. He must have said something," he said, pausing. "You know, before you shot him. Maybe begged for his life, the worthless gimp. Begging was second nature to scum like him."

"He didn't . . . I didn't . . . I mean, shit, why would I shoot him? First time in London, don't know a soul, he's my one link to getting settled—the flat I'd booked. You tell me, what possible reason do I have to want him dead—to kill him?"

Clive's response was to massage his hand, a silent threat.

"Look, Clive," Todd attempted, trying to keep the peace between them. "I'm here on vacation—holiday, you guys call it? I happen to think hotels suck, they drain your bank account and mine ain't that great to begin with. So I found a place to rent out instead. Or tried to. Seemed like a legit operation— what do I know, getting involved with some guy who himself gets involved with killers. I swear, Clive—buddy—I haven't a clue who killed Vance Timberlake—or why."

"Yet the killer chooses the moment of your arrival—same day, hell, within minutes of your appointment, even chooses your exact flat, too. Mighty strong series of coincidences."

"And that's all it is, coincidence."

Even to Todd his words sounded like crap. Because we've already well established that he doesn't believe in the nature of coincidence. Which means what, then? Did he have any idea who was behind Timberlake's killing? No. Honest. His mind was as blank as a blonde's. (Not fair, considering the Cambridge-bound Brandy.) Big picture, though, just because he hadn't a clue didn't preclude his involvement in some roundabout way. The silence was too long, Clive was getting suspicious.

"Obviously you know something, Todd, you're just trying to find the right way to say it. Come on, spill it, what are you thinking?"

"I'm thinking what do you really want from me? Your goons bring me here—with no justification, really—and next thing I know I'm here being used for bitch-slapping practice. What is

Timberlake to you, huh, why do you care so much? Why's it got you running scared?"

"Todd?"

"Yeah?"

"It's probably best not to ask those kinds of questions, you don't want to get in any more trouble, do you?"

The time change and the overnight flight and the abating adrenaline were starting to catch up with Todd, just as was this roundabout conversation. "You know, Clive, we seem to have reached a standstill here, so if there's nothing further to discuss I need to get busy finding a place to crash. My flat's suddenly become unavailable."

"The Savoy."

"Excuse me?"

Clive rubbed his bare chest, the skin beneath his moles ing an angry red. Maybe he had an itch. "I said, the Savo mean something to you?"

"Yeah, the guidebook I read called it a real pricey think I'll look for something cheaper. Thanks for the

Clive gave up on his chest, the itch apparently g mind," he said. He dropped back to his seat, g impression he'd been beaten down by this end' "You're either telling me the truth or you're on liar."

Actually, lying was one of Todd Gleason's if in this particular moment he wasn't appl talent. He had the partial truth on his sid thing about Timberlake. And so figuring part of valor, he said nothing, waiting to tions Clive might come up with.

"What I've decided, Todd, is that Again, please accept my apologies. an unsettling morning, and the re

anything but calm. You see, I was expecting to keep an appointment with Timberlake, too. Rather, he needed to drop off your keys first; he always did have this awful sense of responsibility. A quick drop, he said, then he'd hook up with me. I wasn't sure I could trust him, though, so I sent my mates to keep an eye on him. And while I waited—distracted thankfully by the lovely and long-lasting Fiona, eh?—I in the end get no meeting, no instructions, and little satisfaction. Instead, I get . . . you."

"Sorry."

"Sorry—such an empty word."

"Sorry," Todd repeated. Even empty words filled silent holes.

"Where are you staying, Todd?"

"Obviously not where I originally thought."

"That's not the answer I'm seeking," he said, getting up from his seat. Again, a veiled threat loomed behind that ever-so-polite facade. This Clive, he was one nasty piece of work. Todd found himself leaning back again against the cushions. Wondering if another of those vicious back-handed slaps was forthcoming. None came. Rather, Clive's outstretched hand meant something all together different. "Your wallet—please."

Todd reluctantly handed his wallet back over to Clive. Clive flipped through the series of photographs in the plastic container, stopped short on one particular and unusual shot. He laughed as he flipped it towards Todd.

"What is that?"

"Oh," Todd said, looking at the swampy setting of the photo. "That's, uh, Toad."

"Toad? The frog?"

"My pet."

"Todd has a pet frog named Toad?"

He shrugged. "It seemed appropriate."

"You think you're funny, Todd?"

"Breaks the tension."

"Should, shouldn't it?" Clive said. "I'm starting to get a picture here, Todd. I'm guessing you're not really here on holiday, are you? No, don't answer, I don't need one. Doubt very much I'd get the truth from you. No, Todd Gleason—if that's even your real name, ID like this can be faked so easily— you're up to something. Men like us, we have instincts that reach behind the norm, we know when there's a con going down. Don't we? Wait, say nothing, you'll spoil my fun." Forgetting about the photographs, Clive dug into the hidden money pocket, withdrew the piece of paper Todd had used earlier. "Beth Simon. Balcombe Street—and how convenient, a telephone number."

"She has nothing to do with this."

"Still, it's a start. A place from which I can contact you from, I assume?"

"I thought we were done."

"For now, Mr. Gleason. Only for now."

Todd was handed back his wallet, which he hoped meant his dismissal. He rose from the sofa, made his way toward the door. His hand on the knob, he was that close to getting out of there when Clive once again spoke his name.

"This is not the end, my new friend."

"So you've said."

"See you around."

As the door closed behind Todd, he heard Clive yell out for Fiona. Poor girl, with no appointment for Clive to keep he seemed at a loss for activity. So why not another marathon session of lovemaking? Todd found his bags waiting for him in the hallway. He gathered them up and emerged onto the street, shutting the door tight, the reverberation shaking the building.

Or maybe that was Clive entering Fiona.

Outside, London's famous rain had begun to fall.

"Now what?" Todd asked aloud.

The street, so foreign and devoid of life, left him answering his own question. Get settled, that's what. Good thing Bobo and Larry had seen fit to bring along his luggage, the last thing he needed was to search out the street where he'd tucked it, he'd never find it. He wasn't even sure where he was now, much less where he'd been.

Once settled, "Then what?" he asked aloud again.

Well, that was easy. Even had Clive not mentioned it, Todd had every intention of making his way to the Savoy Hotel, and fast.

The Savoy, one of London's finest and swankiest hotels, was tucked away off the busy Strand, glittery on this rain-soaked afternoon. It's where the rich and beautiful met, lunched on fine food and desserted on delicious power. But just because you traveled in such rarefied circles, that didn't mean you received special dispensation over the laws of traffic. Which is why their cab had yet to get them to their destination, even though the airplane had landed nearly two hours ago. Immigration first, baggage claim second—and lots to claim there was—and now they were inching their way along Piccadilly, headed, eventually, for the Strand via the famous Trafalgar Square. A bit of sightseeing while getting to their hotel, except neither of them seemed interested in playing tourist. So tired of waiting was she, she was craving a drink and made the mistake of saying so.

"You had enough on the plane."

"Hardly."

"Then why did your liver bail out over the Atlantic?"

Fully frustrated over the lack of liquor and the preachy prose from her harping husband, she leaned against the backseat and thought about the nice accommodations in first class—upper class, that's what the airline had called it and she had to agree.

That was style, which she felt should have been her birthright, yet which had escaped her during her first thirty-five years on the planet. Now forty-five—and looking great, too—she knew there was no going back to that old life now. Nope, she was feeling rich. Hell, she was rich, and soon—very soon?—she'd be even more so. So far, so good.

"You know, I do have that duty-free bottle of Skyy in my bag," she remembered.

"Elise, you haven't stopped drinking since we left New York."

"I hate flying."

"We landed so long ago the plane's halfway back to the States already."

Elise replied by searching through her bag for the shapely blue bottle which was calling to her. Too late, though, they'd reached their destination. About time, she thought.

It was twelve-thirty in the afternoon, and after a long overnight flight that threatened to wreak havoc on their body timetables, eccentric Elise was determined not to nap. Hubby Henri, he'd tossed and turned the entire flight, and was no doubt now dreaming of more rest in their luxurious king-size bed. He even yawned. And as much as she tried to dissuade him, Henri took control of his own situation.

"I'll sleep if I want."

Sounding like a petulant child. So she sounded right back as the dutiful wife. "Yes, dear."

Truth was, she was smiling inwardly at her masterful manipulation of the aging fool. In a way, that was more satisfying than thoughts of the chilled vodka that would soon course through her pickled bloodstream.

"Here we are, Mr. and Mrs. Procopio," the driver announced, turning into the courtyard which served as the entrance to this grand palace. Green neon letters spelled out the hotel's name, while a gilt-edged statue welcomed them, his scepter thrust proud to the heavens.

Henri Procopio, chairman of the Looking Great Cosmetics Corporation, along with lovely and leggy fourth wife, Elise, had at last arrived at the start of their new life together. Or what they'd told each other was a fresh start. At sixty-two, average height and slightly round, his head covered with thick black bristles of hair, he was here for a small amount of business and lots of pleasure; she was here for pure pleasure. Funny, though, each of them with a mutual goal—and their own method of achieving it.

The nice thing about the Savoy, check-in was easy. Their copious bags were brought up to their suite separately, the simple swipe of a credit card the only ticket necessary to gain them entrance to all of the hotel's spoils and amenities. So Elise and Henri were inside their money-drenched room within ten minutes; their bags were piled in a corner. Henri went right for the television, searching on CNN International for any news of the financial markets, while starting to undress for that rumored nap. Elise checked the view; the Thames and the London Eye Ferris Wheel within easy reach. She figured she might as well get her bearings before she ventured outside; she was new to London.

Henri found the channel he wanted. "A helluva time to go away, Elise. Looking Great's stock fluctuating daily, the business press hounding me about the launch of our new line, not to mention that damned lottery win that's still hanging over us. Really, how embarrassing, my well-off wife playing the state lottery like some trailer trash, makes me look desperate for cash. Still, it's not a bad idea to get away—anything for you, for us and our future. This week, it's all about the fulfillment of our deepest dreams."

She didn't seem to hear him. "I'm famished," Elise announced.

Deflated, he said, "So order room service."

"No, I think I'll venture down to the restaurant. The Grill is legendary, Henri." Or so she'd read in her Fodor's.

"By yourself?"

"I'm very self-sufficient," she said in a snippy voice that didn't need jetlag to surface. "Really, Henri, you act as though I can't function without you. I can, I did, and I will."

Henri dropped his pants in anticipation of his nap. Elise, that was her cue to leave; she'd seen enough.

She rode the elevator back down to the lobby, checking her appearance in the gilt-edged mirror. She quickly touched up her lipstick. She liked MAC, but don't tell Henri. Then she checked that her yellow scarf was draped over her left shoulder. As she crossed through the main lobby, bypassing numerous people who had gathered on the soft chairs in the expansive lobby, any of whom really could have been someone of importance, she darted her eyes about, searching for someone she'd never met. And when no one made immediate contact with the lady with the yellow scarf over her left shoulder, she continued down the stairs to the restaurant. Actually, what she wanted more than food was a drink, and so she retreated back to the lobby, journeyed up a short flight to a place called the American Bar. She slinked her way inside, where she was met by a white-coated waiter who escorted her to a small table. She liked the quick attention, attributing it to her unfailing entrance. Rarely did she ever fail to grab a man's eye; it was what had secured her job (read: marriage) with Henri. She ordered herself a vodka.

"Grey Goose. Straight up. Freezing cold."

"Surely, ma'am," the waiter said. She loved his accent.

While she waited she nibbled on the peanuts and chips and green olives that were placed on each black lacquered table. Once she was served her drink, she crossed her slim legs and began to scan the room. Lots of imbibers, even though it was the height of lunchtime. She liked these Londoners, they knew how to get into the spirit—and spirits—of things. Unlike her friend Mimi Ledbetter, who was currently losing weight by way of alcohol abstinence and liposuction. How Elise had endured that endless lunch at Le Cirque back in November, she'd never know. Lots of vodka on her part, tea for Mimi. Imagine, tea during mid-day, what was poor Mimi thinking? Elise talked all that day of her favorite things about London, all the while catching the flirty eyes of the cute young man with the dimples at the neighboring table. Now there lay potential.

And so now Elise waited. For an appointment that never showed, not after her first vodka, not during her second. Worry threatened to crease her brow, when she reminded herself the man had said the rendezvous might not take place the first day. But lunchtime, be there at lunchtime. Perhaps the traffic had delayed them too long? In the end, she gave up on meeting with her mysterious guest, ordered a third drink. She savored it, knowing her only other choice was to return to her suite. And Henri.

She couldn't hide all day in the bar, certainly not all week. So she returned to find Henri wasn't sleeping. The shower was going, and she wondered how long he'd been under the hot spray. Henri liked his showers, especially if he wasn't paying for the water. Hah, he paid for everything, whether he realized it or not. The Savoy was no Motel 6 found off some faceless interstate. The television was still on, and so Elise settled down to watch the latest news. She hated CNN, though, so she switched to the BBC. They were barely into a story about a rail crash when the shower stopped and Henri emerged from the bathroom. His bottom was wrapped in a towel, another was being used to dry the thin layer of dark fuzz on his head.

"Oh, you're back."

"I was bored without you. I'm glad you're not asleep."

"No, I decided a shower—"

Henri stopped talking, because Elise had moved to the bed and begun to undress. There came a slight rise from the towel wrapped around his waist. By the time he made his way to the bedside, Elise had removed her clothes and positioned herself on the bed.

"How was your shower?"

"Hot and steamy," he replied, panting now. Getting the message.

Elise kept herself in great shape. And she didn't show it much, not to him. This trip was starting out great.

"Speaking of hot and steamy," Elise said.

"You're had a couple martinis, haven't you?"

"Makes me horny."

"Well, lucky me."

Elise slid up beside Henri, feigned pent-up passion as his tongue probed deep into her vodka-soaked mouth. She had no choice but to return the kiss, was surprised when his mouth sucked on her earlobes, she actually felt arousal. So she gave in to the moment, running her hands across a still-strong chest that was covered by thick whorls of black hair going to gray, hair that grew up and over his shoulders and all the way down his back in thick tufts. As she slid her fingers below the line of the towel, grabbing at the fuzzy fur at the small of his back, he groaned with pleasure. That erogenous zone never failed to arouse him, and today was no exception as his penis made a passable imitation of an erection. Better than lately, certainly. Thrilled by this rare opportunity presented to him, Henri's stubby fingers went exploring all over Elise's fantastically kept body, those pert breasts, oh, and below, that elusive . . . you know what we're talking about.

"Happy Almost Tenth Anniversary, Mrs. Rich Bastard," he said.

"Yes, Almost Happy Tenth Anniversary, Mr. Rich Bastard," she said.

That's when he threw her on the bed and climbed atop her. One easy thrust and he was in, Henri now focused on the task at hand—pleasuring himself. As he thrust and thrust, grunting in the universal language of, well, if not love, at least enthusiastic sex. Elise played along more than she expected, legs wrapped tight around his bristly butt. But she couldn't quite match his verbal proclamations, she couldn't be bothered with such noises. She was busy watching the television as he kept plugging away. The BBC reporter was detailing the story of a local murder which had shocked a quiet neighborhood.

"Vance Timberlake was a simple landlord, never harmed a fly," the reporter stated.

Elise, upon hearing those words, emitted a gargled, "Oh!"

Henri mistook her exclamation as a sign of pleasure and uncontrollably shot his load inside her. Elise barely felt it. She became numb, almost as though someone had murdered her.

CHAPTER FIVE

The neighborhood he'd been kidnapped to was called Vauxhall, he learned, and it was on the wrong side of the Thames from where he wanted and he could take the Tube if he knew which station was nearby and what train would take him out of it. Tired, jet-lagged, and still smarting from Clive's two rounds with him, he just wanted to sleep. He found a phone booth and for the second time that day he had to rely on the verbally unchallenged Beth Simon.

"You said forty minutes, tops, Todd. And what, two hours later you call and say, sorry you got lost? Oh, you poor thing. Surely you could have called earlier, alleviated the worry which threatened to overwhelm me. My God, the scenarios I pictured you in, lying dead in some mews, victim of a terrible accident. Or even a cab crash, those happen. Reckless drivers with licenses, that's all they are. But oh, I'm so glad to hear from you, at least now I can eat my lunch. It's been sitting here on my desk, taunting me, but no, I had no appetite, not until I knew you were safe. Oh, Todd, you're a New Yorker, what was I thinking? My mistake, of course you know your way around— London is just like the Big A, huh? Maybe you drove on the wrong side of the road, went the wrong way out of town? Ha-ha, just a little joke. I mean, I need a laugh after all the worry you put me through. Like I need an excuse for more gray hairs, thank you very much. Oh, listen to me prattle on, you called about the keys. Yes, the keys. I suppose I could let you in on my little secret. How ever did you guess I might have a secret stash near my flat—did Andy tell you? I'll have to speak to him, nasty boy, revealing all my tightly held secrets. Oh, I'm starving."

Yeah, probably for some air, Todd thought.

The next sound he heard was Beth's mouth crashing down on her sandwich, prawns with mayonnaise on multi-grain bread from Pret A Manger, a "whole-food" chain that had begun to pop up in Manhattan too. The homogeny of the world, visit any city and eat the same crap. Kind of made you wonder what all the fuss over traveling was.

"Delicious," she said, mid-chew.

When he had the instructions on getting the hidden set of keys, he tried to hang up. But Beth wasn't convinced he could find the flat all by himself. She tried to get him to stop by her office, she'd love to see him, she said.

"Um, you'll see me after work."

"Oh, right—we can have dinner," she replied, still munching on lunch.

"In the meantime, I'll take a cab," Todd stated, hoping that would be the end of it.

"Call me when you arrive, that's always good. Oh, wait, did I really leave the keys there this time? I had a friend visiting from the Scottish Highlands, she might not have put the keys back— oh, what am I saying, I left my own keys at work just last week and needed my emergency set, so of course they're there, I remember placing them in my white flower pot. Silly me, what was I thinking . . ."

Christ.

At last, as she chomped away on the soggy shrimp, he put the receiver back down on its cradle, emerged from the phone booth and considered his next move. Cab or Tube, he opted for the Tube this time, having had such a bad experience already with taxis. He liked the idea of anonymity again, himself tossed into the throngs of London on the move. Looking for a street sign, he found one posted on the side of a building; that's where all the signs seemed to be found. Kennington Lane. Wasn't he just in that neighborhood? No, that was Kensington, a big difference between an "n" and an "s," and there was a South that went with the Kensington. Todd walked in what he hoped was the right direction, looking for the Underground. And for the first time since yesterday—when that nut had come banging on his New York apartment—luck found him. There was one of those signs with the round symbol used to identify London's Underground. Vauxhall Station. Could have said Timbuktu for all he knew. He studied the map. Victoria line to Green Park, switch to the Jubilee line to Baker Street. Blah blah blah. From there, he'd have to manage on his own in finding Balcombe Street. And Beth's keys, supposedly hidden inside a little flower pot.

Turned out, the trip was easy and fast and successful. Despite a long transfer at Green Park, the ride went smoothly enough, and Todd began to relax. He carefully avoided eye contact with the locals, just like riding the subway in New York, though usually he didn't ride it with a bruised cheek, something for everyone to gaze and wonder about. Hey, did you hear about the guy found murdered in South Kensington? I found him. They'd freak if they knew the truth. Soon after, he had returned topside, where the rain once again reminded him of where he was, dreary old London. This trip had better produce results; in fact, he'd already contemplated increasing his fee. Just because of the hassles.

By now the time was after three in the afternoon. Todd, who hadn't slept, hadn't eaten, hadn't brushed his teeth in too many hours to contemplate, wished for nothing more than a hot shower and a return to feeling normal. So when he finally found Balcombe Street, he followed Beth's easy instructions on finding her spare keys. Once he had them, he opened the front door, walked up the flight of stairs and then again fiddled with the keys until he had at last arrived inside a London flat. This one without a body.

He checked.

The flat was appealing in a feminine way, lace curtains and burgundy drapes in the living room, framed prints of flowers adorning the walls, a cat-shaped clock positioned above the stove in the kitchen. Todd opened the fridge, looking for anything to drink. Beth was a Diet Coke connoisseur; that would have to do. He drank from the bottle, didn't stop until he'd drained the plastic container of the last drop. He set the bottle on the counter, then went in search of the bathroom.

"Oh, yes, thank you, a shower."

He disrobed in Beth's bedroom, glad to be rid of those same clothes he'd put on . . . when? Two days ago? Maybe he'd burn them, he thought, his last for quite a while. Todd didn't make it to the shower, no, because fatigue overcame him and he fell to the bed, dead asleep, his mind so tired that it refused to dream.

Just who is this Todd Gleason, and what's he up to? He's a nice enough guy, just has a problem with authority figures and rich people, father figures really, if you want to boil it down to psychology. Sometimes those were the same people, which only made the situation worse. You know about the lunchroom bullies who helped in his formative years to establish his character. But really, you can't blame your own character faults on a couple of oversized teenagers who didn't know how to deal with their own hormones. Lucky for Todd all they wanted was his pizza money. So, what was it that really motivated him?

Here's Todd in college: Living in the dorm with five other roommates in a three-room suite in a high-rise building at a state-funded school, cheap on costs and even cheaper on educational benefits. Still, for him, coming from the wrong side of the tracks and being the only boy out of a family of four, there wasn't much money, certainly not for him. "You want to go to college, go yourself. It's your degree, so it should be on your bill." That was Mom's piece of wisdom; he would have asked for his dad's, but he hadn't been around since Todd entered kindergarten. It happens. And so he did anything he needed to do, slung burgers, slopped up puke, popped corn at the movies, to pay for his education. Because getting the proper training was tantamount to making a success of yourself in life. Yeah, that and two pounds gets you on the Tube.

Here's Todd after college: Getting a business degree took him five years, those numerous part-time jobs eating away at valuable classroom time. Still, he made it through, no thanks to anyone or anything other than his own ambitions. Not even smarts, anyone could get an A in a class if they studied. No, what Todd had gained from the experience was the nature of survival, and that instinct took him to New York. He joined his college friend, Andy Simon, who had landed himself a job as a trainee at an investment firm, while their other friend Patrick headed off to the golden sunshine of Los Angeles with his new wife in tow. Todd got himself one of those stockbroker jobs, quit after just nine months. Well, quit was a euphemism for being fired; a confrontation with the boss over who actually was the boss. So Todd found himself out of work and determined he didn't need some damn office job to prove his worth. Problem was, money.

Here's Todd dream: Win the lottery. It's as simple as that, pick a bunch of numbers, then have that cheery Yolanda Somebody from New York State's lottery association pick them too. He'd keep his share—the lion's share, he might add—and the government could take their hit. He wasn't completely greedy, he was perfectly willing to pay his taxes. When, after two years had passed and his numbers hadn't yet come up—not even close—Todd needed to rethink his farfetched plan. His landlord was forcing him to, threatening eviction actually, another damned authority figure holding all the cards. The idea was actually already planted in his mind, an outgrowth of a disturbing practice of his. Even though he'd failed to win the lottery, well, others sure had and when they did, Todd had a habit of clipping from the newspapers the feature articles on those lucky people.

He executed his first scam three months to the day he set it into motion. Paul and Debby Goodrich (how's that for a name of some lottery winners) of Fayetteville, New York, some forgettable little village in the snowbelt, won fifteen million dollars, and, according to the article, they opted to take the lump sum payment. Todd took Amtrak to Syracuse, rented a car, knocked on the Goodriches' door holding what looked like a legitimate business card. RICHARD BOOKER, Financial Services. So he gave Debby his spiel, how they needed to wisely invest that cash, if they wanted it to last their lifetime.

"Oh, well, that's Paul's business, the money. I just picked the numbers. My birthday and those of my sisters. I have three of them."

"Me, too, all older," Todd said magnanimously. His dimples got him inside the door.

Debby invited Todd in for coffee. He departed thirty minutes later, having left a series of brochures he'd taken when doing temp work at some financial firm. A few days later, Todd received a call from Paul Goodrich, who wanted to discuss a plan of action. So Todd turned on the charm again and actually convinced the guy to let him handle "one little investment" for them—a trial effort, Todd said. Paul Goodrich handed over a check for fifty thousand dollars and never heard from Todd again.

Here's how Todd handles his guilt: He has none. The Good-riches probably learned a very valuable lesson in handling money, more so than they would have listening to advice from family and friends. No, they needed a fast, hard education in the value of money. They'd won fifteen million, what's a mere fifty thousand to wake them up to the realities of being rich? As for Todd, he was able to pay all his back rent. He even dragged Andy into his new world. The stockbroker helped in setting up a dummy corporation, "Booker Services." That had been eight profitable years ago. Of course, Todd didn't like preying on the unsuspecting or the naive or the just plain innocent, so he tended to take more time in executing his plot, getting to know the people involved. See if they had any exploitable foibles or bad traits or made bad judgment calls, like that idiot from a few months ago, Donald Birdie, screwing the secretary any chance he got. He got off easy (real easy, Bertha had said) with only a fifty thousand dollars penalty fee. Okay, sixty grand, but ten had been for Bert.

Here's what's going on now: Todd is fast-approaching thirty and he's getting tired of the cons. He'd like to settle down, the dating scene in New York sucked, especially when all the dressed-in-black women ever wanted to talk about were their fucking-great careers that were on the fast-track to emotional emptiness. Sure they opened themselves up to him, he was funny and handsome and didn't threaten their femininity. But this existence, this, what—waiting?—was wearing thin. That, and the one close call two years ago had almost made him forego the rest of his goal and run off to a Caribbean island and buy a bar. Then he reminded himself, ambition cannot be denied. Not his. A million bucks, that's all he wanted and then he'd retire, live off the interest in a modest, but comfortable fashion. Continue to play the lottery until he won, maybe pay everyone back who had involuntarily helped him over the years.

And so Todd waited, played his numbers and watched the papers for stories on big winners. In September, in the midst of one particular millions madness campaign that the State ran, a single ticket owner claimed the big prize, thirty-five million dollars. Her name was Elise Procopio, wife of cosmetics king Henri Procopio. Well, that had pissed Todd off, a rich society wife who needs another million like she needs another collagen shot.

And hence, here we were, London, hot on the trail of the unnecessarily more-wealthy Procopio duo. All that would wait, just another day. Because Todd was currently sleeping the sleep of the innocent. There was time later for the actions of the guilty.

Todd awoke to darkness, tried to focus his pupils. A splash of water would help wash out the sticky goo from the corners of his eyes. But why couldn't he find the bathroom, it was to the right of his bedroom. Then he remembered—just as he crashed into a closet door—that he wasn't home. Nope, not even close.

"Todd—is that you? Oh, you're awake, good, I was beginning to think you'd sleep the night through, what fun would that be?"

There were other words too, a constant rambling that brought it all back. Beth Simon, her flat in London and he . . . shit, he realized . . . without any clothes on. He hastened back to the bedroom just as a bath of light enveloped the hallway. Wrapped himself in the first thing he could find—her bathrobe it turned out—he was tightening the belt as Beth walked into the room.

"Oh, don't you look nice in pink."

He looked down at himself. Not just pink, but hot pink with ruffles. "It's the latest on the runways—Paris is positively aglow in hot pink."

Beth laughed, real horse-like, beaming with buckteeth as she did so. "You're so funny."

"Thanks," Todd said. "What time is it?"

"Eight o'clock. I just got home from work about an hour ago, saw you sleeping like a baby, I put a blanket over you."

She winked at him then.

Todd realized he'd been naked atop her bed; had he been on his stomach at least?

Beth Simon. Andy's older sister, what was she, thirty-seven? Had she ever seen a real live naked man in her life? A spinster, he supposed they might have called her in olden days. Now, just not very attractive, physically or personality-wise, poor thing, she always meant well. She was only five foot—even—and her body was round, her legs, her torso, her face, even that nose of hers, which helped hold up thick black glasses. Last Todd knew, she was an editor for one of the British publishers, the name escaped him. He had met her back during the college years with Andy, and upon their return to the campus Andy had announced Beth's major-league crush on Todd. Over the years, Beth had popped up occasionally in his life, Andy insisting that whenever Beth visited they have dinner, her attraction to him renewed each and every time. And here he was, in her bedroom, dressed in a bathrobe that barely covered his, uh, legs. Yeah, let's go with that. He supposed this was as close as he'd get to requiting her love for him.

"So, maybe I should change."

"Okay, you want something to eat? I could cook us up some food, or maybe just order in Chinese?"

He agreed that latter choice sounded good, made him feel a bit more at home. Order whatever, he wasn't picky. Neither was Beth, she admitted. So while Beth started back to the kitchen, Todd finally made his way to the bathroom, where first he peed, second he looked at himself in the mirror, third he looked away. Jesus, he looked a sight, the welts on his cheek prominent in the glare of the bright overhead light. Nice of Beth not to comment on his appearance. He hopped into the shower, and despite low water pressure, he luxuriated as the warm water dripped down his body. Ten minutes passed before he stepped out, and still he wasn't sure he felt entirely clean. He combed his hair, ran his hand across his face and, even though he was in desperate need of a shave, he figured it could wait until morning. Besides, the phone rang in the other room. Todd assumed the food had arrived. So after a quick brush of his teeth, which went a long way in making him feel human, he headed into the living room.

"Oh, good—Todd, the phone's for you."

"Me?" Who knew he was here? A sharp spasm of fear ran through him, remembering that his new best pal Clive had made a note of Beth's number. She handed him the receiver, and he took it reluctantly, touching his sore cheek in remembrance. "Hello?"

"Hey, Todd—it's Andy."

Thank God, not Clive.

"What the hell's going on, man? I called the number where you were supposed to be staying, some stranger answered. Said he was a cop, why was I calling there. I panicked, man, I hung up. And now I find you're at Beth's—surprised the hell out of me, I just called her to see if she'd heard from you."

"Look, Andy, I can't get into it right now. It's been a crazy day, more so than you could ever imagine. I'll fill you in—later," he said.

"Okay, can't wait to hear it, let me know if there's something I can help with. Meantime, I think you may have trouble back in New York."

"Why, what happened?" he asked, his voice rising with concern.

"What's wrong?" Beth asked.

He brushed her off as her brother filled him in on the break-in at his apartment. As he listened, Todd thought back to the day he left, the pounding on his door from that stranger. Got in by breaking the window, tossed the place up but good. The question was, did he find anything? Was there even anything to find? What might he have been looking for anyway? Whoever "he" was. Todd kept his apartment fairly free of important details of his past activities, and even so, those he had were well-concealed. Very well-concealed. So he couldn't imagine anything useful being uncovered.

"The police, they didn't seem to care much, only if you want to make a stink. I did tell them that you were out of the country, so hopefully you can just put it out of your mind, one less thing to worry about, right? Though maybe you should be worried—who do you think broke in?"

"Beats me, Andy. But I'll have to concern myself with it later. Thanks for the update though. Right now I'm going on like three hours sleep and no food. Let me think what I need, I'll be back in touch. Oh, hey, how's Toad?"

Andy chuckled. "Only you, Todd. He's fine, the cops let me take him, tank and all."

"That's good to hear. Don't overfeed him."

"Todd, I've taken care of the damned frog so much he calls me Dad and refers to you as that distant uncle."

"Andy?"

"Yeah?"

"Frogs don't talk."

"Good thing, he'd spill all your secrets."

There was more truth to that than even Todd wanted to admit to.

Todd set the phone back down, joined Beth on the sofa, where she had already delved into a plate of shrimp with lobster sauce. Hadn't she already had shrimp today, that icky-sounding sandwich? He feared now she might start asking questions, but turned out food was important to her (big surprise) and so they ate without interruption, watching a ridiculous sketch comedy show called *Little Britain.* Some guy in a purple dress and riding a bicycle kept proclaiming himself to be a lady.

"My favorite is when he plays 'the computer says no' woman," Beth said.

Todd shot her a sidelong glance. This is what she thought was funny? A guy in a dress? Hadn't Benny Hill done this like . . . a million years ago?

"Uh, isn't *The Office* on?"

As the food was cleared and the show ended, Beth switched over to the local news on BBC One.

And there it was, first item: "Murder rocks the quiet neighborhood of South Kensington."

Todd's feet were planted in the middle of the living room, he still with his empty plate in his hands, his face fixed to the screen. He didn't notice Beth noticing him.

"Vance Timberlake, a local properties manager, was found shot to death in one of his own properties. Police at this time have no suspects, but claim to have a couple leads, including, according to paperwork discovered in his offices, the name of a man who had booked the flat from Friday on. He never showed, they stated. Police are withholding the man's name pending further investigation."

Todd flipped off the television, turned back to Beth.

"You want to tell me what's going on?" she asked. "I mean, Todd, give me a break, you lose your flat and show up on my doorstep with a face that looked like it went one quick round with Lennox Lewis—I didn't want to say anything, not my place, you know? But now? Todd, what have you gotten yourself mixed up in?"

"I have no idea," he said, which was the absolute truth.

He had found a cheap hotel along a road called the Cromwell Road. He was holed up inside his room, a bag of chips at his side, along with a four-pack of Carling lager. Crumbs rested against his bulging stomach, some even were laced in his messy, gray hair, placed there unknowingly in his state of frustration. He was down to his last can—what happened to good old American six-packs?—but still his nerves hadn't settled.

A long flight and no sleep. His life in shambles. And now this.

And to top it off, bad television, too. The last thing he needed to see was a man in a dress.

"What am I doing here?" the man asked the empty room. Then he threw the empty can at the television.

All day long he'd been watching updates on the same story, the murder in South Kensington. With really no new information, certainly no arrests. That, the man realized, would have been the only saving grace in this horribly-gone-wrong incident.

He stood up, needing to pee. Instead, he dug around in his suitcase, fearful that he'd lost it when running away. Nope, tucked beneath his underpants, the feel of it cold, hard. He pulled it out, looked at it in the dim light of the hotel room. Still, it gleamed.

Before today he'd never even held a gun in his hand. Why he'd taken it, he didn't know. Panicked in the face of fear. Remembering the awful scene, he suddenly got up and raced to the bathroom, where he thought he might just puke. Again.

Instead, he peed.

Afterwards, he returned to the bed, where he picked up the telephone and dialed direct because there was no way in hell he could ask an international operator to place the call. No, that would give away the fact he was no longer in New York.

The phone was answered on the first ring.

"This had better be you," a woman's voice demanded.

"Yes, it's me of course, calling with my daily check-in. Sorry, no luck, not yet. I got close," he said, his voice trying to be hopeful. "Real close."

"Well, close doesn't count—not in the lottery, and not in life," she said. "I wasn't kidding, get our money back or don't bother coming home."

He was left with an empty dial tone in his ear, and the memory of her annoying voice. Actually, she kind of reminded him of the man in the purple dress from the television; you know, not attractive? There was something else he found unattractive. That gun. His eyes once again zeroed in on that menacing piece of metal. He picked it up, wondered too if the gun was the end of his bad luck, or just the beginning.

CHAPTER SIX

Since before his trip had even begun, Todd had quite simply not been in control, and it was a feeling he was unaccustomed to. Usually his cons went so smoothly, he barely noticed them happening, even less so his victims. If victim was even the right word; really, was the money he collected from these decidedly wealthy people going to make that much of a difference in their lives? No, no, no were the first three answers to his single question. That's why, when he awakened after a surprisingly good night of sleep—that on top of his three-hour nap the previous afternoon—he was determined to take back charge of his own creation, his con.

He had slept on the sofa bed in Beth Simon's living room. When, at eight o'clock, he realized his body could sleep no more, he got up, brought his suitcase into the bathroom with him. He needed his one suit, which had been uncomfortably stowed inside the tight confines of the bag; couldn't be good for it. And he was right, the dark blue Kenneth Cole suit was wrinkled at best, in need of a clean at worst. He showered, this time keeping the water as hot as possible, while the suit hung on a hanger in the hopes that the stream would render it wearable. Maybe he'd ask Beth for an iron to touch it up. Because he needed to wear it this morning, he had an important appointment he couldn't afford to miss. Literally. When he turned off the shower, his skin was pink from the hot bristles of water, but his suit wasn't in much better shape. When, wrapped in a towel, he entered the living room and found Beth making cof-fee, she instantly volunteered for the thankless job of de-wrinkler. Anything, she said, for a man in a towel. Heck, maybe anything to *get* a man in a towel—and out.

She did a wonder of a job, and by ten o'clock he was gone from her flat, glad to be rid of her constant chatter. While she'd ironed and while he'd dressed and shaved—oh thank God for razors, he felt so much more refined—and while they had shared a simple breakfast of honey-flavored cornflakes, she had kept at him, asking after his plans, why he needed a suit. "And on a Saturday for goodness sake, no one wears a tie on the weekend. No one I know, I mean, maybe you know special people, those who won't mind the fact that your face is swollen from whoever punched you out yesterday."

"You want success, you dress for it," Todd had told her.

Admittedly, the combination of bruised face and fashionable wear were an ill-suited pair. But he couldn't please everyone, and with that bit of truth fueling his newfound determination, he departed from Beth's flat located in the Marylebone section of Central London, finding his way easily to the Tube stop around the corner. Beth herself had been yammering on about helping him get around town, more words spitting out from her mouth than were necessary on such a peaceful morning. He hadn't bothered to respond, just left, not even attempting to confirm his scheduled appointment. This wasn't a meeting that would be put off; Todd certainly knew the man had arrived in London, same flight and all, right? So he hopped on the Baker-loo line and traveled straight on for several stops to Charing Cross Station. When he emerged into a surprisingly calm London day, the sky above a mix of sun and clouds with no rain in sight, he felt the knot of tension in his shoulders dissipate, and he even managed a smile. Maybe the clouds which had hovered over his own life the past couple days had finally left, swept away by some overnight storm front. Leaving clear skies and, using a metaphor borrowed from the high seas, smooth sailing. Todd could feel the energy pulsing beneath his skin, that sense of raw power brought on by the promise of productivity.

His destination was just up the street, easily identifiable. The Savoy. But he had to be careful, Todd did, not to be recognized. It wasn't that he was known in London, God no, but when the police knew you had intended to rent a flat from a man who had just been murdered, the possibility existed that they had found a photograph of him. Of course, he hadn't given Vance Timberlake his real name, no, truly Richard Booker had, uh, booked the flat. But who knew what talents the cops had these days; what resources they were able to tap into in this invasively modern technological age? Who did not have his picture, he was certain, was Henri Procopio, which worked to Todd's advantage. He could ensure that Henri was alone before approaching him; that had been the deal, no one else, not even "the wife."

Especially as she might remember Todd from that afternoon at Le Cirque.

Todd walked up a few blocks on the Strand, slipped down the courtyard where cabs could drop off guests without the pressure of motorists behind them blaring their horns, went through the revolving door and into the beautiful lobby of the Savoy. Bustling activity breezed by him, well-heeled tourists headed for lunch, theatre, sightseeing, all of them seemingly taking advantage of the unseasonably pleasant day brewing. Todd sat down on a plush red chair, his eyes scanning the crowd, his mind thankful to see other men in suits. Made Todd stick out less, though admittedly he was one of the younger faces to be so dressed. Just then the elevator doors pinged open and Henri Procopio emerged, wifey Elise at his side. Shit, Todd thought, he should have brought a newspaper, something to hide behind. Was this any way to conduct business, bringing along someone when he had specifically asked that he not bring someone along? Really, how unprofessional.

But then Elise separated herself from her husband's hold, not without a bit of pulling away, Todd noticed. Subtle, but meaningful, Mrs. Rich-All-Her-Own was showing some resistance to the affections of Mr. Rich-All-His-Own. Still, he coaxed a kiss out of her, and then she was off, her heels clattering against the floor as she was swallowed up by the moving masses of matinee mavens. The time had arrived for Todd to make his move. While Procopio seemed lost still thinking about that kiss. Todd rose from his seat, straightening his tie as he did and put forth his most professional manner.

"Mr. Procopio?"

The balding businessman, himself impeccably tailored in a blue pin-stripe suit and bright yellow tie, swung around and found Todd standing inches from him. He was real close up, so his features were momentarily blurry to the eyes. Todd found this technique a good ploy, disorienting the subject.

"Mr. Booker?"

"Yes, Richard Booker."

"You're a lot younger than I expected," Henri stated with the authority of years of being the boss. Todd himself was victim to a moment's disorientation, his age never before a factor. These days people preferred young upstarts to dying old dinosaurs. "The kind of deal we're talking, lots of money could be exchanging hands, Mr. Booker. I want to know up front that you're legit."

"Youth no longer means poverty, Mr. Procopio."

"No?"

"A dot-com idea, some investors, an IPO, a quick sale. Take the money and run. It's the millennium math. Even now."

"While the project itself goes under—that's old news, Mr. Booker."

"That doesn't mean the money we Internet pioneers made went away. Dot-com companies are about as real as the virtual world from which they sprung, the cash is hard, cold, and spendable. And the strong have survived. Henri—may I call you Henri? Thanks—Henri, I've put the technology world far behind me, I'm looking for something a bit more substantial, something with history and credibility and great potential. Untapped potential, Henri. Looking Great Cosmetics has been around for over thirty years and is a respected name within the cosmetics industry, but it's a bit dated in its products and its perception. Call it the CBS of cosmetics; no one wants to see an overly made-up old person. And as for the future, that previously mentioned untapped potential? Well, I believe that's what this meeting is about. We need to FOX-ify it."

Well, that got the man to smile; he'd built the company from the ground up and had maintained a longer relationship with it than with any of his wives. High praise was the ticket to his heart.

"Shall we lunch?"

"Actually, sir, it's a beautiful day, especially for London— why not take this outdoors. You know, really keep things private."

"A fine idea, quite stuffy in here, isn't it?"

They walked along the Strand, turning down the much quieter Savoy Street, until they emerged onto the busy Victoria Embankment thoroughfare. Waiting for the light to change, they then joined a hoard of tourists as they crossed the street and found themselves walking along the Embankment, the Thames River listlessly floating below them. During this walk, which took them under the Waterloo Bridge and toward the financial district called The City, small talk ensued, the weather, things to do in London, favorite haunts in New York, before Procopio turned back to the subject at hand.

"You know, obviously, that I've been toying with the idea of selling my company, but if that does happen, it will only be to the right—and by right, I mean perfectly ideal—person. While I admire your youth, certainly, and your enthusiasm—not everyone would come all the way to London for such a . . . clandestine, shall we say, meeting. Still, I have to say I remain skeptical. You see, Mr. Booker, I've done my research on you. And guess what I found?"

Todd had always operated small-scale and Booker Services hadn't even registered on the financial meter of New York, no reason it should. Heck, it was fake, a dummy corporation that served only to filter his cash into a high-interest account offshores. So he already knew the answer, wondered now if perhaps he'd overstepped his boundaries . . . and his talents. Bitten off more than he could chew, the saying goes. Todd was certainly fishing in deeper waters than ever before, which only increased his odds of snagging a shark. Todd stared not at Procopio but at the river.

"Mr. Booker, let's be frank."

"I prefer Richard. You can be whomever you like."

"Amusing," Henri said, looking anything but. "Let's cut to the chase—you have no intention of making an offer for Looking Great, do you?"

Well, that was honest, to the point, and Todd needed to do some fast talking.

"Henri—" No, he'd lost the first name privilege, a twist of the man's eyebrow said so. "Sir, it's like this. I'm a financial consultant, one who tends to keeps a low profile, admittedly, as my clients prefer it that way. One of my more well-to-do clients, whose wish it is to remain anonymous at this time, has showed tremendous interest in acquiring your firm and has sent me on what I suppose you could call a fishing expedition. That's why meeting in London is ideal, away from the prying eyes of the piranhas of New York. I'm certain that's why you agreed to meet here, as well. You know how rumors get started. She . . ."

"She? A woman wishes to buy my company?"

"A cosmetics company, sir, wouldn't that be a natural fit?"

"Women should wear cosmetics, not make them, lad."

The use of the word lad, that socked it to Todd. Like he was a petulant child and Henri the domineering parent, scolding the boy. Todd had to swallow that bitter pill. Even with that unexpected setback, he thought he was doing pretty well, he managed to put Procopio on unfamiliar ground: a defensive one. Todd was pleased, figuring Henri couldn't be certain what parts Todd spoke were legit (none being the answer there). Not bad for being out of his league; this might just work.

Todd decided to wait before saying anything further, let Procopio stew in his own words.

So he sat on a bench and stared at the giant London Eye across the river. It was moving slowly, and the sun gleamed through its metal spokes. The view from atop was supposed to let you see all of London. He'd have to give it a try, Todd always envied the view from the top.

Procopio joined him, sitting real close.

"Tell your *client* that if she wishes to talk seriously, to set something up. First with my lawyers. I don't know who she is, what kind of money we're talking, even what her ideas are for . . . for the future. Or why she let you make the initial approach. This has been a complete waste of time, young man. I don't know how you please your clients when you can't pull off the simplest business meeting. In mine, it's not about flashy clothes and fast-talk, no, we're serious about our money, our product—and, as you said, our history. But what we care most importantly for is our credibility."

Bingo.

Procopio's weak point, the sense of pride in all he'd built up.

The old man continued. "I suggest if you want to retain any

shred of hope for this supposed deal, you had better come up with something fast. Real fast. A name—and a legit one at that, Mr., uh, Booker. You know where I'm staying—for now."

Henri Procopio, running his hand over the bristles which grew up over his otherwise smooth head, got up from the bench and started to walk off. Todd sat there, thinking, thinking, of the perfect something to say. Anything. And then he did, jumping to his feet.

"I can destroy you."

Harsh words, dangerous words, especially in such a public place. And on a weekend, yet. These were days intended for relaxation, not the stresses of business. Who knew who might be listening. But Todd couldn't worry about that, not about other people. Just Procopio, and turned out, yup, he was listening. He stopped walking, turned on his heel and gave Todd a look that reminded him suddenly of that polite bastard Clive Remington. Evil lurking beneath a calm facade. He was definitely in newer waters; possibly drowning in them too.

"What did you say, you little bastard?"

Todd tread lightly. "Perhaps we should find someplace more private."

"The wife is off seeing some weighty O'Neill play—"

"*Long Day's Journey into Night,*" Todd said.

"Certainly is," Henri replied.

"Drink?"

"Please."

"Whiskey."

"What else is there, sir?"

That made Procopio smile, at least Todd had some sense of how the business world worked. None of those blue or pink or purple concoctions for him, no, a real man's drink for a real man's discussion. And once both real men were settled with their manly drinks inside the Procopios' suite at the Savoy, the real business began.

"You quite boldly stated you could destroy me. Okay, how would you plan such a preposterous thing?" Henri asked.

"My client—she, well, she does exist, despite your skepticism. And she could easily take your company away from you. Away from anyone, actually."

"Meaning what?"

"My client, sir—"

Procopio interrupted. "Look, I've got things to do, this trip is supposed to be a vacation. Just spit it out, enough dancing around the issue."

"Fine," Todd said, his mind racing as fast as his pulse. The moment of truth, so to speak. "Charity Willow is an actress friend of mine, has done some modeling work, too. So her face is her fortune, I'm sure you can appreciate that. Or at least, her face was. She used your products, Mr. Procopio, Looking Great cosmetics. Suffice it to say, the burning she received from applying your make-up on her precious face has ruined any chance of her working again. Unless it's a company that sells bags to wear on your face."

Henri guffawed. "That's preposterous, there's never been an incident like that in the history of my company. My products are completely safe. You have proof?"

"Of her disfigurement, yes sir."

"But not proof that my products caused it."

"Now who's being naive? The press, they wouldn't need such proof to run the story, just the alleged incident would be enough for them. For them, and for all those consumers who believe everything that the press prints."

Just then Procopio's eyes lit up, as though the light switch in his head had brightened them. "I get it now. I pay you to make the whole thing go away, or else you go to the press."

"And the reputation of Looking Great Cosmetics goes down the proverbial toilet. Not to mention you'd lose any hope of selling the company, especially at the price that's been rumored about in the financial pages."

"That's preposterous, why would the press care about such a thing?"

"Because, Mr. Procopio, you—thanks to your wife's very public lottery win—are big news in New York. You and the Mrs., you're always getting your names in the gossip columns, Cindy Adams and Liz Smith and all that Page Six nonsense in the *Post*. They've even run photographs of the two of you at charity events, hobnobbing with Regis and the Donald and all those Manhattan socialites. Face it, since the lottery win the two of you have become public fodder. And who eats up all that gossip, taking it as truth? The public, and that's who you should be concerned with. All those women who trust you, those teenagers who have made your start-up Youth America line such a top-seller, all they care about is their looks, little Britney or Lindsey wannabes."

"Why not just sue the company? That's why I have a legal department, to take care of such claims—frivolous as they may be."

"What, and let the lawyers drag this out for years, and end up taking far more of the cut than we want? I don't think so."

"You're clever, capitalizing on my wife's—and subsequently my own—notoriety. Very clever, young man—*Mr. Booker*, which I doubt very much is your real name." He drank down the remainder of his whiskey before standing up, his motions seeming to indicate the end of their meeting. Almost.

Todd remained seated; he knew there was a bit more.

"How much?"

Todd's usual fee was fifty thousand dollars. That sounded

low, penny-ante in these leagues. "One hundred thousand dollars."

"You're letting me off easy, son."

Son. Don't call me that, Todd felt like saying. Son, lad, boy, condescend to someone else, dammit. Todd took a moment to breathe, to let the moment pass. He had to focus on the here and now, not a past that was over and done with, unfixable. "We're not looking to bankrupt you, Mr. Procopio. Just a bit of compensation."

"But you are willing to destroy my business—or threaten to anyway—to get that compensation, aren't you? Your methods don't exactly match the money, do they now? Tell me, why should I give in to what amounts, really, to blackmail?"

"Because, one hundred thousand dollars is a pittance for you. Because you want to retire and sell the business, live like a king for the rest of your life—with your well-to-do queen, I might add. Because the barest hint of a scandal will send your already declining stock price even lower, which will scare away a number of legitimate investors, and certainly lower how much Looking Great is worth. Because maybe the company is already in trouble, and you need your wife's windfall to bail you out."

Henri was nodding, he was smiling. He was also slightly sweating, a thin layer of moisture appearing on his upper lip. "Well, you have done your research, there's credit to you. I'll tell you what, lad, you bring me the proof you were going to give to the press and I'll write you a check. Sound simple enough?"

"Proof?"

"Yes, a photograph, I suppose. The actual woman—Miss . . . what was her name?"

Good question. Uh . . . "Charity. Charity Willow."

"Yes, put her before me and I'll happily pay you one hundred thousand dollars."

"Two-fifty," Todd blurted out.

"Excuse me?"

"I provide the girl, it'll cost you."

Again, Procopio smiled. "I have to admit, Mr. Booker, this meeting of ours has been much more fun than I anticipated. Thought it might be just a boring little business transaction, the kind that has made me realize how bored I've become. You've got gumption, so much so you'd probably do well in the business world if you applied yourself. Fine, bring me the girl with the ruined face and I'll give you a check for two hundred and fifty thousand dollars."

Holy shit.

And so the meeting ended with a surprising shake of the hands and a promise, on Todd's part, to be in touch.

"Oh, I look forward to it. Goodbye, Mr. Booker."

Todd could barely find his voice and settled on a polite nod as he left the suite. He thought he was very much in need of another drink—and fast. Talk about hitting the jackpot. Now all he'd need was the girl.

So he went to the Savoy's American Bar, where the walls were decorated with autographed photographs of Hollywood's finest film stars, and ordered an Absolut martini from the waiter. Very dry, very dirty, he said, sucking up the vodka that had soaked through the olive. The waiter watched in amusement. Todd was celebrating, albeit prematurely.

Two hundred fifty thousand. Which would place his secret account at just over a million dollars, just as he'd always dreamed. Maybe this was the last con, the best con. Sure, it had gotten complicated rather quickly, but Todd had always done well thinking on his feet. Charity Willow, what a name, charity indeed. He enjoyed this brief victory, lasting as long as his drink, because then reality began to settle in. Where the hell was he going to find this wonderful friend of his, this Charity, who was such a looker that she got modeling jobs, who was now so disfigured that she couldn't get work?

As he was pondering this insurmountable problem, a woman sat down at the table next to his, she gazing out the window at the falling darkness of London's early evening. You could see the Thames through the rectangular glass, and beyond to the Royal Festival Hall and the impressive dome of the IMAX theatre, lit with a blue glow. What you couldn't see, at first, was the woman's face, and then when she turned to order herself a martini, Todd's face widened with surprise. So did hers, and it wasn't over the fact they had ordered the same drink.

"You," she said.

"You," he said.

Todd Gleason had inadvertently just hooked up with Elise Procopio.

Shit, he thought, she was supposed to be at a play. A long one, O'Neill, for Christ's sake, she should have been gone for hours. Had that been part of Henri's plan, was he using his wife to spy on him? No, that made no sense. Elise had never had anything to do with Looking Great, she was just window dressing. A society wife who'd bought her way into the "in" crowd with hubby's money, her lottery win now her own ticket to the ball. So, then why was Elise Procopio, drink in hand, grinning like a dentist's model?

"I have to give the man credit, you certainly do your research. Running into me in New York wasn't any accident. He sent you then, and he's sent you now. Though I was looking for you earlier, lunchtime, yesterday and today. Had the yellow scarf and all then, though it looks like I didn't need it. I suppose he gave you the wrong info; or maybe I got it wrong. Whatever, I'm glad we've at last connected. Why don't you join me at my table?"

Todd was completely lost. What was Elise Procopio talking about? Still, discretion seemed in order, so he transferred himself to her table, stole an olive from the dish and chewed while contemplating what to say. The direct approach seemed best in this instance. So he asked her.

"I'm afraid I don't know what you mean."

Elise's face just gleamed, as though this was a game of tennis and she was enjoying this sudden volley. "Oh, right, keep things distant, as though we've just met. Really, he's done a fine job, not only will you do the job for me, but you're a nice one to look at too. Truth be told, I wasn't quite sure what to expect."

"You keep saying 'he.' Who is 'he'?"

"Oh right, I suppose you need confirmation."

Todd nodded. Spill it, lady.

"Why, Timberlake, of course," said Elise Procopio, sliding her foot up his pant-leg, graduating from innocent meeting to full-blown conspiracy.

Todd spit the pit of the olive out of his mouth, where it smacked against the framed photograph of Dustin Hoffman, appropriate if you think about it.

CHAPTER SEVEN

"Now isn't the time—to talk."

That's what Todd came up with when he finally got over his shock. Though in that elapsed time questions upon questions flooded his mind. How was it Elise Procopio knew who Vance Timberlake was, and why? For a dead guy, he sure was popular. Was she looking for a flat to rent from him, searching for more of a permanent residence than the Savoy? And was dear hubby Henri aware of this plan of hers? Was she ditching him now that she'd found her own stash of cash? Or, as he feared, did this have anything to do with his murder? That last one, that was a biggie, and at the moment, unfortunately unanswerable. Todd needed to stall. Because what with all those questions, not one damned answer had presented itself.

Luckily, Elise kept things on the sly, and agreed with him. "Of course, I understand. My husband, he's out at some business meeting and could return at any moment. If he doesn't find me in our room, let's just say he'll know where to find me." She ordered another martini, hers with Grey Goose. "So, when can we meet?"

"Name the time, name the place." Todd was about to jot down on a cocktail napkin the phone number of Beth's flat. Instead, he gave her an e-mail address: frogman13, finishing with the Internet provider. "This is the best way to contact me."

"Oh, yes, of course, how . . . how very *now*," she said, patting his arm. "Tomorrow, check your mailbox. I'll know then where

103

to meet. Unless I change my mind." And then she laughed as her long-stemmed fingers took hold of the long-stemmed glass. "As if. I'll be in touch."

Todd slipped away, hoping his presence aside the lonely lady had gone undetected. By the other denizens of the bar, sure, they were too busy drowning in their own self-importance. No such luck outside, though, because as he stepped into the dimming light of day, rain spritzing down now from a darkened sky, a familiar-looking cab pulled up right beside him. The window rolled down and good ol' Bobo stuck out his ugly mug. In the back, Larry waved at him, his hand lost inside his sleeve. Todd didn't need two guesses to know what else was hidden up his sleeve.

"Doesn't your uncle ever need this cab?" Todd asked.

Then he got inside it. Best not to fight them.

Another day, another cab ride, another trip to the same destination. At least he wasn't welcomed by the harmonious sounds of Clive and Fiona making their brand of music; they seemed to have just finished. Fiona was getting herself a beer, a near mirror of the situation from the day before. Yet rather than Clive coming before Todd, Todd himself was granted an audience with the master as he lay languidly in this throne. Pillows propped him up, a thin sheet fortunately covering the parts Todd could go without seeing.

"We meet again."

"Wouldn't be like that, but your—what do we call them, anyway—goons? thugs? henchmen?—"

"Associates."

"Right, more PC sounding, even the bad guys need some social encouragement. Good of you. Anyway, there I was, innocently standing on the street corner, not even looking for a cab. Lo and behold, one shows up for me anyway," Todd said, unable to control his smart-ass remarks. Maybe Clive was too tired for one of his slaps. It was something to hope for. "Never happens like that in New York, you know? Especially when it's raining, damned cabs always go off-duty during inclement weather."

"You don't shut up, you'll be feeling inclement," Clive said. He spoke then to Bobo, asked, "Where'd you pick him up?"

"One guess."

An eyebrow raised, more intrigued than surprised. "Really, Todd. Good friend of mine, what possibly could you have been doing at the Savoy?"

"High tea?"

"Very civilized. What did you have?"

"Those little cucumber sandwiches," Todd said, "Oh, and tea."

Okay, one joke too many. Clive was off the bed faster than a shot of lightning, his impact just as powerful as before, as Todd was thrown against the far wall. He landed on the floor with a loud thud; great, just when the wounds from yesterday were healing. He couldn't help it, but he groaned. He hated showing weakness, but dammit, that hurt. Others may have wanted to beat the crap out of him for conning them out of cash, but none had followed through on their desires. Clive, Todd had done nothing to him and yet here he was, nursing a bruised everything, and on account of what?

"Bring him to me," Clive said to his two silent associates. He didn't bother to hide the fact that he wore no clothes. Not that he had any reason to be ashamed, quite the opposite. Todd looked away.

Bobo and Larry gathered him up by his arms, dragged him until he stood right before their ever-commanding boss. Todd waited, bracing himself for another slap. Which is why Clive changed tactics, and landed a punch directly to the solar plexus.

105

Todd let out an "oof," just like from that old *Batman* television show, and wanted to crumble to the floor; those two goons—sorry, associates—kept him from falling flat on the floor. He thought he might feel better if he vomited. Or if he had joined Elise in a second, numbing martini.

"Okay, boys, let him go."

Todd was surprised his shaky legs held him up. "What was that one for?"

"I hate cute remarks, I hate people who think they're funny," Clive remarked. "And I hate dimples."

Todd, who had had nothing to smile about since arriving at Clive's Vauxhall flat, frowned at the comment. Those dimples always worked against him.

"Come, Mr. Gleason. You and I need to have a serious chat."

Clive was putting on clothes, his overcoat too. Todd, not having been invited to remove his jacket when he'd arrived, was already ready. Clive led him out the door and down the stairs, escorted him inside the local pub, the Frog and the Firkin. How appropriate, Todd thought, with a subtle smile, feeling for the first time that London was finally driving on the right side of the road. His side. Though for the life of him, and wasn't that the truth at the moment, he couldn't bloody tell you what a bloody firkin was. He stole a look at the pub sign, at the illustration of a frog leaning against a wooden cask topped off by a tap. "Oh," was what crossed his mind.

Clive ordered two pints of bitter and then took up position at a far table, away from the football-watching fans at the other end of the pub. "Bet you fit in nice at the Savoy—nice duds."

Todd said nothing, started to undo his tie. "You mind?"

"Be as comfortable as you like."

This, from the man who had attacked him dressed completely in nothing.

"So, Todd Gleason—any relation to that *Honeymooners* actor, what was his name, Jackie?"

Todd shook his head. "Not even close."

"Good, because you're not funny. So can the jokes and we'll get along just fine."

This time Todd nodded. He was full of compromise now.

"The last time we spoke, we very clearly established that you were American by birth, a New Yorker by lifestyle. What we failed to get from you, though, was your profession. Let me guess, yesterday you show up in London looking like a drowned rat, unshaven and dressed in clothes that seemed to have had a break-up with laundry services. Today you're all spiffy, aren't you, designer suit and tie, looking like the entrepreneur I'm quite certain you're not. You fly in on the weekday, conduct your business on the weekend. You know what that signals to me? An unconventional life for Mr. Todd Gleason. You also have very unspoiled hands; haven't had to work hard in your life, have you? I mean, really strenuous work where your back is near to breaking, where the grime under your fingernails takes on permanence. But you're not quite the smooth operator you pretend to be either. So that begs the all important question: what are you?"

Todd hadn't said a word during this monologue. Clive had everything worked out on his own, what more could Todd add? So he sipped at his warm beer, trying not to make a face. What was so wrong with chilling this stuff?

"You know what my conclusion is, Todd?"

"No."

"I think you're a crook."

Had he not been warned earlier about smart remarks, Todd might have said "Takes one to know one."

"Not a particularly resourceful one, I'm guessing, getting yourself embroiled in a murder nearly the second you arrive in London. Poor Timberlake, for him I hope it was quick and painless. His death, or your stumbling upon it, if indeed it's as innocent as all that, it can't be good for whatever it is you're planning. Tell me, Todd, what exactly are you doing here in London?"

"Is that a rhetorical question? 'Cause you've been full of answers already, thought you might be searching your imagination for some more."

Clive drank from his pint, his hand shaking as he set the glass back down. Was his temper rising? Would he dare try something in public? Todd had blurted out his comment before thinking and now prepared himself for retribution.

"Lucky you, I'm going to let that one go. Really, Todd, co-operation is the better part of valor here. You want me out of your hair, I'm sure, and the quickest way to achieve that is to answer my questions. I get what I want, you'll get what you want, and everyone will leave happy. So, I repeat, what has brought you to London in what is affectionately referred to as the off-season?"

"A business appointment is all. That's why the suit, even on Saturday. Nothing sinister, nothing crooked—and nothing that involves you."

"See, that's where you're wrong. First you show up and blow my impending meeting with Timberlake—his dying having with left me with just one little detail about my new assignment. The Savoy, which no doubt you recalled from our discussion yesterday. Then, where do my associates find you today? And all dolled up like a big-time money roller? At the Savoy, of course. Do you see where I'm going with this, Todd? As—like you—someone who lives life a bit out of sync with the rest of the world, I don't believe in coincidence. Yet here we are, victims of two rather remarkable ones in two days. Now, since I'm asking for honesty on your part, let me be a bit forthcoming myself. Timberlake's death has stalled my getting a certain job done.

So I find myself in need of a, uh, distraction. A new opportunity."

Todd tried not to imagine (and failed in that endeavor) what the arrangement was between Timberlake and Clive. His mind came up with several scenarios, the least dangerous of which had Clive playing the heavy to delinquent renters. Pay the rent or pay the price. Clive certainly didn't lack menace, or the desire for violence. As for what qualified as the most dangerous, let's not go there just yet. Let's not wish that. Todd shuddered, hoping Clive would think it was the bitter he was drinking.

"Todd, I've decided that whatever scam you're pulling—and trust me, we both know that that's what you're doing here—consider me in it for half."

"Half?" Todd wished he hadn't said that. In the air between them hung what sounded awfully like a confession.

Clive was grinning. "Bingo."

"Shit," Todd said.

Before another word was spoken, the front door to the Frog and Firkin opened, and in walked a woman Todd at first didn't recognize. But it was merely Fiona. She was wearing clothes, that accounted for the new appearance. She wandered over, placed her arms on Clive's shoulders, her fingers snaking down the front of his shirt. Her own sweater was pointing out the mood she was in.

"I was getting tired of waiting, baby. You said you'd only be a few minutes."

"Do me a favor, love, get us boys a couple more pints and then wait by the bar. Shouldn't be more than a few more minutes."

Fiona was a good girl, she did as she was told.

"Sorry for the interruption," Clive said, drinking then from the fresh pint Fiona had fetched for him. Todd had no choice, he joined his new—what?—associate in a reluctant cheer. "To new ventures."

As they drank, Todd's gaze fell on Fiona, cute little Fiona with the strawberry-blonde hair and the nice body, model quality if you asked him and seeming to be up for anything. An idea popped into his mind.

"Clive, I have a proposition for you—no questions asked, but with your cooperation, you'll get your money."

"I'll get it anyway."

"Clive, come on, don't you trust me?"

"Ha. Trust you, the world's worst con man ever?"

"Oh, I may have a few surprises yet."

"Such boasting. Okay, Gleason, what do you need?"

"More like 'who' do I need."

He drank again, his eyes falling back on lovely Fiona. He knew his dimples were on full display this time.

Detective Chief Inspector Albert Brury of the Metropolitan Police, Kensington Branch, who in just two days would turn fifty years old and who had a perpetual disagreement going with his stomach, was sitting inside his office on Earl's Court Road when the phone rang. Damn, he hated murder cases, more so when he hadn't a clue why the hell the bloke had been offed. He chewed another Tums tablet as he read over his file once again, for like the umpteenth time today.

Vance Timberlake, himself just fifty-two, in relative good health, had ended up on the wrong side of a speeding bullet. It had entered his chest and exploded there, pieces of metal tearing into his heart and ending his life in just seconds, if that long. He'd been shot where he'd been found, inside a fully furnished flat that he managed. It had been empty of a tenant for two weeks, according to the records which Brury had already had confiscated, but was expecting a new tenant just that morning. The new guy, an American chap by the name of Richard

Booker, had failed to show up. Why? That was one of Brury's many questions. Could be an innocent happenstance, finding out the man he was to rent the flat from was killed in that very place. Heck, if Brury had been in that situation, he wouldn't want the flat either. Trouble was, that being the case, when had the tenant learned of Timberlake's untimely death? Maybe after it had happened, or maybe only after he'd shot the bullet from the gun which had killed him. Yes, in all likelihood, Mr. Booker, whoever he was and wherever he was, had almost certainly killed Mr. Timberlake, the motive still unclear.

But motives, in Brury's experience, were often the last piece of the puzzle to reveal themselves. Suspects first, figure the rest out later. So he had to trust his well-honed investigative instincts, in use now for the constabulary nearly thirty years. Nope, either this stranger named Booker had done it, or perhaps Timberlake's wife had. Always suspect the wife, right? What Brury was waiting for—right at this moment, actually, nursing his gastronomically challenged stomach—was news from ballistics. The call came ten minutes after his eyes had blurred over those same damned inconclusive words of his report.

"Brury," he said, grabbing the receiver before the first ring had ended.

Was this guy anxious?

"McCullough here, from Ballistics, sir. Just got back that test. Caliber of gun was a .45, put a real nasty hole through someone, no chance he'd survive."

No kidding. "Right, thanks. Brilliant."

Brury rang off, then got up, realized he'd eaten the last of the antacid tablets. He couldn't live without them and stopped at the Food Corner just across the street from the station house to replenish his supply. Wasn't that just the icing on the cake, his birthday just a couple days away, probably just stick a candle on one of those dissolving tablets and be done with it. Pushing worries of aging to the back of his mind, he realized he had solid info now, so it was time to see about the business of this gun. Guns, they could fix any worries about aging.

It was a quick ride down the Cromwell Road to Queen's Gate and from there just a couple more blocks south to Vance and Clara Timberlake's home in South Kensington. The prosperous couple had lived there for the past ten years, ever since Timberlake's business had exploded, really started raking in the money. No kids, but that had seemed to suit them fine, that's what the Mrs. said late yesterday after Brury had conducted his initial interview with her. She'd been broken up, understandable under the circumstances, unless of course she had killed him and was now shooting for an Olivier. With Albert Brury, no one was free of suspicion; had they a pet, he might have done a residue test on the furry and faithful Fluffy. That was his thinking as he rang the bell at the Timberlake home on Onslow Square.

Clara Timberlake, pear-shaped and standing five foot seven, peered behind the lace curtain that covered the windows on either side of the front door. Brury nodded, and she opened the door.

"Oh, Inspector. Any . . . word?"

"Could I come in? I promise not to take up too much of your time."

She opened the door wide and escorted the detective into a tastefully-decorated living room, plush carpeting and oak furniture, a glass and polished brass chandelier which hung from the ceiling. Yesterday he hadn't taken much notice of it, concentrating his attention on the widow Timberlake, on her body language and on her eyes. On how much contact they made with his.

"You have a lovely home."

"Thank you. Only because Vance did so well, you know, with

his business and all, were we able to afford such nice things."

"But you worked with him."

"I managed the cleaning staff, the help who came in and fixed up the flats between renters. Not much to do, really. He wouldn't let me near the office. Sometimes I would show a property—you know, if there were special demands. Party planning, catering, that kind of stuff. Everyone should have interests other than their job."

"I see," said a suspicious Brury, who was a policeman first and a policeman last. "Now, Mrs. Timberlake, I need to ask you a couple delicate questions. I expect total honesty; it's the only way we can determine who did this terrible deed."

"God's honest, Inspector."

"Right," he said, flipping open his notebook. "Let's review first of all, where you were at the time of the killing. You said . . ."

"Oh, Inspector, is this really necessary? Treating me like . . ."

"Like a suspect? I'm sorry you feel that way. It's just my way of eliminating you from my list."

"Oh . . . how, clever."

"You said you were at home."

"Yes, taking care of some paperwork in Vance's office."

Brury jotted down a note, looked up at the widow. "Thought you said only your husband took care of the office."

"Oh, I didn't mean I was attending to his stuff. I keep my own records in the file cabinet . . . you saw that yesterday, in your search."

Brury made another note. "Of course, my mistake. Now, moving on, did your husband own a gun?"

Clara Timberlake shifted uncomfortably on the sofa. "I was afraid you'd be getting around to that. Yes, Inspector, he owned a gun."

"Do you know its caliber?"

"I don't know much about guns. But I did take the liberty of digging through his paperwork. I urged him not to get it, but in his business—renting to strangers, you never know who might show up, what they might really want—he wanted protection."

"So he would bring it with him on occasions such as yesterday. When he was meeting a new tenant."

They were statements and not questions but she nodded along.

"Could I see that paperwork?"

"Be a minute."

More like five; he wondered what could be taking so long. At last she returned with a file folder in her pudgy hands, apologizing for the delay.

"He keeps this stuff in his safe, sometimes I forget the combination and have to start again from scratch."

She handed it over and Brury began to flip through the documents. Gun registration, license to carry, all the appropriate stuff. It was all in order, strictly on the up and up. The most telling detail was of course, the caliber of the gun, a .32. Interesting, not the same caliber as the one he'd been killed with. Someone had come prepared, which struck Brury as a simple case of premeditation. Whoever had killed Timberlake, they'd been angry, they'd been determined, they'd wanted the man dead.

"Mrs. Timberlake, is your husband's gun in the house?"

"No, certainly not. He leaves it in his safe when he's home, and the gun is definitely not there. He must have had it on him, like always. Quite attached to the bloody thing—oh, sorry, but as I've stated, I disapproved of his owning it." She paused. "Surely you found it on . . . well, among his things."

Brury shook his head. "I'm sorry, no."

"No? But that's impossible . . ." she started to say, only to clam up. Her eyes fell to the floor, as though a piece of lint had suddenly distracted her.

"Mrs. Timberlake, whoever shot your husband seems to have made off with this gun—why, I can't imagine, considering he brought his own. Adds a whole new dimension to the crime. His gun, along with the murder weapon, could be at the bottom of the Thames by now, little help to us now."

"Oh my, how puzzling. Can you believe such a thing, Inspector? I mean, my husband, shot to death right in his own neighborhood. Getting's so no place is safe."

"I quite agree. South Kensington is not only my territory, it's my home, too," he said, working the sympathy angle to see if it would help open up Mrs. Timberlake's memory banks. "Can you tell me more about this Mr. Booker—the man scheduled to rent the flat."

"A standard booking, Inspector, like we'd done hundreds of times over the years. There was nothing remarkable about it. Found us on the Internet, rang us up and asked the right sort of questions, had no reason to think he was anything but a legitimate booker. Oh, now isn't that an ironic name."

"Yes, it is. Have you heard from him?"

"No, not a peep."

Brury made a note in his pad.

"He killed my husband, didn't he?"

"Well, we're certainly interested in questioning him. What his involvement is, if any, only time and cooperation will reveal. Now, there's one more question, ma'am, and I should preface it by saying you may not like the question, the implication. It's true, you have no children, right?"

"Correct, sir. A regret now, I suppose, I'm all alone."

Brury nodded sympathetically. "The reason I ask is, well, do you use the Internet, e-mail, that sort of modern stuff?"

"Certainly. Opened up such new possibilities in marketing our services. Why?"

Brury paused, as though considering whether to pass along a

piece of information which to this point had not been revealed to anyone, certainly not to the press. He decided to go ahead with it. "I'm going to reveal this to you, ma'am, because, as the victim's wife, I need your unique perspective, your history and your knowledge. There was a faint impression of an e-mail address on your husband's neck. Not the entire address, unfortunately, not the service provider. But the first part, that was clear enough. Looked like ink from a felt tip pen, don't know how it got on his neck."

"I'm afraid I don't understand what you're driving at."

"Mrs. Timberlake, was your husband having an affair?"

Despite the fact they were discussing her husband's brutal murder, Clara Timberlake laughed heartily, the rolls of her stomach jostling like jelly. "Lordy, no, Inspector Brury, that's impossible. Vance? An affair? No, he and I were very happy; he and I were not the most attractive couple around, we knew what we had, something special. Beautiful people should be lucky to have what he and I had—from our teen years on. Vance and I were as close as two people could be, he'd never keep that kind of secret from me. Any secret, for that matter, he knows what's good for him."

Nothing was good for him anymore, Brury thought.

But what he said instead was, "That's lovely to hear, Mrs. Timberlake, the nature of your relationship, quite a testimony to your husband's memory." Brury tossed a Tums into his mouth. "Still," he said, mid-chew, "I have to wonder, if he wasn't having an affair and he didn't have any children, who then is 'daddysgirl'?"

CHAPTER EIGHT

Still at the Frog and Firkin, still with Clive. And no closer to leaping out of here.

"How much?"

"Two-fifty."

"Each, I assume."

Each? Two-fifty a person? Shit, it had taken all of Todd's thinking-on-his-feet smarts to get the money up that high from his originally planned fifty grand. He shook his head. "Total. And that's only if I produce the woman herself. I've already negotiated upwards, two-fifty max."

"Todd?"

"Yeah?"

"This is literally the stupidest plan I've ever heard of. Bloody foolish, if you ask me. If this is the level of crap you pull, it's a wonder you're not rotting in prison yet. Personally, I'm amazed this guy listened to your whole spiel before he had the wherewithal to throw you out."

"But he did listen, and that's the key. He's already agreed to the payoff."

"Only if you can pull it off—convincingly."

"That's why I need the lovely Fiona," Todd said. "She seems to be quite the little actress, you know, from what I've heard through thin walls."

Clive held a look of disdain at the supposed insult. "She's more into method acting, feel it, react to it."

Poor impressionable Fiona, twirling her hair at the bar all by her lonesome while these two men discussed whether her screams of passion were live or Memorex. Whatever the truth, their discussion ended in a stalemate—Todd was convinced she could pull it off; Clive less so. These two couldn't agree on whether the Earth was flat or round.

"Yeah, but since it's my scam, I get to make the decisions. And I say we go with Fiona."

"It's my investment," Clive stated. "And your health if it doesn't pay off."

Again with the threats. This guy was a one trick pony. An effective trick, sure.

In the end, and maybe that third pint had something to do with it, Clive agreed to the plan. With one provision. "You've got one try to separate man and money and then I take over. Should take a day or so to get Fiona ready—I have a contact in the West End who should be able to help us. I'll be in touch." He stood, then thought better of it. One last warning, best whispered. "Oh, one last thing."

Great. Todd couldn't wait to hear this one. "My cut is two-fifty, nothing less."

"But that's the whole pot."

Clive dropped his head in shame. As though the student had failed the mentor. "It doesn't have to be, Gleason. Use your head."

Then Clive drained the murk from the bottom of his glass and grabbed hold of Fiona, leaving Todd with the suddenly-from-nowhere arrival of Bobo and Larry. With instructions that they "keep an eye on him."

This time they drove him where he wanted to go, directly to Beth's flat, extending a courtesy Todd hadn't previously seen much of. As Todd stepped inside, he noticed that Bobo had parked outside the building, taking this watchdog job seriously.

Shit. Couldn't things go his way for just once?

Well, yes. Todd found the flat empty, a note from Beth saying she had plans with a friend, make yourself comfortable, she'd talk to him later. Talk at him, certainly. For now, he relished the silence, the first such serene moment since this entire insanity had been unleashed. He shed himself of the suit and put on jeans, more his natural skin. Grabbing a Coke from the fridge—enough of those warm beers—he dropped to the sofa. No TV, no music, just the steady drone of the rain outside. He imagined Bobo and Larry sequestered in the cab; what did those two talk about?

The silence gave him a chance to review. Todd Gleason, the concerned con and dimpled diatribe, was looking to score his biggest payoff yet, the two hundred and fifty thousand bucks that would put him past his goal of one million dollars; retirement money. For Henri Procopio, the money was a drop in the bucket; to Todd, life-changing. Seemed easy enough in theory, yet its execution was anything but, given that pest, Clive. Fix that—*dangerous* pest, Clive. He was now demanding the entire cut, and for doing what? Not breaking Todd's legs, or worse. Todd knew he had one choice: convince Procopio to double the fee.

How?

"Shit," Todd said to the empty apartment.

In his eight years of pulling small-time, small-town scams, none of them had gotten quite so complicated so quickly. He was chased out of his apartment in New York, he stumbled upon a dead body in London, he got caught up with a bad bloke named Clive, and now, after setting his plan in motion with Henri Procopio, he was in danger of not only not yielding a profit, but losing money on this deal. These operating costs like flights and designer suits and flat rentals (okay, so he could deduct that from his list), they didn't fall off trees, you know?

There was an ace up his sleeve, though. Or better yet, a queen. Her name? Elise Procopio.

This was truly the first moment he'd had to analyze his impromptu meeting with the woman whom he originally viewed as his uninjured victim. She, after all, was the winner of the lottery and the reason Todd set his plan in motion. Thirty-five million, what would that be like? Todd, with his pittance of fifty thousand dollars per scam, realized he was still ranked an amateur. This crew, Procopio, Clive—an unknown someone else who was probably Timberlake's killer?—they were in whole new league, the majors and Todd felt like he'd just been called up from A Ball. And of course, Todd had to assume there was some kind of connection between them all. Timberlake had told Clive he would be meeting his "assignment" at the Savoy, but died before he could impart him with any more information. Todd's own meeting had previously been set up to take place at the Savoy, as well. With Henri.

And then, of all things, Elise sidles up to him and plays coy with him. About what?

"Beats me," Todd said aloud. "Other than it involves Timberlake."

And then again, maybe he did know. Todd began to laugh, so heartily that he wondered if even Bobo and Larry could hear him. Still, as convinced as he was of his newfound suspicions, there was only one way to know for sure.

He ran back to Beth's bedroom, grabbed his laptop. He flipped it on, went on-line and—after being bumped off three times by the slow dial-up—his persistence paid off. There, along with a message from Andy—"Toad the Frog is doing well in his new surroundings" at Andy's apartment—was another, newer e-mail from an address he wasn't familiar with. Still, he knew what it was about. The screen name was "ladyluck." He double clicked and the message appeared:

Sunday. 5:00 P.M. Buckingham Palace. Beneath the statue of Queen Victoria. Let's hope for rain, we can huddle under an umbrella and make plans.

Of all places to meet, she picks Buckingham Palace? What did she think, they were going to have fricking tea with the Queen? Yes, I'll 'ave a scone and, and what?

What indeed.

"What are you plotting, Elise?" Todd asked the computer screen. "And does Clive have anything to do with this?"

Todd sent a reply, confirming the appointment. As he put the computer away, he noticed that his hands were sweating. He settled back down on the sofa and that's when Beth arrived, talking non-stop about the frustrating date she'd just been on.

Stuffing potato chips—crisps, eh?—into her mouth, and still talking, by the way, she admitted it had been "a blind date."

Deaf, that would have been good too for the guy.

"Oh, Todd, it's so nice to have you to come home to. Do you mind if we talk for a while, I just don't get it, what's wrong with me? Didn't even bring me home, just pushed me into a cab, mid-sentence for goodness sakes. I'm nice and friendly and oh, I'm a great conversationalist, don't you think? Any lull in a conversation, I've got the perfect solution, I can pick a topic out of thin air and get the dialogue going again, an unappreciated talent if you ask me. Well, his loss . . . I'm thirsty, how about we head down the street . . ."

Blah blah blah, he tuned it out and resumed thinking about the con he'd set into play.

Sunday arrived. Todd heard nothing from Clive all day. In front of Beth's flat there was no cab, no Bobo, no Larry. He remained indoors, watching it rain and watching terrible movies on the television, but at least they kept Beth from chattering on. She had suggested dinner at a Turkish restaurant over on Cleveland

Street, "just the two of us, we'll have a grand time. They have this dipping sauce that tastes just like caviar, oh, I forget what's it's called. What do you say?"

Todd confessed to having an appointment.

"With who?"

"Beth—what did brother Andy tell you about my visit?"

"Nothing."

"What have I said about my visit?"

"Nothing."

"Are you sensing a pattern?"

"Oh." She seemed more disappointed than she had been with the blind date.

He left at four to give him plenty of time to get to Buckingham Palace. From the Tube map it was clear getting to the Queen's quaint home wasn't all that simple; maybe she preferred it that way. You want to get here, walk, dammit, crawl if you must, my loyal subjects. As he stepped out of Beth's building, he raised his umbrella, partly to shield himself from the heavy rain, partly to shield himself from any possible curious onlookers. Cars lined the street, but none were cabs. Hopefully that meant Clive's thugs were nowhere to be found. Could they have lost interest? He sincerely doubted that. Which meant they were better at tailing than he'd given them credit for. Todd had to assume they were near, Clive wasn't likely to make any mistakes, not with quarter of a mil at his lazy fingertips.

Todd stayed cautiously alert until he'd disappeared into the complex Tube system, joining other faceless individuals on their silent journeys. He hopped the Jubilee line, which took him south to Westminster, where he transferred to the Circle Line. London's version sure was different from New York's, seemed here you had to transfer every stop, he thought, glad he could think light, distracting thoughts. He realized he'd smiled and a woman had smiled back at him. Sometimes those dimples worked well enough. Too bad she didn't get off at St. James's Park, his stop. Oh well, he reminded himself to stay focused on business.

Back topside, Todd followed the signs to the palace. Even with the crappy weather brewing above, there were lots of tourists milling about. Perhaps that was the brilliance of Elise's plan, meet where there were guaranteed crowds, even on a rainy Sunday afternoon. And where would you most expect to see crowds than at the grand home of the Queen herself? Everyone loved a taste of royalty, and here you could get close enough to at least smell it. Todd himself took a whiff, liked what his nose picked up, the scent of riches, of avarice. Other senses were heightened as well, his eyes foremost. He'd never seen the palace before, and tonight it was aglow with warm light against a cool, rain-streaked blackening sky. Now that he was here—and early, so it appeared—he stared ahead with obvious envy, beyond the big iron gates that separated royalty from poverty, and into the majestic palace in his mind. He could live here.

Tourists with cameras and camcorders began to crowd him near the gates and before he ended up a bit player in someone's home movie, he made his way across the street toward the Victoria monument, where Elise had specified—and there she suddenly was.

"Darling," she said, kissing him full on the lips. Todd detected some tongue.

Pulling away, he said, "Uh, hi, sweets."

"Play along, we're passionate lovers."

What was this, *The Graduate: The Next Generation?*

Elise slipped her arm through his, snuggling in tight. "See, I got my wish, it's raining and here we are, our bodies tight against one another." Then she patted his butt for added effect, her smile brighter than any camera flash.

Todd was mulling over that maybe this whole escapade of

hers was just Elise wanting an affair. Was Clive some kind of call boy, there to service the needs of a lonely married lady? If so, why was Clive getting so angry at Todd, slapping and smacking and punching because he didn't get to boink the rich lady? Fiona seemed an awfully fine consolation prize, even if there was no cash reward. Then Elise went ahead and spoiled the innocent image.

"So," she said quietly, "you don't look like a killer."

Todd only missed a step, barely unnoticeable. "A killer."

"Oh, I know, I shouldn't speak such a word in public." She looked around at a group of Japanese tourists. "No one's paying attention to us anyway, they probably don't understand English. It's just, well, I find your choice of profession very intriguing."

"It's best not to look too deeply at it."

"Do you have a conscience?" she asked him.

Todd withered her with a glaring look. "Do you?"

She looked away. "It's the only way."

"Tell me more."

"Timberlake told me . . ."

"Forget Timberlake, he's dead and of no use to either of us anymore. And while we're at it, let's forego all names. Yours, mine, any others involved," Todd suddenly said, anger cutting through his words like a sharpened blade. He figured a hired killer would have a temper. Method acting, just as Clive had mentioned.

"Oh, I'm, I'm sorry. I won't . . . pry. Oh my, did you kill . . . ?" And then she wisely shut up.

"I told you, forget him. His death is . . . unfortunate, but we were able to hook up anyway, shows how unnecessary he really was."

"I suppose. Did he tell you what I needed done?"

Here was one moment of truth, Elise Procopio's own plot soon to be revealed. They'd left Queen Victoria faster than had

Prince Albert, and were now walking along the Birdcage Walk in St. James's Park, going against the flow of human traffic. Headed for the Houses of Parliament and discussing murder. Or, at least, about to.

"It has to look like a random . . . occurrence," she said. Didn't say what, didn't say who, didn't have to.

"That's going to cost you."

"Timberlake and I already settled on the price—a cool mil."

Okay, this time Todd's feet failed him and he stopped mid-step. Foot actually still in the air. When he turned and looked at Elise, it was apparent even she was uneasy about this part of the conversation. Discussing the contract killing of her husband, it was nice to know she was showing some level of remorse. But why, Todd had to ask himself, why not just divorce him? She had the money herself, surely Henri would give her more just to get rid of her. To resort to killing him? Todd shuddered, and not from the cold wind which was cutting through to his skin.

"One million dollars."

"Pounds," Elise said, too quickly to retract.

"That's quite a bit more than U.S. currency. With Timberlake out of the way, you could have stiffed me and I'd never have known."

"You do the job, I won't care about the money."

"What'd you do, lady, win the lottery?"

Todd's little joke.

She ignored the remark and forged ahead. "I mean, it doesn't have to look like an accident, like running him down with a cab. I'd rather it be quick, but just, well, as I said, it's to look random. As though you could have chosen anyone and Henri was the unlucky choice."

"It's to look like you couldn't have had anything to do with it."

"That's why I'm hiring a professional."

Todd nodded. "When?"

"Saturday is our tenth-year anniversary. We leave London the next day."

"The anniversary—and tenth one. That's cold."

For the first time, Elise flashed a look of pure malevolence. "You don't know what that bastard tried to do. It serves him right."

"Please, I don't want to."

Actually, he was dying to know.

"What are your plans for Saturday? I assume big plans?"

"That's the problem, he won't tell me. 'It's a surprise, dear,' he tells me. It certainly will be—for him."

"This won't be easy."

"For a million fucking pounds, I shouldn't expect it to be a walk in the park."

A well-timed remark, as their own little walk in the park came to a close. They had reached Whitehall and Big Ben was just down the street and was minutes from announcing six o'clock.

"Well, I guess this is it, then," Elise said.

"So it seems. Uh . . ." Todd was hesitating, surely a trait that would elude a trained hired gun. "Are you sure this can't be done another time?"

Elise looked up, puzzled. "I thought I was the one who was supposed to have second thoughts?"

"Sorry, it's just . . . I want to be sure you know the full implications of what you're asking. This isn't like ordering off a menu. You don't like what you get, you send it back. There are no returns here."

"I understand—and as for the timing, it has to be just perfect. The anniversary date is ideal, and preferably in the evening— ten o'clock to be specific. I'd like to time it with when he and I first . . . you know. He got his rocks off, now I finally get mine," she said. "As I know more details, the when and where of our torrid celebration, I'll let your know—e-mail, it's such a great invention. It's so, impersonal."

"Yes, it's perfect for you," Todd said.

Before leaving, Elise kept up the image of "young lovers." She pressed her lips to his, forced her tongue deep into his mouth. Her hands gripped his butt, made their way around to the front package. Todd wanted to recoil from her touch, knew he shouldn't.

"Perhaps when all is said and done, we can celebrate."

"I celebrate alone," Todd said, and then blushed when he realized exactly what he'd said.

"You're funny—for a killer."

Tell that to Clive.

She stopped for a moment. "You know, I expected at a least a British accent."

Oh, good point. "Where I'm from originally and where I live have little in common. It's best to be able to blend in anywhere."

With a hearty laugh, Elise slipped away. She took the umbrella.

As for Todd, thankful for that improv class he took in high school, he was left standing in the rain. He walked for some amount of time, how long he didn't know. Big Ben was the other way now, out of reach and seemingly out of sync with the world Todd found himself in. Time was standing still, despite the constant shuffling of bodies all around him. He walked through Piccadilly Circus and up the sweeping sidewalks of Regent Street, emerging onto the claustrophobic sidewalks of Oxford Street, quite far from the palace and quite drenched from the rain. He remembered what he'd read in his Fodor's: anything could be bought here on Oxford Street. Perhaps even a killer?

★ ★ ★ ★ ★

Could he really return to Beth Simon's flat right now? She'd been alone and was probably starved for conversation and that was the last thing he needed. More words. Words held such damaging potential, they had the power to kill. Did they have the power to save a life, too? Should Todd go pay a visit to Henri Procopio and tell him his wife was planning to kill him? He'd be laughed out of the man's room, just another stunt to grab some cash, couldn't find the woman with the facial disfigurement, huh? His con blown up in his face because of an attack of conscience. Todd's sole consolation at the moment was the fact that the only people who knew about the contract killing were Elise and himself. And so really, it's not like the hit would actually go down. Todd was no killer, not even for a million pounds, which in today's market was damn near close to two million American. Did the fact she hadn't connected with the real hit man mean when Saturday's anniversary went off with Henri's version of a bang instead of Elise's the threat to his life ended there?

Todd walked all the way back to Beth's in Marylebone, a healthy walk, though in this cold, dreary, rainy weather, did the exercise to his heart really outweigh the threat of catching a cold, the flu, pneumonia? He was tired, drained, both physically and emotionally, and at first he didn't notice that the front door of the building was open. Only when he pushed against it with Beth's spare key did he realize how needless the key was.

A tiny voice told him to turn around, get out of there, run, run, fucking run as fast as you can, anywhere but here, back to New York and out of this crazy mixed-up con. Concern for Beth overrode his instincts; after all, the last time he came upon this situation, he'd found a dead body. Please, God, no, not Beth. She had nothing to do with this. An innocent who had only offered her friendship, making Todd feel like a shit for how he'd thought of her. What was wrong with a talkative person, took the pressure off yourself, didn't it? As he made his way up the steps, he told himself that even if Beth was okay, he was going to find another place to stay. There was enough danger lurking that he didn't need to expose this kind woman to it, no more.

The door to Beth's flat was open and bright shards of light were spilling out into the hallway. Todd stepped in, calling out Beth's name. There was no answer. Fear gripped his heart. Sweat formed on his brow. He approached the living room, found nothing. The same with the bedroom. There was no sign of forced entry and the flat looked entirely undisturbed, but still there was no sign of Beth. In fact, the only thing that seemed wrong with this picture was the open door; but that was enough to raise the hair on the back of his neck, wasn't it?

Todd entered the tiny kitchen, where Beth had been leaving him notes as to where she'd gone, when she'd be back. Today there was no note. Just the smell of food. Still in their delivery bags, and from a quick touch, still warm. Stapled to the brown bag was a menu; Todd recognized the name of the nearby Chinese food restaurant, Phoenix Palace. If Beth had ordered food, where was she now? Run off with the Chinese delivery man? Todd didn't think so. That's when he noticed a hastily jotted note on the menu.

She'll do for now. I will find you. And you'll pay.

"Oh, shit," he said.

This wasn't good, not good at all. Beth Simon had been kidnapped. Trouble was, this didn't smell of Clive, they'd already established a detente of sorts. So then, what the hell was going on? Did this have anything to do with Timberlake's murder? There was a similarity, the open doors to his flat and now Beth's. Damn, where were the neighbors in all this, didn't they hear anything? Todd didn't think he had time to ask. No, Todd didn't think he had time for anything except a fast escape.

He ran to the bedroom and then thought better of it, he didn't need to be saddled down with his suitcase. He'd need access to his e-mail, though, so he went to reach for his laptop.

Which of course was missing.

"Oh, fuck."

Maybe coming to London had been a bad idea.

★ ★ ★ ★ ★

PART TWO
CAMBRIDGE CIRCUS

★ ★ ★ ★ ★

CHAPTER NINE

Be there, be there, be there . . .

That many pleas, that many rings. Then the machine picked up, again.

"Thanks, never mind," Todd said to the overseas operator, so helpful in placing the collect call. He replaced the receiver and stepped out of the phone booth and returned to the rain that had already made a mess of him. Two hours had passed since he'd escaped from Beth Simon's flat, and in that time he had attempted four times to call Andy. Sunday late afternoon in New York, no doubt he was at the movies or an early dinner or watching some sporting event in some bar, the financial wizard in play mode. Now midnight was approaching London and Todd had no place to stay, no clue where he might begin to find a suitable hotel (and with no luggage, that wouldn't raise any eyebrows, now, would it?). His only option, really, was Beth's.

Which meant he had no options at all.

Luck found him. Walking along the deserted Marylebone Road he came upon an Internet cafe, coffee and computers for the new age, and conveniently open twenty-four hours a day. As he stared at the brightly-lit shop, inspiration struck him. He entered and plopped down two pounds for an hour's worth of Internet access. The clerk didn't even pause over Todd's appearance; no doubt he'd seen worse, working the graveyard shift as he was. Grabbing a cup of coffee first—to keep him awake— Todd made his way toward the back of the shop, sat on a stool and got to work. One other person was surfing the net, he not bothering to look up from whatever wave he'd caught.

Todd went right for his service's home page, then typed in his screen name and password. The taunting voice told him he had no new messages. Some people took that as an insult, Todd took it to mean Elise might be having second thoughts about killing her once-beloved husband. Or she'd been unable to come up with new information. Cracking his knuckles, he set about typing.

The first was a message to Andy. *I tried to reach you, but you were out. My computer has been stolen, I think, by the same man (men?) who has, brace yourself, kidnapped Beth. I'm sure she's fine, it's me he wants. I think. I'll handle from here. Sorry for the complication. Not one of my easiest, huh? How's Toad?*

The second message he sent to himself. Or at least, to whoever had run off with his laptop; damn, he hoped to get it back, sucker cost two grand. His request was simple. *Let me know what you want. Reply to same.*

Wasn't it nice, this technological age that allowed you to contact kidnappers before they'd even had a chance to make their ransom demand? Although with Beth Simon the captive, they might need a temporary ransom until any money could be delivered. Tape strong enough to keep those jaws of hers from yapping. Maybe they'd tire of her, let her go? That was, at best, hopeful. They could decide to just rid themselves—and the world—of her, you know, permanently. That was, at worst, terrible. He hit send, and his message shot its way through cyberspace.

He waited, content to surf the net himself, even though the other guy had long given up and taken his board home. At one in the morning, no return message, at two, same status. Todd was beginning to think the computer voice was mocking him. Anyway, through a very long night in which only one other person came in, a bit drunk and sending pornographic messages to an ex and cackling as he did so, Todd waited. In the lonely stretch between four and five when it seemed the entire world was asleep, the clerk at the cafe's front desk, the Procopios and Clive and even Beth Simon, heck, probably New York City, too, which rumor had it never did, there was Todd, not exactly wide awake but certainly you couldn't call it sleep. He was contemplating whether to contact old friends, his sisters, hah, even his mother who had kicked him out at eighteen so he could pay his own way in the world. He'd need a new screen name for that, though. Instead, he sent a humorous little jibe to one of his more recent acquaintances, must have been the lack of sleep that made him think this was a good idea. Anyway, it was an easy address to remember, even though it had washed off that first day.

How I wish we could have joined the mile-high club. Regards, Seat 46H.

Todd gave up at six in the morning, having paid out his last pound. He needed cash, he needed sleep, and most of all, he needed a response . . . from anyone. Why steal his computer if not to be able to communicate with him? His password was automatically remembered by Windows. So helpful. Of course, whoever Todd was dealing with could have been sleeping; it was that time of day, er, night.

Actually, day was technically correct. Outside, the rain which had flooded London yesterday had blown past, replaced by a sky that held promise. Too early for the sun, but the smell in the air was cool and crisp. It almost gave him hope. Hope, though, was nothing without a plan of action, which is what he tried to come up with during his aimless walk through the city's streets. He came upon a newspaper vendor, setting out the day's morning papers and taking out a black marker to write on a paper placard the day's hottest headline. Anything to get passing folks to stop and pick up a paper on their way to work.

"Holy shit," Todd said when the vendor finished writing.

"Newspaper, sir?"

"Yeah—that one," he said, pointing to the headline.

Thirty-five pence, that he had in his pocket. The sale a success, Todd anxiously flipped through the paper for the article that the headline had teased. The ink was staining his sweaty fingertips. He couldn't find the article, dammit, it had to be here, somewhere . . . calm down, Todd, calm down, mate. Focus on your needs first, then concentrate on the problems. So, for the second time that night, morning, whatever, inspiration found its way to Todd's tired mind. Cash, he needed cash. That was an easy enough request, an ATM nearby. A cab, now, he needed a cab. (And this time, no Bobo or Larry, this bloke was legit.)

"I want to go to Cambridge."

"You smart enough?"

"Ha ha."

"Good to start the day with a joke, eh?"

Not this morning. "Can you get me there?"

"Not to Cambridge itself, sir, way out of my zone. But I can get you to the train station, no problem. King's Cross, right across town."

Before committing to the ride, Todd stole a glance out the rear window. Was he being followed? He hadn't seen any sign of Clive's henchmen, hoped they too needed sleep. That's what had happened to him over three days, paranoia had crept in, crowding into his mind with sleep deprivation and evil plots of murder.

"Step on it," Todd said.

"Right, sir," the cabbie replied and they sped into the early Monday morning traffic.

Then Todd returned his attention to the newspaper and found, on page five, the article he wanted: WHO IS DADDYS-

GIRL? the headline read with big bold black type. How had the police learned about that, and how had the press gotten their greedy hands on it? Oh, this wasn't good. It was the latest detail to be revealed in the murder of property manager Vance Timberlake. A partial e-mail address, a mark left on the victim's neck. Todd could have laughed if he thought it was remotely funny. When he'd gone to check for Timberlake's pulse, the address must have rubbed off—or part of it.

But Todd knew the missing portion, because only a few hours ago he'd been sending a message to that very same e-mail address.

Monday day and Brandy Alexander was quite simply bored out of her educated mind. The lecture was endless today, just like always, nothing had changed in the week she'd been gone to attend Granddaddy's funeral. If anything, it was worse. Today's topic? The twenty-first century (and probably twenty-one millionth) interpretation of Lady Macbeth's behavior. "Tell me how you see 'Out, damn spot,' " was one of the inane questions posed. Brandy thought: This is Cambridge? The Highest Center for Learning in the Universe? That capital-letter description courtesy of her father, who today wouldn't pick up a book unless the gold-foil on the cover read Patterson or Grisham, and even then he'd probably opt for the audio book. Bastard probably had the books personally read to him by the authors; that's what money could do. And it's not as if the weather was any great distraction either; rain, rain, and more rain, four days straight and not a ray of light—or hope—in sight. Nope, there was something else eating away at her, something she couldn't quite wrap her mind around.

With the *Macbeth* lecture at last droning to its foregone conclusion—yes, even today wives could plot to kill their husbands—Brandy grabbed up her books, keeping them tight against her chest. Body language for eager coeds to stay away, a fruitless effort, just like every day. She felt a presence behind her.

"Wanna grab a pint at the Pickeral?" asked a thick-necked bloke named Liam.

Well, that hadn't changed either, Liam was always asking her to do something after each lecture; they were at the same level at Trinity and he seemed to think that gave him rights over the other guys. Back last fall when the weather was nicer he'd proposed that they "go punting on the Cam." She'd almost punched Liam, until she learned that meant just going for a boat ride on the river. Still, it had implications, as did every invite she received from every man. A pint or a punt, it was all a first step toward getting into her pants. Since arriving in Cambridge she'd refused every offer, sticking close to her friend, Jennifer Most, who was anything but. Bespeckled and studious, a fashion victim who should be imprisoned for some of the color combinations she came up with, she was the least likely person at college to be asked out by this randy bunch, Liam their forward leader. So with Jennifer always dateless, she was always free, and a good companion to be with. Brandy liked how she intimidated the guys from the rowing team.

Today she had no trouble dispensing with Liam; she had something else on her mind. Her friend had noticed.

"What's with you, today?" Jennifer asked, clutching her books the same way as Brandy. Really, it had been her invention, the boys didn't mind staring at her breasts, better than at her facial features. She was the smartest one around.

"I'm officially bored," Brandy admitted.

"As opposed to last night? What was that?"

"Unofficial—undiagnosed."

"You still sad about your grandfather?"

More like mad. Really, it was his fault she was in this predicament and likely she'd never forgive the old goat for it. Grandfather Alexander—Daddy's Daddy—had treasured her and promised that he would take care of her when he died. Only, he hadn't exactly gotten around to taking care of that little detail before croaking just after New Year's. She'd flown back to Saddle River, New Jersey, mostly just to learn about her inheritance, not really to see him buried. That was a long trip to take just to see some box laid in the ground. Her father, that brilliant scholar and financial tight-ass, had insisted she stay for a couple days, "grieve, honey, like the rest of us." Yeah right, ol' Pops had inherited the whole shebang, nothing for him to mourn. So with him controlling the purse strings, there was no way she could chuck this academic hell she was living in. As far as Brandy was concerned, the admissions board only let her in because she could, uh, beautify this homage to medieval life.

"A walking statue, perfectly carved," she'd overheard one of the architecture fellows state one day. In a freaking classroom, no less.

"Well, I've got to get to library, study that *Macbeth*," Jennifer said.

Brandy parted ways with her friend at the entrance to her room at Trinity. Once upstairs, she tossed her books on the floor and tossed herself on the bed. She grabbed for *Cosmo*, skipping past an article titled "Your IQ or Your Rack—Which Is Bigger?" They had to be kidding. Still, the combination of the dumb *Cosmo* quiz and the lecture on *Macbeth* had her thinking about that cute guy from the plane, Todd. She wondered what he was up to. She worried if she'd ever hear from him. She wondered how good in bed he was. She worried if she read *Cosmo* too much.

"Oh, why didn't I get his e-mail address too?" she complained aloud.

Her phone rang at that moment and hope filled her face.

"Hello?"

"Brandy, it's your father. Why aren't you in class?"

"Because, it's after five and I'm done for the day."

A slight pause. "It's only noon."

"Yeah, in New York, Dad."

"Ha ha, just testing you, my Little Miss Smarty-pants," he said. "Now, the reason for my call—and don't get alarmed, it's nothing serious—but I've had a bit of a financial setback. Cash flow, they call it. So there might be a slight delay in getting you your allowance. It should only be a week; I'm sure you'll get along fine, it's not like you're destitute, right?"

"No, Daddy, I'll be fine."

"That's my daddy's girl."

He hung up and she threw down the phone. What an idiot.

"Oh, what I wouldn't do to get out of this stupid life."

She ran to her desk then, opened her laptop and logged onto her e-mail. There were two messages, the first of which was from her father, the second from an address she was unfamiliar with: frogman.

"Frogman?"

And then she exclaimed loudly, her legs rubbing together in anticipation. She clicked that one on first, laughed at his comment, kind of agreeing with it, too. She stared at the message so long her screensaver came on. So she activated her screen again, deciding she might as well check what Daddy had to say. Basically it repeated the same thing he'd said over the phone. He used the stupid icons to form a smiley face at the close of his message.

Yup, Daddy was an idiot.

But still, that yellow smiley icon had its place, planted right there on Brandy's very pretty face. She quickly typed in a reply to her frogman. Then she wondered what she could do with her evening, studying not even hitting her radar.

"I'm looking for a blonde."

"Hah, who isn't, mate?" the guy said, sucking down half a pint of his bitter in one big gulp.

"No, a specific one. She's kind of memorable."

Todd had tried this line of questioning at six pubs already, ever since arriving in Cambridge and getting his bearings. He'd slept on the train, had to be awakened before he found himself fruitlessly headed back toward London. The one-hour trip had energized him slightly, and after a fifteen-minute walk from the train station down the main stretch of road, which kept changing names, Regent, St. Andrews, Sidney, etc, he found himself embroiled in the genius world of one of the greatest universities in the world, hallowed halls of higher education that had produced such notables as Sir Isaac Newton. Now there was a Gap on every corner, in between churches built centuries ago. Gap indeed . . . generational. And what was Todd looking for here? A greater plane of learning? Rare books on English literature? The theory of relativity? Nope, a blonde.

"Sorry, mate, can't help," was the standard response.

He'd even volunteered to buy a pint for whoever could help him. No one could, at least not until after five p.m. when he was ready to give up his search and find a cheap hotel room. He'd stumbled upon a divey-looking pub just on the other side of the Magdalene Bridge called the Pickeral, started his line of questions with a table full of thick-lensed scholars, none of whom looked like they could get within ten feet of a blonde. But this one guy, over by the bar, getting himself a refill on his Courage, waved Todd over.

"You buying?" he asked Todd.

"If you've got answers."

So a fair deal was negotiated, Todd bought the man a pint,

grabbed one for himself just so the guy wouldn't think he was blimey—shit, where is this language coming from? They took a table and Todd proceeded to describe the woman.

"She has a memorable name, too," Todd said.

"Brandy Alexander."

"You know her?"

"Yup. Knew too who you meant the second you opened your mouth," said the guy, who was named Liam. "Good luck, mate, pants are locked tighter than your Fort Knox. She'll never be Fort Knox-ed Up, if you know what I mean. Ha ha."

Todd was amused. He even laughed.

But in the end he got the info he wanted, the address of which building she was living in. But not until after he'd sprung for two more pints. Todd got up to pee, then when the guy wasn't looking, he escaped from the pub, glad to be back into the fresh air. He smelled now of cigarettes, he hadn't showered or shaved, hadn't changed his clothes, he was tired and slightly tipsy from not having eaten and having consumed three pints of bitter. Now it was time for a nightcap, and he hoped it was Brandy.

He found her building with the help of the map he'd bought at the train station. Trinity College was the largest of the universities, but if Liam had known Brandy from what was admittedly a rather sketchy description, well, Todd had hope that Trinity wasn't too large that he wouldn't be able to find her. Now he was faced with the question Liam had faced, how to get inside.

"Come on, can't I catch a break in all this?"

He walked along the cobblestone path that ran the perimeter of a lush green quad that, while totally dissimilar, reminded Todd of his own dumb college. It was a gathering place, though in the winter and in the dark and in the rain, not too popular. Only a few students showed themselves, crossing from building to building, through vaulted arches that led from the chapel to the library. After an hour of watching these comings and goings, none of whom came even close to resembling Brandy, he was about to give up. He worried someone might not like his lurking around and phone the police. He wondered how seriously to take those blue signs that halted visitors from exploring the campus too far. That would go over well, oh officer, I'm just stalking the hot blonde who lives in this building.

As much as he didn't want to admit it, his plan had flopped. No Brandy; Cambridge was proving to be the only bust he'd get. And now the rain was starting to fall harder. Todd left the quad, made his way back up the quiet street as his shadow taunted him, pointing out how alone he was in this unfamiliar territory. He returned to the Pickeral because at the moment a drink sounded like the perfect antidote to feeling miserable.

Liam was still there, no surprise there. Or was there because he had new company.

Todd noticed her legs first, his eyes following upward to her sweater and then to her hair, that lovely blonde hair that had smelled so nice on the plane. He couldn't believe it, Brandy.

Just then Liam pointed at him, nudged Brandy on the shoulder. That's when she turned around. She smiled, white teeth the only spark of light in the dimly lit pub. Todd returned the grin.

"Frogman?"

"Daddysgirl?"

And that's how the happy reunion happened between two virtual strangers who had nothing more in common than being placed in the same row together on the same flight. See, sometimes it pays to be friendly, talk to that person who keeps looking your way for conversation.

She got up from her stool and they embraced.

They didn't stay long at the Pickeral, just long enough to

thank Liam, who had been telling the fabulous Brandy about the stranger with the American accent who had come looking for her. He gave Todd the thumbs up and asked how he knew the combination to Fort Knox. Todd just laughed as the door to the Pickeral closed behind him.

Once they returned to Brandy's room, Todd said, "I need a shower."

"Yes, you do."

"I need to get some sleep," he said.

"That's probably a good idea, too."

"Oh, and I need to get something to eat."

"I can provide that, too."

She waited for his next request.

Had he been more awake, he might have read what it should be.

"Maybe later," she remarked. "You know, this is remarkable, Todd, you being here. I just got your e-mail, and oh, how it made me laugh. I needed one, it's been a pretty horrible first day back in classes. After spending the weekend just trying to get my body clock readjusted, I go to this boring lecture on *Macbeth*. My God, it's like I dreamed for you to show up and then, poof, like magic you're here. I hardly ever go to the Pickeral, must have the power of suggestion on Liam's part."

She may talk as much as Beth Simon, but he liked Brandy's sweetly-toned words a whole lot better. The package they came in, too.

Brandy said she'd order in food—do you like Indian? Sure, why not?—and then Todd found his way to the bathroom. He shed himself of his dirty clothes and then turned the shower on, waiting until the steam was rising up. He stepped in and conjured a sigh from the bottom of his toes. After a miserable, sleepless night on a stool in an impersonal cafe, this was the best feeling in the entire world.

Okay, second best.

Because the glass door to the shower opened and a naked Brandy found her way into the shower stall. Because her lips tasted like sweet wine. Because her hands felt wonderful on his aching body. Because her mouth felt wonderful . . .

Darn if the steam became too thick to see what happened next.

CHAPTER TEN

Another day, another stakeout.

"This one is more boring than the other day," Larry said, scratching his nose.

"Since that one ended up in murder, consider our boredom a blessing."

Bobo and Larry again, again with Bobo's uncle's black cab. This time they were stationed in front of a small family-run hotel along the Cromwell Road, this one called the Doric. It had two thick white columns that held up a tiny portico above the entrance to the place; neither man knew why it was called the Doric. Maybe the family crest? In any case, in nearly ten hours of said stakeout, they had reached the lowest depths of conversation.

"What is snot, anyway?" Larry asked, examining the results of a real good nose dig.

"Christ."

Near the end of *Tom Sawyer,* that was reason enough to want this impotent watch to come to an end. A visit to Waterstone's bookstore on Charing Cross Road was required, get a new volume of old literature. That was his favorite street in all of London, all those pristine books ready to have their spines cracked. Now, with the snot comment, he had a second reason to want to get on with things.

"So, how come your Uncle Clyde don't need the cab much these days?" Larry asked.

"Because he fell down the stairs, broke his leg in three places. Can't exactly accelerate without screaming out in pain."

"Fell, huh?"

"Probably his old lady, in a fit of drunkenness."

"Aunt Bonnie, right?"

Bobo looked up from his book. "Don't laugh."

"Ah, come on."

"No kidding, Larry, Aunt Bonnie and Uncle Clyde. Not like reading Twain, you can't make this shit up," Bobo said. " 'S what made them hook up in the first place, scared the crap outta folks by their very names. Now all they scare is each other. Probably do each other in someday, leave me the cab permanently. So that's the long version of why I've got the cab."

Of course, having temporary possession of the cab, Bobo was supposed to be picking up the occasional fare, if only to pay for the used petrol. He'd yet to fulfill his portion of the obligation. Kind of difficult, when you were busy staked out in front of some hotel with your off-duty light lit.

"I don't think that guy's coming back, Bo."

Bobo checked his watch, noticed it was now, officially, after five in the afternoon. They had been on duty for over twenty-four hours and they had shit to report back to Clive. Actually, less than shit, because their original assignment had been to keep an eye on good ol' Todd and he had managed, somehow, to slip through their careful watch. Actually, Bobo knew exactly when it had happened, when Larry had needed to pee and gone to the local pub and ended up being coaxed into having a pint, while Bobo himself got caught up in some funny-ass stuff that Tom and Becky Thatcher were up to. A span of ten minutes, max, and their quarry had escaped.

But they stayed, parked down the street from the flat on Balcombe Street, waiting hopefully for Todd's return. That's when the activity had started. First up, a Chinese delivery man headed for said destination while whistling a happy tune. Bobo and Larry had perked up at the song, kept four eyes on what was to develop. The delivery guy was mugged, right there in broad daylight; okay, it was seven at night and dark, but still, mugged. For a plate of moo goo gai pan or something. But then the unexpected happened, the big bloke who stole the food rang the buzzer at Gleason's friend's flat and gained entrance, it was that easy. Not even five minutes passed before the guy was escorting the rotund flat owner—Gleason's friend—outside and into a passing cab.

"That guy," Larry had said. " 'E looks familiar."

"How can you tell, it's dark."

"A feeling."

"Yeah, you've got a feeling. And I've got a headache."

Bobo had wanted to stay at the flat and wait for Todd's return. Larry, though, came up with evidence enough to warrant following the duo in the cab. He reminded Bobo that they had maybe let this guy go once, after he'd maybe murdered Timberlake.

"Lotta maybes. You can't be sure it's him."

"You got a better idea? It's our best bet in finding Todd. He'll chase after whoever took his friend."

"Maybe," Bobo stated.

In the end, Bobo conceded to his usually dim-witted friend, knowing it was Todd they needed to keep track of and, having lost him already, drastic measures were in order. Wherever the little fat lady went, Todd was bound to show up eventually. As he drove off in pursuit, he thought Todd would have had better taste in chicks. They had followed the cab through half of central London it seemed, finally cruising down the rain-soaked streets of Park Row and Brompton and Knightsbridge, wondering if maybe they were headed for the M4 motorway and Heathrow. Nope, they stopped on Cromwell, where the big guy and the short gal went into the dumpy hotel. That was around eight last night. Since then, only one piece of activity had been noted, the big guy left about twenty minutes after arriving, and he left alone.

"Maybe she's a hooker," Larry had said, "and he's gone for a condom."

"Yeah, a round, ugly hooker, she's gonna make a fortune."

The man did not return, not that night and not this morning or afternoon and it didn't look like this evening held much promise. Nor had the woman left, they were positive about that one. Another nor, Todd had failed to show up, so both men were understandably bored by the end of their twenty-fifth hour of surveillance.

"Got any brilliant ideas, mate?" Bobo asked.

"I think he's killed her."

Bobo shook his head in exasperation. "You've got murder on your mind. First you think this mystery man killed Timberlake, now he's plucked the life out of our little mystery woman. You watch too much American television, try reading once in a while."

"But then why hasn't she left the hotel—not even for a sandwich."

They themselves had gotten takeaway from the nearby Pret A Manger, and it was the remembrance of the chicken club sandwich that had Bobo realizing that Larry made a good point. A round girl like her, bet she liked to eat. The Doric didn't look as though it had much in the way of room service.

Concern overrode common sense, and next thing Bobo knew he was out of the cab and crossing the street against traffic, Larry chasing after him. They entered the Doric and were met immediately by an unpleasant smell and by the sour-faced matron who ran the joint. She wore a housecoat and from her mouth dangled a cigarette. Couldn't tell if it was Momma

Matron or the hotel itself which reeked.

Bobo put on his best gentleman's voice. "There is a young lady—my cousin, actually—who is staying here. She arrived last night with a . . . gentleman, rather oversize, if you know what I mean. They would be a funny-looking couple, because my cousin, she's oversize in a smaller way, if you catch my meaning."

"Go away," the woman said. "I don't discuss my guests."

"I'm not asking for information, I just need to see if my cousin is all right. You see, that man is her ex-husband and he's an abusive sort and well, I'm afraid he may have done something awful to her. You wouldn't want to get the police involved now, would you?"

Places like this, they'd rather hear a guest screaming about having seen a rat than have the police stopping by for a visit. The threat worked, Broome Hilda was handing over a key.

"Better than having Godzilla breaking down all my doors."

She meant Larry, who was hulking behind Bobo.

"Obliged," Bobo replied in his best Mark Twain southern. Then he grabbed the key and the two of them dashed up a flight of stairs in search of Room 6. Easy enough to find. They approached the door, put their ears to it for a good listen. Nothing, not a sound. Maybe Larry had been right, the big guy had offed the little gal. Bobo inserted the key and threw open the door, prepared for . . . anything. The room was tiny, you couldn't miss a thing. Certainly not the body, lying face down on the bed. He didn't smell death, didn't see blood, but he was no doctor, didn't know how long it would take for a body to reek. (Not that this rancid hotel lacked for foreign odors all its own.)

Then a snorting kind of snore came from the bed and both Bobo and Larry jumped back, scared out of their wits. Dead bodies don't snore, and they didn't toss and turn in their eternal rest, otherwise wouldn't caskets be made wider? No, she wasn't dead, thank God . . . but she might as well have been. She was a heavy sleeper, the bumbling break-in efforts of Bobo and Larry failing to awaken her.

Bobo pushed Larry forward. "Wake her up."

"You do it."

Bobo gave his partner a weary look. There was nothing to be afraid of. Right?

So Bobo moved forward, tapped the sleeping beauty-less on the shoulder. Nothing. He shook her little round body and suddenly not only was she awake, she was laughing. Guess she was ticklish. She stared up into Bobo's brown eyes and she smiled.

"You're not Todd," she said. "I was told to wait for Todd, have you come to take me to him?"

"Um . . ." Bobo said. He couldn't help staring at the woman before him.

Larry had to tug at his sleeve to bring his partner back to the here and now.

"Oh, yes, Todd is tied up—he can't make it, not now. You're to come with us."

"Give me a moment to get myself pulled together," she said, rising from the bed and heading for the bathroom.

"Needs more than a moment," Larry said.

"Shut up," Bobo instructed, his eyes boring through the closed door of the bathroom.

At last she emerged and what did she do then? Fully awake, she began to talk. "Do you work for Todd, too, just like that other man? You two, you're British, right? The other, he was American, so I guess Todd's got associates from both sides of the pond working with him on his business deal, good for him, I'm glad he's got some support. But I don't understand why I needed to wait the entire day here, had to call in sick to work and then not even a peep from Todd . . ."

She was still talking as they escorted her outside, tossing the

151

key back at Miss Gulch on the way out. She followed them to the cab, and only then did it occur to ask them who they were. It was good to know who you were dealing with, such fine folks as these.

"I'm Larry, he's Bobo."

"Bobo?"

"Yeah, you gotta problem with that?" Bobo stated.

"On the contrary. I'm Beth Simon."

"Pleasure," Bobo said.

They both smiled at each other, and Larry, he pretended to gag. Okay, he wasn't pretending.

"Will you take me home now, Bobo?" she asked.

That's when Larry and Bobo exchanged looks of their own, both of them wondering exactly what they were going to do with her. They hadn't exactly thought this one out in advance. Finally, it was Bobo who said, "Uh, sorry, can't do that. You're . . . valuable to us."

"You don't work for Todd, do you?" When neither answered, Beth's face paled. "Do you work for that other man?"

When neither answered, Beth nearly fainted.

"I was kidnapped, only I was too stupid to realize it, what was I thinking, Todd always works alone," she said. "And now I'm being kidnapped by the men who rescued me from my original kidnapper?"

"Suppose you could look at it that way," Larry said. "Now get inside the cab."

As they drove away, she noticed the Twain book on the dashboard.

"Oh, he's one of my favorites. His use of words, though excessive, is quite brilliant."

Bobo drove, conflicted by a sense of duty and a sudden, unknown desire.

★ ★ ★ ★ ★

If any of her neighbors and fellows students were listening, they'd know she wasn't exactly brushing up on her Shakespeare tonight. Even Romeo and Juliet had been chaste compared to what was going on inside Brandy's bedroom. The shower was over and they were enjoying the juxtaposed world of being both clean and awfully dirty. Currently, Todd was beneath the covers and Brandy wasn't and only nuzzling sounds came from Todd's end of the bed, while from Brandy came, at first, slight, gentle moans. As time went on and the passion heightened, well, those moans became groans and they took on a whole new level of volume. His scruffy cheeks scraped against her milky thighs, and she was glad he'd opted out of using her delicate lady razor. She grabbed at the bedposts, her fingers raw from gripping them so tight. But it was either that or just explode and she wasn't ready, not ready, not ready . . . oh, she was ready now, so ready . . .

. . . one more flick of the tongue, oh yeah, that was it, one more . . . that was it, oh was it ever. Brandy's body arched in absolute ecstasy, only to fall back against the soft mattress in need of air, breath, sustenance to keep her from dying after feeling such an incredible rush of life.

That's when Todd poked his face up from the blanket, smiling.

"Not everything can be learned in books," he said.

"I always liked extracurricular activities."

Mutual pleasure had been explored, exchanged, given, and yet the two of them had not succumbed to the full expression of their intimacy. Fancy words that really just meant as much as they enjoyed their oral excitement, only a pesky amount of time separated them from screwing their brains out all night long. But first, Todd knew he needed food and said so, otherwise he might just drop here and now, spent and exhausted. So Brandy hopped out of bed, went over to her small kitchen and pulled out a series of menus. Chinese, Indian, Thai, Pakistani, Turkish, Burger King, "anything but English food, please."

They settled on Thai, a couple shrimp dishes, some chicken satay, a bit of pad thai—love that peanut sauce. Delivery time, forty-five minutes.

"Surely we can invent something to do while we wait," Brandy had said.

"Yeah, we could talk," Todd said.

Did he really just say that, with the hottest piece of ass he'd ever had just a few, well, many inches, away from him?

They lay in bed then, cuddled up close. He drew his fingers over her soft arm, his touch tingling her nerves and sending shockwaves to all her important areas, while she stroked a strong chest matted with dark hair. She followed the fuzzy trail down his stomach until it disappeared beneath the covers.

"Hmm, I like how that feels," she said, kissing his chest. "So furry."

Todd kissed her in return, enjoying the feel of her full lips against his.

In the darkness of the room, Brandy broke the silence and said, "Is your dad?"

Todd's eyes flickered wide. "Is my . . . um . . . is he what?"

"Hairy, did you get it from him?"

He was gazing into eyes as blue as the seas and wishing they hadn't ventured quite so soon into meaningful conversation. Surely it was too early for pillow talk, too soon to reveal the certain darker regions of their hearts. Still, he didn't want to spoil the mood and so he gave her the short story.

"I don't discuss my father, he's not a topic that ever bears mentioning. Not since I was five years old and he packed up and left home. The proverbial cigarette run," Todd responded, his voice sounding distant even to him.

"Oh, I'm sorry," she said, and kissed him tenderly.

"Don't worry about it, I don't."

"Sometimes I wish my dad would just go away."

Todd snuggled in closer, whispering into her ear, "You shouldn't ever wish away things that most people take for granted. I sometimes think I would have turned out a lot different if I'd had a father figure around. Instead, it was just me and my mother and three sisters. Ask me about that time of the month, I know plenty."

Brandy might have laughed at his comment had she not realized Todd was trying to be honest, truthful. How strange, to go from such animalistic behavior where the basest pleasures were physical to such revelatory insights into a person's lost soul. In the shadows of the night, things had turned decidedly serious. Todd wanted out of it.

So the smart-mouth returned.

"Did you inherit your big breasts from your mother?"

She laughed at that, climbing atop him as she did. The fun was back. And suddenly their eyes locked, both of them realizing what they'd both fantasized about on the plane was mere seconds away, the moment where passion met fulfillment. She was ready, so was he (his readiness easier to interpret), but before Brandy lowered herself on him, she said one thing to him.

"Who are you, Todd Gleason?"

"You'll hear as much as you want . . . later," he said.

She accepted that, and then opened herself to a world of untold pleasure.

Maybe it was because so much time had passed since her last bedroom antics, but for the next twenty minutes he and she went at it like, well, not exactly first-timers, those were always filled with such awkward moments and this, this had none of the awkwardness, but all of the intensity and enthusiasm of teenagers at the height of their powers. Position after position, it was like a choreographed ballet, one that built to a thrilling, dramatic conclusion, no words, just dance, just motion, and what glorious, fluid motion it was. When it ended with its predestined explosion, both could imagine thunderous applause, though they doubted they would have heard it, so loud was the thrumming in their minds, the sound of them catching their breaths, the knowledge that only they existed in this otherworld.

That's when the buzzer sounded.

"Oh, shit, the food," Brandy said.

"Good, I'm starving," Todd remarked.

She smiled at him. "You should be."

Brandy pushed her tousled blonde hair out of her face, got up from the bed, wrapping herself in her thick downy comforter.

"Hey," Todd said, noticing he'd been left exposed.

So he got up too, retired to the bathroom while Brandy handled things with the delivery boy. Might as well give him something to talk about with the boys back at the restaurant, the hottest chick in all of Cambridge University answered her door wearing nothing but a blanket, he wouldn't even be looking for a tip. No doubt they'd keep track of the address, fight whenever an order for delivery came through.

Todd heard Brandy say, "How much," while he splashed his face with water, an attempt at revitalizing himself after such a fine session. In fact, all he could think about was Brandy and that responsive body of hers. So his con of Henri Procopio and his involvement with Clive and the Gang, the murder of Vance Timberlake and even the disappearance of poor Beth Simon, it was all relegated to some distant place in his mind, a place that had itself been kidnapped by the part which sought pleasure, constant, wonderful, nearly painful bouts of erotic thrills. Oh, it was going to be some night. He'd come seeking a place to think, instead he'd found a place to come.

A knock came at the bathroom door.

"Todd, hurry up."

Todd stole a glance back at the mirror, smoothed his tousled hair, before returning to Brandy's side. He grabbed her, telling her how famished he was. Brandy was strangely unresponsive and he quickly learned why. They weren't alone. Todd might have been self-conscious about his nakedness, but the mere fact that a gun was pointed at him made those fears retreat. And not just his fears.

"What the hell . . ."

"So, it's Todd, huh? If that's even your real name. Huh, Mr. Booker?"

Henri Procopio sat in his hotel suite at the Savoy all by his lonesome. Elise had gone shopping at Harrods, determined to buy out the store. Ordinarily he would have objected, he only earned money—and not that much, his salary at Looking Great Cosmetics was low, for tax purposes—but she acted like he worked for the fricking U.S. Mint. And could take home samples at will. But ever since Elise's unlikely lottery win—what other millionaire's wife played the weekly lotto? and then wins, for God's sake?—she had become much more of an independent spirit. She made plans without him, went to bed long after he'd gone off, attended functions alone even when he was in town. He missed the woman he'd married, the innocent babe who knew more about whine than wine, who used to ask if she got fries with her haute cuisine.

Truth was, Elise was different now.

Sure, they had had that one great lovemaking session the day they'd arrived. But Henri was convinced it was more the booze telling her she could than Elise thinking she should. She'd always had a healthy sexual appetite, that's one of the prime reasons he'd married her. His three previous wives had been cold fishes when it came to loving, producing only one child in all that time, which would explain why he'd gone in search of other outlets, why he was currently on his fourth wife. He liked Elise, he missed the Elise he'd married. Sure, he was rich, he could have anyone. But he wanted the old Elise back. Didn't she know, he would have done anything for her?

Anything, he thought.

Just as he would do anything to protect the firm he'd built up from nothing. From one lipstick shade and hopes of a complementary eyeliner, Henri Procopio had steadily increased his product line and his distribution, until his cosmetics were the talk of the industry. Low-priced quality cosmetics, competition for the major labels like Revlon and Estée Lauder and a host of others. With Looking Great, it had been economics first, flashy ads a distant third. In the middle, there was the issue of safety. Here was a priority of his, the testing of his formulas and chemicals closely safeguarded, so the very notion that one of his products had harmed, scarred, a woman, well, that was laughable. In fact, the very notion of such had been responsible for his one laugh this entire trip.

Richard Booker. A small-time con, latched onto the Procopios in anticipation of a big windfall. Henri had to give the boy credit, he had balls the size of Big Ben to come to him personally, even utter the words, "I could destroy you." Truth was, even the slightest hint of a scandal of such magnitude could, well, maybe not destroy Looking Great, but it could seriously hamper his plans to sell the company. Gossip columnists trailed Elise these days like she was a goddess just come down from Olympus. That much Booker had right. But he'd dispensed with that bit of trouble, not having heard a peep from him since their meeting on Saturday. Okay, only forty-eight hours had passed, but Henri sensed this guy wanted in, wanted out, fast and smooth and no fingerprints.

Henri was pleased that distraction had removed itself. He had plans to make.

He phoned New York, got his secretary, a fiftysomething spinster who looked about as appealing as a pug dog. Elise, his former secretary, had insisted on hiring Althea herself.

"How are the plans going, Althea?"

"Oh, Mr. Procopio, just wonderful. I've lined up what I think will be the most exquisite setting, so romantic, oh, it just makes me green with envy. I mean, you know, for a man to do such a thing for the woman he loves. You must love Mrs. Procopio very much."

"Yes, Althea. E-mail me the details, I'd like to check it out myself and speak with the landlord personally. What's her name?"

"Clara Timberlake."

"Thank you, Althea. Everything else okay at the office?"

"Looking Great, sir."

Henri laughed. That was their little joke. "Goodbye, Althea, and thank you."

He replaced the receiver and, his mood suddenly buoyant, he made himself a whiskey. And then he thought about this coming weekend, how his and Elise's tenth anniversary would go off with such a bang. He couldn't wait for Saturday evening, just five nights away now, what a surprise he had in store for the woman he'd adored all these years.

Chapter Eleven

Todd Gleason's past had caught up with him, and really at one of the more inopportune moments he might have envisioned. Caught in bed with Miss January, caught with his own pants down too, no one could mistake what he and the calendar girl were currently engaged in. But the man with the gun, he didn't seem to mind. In fact, he seemed distracted by what he held in his other hand—a bag from which came the most delectable smells imaginable, hot and spicy Thai food. Todd's stomach had been craving it since even before they'd ordered. He was that hungry.

Apparently, so was the man with gun, who said, "I don't see any reason to waste all this food. Shall we eat?"

Todd and Brandy gave each other surprised looks and then shrugged, why not, the man didn't seem eager to use the gun and they'd worked up quite an appetite.

"Could we, you know, get dressed?" Brandy asked.

"You can," the man said. "I don't trust him—*Todd.*"

"So I'm to remain in my birthday suit for the duration of what, the meal? The next few hours? The rest of my life?" Hoping his life would last beyond the meal and those next few hours.

"If you knew what was good for you—*Todd*—you'd shut up with the smart remarks."

Todd had to wonder if this humorless man was another of Clive's associates. No, not with that obvious American accent. So, then who was he working for? Who was he? Truth be known,

Todd hadn't really given the guy that close a look, preoccupied with the gleaming weapon he held in his noticeably shaky hand and his own obvious nakedness. And what with his attitude, saying Todd's name with such . . . derision.

"Do I know you?" Todd finally asked.

"Ha—that's a good one, *Todd*."

"Would you stop saying his name that way, it's annoying."

"You two are awfully bossy considering I'm the one with the gun. Now, enough chatter, boy have I had enough of that to last me a lifetime. Let's eat."

Brandy had wrapped herself in a robe and Todd had been allowed to put a towel on, the man admitting he didn't need to be looking at Todd's privates as he dug into one of the Thai spring rolls. They ate in silence, not even the utensils made noise because they were using plastic forks (the gunman) and wooden chopsticks (the gun-threatened). How Todd wished he could feed Brandy; he'd fantasized what such an erotic picture could lead to. All around, it was a ridiculous situation, as though Todd and Brandy were delinquent teenagers, caught in the act by her father and forced to endure this torture, a meal that probably tasted great going down but could inevitably only lead to indigestion.

Was the gun dessert?

Todd at last got tired of sitting in a towel; he was getting cold. "So, mister, you want to fill us in on what's going on?"

"You still don't know who I am, do you, Todd? Or should I say Mr. Booker?"

Well, Todd had already begun to figure that part out. One of his previous victims; really, this was unprecedented. Never before had someone come after him; he'd always done a good job of covering his tracks. And now here was this . . . guy. Todd gave him a closer look, the steel-gray hair and the bulbous nose and the bulging stomach, he pinned him at close to sixty. For a man who had won the lottery, money certainly wasn't improving the way he dressed or presented himself in public.

"Sorry. I'm not good with faces anyway, it's one of the disadvantages of my profession."

"You remembered her," the man said, waving the gun at Brandy.

"How would you know that?"

"From the plane."

"You were on the plane?" they both asked.

The man nodded, obviously pleased that the upper hand was still his. "Allow me to introduce myself, Mr. Booker—by the way, is it Todd Gleason or Richard Booker or something else altogether? I'd much prefer to know exactly who I'm dealing with."

This confusion over Todd's name, it had even garnered Brandy's attention. Maybe she was wondering who she'd screwed earlier, Todd or Richard or, as the still unidentified man said, someone else altogether. Todd's answer might not satisfy either of them.

"No, Todd. That'll do."

"Good," the man said, setting his plate aside and reaching for a stick of gum. Clean the palate, Todd supposed.

Gum. That stuck to his mind. What was it . . .

"My name is . . ."

And then Todd remembered. "Holy shit, you're Donald Birdie."

"Who's Donald Birdie?" Brandy asked.

"Him," Todd said, pointing.

"Me," the man said, confirming.

Todd, trying desperately to make sense of this new development and to maybe keep the truth from spilling out in front of the delectable Brandy, said in his best friend kind of voice, "Birdie, what brings you to Cambridge, I mean, man, it's been years. You've changed, you look great, how's the wife?"

Oops, wrong subject. And actually, he looked a hell of a lot worse than that time he'd seen him last fall. "Nice try, Todd. He's something, a real con," Birdie said to Brandy. "You do know what he is, how he makes his living, don't you? And if you tell me he's a financial consultant, I just might pop this gun right here and now. How much is he taking from you? Bet he's got a rock solid investment for you, just a mere fifty thou and you'll be swimming in money. That's what he tried with me and I saw right through him, tossed him out of my gum factory office. Then he shows up one afternoon, I'm innocently eating lunch at Sam's, that's the local diner, nice enough place, they treat me nice, nicer since the big windfall, did he tell you that, too, I'd won the lottery and he wanted a piece of it. So when his investment scheme died on my doorstep, he tried another tactic. And lo and behold, that one worked like a charm."

Brandy was listening intently to Birdie, but Todd noticed her studying his face. Todd was careful not to let his expression betray anything, as though he were listening to a story which bored him, or maybe one he'd heard before.

"See, little lady—by the way, what's your name?"

She returned her attention to Birdie, said, "I'm Brandy."

The man roared over that one, gave Todd lots of credit, a real looker, a name like that, and she had bucks to spare, no doubt, otherwise what's he doing here. Todd raised an eyebrow at that question and Birdie conceded that Brandy might just have more to offer than cash. Though he did remark that the fringe benefits on this particular scam seemed to outweigh the end result. Money grew on trees compared to women who looked like her.

"This isn't a scam," Todd said, more to Brandy than to Birdie.

"Uh-huh, sure. Anyway, my story, where was I? Oh, you know, Brandy, men have weaknesses and primary among them are women. Or at least what women make them do, or want to do. Another is money. Oh you can never have enough money in the wallet, cash in the bank, or under the mattress or wherever you feel it's safest to keep. Now, combine those two things, women and money and the very devil himself will show up. Or in my case, this little devil, here. *Todd.* I'm a regular guy, married my high school sweetheart right after graduation, went to work for the local factory and worked my way up, raised a couple kids, the American dream, right? If I have a problem, it's I like to gamble, at the local casino run by the Indians or play the lottery—and wouldn't you believe the one in a million happens, I hit the big jackpot, New York State lotto and my take, oh, it's big. How much, Todd?" Sweat had appeared on the man's upper lip.

"Forty-two million."

"You don't remember faces, but figures, sure." He shot Brandy a look. "See?"

"You know, this is all very interesting, Mr. . . . Birdie, is it? I would be more comfortable if you would put the gun down, we don't want anyone getting hurt, right? I promise, no one will try anything funny—Todd?"

"There's nothing up my sleeve—I'm in a towel after all."

"You have my assurance," Brandy said.

Birdie was hesitating, and at last he gave in, setting the gun down on the floor in front of him. They'd been sitting cross-legged while dining on the floor on a blanket Brandy had spread out. Good friends and good food, a loaded gun, all the requirements for a friendly picnic.

"Now, why don't you tell me—the short version—what Todd did to you. And then let's see if we can reach an equitable solution."

Birdie nodded. "He stole money from me, blackmailed me. I did the unforgivable, I had an affair with my secretary right after I won the lottery. I was king of the world, like that hotshot

Hollywood director a couple years back, could do nothing wrong. Todd, I still don't know how, but he found out about it and said his silence would cost him sixty thousand dollars. Pay up or he tells the wife, and then . . . then I'm the one who gets screwed."

Brandy gave Todd a sidelong glance; he couldn't read whatever she was trying to say.

"Well, two months ago the wife found out about the missing money and she demanded to know what I'd done with it. I'd been wracked with guilt anyway and so finally I broke down and confessed to everything. The affair, the blackmail; she'd even met our friend Todd, who we knew as Richard Booker, he'd been to see her too initially about his supposed investment. Prey on the wife first, who would then convince me to make my fortune ever bigger. But Marta's no pushover and didn't buy Todd's scheme for a second. After my confession, Marta threatened to divorce me and take all my money. I begged her not to, said I could fix it."

Todd supposed they were getting to the heart of the matter. The reason why Birdie was here.

"How were you planning to do that?" Brandy asked.

"Easy, I told Marta, 'I'll find Booker and get my money back.' "

"Here's what I figure."

Birdie was still talking, suddenly reminding Todd of Beth Simon's many marathon monologues. Of her kidnapping, too. Was Birdie her kidnapper, and if so, where was she now?

"You stole sixty thousand dollars from me, plus I spent five thousand on a private detective to track you down and another ten thousand on this trip—do you know how much a first-class ticket to London at the last minute costs? But I couldn't fly coach, I knew that's where this cunning little cheapskate would be. And lucky me, packing my passport—I anticipated every-thing, including you fleeing the country."

Todd wanted to point out that Brandy had been in coach, too. Birdie wasn't doing a good job of winning over Brandy, what with his veiled insults toward her.

"Plus emotional duress and interest. So here's what I'm of-fering: pay up one hundred thousand dollars, Todd, and I'll forget the entire thing. I'll walk out of your life and you'll never hear from me again—and vice versa, I assume."

"It's a nice dream, Birdie, but that's all it is," Todd said. "I haven't got the money."

"I'll take whatever you're getting out of her—for starters."

Brandy raised an eyebrow. "Oh, and how much am I worth?"

"Nothing," Todd said, quickly amending his statement. "I mean, everything, the world, the moon and the stars, there's no price tag. No, wait, Brandy, I'm not here to get money from you. No, I'm here . . ."

"Because I was an easy lay?"

She'd made the first move, he might have pointed out. But decided there was no use in reminding her. "No, I'm here because I really like you—meeting you on the plane and then separating at Heathrow with just the barest hint of a kiss, it wasn't enough, not for me. I wanted to see you again, the entire weekend I couldn't think of anything else. That's why I'm here."

"Oh, what a load of bull," Birdie said.

Shit, why'd he go and ruin it, Brandy had begun to melt again, batting her eyes at his still towel-clad self.

"Don't listen to him, Brandy, he'd say anything, he's a desperate man, scared of losing his wife . . . or worse, his fortune," Todd said. "He's the one who broke in here with a gun, not me. You let me in voluntarily, and not only to your flat." He produced those dimples of his, hoping the remem-brance of what they'd shared would override the ravings—albeit truthful ravings—of this semi-crazed gunman. She touched his scruffy cheek, smiled.

"You're so sweet, so cute . . . and really sexy," she said. "But I agree with Mr. Birdie, your story is a load of bull. I happen to believe every detail of his travails, I think you have enough charm, Todd, to convince Granny Poorbucks to part with her knitting money. Which means so far, of the two of you, Mr. Birdie is the only man in this room to tell me the truth. We began as a lie—you told me you were in England to do research for a screenplay—but who knows what you've been up to the past couple days since arriving in London. Another scam? Who's the victim this time? Is it me? Oh, Daddy would have a cow over that."

"Look, Brandy, whatever I've been up to, it has nothing to do with you. I . . . I just ran into a bit of trouble and needed to get out of London, lie low for a couple days and figure out what I was going to do. Cambridge was the first place I thought of, because of you. But I swear, you're not part of this."

"Well, I am now," she said. "Whatever *it* is. Care to fill in the blanks?"

Todd shook his head. "It's better you don't know, safer. Right, Birdie?"

"What's that supposed to mean?"

"Oh, it's simple. You see, the thing with cons, they have to be orchestrated down to the very last, well, note, to keep the metaphor alive. One wrong note and the entire song is ruined. Admittedly my, uh, new venture has taken a wrong turn. But I daresay yours has too, and far worse than mine ever could. You see, I've never killed anybody."

Brandy let out a chirping sound that could only have been described as fear. She did it again as Birdie reached for the gun and pointed it at them, his hand quivering even more than when he'd first arrived. Clearly he was uncomfortable even holding it; they were uncomfortable with him holding it, too.

"I didn't kill him . . ." The gun fluctuated in his unsteady hand.

"Timberlake, sure you did," Todd said. "He was killed with a gun—and here you are, with a gun."

Birdie hung his face in his hands, the cold steel of the gun cracking against his forehead. When he looked up again, tears had streaked his face. "I swear, I didn't do it. I . . . I was there, yeah, and I found him there. I went looking for you at that apartment—the door was open, so I walked in. Easier than getting into your New York apartment, nearly cut my leg breaking that window. Anyway, I walked up the stairs and I found the guy lying on the floor. He was still alive—barely. His eyes looked at me and he tried to speak. I went to his side to hear but only blood gurgled out of his mouth—and then he was dead. The poor man, he died in my arms, there was nothing I could do. Except call the police."

Brandy felt sorry for the man, for this story, and went and hugged him. Todd watched this display with amazement. Why was it she believed every word of out this stranger's mouth? Though, in reality, what reason did she have to doubt him? What reason did Todd have? He was glad to get some answers, like who had been banging down his door in New York, but he didn't know who had killed Timberlake or why (he was still hoping it was Clive). What next, though? Had they defeated Birdie, crushed his resolve by forcing this confession? Was this over?

From the bathroom, Brandy sought a wet towel, which she gave to Birdie. He wiped his face, and when he'd composed himself, he was staring directly at Todd. "I know you don't believe me, Todd, probably think you can get out of this by accusing me of murder. But I did nothing wrong . . ."

"You have the murder weapon, Birdie."

Todd pointed to the gun that lay on the floor between them.

Birdie shook his head. "No, I mean yes . . . oh damn. This isn't the gun that killed him. The man had it on his body and . . . I thought it would come in handy, you know, if you gave me trouble at some point. So I took it."

"You messed with a crime scene, ran from a crime scene after calling for the police; you're not guiltless in this, Birdie."

It looked like they'd reached a stalemate. Sure Birdie could be in trouble, but the authorities would probably even give him immunity from those lesser charges if he helped them solve the case—or handed them a new suspect. Todd had to think fast to try and figure some way out of this mess.

Birdie began to babble, a string of nonsensical words that attempted to explain away his guilt, the words sounding hollow as they hung between them all. And that's what made Todd remember.

"You know, Birdie, there is one major crime you are guilty of."

Birdie looked up with surprise.

"Kidnapping. Birdie, what have you done with Beth Simon?"

"Who's Beth Simon?" Brandy asked.

"I did not kidnap her. She's fine, unharmed. I left her in my hotel room."

"What did you do to her?"

"Nothing. Only I told her you were in danger and subsequently, so was she as long as she stayed at her place. So I convinced her to come with me to my hotel, told her not to move until she heard from you. That woman, she talks a lot, and one of the things I figured out from all that chatter was how much of a crush she has on you. She'd do anything for you, Todd, like hang around a hotel room all day long. So, no crime there."

"Sure, we'll see what Beth has to say about that, Birdie."

Todd asked Brandy for a phone book; she didn't have one for London and so Todd found himself calling information. Birdie provided the name of the hotel and soon after the call was put through to the Doric. He asked the woman who answered to connect him with room six, only the woman just laughed at him. Todd listened, the blood draining from his face as he absorbed the information.

"Oh, shit," he said, putting the receiver down.

"What?" Brandy asked.

"Beth's gone, the room's empty. A couple guys came for her, claimed to be relatives."

"Meaning what?" Brandy asked.

Birdie answered. "Meaning she's been rescued, right? So I can't be charged . . ."

"No, Birdie, she's not been 'rescued,' she's in even worse hands." Todd shook his head with despair. "Professional hands. If something happens to her, Birdie, it's your responsibility."

"Oh God, what have you done to me, Todd? You've ruined my life," Birdie said, starting to cry again. He was in over his head.

"So, now what?" Brandy asked.

The question seemed to hang in the air, waiting for someone to grab it and conjure the answer to this confounding complication. Turned out, it was the one who was least involved, she about to toss herself into the middle of this mucky mess.

"I'll fix this," she said, and then with an authority that neither man expected, Brandy stood up and said, "Okay, gentlemen, we first need to get this Beth Simon situation resolved. Really, you've both got a gift for dragging women into your silly little games. We also need to find a solution to the earlier problem—in short, Todd getting Birdie his money back. We have what we call a stalemate, since Mr. Birdie, you want your one hundred thousand dollars that's owed to you and Todd, you say you don't have it. Let's work with that, and see what we can come up with. And who knows, maybe when all is said and done, we'll all go home happy, and just a bit richer."

Todd thought that at that very moment he fell in love with Brandy Alexander.

"First things first, just as Brandy stated," Todd said. "We need to rescue Beth."

"So that means what?" Birdie asked.

"It's back to London—for the moment, Birdie, like it or not, you and I are working as a team," Todd said.

"Hey, don't forget me, I want my cut."

"You have classes tomorrow, Brandy."

"Bo-ring."

Todd shrugged. "Suit yourself." Actually, it suited him, too, having her near, close.

As they gathered to leave, Todd finally allowed to dress, he kept thinking about one of Brandy's comments—what exactly did she mean by wanting her cut? Her cut of what?

"What the hell is that?"

Not who, what.

"She's . . ."

"I'm Beth Simon, who are *you?*"

She was mad, not having appreciated being referred to as a "what."

"Yes, right, hello. Friend of yours, Bo?"

Bobo shook his head. "Friend of a friend. You know him."

Clive, who was in bed again, was suddenly interested in something other than the lovely Fiona, who was still at his side barely covered by the blankets. He beckoned Beth closer to him, his breath smelling of garlic. He and Fiona had dined on Italian. Beth nearly reeled back, but his grip on her wrist was too strong.

"So, you know Todd?"

"He's a friend."

"You like him?"

"He's . . . nice."

"Nice? I'd say you've got a case of the itchy pants for him. Do anything for him, wouldn't you?"

Larry was grinning and Bobo elbowed him.

Beth was shaking in her shoes. She knew she was in trouble. "Not really, don't know, he's . . . my brother's associate."

"How interesting, Todd has an associate. I have associates, you've met them."

Beth looked over at Bobo and Larry, who still stood in the doorframe. Bobo stupidly waved at her, stopped when Clive shot him an angry glare.

"Bo—what are we doing with her?"

"Figured she could lead us . . . you know, to Gleason."

"Why is it we need her—what happened to the Great Cab Surveillance?"

Larry nervously stepped forward. "We lost him, sometime yesterday afternoon."

Clive was no longer interested in Beth. He got out of bed, fast like a fox, and landed backhanded slaps, first on Larry, then on Bobo. "You bloody idiots, why am I just hearing about this now?"

"We were searching for him, but . . . well . . ."

"You were reading that book again."

Bobo nodded.

"And where were you?"

"Had to pee."

"Jesus, the talent I surround myself with."

"But we brought you the next best thing; Beth is the woman Todd's been staying with. When he finds out we've got her, you know, he'll come back all right," Bobo said.

"Until then, we've got something better," Larry said, stepping forward, as though he'd just melted the Wicked Witch of the West and taken possession of her broom. "Look."

Clive stared at the black case. "So, it's a computer—a laptop."

"Gleason's computer."

Well, that was the first bit of good news Clive had heard all night. "How . . . fortuitous."

"So, in the meantime, what do we do with her?"

Clive returned his attention to Beth. Shuddered at the sight of her and had to look at Fiona to repair the damage to his eyes. Still, this ugly duckling might be useful.

"I don't know, keep her, I guess. You hungry, Beth?"

She nodded.

"Yeah, figures. Bo, Larry, take her to the pub, get her some grub. Leave me and Fi some peace. Oh, and leave the computer, too. Now get the hell out."

The door closed behind him, leaving Clive alone with his swan. He was glad to focus his attention back on the beautiful babe in the bed. As he hungrily mounted her, he slapped her across the face—because he was still a bit angry and she was the only one around.

"Ow," she said, squirming beneath him, "what the hell was that for? Daddy sees me like this, he'll have some real questions about my new boyfriend, now, won't he?"

He'd forgotten, he apologized, and then he resumed normal operations.

"Ooh," was what she said next.

That time there was no complaint implied.

CHAPTER TWELVE

Todd and Brandy and Birdie, a ménage à trois dreamed up only by the truly desperate, arrived back in London Tuesday morning via British Rail from Cambridge to King's Cross Station, rainy skies there giving way to blue ones here. All three had shared Brandy's flat the night before, nothing happening of course, not even between Todd and Brandy, who both felt as though they were sleeping in the same room with Daddy. He with a watchful eye, not to mention the gun he insisted on keeping close at hand. Truth was, Todd could use the sleep; tomorrow, as they say, was another day. And so it was. He spent the train ride filling Brandy in on what had been happening since they'd parted ways at Heathrow.

"And you wanted me to stay behind and study," she said with a wave of dismissal.

"Probably should have," Birdie told her. "Better than being involved with this guy."

"Hey, we're all in this together now," Todd reminded him.

"Don't expect me to like it," Birdie said.

Todd had heard this was the off-season in London, but he'd yet to see evidence of such. It was noon already when the three of them hopped the Tube, crowding amongst Londoners and tourists alike. There were as many languages spoken as people, it seemed. The unseasonably likeable weather had brought everyone out, and so the three of them kept close, kept tight, kept silent. What they had to discuss, it wasn't for other ears, whether they understood English or not.

Their first stop? The Doric Hotel, which Brandy pronounced as seedy, which Todd decided would have been a decently bad place to hide out, had its location not already been compromised by Clive's men. Birdie just called it home—for the moment. It was Brandy who pointed out that, of the three of them, Birdie was the richest—lotto winner and all—and he was the one with the crappy accommodations.

"Marta's fault—she insisted this trip should cost as little as possible. She doesn't even know I've left the country. My God, if she found out, the hell I would pay."

Todd didn't want to think about that complication right now, they had come to retrieve, he hoped, his computer. Birdie had admitted to taking it, and now he admitted to leaving it on the bed, he swore.

"Well, it's gone," Brandy said.

"Shit," Todd said, the economical version of "Well, it's gone."

"What now?"

Todd's idea was to leave Birdie at the Doric, since there were a few details to be taken care of before they could attempt to rescue Beth from the evil clutches of Clive. Birdie decided that was a good idea, providing Brandy remain behind as insurance.

"I still don't trust you," Birdie admitted.

"You'll be fine," Todd told Brandy and to Birdie promised, "I'll be back."

Brandy gave him a kiss, as though he were a soldier going to do battle who knew a bullet might end this grand romance of theirs at such an early stage. In other words, a nice big wet kiss that held promise of much more, so watch your ass. How lucky could he get, even after all Brandy had learned about him, she was still hot for him, still wanted to be with him and was even willing to chance mucking up her studies at Cambridge and risk the wrath of Daddy Alexander. So with a bounce to his step, he returned to the London streets, hopped the Tube again and as it traveled back up to Marylebone, he thought of nothing else but Brandy. Okay, a bit about Beth, since he felt terrible about how she'd gotten mixed up in this, but once he'd assuaged his guilt over that, yup, it was back to Brandy.

He returned to the same Internet cafe as before, figuring he'd spend more time looking for a new one than traveling across central London to get to this one. He paid his pounds and grabbed a computer; it was mid-day and the place was much busier. He had no choice but to sit between two students who looked as though they could crack the government's code and risk nuclear war. He merely smiled at them.

Again, he logged on and typed in his screen name and password and voila, like magic, he was connected with a world that existed in electronic wonder, by pixels and words that floated around in some undefined nexus. He had one new message, as well as two old ones, both from Andy. Which meant in between the time of this one message and those other two, someone had logged onto his computer and read his mail and forgotten to "keep as new." Someone. He had to assume Clive.

Todd checked the previously read messages first.

What the hell is going on over there?!!! Sounds like you should get out, and fast. Heard from Beth, though, she sounds fine, though not exactly free to leave wherever she is. If you get a chance, call me. I'm tempted to come over and kick your ass for involving my sister in your latest scheme. And yeah, the fricking frog's fine.

The second message he read was actually Andy's first reply. He'd used several expletives, mostly because he hadn't yet heard from Beth. Todd deleted both, glad that at least Beth had been able to reassure her brother that she was okay. Meaning: alive. Then he turned his attention to the latest message, the new one. Ironically, sent by himself; or rather, the masked man behind the kept keyboard.

Hello, mate. A friend of yours has stopped by for an extended stay. If you want her back, it's going to cost you. We have previously discussed a sum of two-fifty and I have decided to increase it to an even five. I'm sure she's worth even more. Consider the increase a penalty for disappearing on me. Shame on you, Todd. Please send reply to this address, once you've completed your transaction. P.S. Ingenuity, my friend, and you could still turn a profit. Regards, C. R.

C.R. Clive Remington. Cheeky bastard.

"More like greedy bastard," Todd said, not realizing he'd said it aloud. A few pairs of eyes turned to him.

He logged off and got the hell out of the cafe.

Only then did he realize the one message he'd been expecting hadn't been there, the one from Elise Procopio. As far as he knew, the hit on her husband was still on. Though she had worried she might not have the info until the end of the week, Todd was for once glad for the delay. With the computer in Clive's hands, there was no telling what he could uncover—or who he could get in touch with.

Todd rushed back to the Doric, announced that they needed to find new digs—"Not the Doric, not Beth's . . ."

Brandy shushed him with her finger, and Todd realized Birdie was on the phone.

"Yes, honey, I'm getting close, I should be finished in a couple more days. No, no, that was room service, no, it's not an expensive hotel but, well, a man's got to eat. What, every receipt? This isn't a tax write-off, you know? What? Yes, and more." He gazed back at Todd, then said into the receiver, "Just like I said I would. Yes, New York is very nice, a bit rainy . . . what? Well, those weathermen are never right. I love you. Hello?"

He hung up the phone, unnecessarily said, "Marta."

"I've heard from Clive, he's upped the ante. I suggest we find a new base of operations and then launch our attack—at dusk."

"Attack?" Birdie responded, not without a bit of nervousness.

Nightfall, black skies and cold, crisp air and around the Thames, thick rolling fog, the kind of scene that Hollywood loved to mimic because it was such a good mood setter, you knew something was afoot. Danger, intrigue, suspense?

Yup, all of that was on hand. Todd, dressed all in black and sporting shades that pinned him as either a crook or maybe an actor, was accompanied by Brandy, she cutting a stylish criminal edge of her own garbed in black pants and leather jacket. As for Birdie, he came equipped with brown cords and a ratty winter coat and a frown of frustration on his face. You work with what you've got, right?

They were in a black taxicab, traveling through the Tuesday night traffic across the Vauxhall Bridge, its headlights guiding them through the murkiness that swirled outside. Todd wasn't positive he could find Clive's place in the daylight, much less at night, but still they'd decided to chance it and at night yet, that cover of darkness better for skulking around. They had one place of reference, the Frog and Firkin pub and all they had to do was find it and they'd found Clive's lair. If only the rest of their plan was as easy. The cab dropped them off just around the corner from the bridge, along the Albert Embankment. Close enough, Todd knew. It was just past nine p.m.

"Well, pay the man, Birdie," Todd said.

Getting angrier with each spent sterling, Birdie took out his wallet and passed the driver a ten pound note. "I'm keeping track of every damn pence."

They would separate on the corner of the Embankment and Glasshouse Walk, and would meet up a few blocks down— hopefully at the Frog and Firkin. Todd pointed south and said, "I think it's that way." The plan was for Todd and Brandy to walk in first, Birdie two minutes later. Traveling together they would have captured everyone's unwanted attention; this way, no one could guess this threesome was working a con together.

And that's what happened, with Birdie adding, "I hate this, and I don't like being left alone in this rather questionable neighborhood" as Todd and Brandy linked arms and nonchalantly strolled down the darkened street.

It had been a busy afternoon which had gotten them to this point . . .

After leaving the Doric Hotel, they had hopped into a cab and were taken to a far nicer place: the lushly elegant Savoy Hotel. Immediately, Birdie protests, saying he couldn't afford the place, no way, no how, when Marta sees the bills she'll have a cow and moo all at the same time.

The cabbie had shot Todd a look, meaning should they search elsewhere.

"Come on, Birdie, be a man and live a little, you won the lottery," Todd said. "You'll make back money enough to live here for a year and not even make a dent in your lottery savings. Marta will be so happy she won't have time to even milk a cow."

Under her laughter, Brandy murmured in Todd's ear, "I'm guessing you have a reason for choosing such lofty accommodations?"

"Of course."

As they'd approached the reception area of this very posh-looking place, Birdie said, "This had better work." It did, because they looked legit, a young man and his wife, her father along for the trip after the death of his wife (such hopeful thinking). Each of them had their own luggage, even Todd who had retrieved his from Beth's empty flat. The single swipe of a credit card—Birdie's, natch—and they were in, the newest guests at the Savoy, and for not a bad price at all. Thank goodness for the off-season. They had settled in two adjoining rooms on the second floor and busied themselves unpacking, getting some rest and getting geared up for their night's excursion. Todd ran through the plan with them—it was simple really: break in, grab Beth, run for your lives. Hope to avoid Clive at all costs. There was no way Todd was going to be paying Clive that five-hundred-thousand-dollar sum he'd summoned. It was bad enough Birdie was still harping about the one hundred thou he expected to be paid. Brandy had asked if Todd had a back-up plan and this time he had to admit to the truth, no. Birdie then showed what he could bring to the table, Timberlake's gun, still very much in his possession despite the camaraderie that had developed between him and Todd.

That was then, and this was now . . .

Todd and Brandy were within a block of the Frog and Firkin, its wooden sign barely distinguishable in the mist. Music could be heard spilling from its doors.

Todd spoke. "I've heard about foggy days in Londontown—ol' blue eyes himself used to sing about them, great song. Seeing it, walking in it—that's a whole other story. This is some thick frog."

Brandy laughed. "Did you say frog?"

"Sorry, I guess I did," he admitted. Missing Toad.

"You okay? Ready for this?"

He shrugged. "Guess I've got a few things on my mind. Like, how the hell did we get to this point, anyway? Maybe my subconscious was wishing me home, scratching off stupid losing lottery tickets and feeding my damned frog."

"You mentioned him on the train, even in the midst of this you're worried about Toad, huh? You really love that stupid frog, don't you, Todd?"

"Don't call him stupid."

"Why—you just called him a damned frog. What about the frog's got you so sensitive? Bet he calls you Dad."

He tried to find his voice, but it croaked. He didn't use the word Dad, doubted anyone would ever use it to refer to him. Finally, he managed to say, "Toad doesn't talk, Brand."

"Sure thing, my London Frog."

Silence for the next block, and then, standing before the entrance to the rundown-looking pub Todd announced it was time to focus, keep your eyes peeled for any unsavory characters who might take a disliking to some lovelorn interlopers at their local. It was possible Clive himself might be here, he thought, opening the thick wooden door and escorting Brandy in. A few eyes looked up, none of them familiar looking, some returning quickly to their pints, others happy to gaze at their new guest; oh, and the guy next to said new guest.

"Two pints, mate," Todd said to the bartender, pointing to the Fuller's London Pride.

They paid their four pounds forty pence and retreated to a corner table, one which usually would have had a nice view of the street. The fog, though, held visibility at a minimum. As they sipped at their lager, Birdie walked in and gained not an ounce of interest from the locals. He ordered a pint, too—Todd has insisted, no Coke or anything sissy like that, don't draw attention to yourself—and then contented himself by leaning against the bar. No eye contact, no nothing, not with each other and not with the imbibers. Todd was busy surveying the place, anyway, looking for any familiar face in the crowd of ten or a dozen men. Just then, from the gents toilet emerged a rather large man, so tall was he that he needed to bend down to fully miss hitting the doorframe. Todd knocked his fist against the table and then shielded his face, deliberately trying to both catch the man's attention and not be seen. It was an action designed to make the man do a double-take, and that's indeed what happened. But he didn't have the guts himself to come over, nope, he went right for the telephone in the corner.

"Bingo," Todd said.

"Who is that man?"

"One of Clive's associates. He's either Larry or Bobo."

"Bobo?"

"Yeah, they've got a Bobo and we've got a Birdie."

"Doesn't anyone have normal parents?"

This, from the woman named Brandy Alexander.

"Though, in all fairness, I believe Birdie is our friend's last name," Todd added. He caught a quick look at Birdie, nodded, swiped at his nose. That was the signal. Birdie slipped out of the bar.

They waited about ten minutes, nursing their pints as they did so. Then the door opened and in walked Todd's most favorite person in all of London and quite possibly the world, one Clive Remington. And what do you know, he was dressed. He and Larry (Bobo?) hooked up, then Clive turned and walked right over to Todd.

But first Clive had the decency to say hello to Brandy, nearly bowing with exaggerated politeness. "I find myself in awe of such beauty, and can't for the life of me figure out why you might be in the company of such a wretched individual."

Brandy looked squarely at Clive and said, "But you just arrived."

Todd couldn't help it, he grinned. Clive could help it.

"But you're right, Todd sweetie, he is awfully polite."

The big guy—Todd was convinced this one was Larry—came up behind Clive, towering over him. His thick paws rested on his hips. A villain vogue-ing. Strike the pose.

"Haven't seen you for a couple days, Todd, am I to assume that you no longer need Fiona for your half-assed plan and went it alone? Or perhaps this beautiful creature has helped you. In either case, I trust it went well and that you have my money. Why else would you have ventured to my part of town, eh? My money, Todd, and all of it. Like my e-mail said."

"Um, nope." Real cocky-like.

" 'Nope,' " Clive repeated, as though tasting it for good flavor. His expression soured. "What an absolutely dreadful word. Not only is it bad English, but its connotation brings out a profound sadness in me."

Todd looked at Brandy. "Do the mates talk that way in Cambridge?"

"Um, worse."

Clive slammed his fist down on the table, causing their pint glasses to jump; Todd and Brandy, too, though both were as amused as they were startled. Todd had warned Brandy to expect such behavior, and to remain cool. Then Todd told her Clive had a low boiling point and Brandy said she could see that, and then Todd said Clive had done that before, the last time they were enjoying a pint at this very same bar, and Brandy said really, you'd come back to such a dreadful place, it brings out a profound sadness in me, and then Clive said, "Are you two fucking finished?"

And then: "Larry, grab hold of ol' Todd there, I'll handle the lady."

"Get your paws off me," Brandy said, getting feisty with the fiendish Clive.

Both Todd and Brandy were escorted out of the pub, brought around to the front of the unexceptional building. They walked up the stairs to Clive's flat, their feet stomping against the floorboards, making an awful racket. Clive informed them to cease with the noise. He unlocked the door and tossed Brandy to the sofa while Larry pushed Todd to the floor.

"What are you going to do with us?" Brandy asked, fear rising up from her throat. She sounded like an actress in a bad horror movie.

Todd nodded at her, swiped at his nose. Keep it up.

"I mean, I'm just out for a drink with this new guy, it's our first date and all . . ."

"Can it, I don't believe you for a second," he said, and then, well wasn't this happening sooner than expected, Clive lashed out again. But at the wrong victim. Because this time he made Brandy his unsuspecting target. His hand smacked across her upper cheek. Todd, wishing he hadn't allowed Brandy to play up the smart-ass routine so much, instinctively lunged for Clive, knocking him down to the floor, getting off a nice punch to the guy's face; he'd deserved at least one from nearly the moment they met. A couple more punches were thrown by each, but their tussle didn't last long because Larry picked Todd up.

By the throat.

"Shall I crush it boss?"

By *it*, Todd had to assume his neck.

"There'll be no crushing—put him down."

Larry turned when he heard this new voice, actually they all did. All eyes fell on Birdie, who was standing in the entrance-way to the flat, his arm extended, the gun affixed to the end of it. He waved it at Larry, who set Todd down. The situation in their control—for the moment—Todd took that opportunity to do a quick search of the apartment, running first into the bedroom, which he found empty. No Beth, not even a Fiona. Damn, where the hell were they keeping her? Could all this foolishness have been for naught? That's when he saw a familiar computer case sticking out from under the bed. He checked it, thankful his laptop was still in it. He grabbed it and returned to the living room.

"She's not here," he said.

Clive laughed. "Is that what this is about—you want that . . . that . . . woman? Sorry, mate, she's under protective custody, and now that I know how valuable she is, it's going to cost you bigtime to get her back. Cost you anyway for this stupid stunt you pulled tonight. I think I'll double my rate. Yes, one million pounds, mate—let's see, by when would I like it? How about by Saturday night? Say we meet at the Frog and Firkin again—I tend to think of it as 'our place' Todd, don't you?"

"Shoot him, Birdie," Todd said.

Birdie gave Todd a look of astonishment, making Todd nod. He hesitated, then thought about it and there came no swipe of the nose.

Clive chuckled. "Nice try, chap. Next time, bring someone who actually knows how to handle a firearm, much less isn't afraid of it. Who is he anyway, Shaky the Shooter? For now I'll consider this a stalemate, so go on, get out—and don't come back until you've got the money. Cash. Remember, we'll be watching you. Larry, get them out of here."

"Right, boss."

Todd, Brandy, and Birdie were escorted out of the flat, Larry slamming the door closed behind him.

"Todd, for a second, I thought you really wanted me to shoot that Clive bloke," Birdie said.

"For a second, I did want you to." The swipe of the nose was their code for a call to action. Without it, Birdie and Brandy behaved.

"Now what?" Brandy asked. "We didn't rescue Beth, and instead we're in debt to that psycho for even more."

"Maybe all is not lost," Todd said, smiling as he held the computer close to his chest. This was their link to a possible fortune, and for that he couldn't think of the night as a total bust. Still, he had to wonder, where had Clive stashed Beth? Probably in the arms of the other one, the one called Bobo. He hoped she was safe, which of course meant alive.

And hey, when did Birdie start using terms like "bloke"?

"I feel more like your date than your hostage," Beth Simon

said, "I mean, here we are, out on the town, strolling like, like, like . . ."

"Say it, you can find the word, I know you can."

"Like lovers," she at last said.

Indeed, that's the very picture that Bobo and Beth presented to anyone who cared to notice them. Bobo wasn't the nicest-looking chap you'd ever see, with his thick brown hair seemingly cut by a hedge clipper and his clothes drooping on his body, and Beth, though her rotund little body at least knew how to wear her clothes (they had to be custom made), her squashed facial features didn't help matters. Still, they walked arm-in-arm down Charing Cross Road, poster children for the theory that there was someone for everyone. They'd been to the movies all afternoon—the fourteenth installment in the Harry Potter series (well, it felt like there were that many)—and were now looking at bookstore windows, Foley's, Waterstone's, Blackwell's, even a Borders. They had just finished slices of not-very-good pizza from some shop in Leicester Square.

"Next time," Beth said, "we pick a romantic comedy. With someone like Vince Vaughn. Did you see *The Break-Up*? Oh, my, that was funny. Oh, listen to me, talking about break-ups and here we are . . . well, not even on a real date. Though maybe next time . . ." And then she got even more flustered, because this wasn't a date, it was a kidnapping. Her words trailed off; they had actually failed her. What had thrown her was that silly comment she made about seeing Bobo again. My God, what was she thinking, this man had kidnapped her and here she was fantasizing about . . . about what? A future? You had to understand, Beth didn't have many of opportunities for company of the opposite sex, so she had to take them where she could. In fact, this being a hostage was going better than the blind date from Saturday night.

It was Clive had given Bobo the money for the movie: "Just

get her out of here. But keep an eye on her—and a better eye than you kept on Todd, whom you lost. Screw up one more time and there's no telling what I might do."

Those had been his instructions, and Bobo was going to see them through, even if it killed him. He was determined to prove to Clive that he wasn't a complete dunderhead. He could be trusted with an important assignment. Yet as the day had worn on, he'd forgotten that he was working, so much so that his heart had swelled when Beth said she felt not like a hostage but a lover. And that she was talking about doing this again, the movie, the stroll, with Bobo at her side? This romance stuff, it was all new to Bobo. Move over, Vince.

"Oh, I'm sorry," Beth said.

"About what?"

"About, well, that next time comment. I know I'm your prisoner—you're the one who made me call in sick to work and I never call in sick, so they must be wondering exactly what I'm up to, though they'd never believe it if I told them. Imagine their faces if I told them that I've been kidnapped by some nasty man who slaps people into compliance—that's Clive, not you—and that his henchman, oh, just saying that gives me a thrill, that his henchman took me to the movies and that's he the most gentle criminal I've ever met . . ."

Bobo leaned in and kissed her, right smack on the lips, shutting off whatever words she might next have spouted. The kiss held, longer than was necessary if all he'd intended was to shut her up for a moment. But, were those bells he was hearing? Sparks he was feeling? New words springing into his mind, as though Beth were transferring them with the kiss. When at last they parted, there was a small gathering of people around them, all of them clapping.

"Oh, my," Beth said, her face tomato red.

"Yeah, oh."

They excused themselves from the appreciative crowd, and when they were alone again Beth looked at Bobo and said, "Why did you kiss me?"

"I thought it was to shut you up."

"What do you mean?"

"Well, you talk a lot. I mean, a lot a lot."

"I do?" She was oblivious. "No one's ever said anything. Why hasn't anyone ever said anything, they say something and I fix it, simple as that, right. I mean, honestly, talk too much! Who ever heard of such a thing, anyway, words are art, they're communication . . . they're . . . oh, how about that, there I go."

After that little outburst Beth suddenly seemed at a complete loss for words, so much so that the lingering silence started to become annoying. Bobo shifted from foot to foot, fearing he'd messed up this date bigtime. He had to remind himself this wasn't a date, and then inwardly told himself to shut up. Wished he hadn't said what he'd said.

"Say something, please."

And Beth did, and he liked what she said. "Let's go shopping—you need something new to read, don't you?"

He'd confessed that he enjoyed reading, something men like him usually didn't admit to. Only Larry knew it, and that's because Bobo was never without a book when on a stake-out. So they entered Foyle's and went immediately to the classics section, where Beth picked out *The Adventures of Huckleberry Finn*.

"Since you've already read *Tom Sawyer*."

They made their purchase and rejoined the crowd on Charing Cross.

It was getting on towards nine in the evening, and Beth was still his hostage. Should he bring her back to Clive's? Nope, he might get angry again, and Bobo realized he didn't want to subject the new woman in his life to Clive's behavioral outbursts. So the question was, where could they go?

"I suppose we can return to your own flat—but I have to watch over you—Clive's orders."

"Oh, oh okay."

They took a cab, because Bobo felt like splurging. How odd it felt for him not to be behind the wheel, to not feel Larry's hulking presence behind him. Nope, instead he had this very nice woman at his side, she who had helped pick out a new book with him. That, more than anything, had signaled a shift in the course of his life, an indication that maybe there was more out there than crime and punishment, there were the classics to be read and shared.

Back at Beth's flat, there was a bit more kissing but nothing more.

"No one gets any further without a commitment," Beth stated.

Still, they spent the night in her bed. He propped himself up against a fluffy bunch of pillows while she opened *Huck Finn* and began to read. " 'You don't know about me, without you having read a book by the name of *The Adventures of Tom Sawyer,* but that ain't no matter.' "

"Oh, good," Bobo said, "Like with Harry Potter, I love sequels."

It was the perfect melding of vices, his incessant need for stories of other lives, her incessant need to talk, talk, talk, and that's what she did, reading about Huck and his pals long into the night, even after Bobo's snoring had threatened her concentration. She realized this was her chance to escape his clutches, and instead, she placed the book down on the night table and snuggled up beside Bobo and fell asleep herself.

Todd who?

CHAPTER THIRTEEN

Todd wasn't thinking about Beth Simon either. So there.

Gently he ran his fingers over her bruised cheek. The swelling had gone done over the last few hours, but now, as they lay awake in this den of luxury, the silk sheets soft against their naked selves, Todd had to wonder why after such a misguided rescue attempt she was still with him. Looking back on the near-disastrous night, sweet Brandy had accompanied Todd, a relative stranger and self-confessed (well, confessed by gunpoint) con man, into the flat of a man who enjoyed striking people for no just cause. Not to mention what he was capable of when he believed the cause just, or high-paying. That man—*Clive*, Todd thought with distaste—had slapped her around, a gun had been pointed at them, and a huge beast of a man had nearly crushed Todd's windpipe. After all that drama, any other woman would have gone running far, far away. Cambridge, it wasn't looking so bad now, was it?

Except, retreat was not what Brandy Alexander had done. Instead, after saying goodnight to Birdie, she had closed the door, locked it, and put on the "Do Not Disturb" sign. She'd undressed and then undressed Todd and then had taken him to bed, where she allowed him to make love to her until both of them grew weary and tired. And unlike last night—was it only twenty-four hours?—when their coupling had been frantic and frenetic, this time it had been sweet, maybe even romantic.

Now, even the shadows had crept off to sleep, leaving only

the two of them awake in this mixed-up world of theirs.

"You were so gallant," Brandy said, her body cupped by Todd's.

He leaned down, kissed her freckled shoulder. "Right, almost got us both killed."

"But you didn't, and what you did I'll never forget. You came to my rescue."

She turned her head back to his, where he gave her a tender kiss, careful of her bruised cheek. But he said nothing, content to just hold her, her body so smooth and silky, so . . . perfect.

"Todd?"

"Yeah?"

"Why do you do it?"

He pressed his hips against hers. " 'Cause it feels so good."

She elbowed him. "No, you jerk. The cons, why do you do them?"

He shrugged, a meaningless gesture in the darkness. " 'Cause I'm jealous of other people having the things I want, because I feel like life has cheated me out of a lot of things, and not just material things. Because they have more than they need, so what does it mean to them if they lose a bit of it, it doesn't hurt them and it helps me. Because I do and I don't know why."

"And how about Birdie, seeing what your con has done to his life, how does that make you feel?"

"That's harder to answer. For the first time I'm beginning to question it—not my motives but the effect of them. I've never before had to face one of my victims after the fact. I supposed I always thought they would just take the monetary loss and move on. I always left them with more than enough to survive several lifetimes. What I didn't anticipate was a Marta Birdie, someone who'd want . . . what is it, anyway, revenge? You know, I could have ditched Birdie at any time, left him to figure this whole thing out himself. Let him take the rap for shooting Vance Timberlake—whether he did it or not."

"So you're not sure he's innocent?"

"Do you really think he'd admit to killing him?"

"Good point," she said. "So why didn't you ditch him?"

" 'Cause this is partly my responsibility and I need to answer to it."

The answer surprised even himself.

He felt a yawn taking over, glad it was. Even though this lonely hour was made for soul-searching and lovemaking, what he truly wanted, for just a few hours, was to forget the mess he'd created. London, Clive, Birdie, the Procopios, the fact that he was in debt up to his eyeballs and had to answer to a psycho. So he snuggled in even tighter, whispering sweet goodnights into Brandy's ear. Brandy. Ah, the silver lining in those English rain clouds. She responded with a grin on her face, a languid stretch of her body.

"I could have left at any time, too," she said.

"I know. Why didn't you?"

"Because, Todd, I think you're in over your head, and I don't want to see you get hurt. Or worse. Because I think maybe I can help. Because I always found life behind the walls of academia boring. You owe this Clive guy a million pounds . . . or else. Plus there's Birdie's one hundred thou."

"Yeah, I know. Thanks for the reminder."

"Have you got a plan?"

"Just my original one."

"Which you never did share with me," Brandy said. "Afraid to drag me into your big scheme, Todd? Don't want to corrupt an innocent girl? I think we've both learned I'm not so innocent, huh? Besides, I'm already in. So you might as well come clean and tell me what's really going on. Come on, can't I help?"

Todd's eyes were nearly closed and the light from the moon was but a slit in his vision and suddenly, they were fully open and awake, sleep no longer on his mind. He sat up in bed, Brandy doing the same, asking him what was wrong.

"Nothing, nothing, just . . . inspiration is all. Oh, Brandy, what you do to me, how you make my mind stand up and take notice of exactly what's in front of me."

"From where I'm sitting, it's more than just your mind that's stood up," she said, running her fingers through his chest hair, down his furry belly and below, to where he was most excited at the moment. "Tell me, tell me, what's got you so . . . you know."

Todd switched positions, rolling on top of her. "It's a two-part plan, actually, and for the first one, in answer to your question, yes, you can help. Because I need the able services of one Brandy Alexander. Though I wonder, being a natural beauty such as you are," he said, kissing one pink nipple, then another, "the million dollar question is, do you know anything about make-up?"

"Don't you remember? Before my father shipped me off to Cambridge, I was studying to be a cosmetician."

"Oh," he said, and then kissed her deeply, this ever-so-resourceful woman. Kissed her again, again.

"Oh, yourself," Brandy said.

There were details to be worked out, sure, but those could wait until the moon and sun switched positions. There were other positions that needed their attention first.

Clive Remington awakened on Wednesday extremely pissed off and very much alone. Fiona had returned home yesterday to celebrate her father's birthday and had said she might not make it back to Clive's for the night; Daddy might expect her to stay for once, but really the lack of the lovely Fi in his bed was not what had put such a sour mood into Clive. It's what had been transpiring the last few days. You see, Clive Remington had a bad habit, several really, but currently there was a biggie that he'd been unable to exercise. Control. He was out of it, and a loss of control meant a loss of power, of pride, and, it seemed, income. What he lost in power, however, he more than made up for in drive.

Here's what he'd lost: The big job. Timberlake was his contact and his conduit, had been for nearly eight years, since they'd first encountered each other. Clive was on the wrong side of a gun one night, facing down Vance Timberlake, who was dressed for bed but with a gun in his hand, also ready for action. The situation was this, a robbery in progress at the Timberlake home. Clive was the two-bit thief who had climbed through a window in the man's flat, caught because Mrs. T had made her notorious bread pudding and had forced a second helping on Mr. T, forcing him to spend part of the night on the bowl. The crash of a vase falling to the floor had alerted Timberlake that something other than his intestinal system was out of whack. Timberlake cornered the thug (Clive) and asked what he was looking for— was this a drug thing? Clive said no way, he didn't mess with that shit, and so Timberlake said he should call the police but instead a boy like you, a gutsy one whose only fault was stupidity and, looking at the shattered remains of the vase, a bit clumsy, maybe he could prove useful. Clive was gutsy and he was darn talented too and so Timberlake hired him. For special projects. It started innocently enough, beating up tenants who didn't take paying rent seriously. Clive had graduated to bigger projects over the years, until he found himself in the enviable position of being "indispensable." Both men had services to offer, and there were people out there willing to pay the price. As a result, Clive Remington had become wealthier than he'd imagined. Now, with Timberlake's untimely death, the gravy train looked to have run out of steam.

As Clive headed for the shower, the memories of his and Timberlake's first meeting gave way to thoughts of this latest job, stalled by the man's death. He knew the gist of it, a simple execution. One bullet, one corpse, one million. As he soaped himself up good that morning, he contemplated, in light of what he'd lost, what he'd gained. Simple, in a word: Todd. Bloody Todd Gleason and his interfering ways, his ridiculous scheme and damn him, that foolish attempt last night at pulling a fast one over Clive. He'd underestimated the American, figuring a two-bit con like him would be working alone. Then he goes and shows up with quite a stunning babe, a shame really to knock her about. But she'd been cheeky with Clive and well, she was with *him*. Made Fiona look like . . . that noisy Beth creature. If the blonde with the bombs wasn't enough, showing up out of nowhere was Mr. Middle-Aged Man and his middle-aged gut, like that dumb old *Saturday Night Live* character, shakily pointing a gun at him. At him! Okay, that round had gone to them, but as stated, that only provided Clive with drive, with an itchy trigger finger.

The shower over, Clive stepped out of the shower and walked into the kitchen naked. He was making tea just as the front door of his flat opened.

"Fi?" he called out.

"Uh, no, boss, me, Larry."

Larry had been sent out on a mission last night to track Todd and Co. down. From the looks of it, the mission had been a bust.

"I've been up all night," Larry said, "waiting in front of that seedy motel where that guy was staying. You know, the place we picked up that Simon chick from?"

Clive sat down on the sofa and contemplated the situation aloud. "I still don't understand from where that doofus showed up. What's Gleason doing with him, anyway, and how does he figure into his con? I had pinned Todd as a lone operator. Then 'poof,' the loser with the gun pulls a fast one on us."

Larry was still standing there in front of his boss, fidgeting. "Um, uh, um, uh . . ."

"Stop that . . . what's wrong, Larry? There something you haven't told me? Right? I can always tell when you've been withholding information. You begin babbling like an idiot. What? You've seen that man before, haven't you? Before last night—shit . . ." He felt his blood boiling, hot enough to make that cup of tea. He forced down his temper, now wasn't the time for violence. He just wanted answers. "It's okay, Larry, just be honest with me and you won't get hurt, I promise. But you better tell me now. Tell me about our mystery person."

"About Todd, sure, we know all about him . . ."

"Not Todd," Clive said, clenching his teeth in restraint. "The other one."

"She was Brandy—that's what he called her. She was real nice to look at."

Well, he'd tried to keep his anger in check. Tried and failed. Larry had pushed his patience too far and suddenly Clive was pulling . . . well, a Clive, a double one actually. His hand moved in a swift two-motion move that had Larry's cheek's stinging and his huge body reeling back, all of it happening in the barest hint of a second. Clive, he had speed and power, enough to topple anyone, their size a non-issue.

"Yeah, uh, sorry, boss. It's just . . . okay, yeah, that other guy. I'd seen him before . . ."

So Larry spilled his guts. Saw him first at the flat where Timberlake was shot, same day, before even Gleason showed up. Saw him again when he kidnapped Beth Simon, followed him to that seedy joint he'd been scoping out last night. As Clive listened, his mind reeled and finally he exploded, a foul-mouthed burst of words and phrases and images, a testament really to Clive's fertile vocabulary more so than his temper. Larry had dropped to his knees in fear of retribution, sputtering

196

his apologies. Nearly crying, this big oaf finally spilled the last drop of news.

"It's Bobo's fault—he said that guy wasn't important, some nobody."

"Bobo did, huh? Where is he?"

"Keeping watch of that Beth woman—where, I don't know."

Clive angrily stomped to his bedroom, where, in the drawer by his bed, he withdrew the nastiest, biggest-looking revolver you'd never want to see. "Find him, Larry. Tell him I need to see him."

Larry gulped. "What are you going to do?"

Clive grinned. He couldn't remember the last time he'd gone to target practice. "What am I going to do, Larry? Why, I'm going to promote you," he said, staring down at the barrel of the revolver.

He pointed it at Larry, and Larry made quick use of the space between him and the door. He was gone in seconds.

Clive had better things to do than wait for Bobo. He left soon after, he had a couple errands to run. Hailing a cab, he instructed the driver to an address in South Kensington, and after a short trip, he was standing on the corner of the Old Brompton Road and Harrington Road, not far from the Tube stop. A street with beautiful row houses seemed to stretch endlessly before him. He found the address he wanted, rang the buzzer. In a moment's time, the door opened and an older gentleman answered.

"Help you?"

"Yes, sir, good morning, I was wondering, has Fiona awakened?"

The man scrunched his face, even though he had no reason to. Clive looked perfectly respectable and he was wearing his best manners right there on his sleeve. Guess fathers were always protective of their daughters, no matter what age they achieve.

Not that Fi was that old, early twenties.

"Yes, we're having breakfast. You must be the new boy. Must say, you appear more composed than the others."

"Yes, sir, thank you, sir."

Fiona was finishing off a croissant, dotting the crumbs with a wet forefinger. She was excited to see Clive, hugging him tightly and then cutting off her affections in light of the fact that Daddy was watching. He had turned fifty yesterday, no need to test his ticker so early into the second half of his life.

With a quick clearing of his throat, Fiona's father excused himself, donning a black overcoat over a black suit. Like he was headed for a funeral.

Turned out, he was.

"Don't know how many people will attend, I feel bad for the widow. Nice lady. Plus, it's my job, you never know who will show up, might lead to a clue."

"Goodbye, Daddy," Fiona said, kissing him on the cheek.

"Yes, sorry about the funeral and all, Mr. Brury, good luck," Clive said.

"That's Inspector Brury, son."

When he'd gone, Clive turned back to Fiona, and with his mouth agape, said, "Holy shit, Fi, you never told me your father was a policeman."

Or that he was investigating Vance Timberlake's murder either.

"You never asked."

"I never asked, huh," Clive responded.

He was surrounded by idiots. At the rate he was going, Toddy-boy had assembled a more capable team of misfits than he. Which meant Clive had better get a move on things, and really, this was good timing finding out about Timberlake's funeral, it meant no one was home at the Timberlake home. The perfect occasion for one last break-in, a memorial in its own right. Who knew what kind of revealing papers his secret employer might have kept. Knowing now how many idiots already filled his life, the odds were good that Timberlake had been one, too. He had to get better friends.

"Come on, Fi, I need your help."

"Where are we going?"

He said nothing further, merely grabbed her arm as she grabbed her purse and the two of them left her home, walked just a few short blocks away to where Vance and Clara Timberlake had shared a life and a business and . . . what else? An intimate knowledge of each other's secrets? Clive had always wondered if Clara Timberlake knew more than she let on. Vance insisted his wife was not privy to his "other" business, she was a good, dutiful wife. Clive hoped that Timberlake had gone to his grave without spilling his guts, doubly hoped his voice didn't hold the power to speak from the grave. Clive hated to do this kind of stuff in broad daylight but he hoped that most people were at work and those who weren't, well, there was always the hope his genial neighbors had gone to the funeral.

Looking confident and innocent, Clive and Fiona walked to the front door as though they lived there. He told Fiona to fix her lipstick or something busy-like to distract whoever might be looking at what he was trying to do. Which was pick the lock, something he'd become more adept at in his years of training with Timberlake. Oh, the sweet ironies of life, the lock clicked and the door opened and next thing, it was like they belonged.

"I've got some looking around to do, Fi."

"What do I do?"

"Keep watch."

"I can't believe it, Clive, you're making me break the law," she said. "Daddy will be so upset."

He patted her on the cheek, real sweet-like. "Daddy's not going to know."

Clive made his way through the living room and kitchen, to a back office where Vance had conducted his business. The usual equipment was in order, phone and fax and computer; he turned that last one on and began to search the files. Lots of properties listed, details about various flats to let, lists of names of people who had booked them, boring-ass shit like that. He flipped through a series of disks, none of them looking particularly promising.

He gave up on the computer, moved to the locked filing cabinet. He popped the lock in seconds and began to search through folder after folder, again, with no results. Just stupid property estate paperwork. Clive wasn't sure what type of paperwork Timberlake might have kept about his criminal activities. Did he just keep it all in his mind? No, Timberlake wasn't that smart. He had to have phone numbers for his own contacts, that's how these jobs came along. Someone who knew someone, a chain of evidence that had the police any ingenuity they might have been able to break. As frustrated as Clive felt about not finding any shred of Timberlake's secret life, that just made him realize that, heck, there was nothing to find. Not here, anyway. So if Clive came up empty-handed, so then must have the Mrs. and no doubt the police, too.

Clive searched further, starting with the desk drawers. They weren't locked, that was his first clue that they hid nothing incriminating. Still, he spent a few minutes flipping through a stack of paper; again, boring, landlord stuff. In the bottom drawer were lots of office supplies, which he quickly dumped onto the floor, thinking maybe something was hidden beneath them. A false bottom? Again, nothing. So he bent down and cleaned up the mess he'd made, and that's when he found what he was looking for.

The floor was made of a series of square pieces of wood and one of them had come loose after having the office supplies dumped on it. Clive lifted the square and underneath it found a gray metal safe carefully imbedded into the foundation. He tried to lift it and was unable to; it was that secure. Clive was convinced that whatever he didn't want the police to find was located inside this seemingly impenetrable safe. He tried a few quick numerical combinations, all with no luck. Damn, he'd have to get the number somehow.

But that would have to wait. He'd already spent too much time inside the Timberlake home. Who knew how long Timberlake's funeral would take; did he have many friends? Those were his thoughts as he wiped clean all the surfaces he'd touched. Replacing the handkerchief to his pocket, Clive stole one last look at the office, his eyes zeroing in on a framed photograph of the happily married couple. Both of them doing their best to look attractive, their smiles serving only to highlight their crooked teeth and odd features. It was in Timberlake's own eyes that Clive saw what no one else saw in the man, a cold and calculating individual, willing to do anything for a buck . . . well, lots of bucks. An honest landlord, an honest front for a man who had over the years built up a network of criminal activity. Clive smiled back at the man; yup, it was nice to find people who shared your common interests.

"Rest in peace, you ol' crook."

He stole another look at the photo, this time focusing on Clara. What do you know? Clive asked. Do you know who I am and what I really did for your husband? Do you know who killed your husband? Do you have the combination to that safe? Too many questions, not enough answers.

For someone who made his living on ending lives, Clive felt spooked being inside the house of a dead man. Cold shivers ran up his spine. So he escaped from the office and ran far away from the house on Onslow Square. Fiona went dashing after him, forgetting to close the door after her.

Meanwhile, back in New York City, Toad the frog was staring out of his glass tank, itself positioned on a table near a window that afforded a magnificent view of the East River. His big eyes blinked and then he hopped away from this particular view. He couldn't care less. Andy Simon, though, could. Manhattanites were willing to shell out big bucks more for the view than for the floor space (or closet space). Andy was one such sucker, immensely proud of his twenty-eighth floor two-bedroom digs in the midst of Sutton Place. The Citicorp Building from one window, the Queensboro Bridge from the other. Landmarks from your bedroom window, now that was status.

"Here you go, a little food from Uncle Andy," he said, sprinkling some pellets into the water. He waited to see if Toad took them; he didn't, once again. "Come on, you stupid frog, you've gotta eat. Todd said you gobble your food like a Great White shark, what's the deal, huh? He'll be home soon, and then so will you. God, I hope so, because I can't take this much longer." He rapped his knuckles on the glass. "You hear me, Toad? Todd said to talk to you and so I am and what do you do? You ignore me. Fine, forget it."

He stood there, as though waiting for an answer. Andy had to get a life.

And at the moment, he had to get to work.

It was Wednesday morning New York time, and he had just finished tying his tie, a two-hundred-dollar silk piece from Armani, beautifully matching the three-button suit from the same maker. Nothing but the best for Andy Simon, financial wizard and fashion plate. He finished his cup of coffee while flipping through the last of the newspapers; the *Post*, his guilty pleasure after the required reading of *The Wall Street Journal* and the *Times*. There were those same two people again, featured on

Page Six. "Looking Great . . . Out on the Town" was the sly headline that accompanied the photo. Followed by a short piece about Mr. and Mrs. Henri Procopio—the cosmetics king and his glamorous lottery-winning wife, the perfect, luckiest couple—strolling along a street in London after having attended the latest play that would soon bore Broadway audiences. No doubt a P.R. move, but a good one. From all Andy had read, the Procopios could use a dose of good press; well, Henri anyway. He'd taken a ribbing from Wall Street and others when it was learned even his wife had lost her confidence in his money-making skills. Why else had she played the lottery? And won, what were the odds of that? Andy remembered the joke running around his office. Hey, how many cosmetics kings does it take to screw in a lightbulb? Two, one to screw it in and another to win the lottery so they could afford the bulb. That was the wit that controlled our economy.

Andy grabbed his jacket and overcoat and then headed out for the offices of Bernstein, Gilbert & Young. Some mornings he took the subway and some mornings he took a cab and because he was in a good mood and the sun was shining he opted for a cab; he just hated to go down underground and miss out on such a nice day. He arrived twenty minutes later and instantly flipped on his computer, the twenty-first century answer to getting coffee. Then he put on his telephone headset, ready for a day of action and transactions. The phone wasted no time in ringing.

"Andy Simon, let's make some money."

"I certainly hope so," said his favorite client. "Let's not waste time, I'm sure you saw it and I certainly did, that photo. I want to buy ten thousand shares of Looking Great Cosmetics."

"You been drinking already, a little nip poured over the corn-flakes?" he asked, joking.

"You're lucky to have such a good track record, making comments like that." And then she laughed and so did Andy.

"Consider it placed."

She disconnected, and Andy considered what was up. Looking Great, sure the rumors of a sale were rampant, but that and four-fifty got you mocha caffe latte supremo at Starbucks. Still, she'd never steered him wrong with her honed instincts; hell, she should be the trader and he . . . what? The rich bastard who could afford to gamble with a fortune. Now there was an idea.

Before he could change his mind—not that he would—he placed a phone call of his own, first following through on the order for his client and then another purchase as well. "Yeah, same stock, no, no, a different client. Let me give you an account number, take the funds directly from there, right. An anonymous risk-taker, yeah, thinks he's on to something. Thanks."

"Either you're smart or stupid," the man on the other end said.

"Separated by a thin line," Andy said.

Andy disconnected the phone, leaned back in his chair and smiled, not even noticing that standing over him was his boss, a stern-faced man with an ugly black mole on the tip of his nose; really, he could afford to have that removed.

"Simon?"

"Oh, sir, good morning."

"Have a hot tip?" He indicated the phone.

"Oh—uh, that. No, just an overanxious client, insisted I make the buy first thing I arrived. Well, I did, guess I can get some coffee."

"Keep up the good work, Simon."

"Yes, sir, Mr. Alexander."

Back at Andy's apartment, Toad the Frog was glad to see his temporary caretaker gone for the day. It was then that he ate his food, surviving, like all beings, on his instincts.

And Toad's instincts told him not to trust one Andy Simon.

CHAPTER FOURTEEN

Clang, clang.

Nope, that wasn't the sound of the trolley and we were way far from St. Louis. It was a less than amiable lunch with Henri and Elise Procopio, as silent as ever, the only sound between them coming from utensils being scraped against their plates, digging for food. Henri had wanted to stay close, maybe go to Simpsons on the Strand located right there at the Savoy, but Elise had opted for straying a bit further, maybe down Piccadilly and of course she had won out, she was winning all week long and that's what had put Henri in the foul mood that had settled over him. Really, this dream-week vacation was turning into a nightmare, the cause of it sitting right across the table from him, the woman he'd vowed till death do them part. (Of course he'd said those words three other times to three other women and they still breathed.) Elise had chosen a restaurant along St. James's Street, insisted on the table up front which allowed her to see out the large plate-glass window, also for her to be seen.

"Elise, no one cares."

"But I was in the newspaper—that's what Mimi Ledbetter said. On your arm, and there was even an article accompanying the photograph, detailing my every move in London."

"That was the *New York Post;* no one here reads it."

She couldn't be bothered with such a rational explanation. "Well, they should."

That's how lunch began, as Henri drank down the first of his whiskeys, listening to more news from New York that had come courtesy of that surgically altered hag Mimi. She had called Elise's mobile just a short while ago, unusually early in the morning for her. Henri found he felt sorry for Elise, she who was beginning to believe her own hype. So she was in London (big deal) and having a grand time (hardly) and wasn't everyone jealous of her (no). Henri smiled in amusement at the way Elise could twist words to stroke her own ego. Elise, her face stern over her stemmed glass, asked him what was so funny.

"With your limited list of topics, did you ever think you should have been named Mimi?"

She frowned. "I don't find that funny."

"I shouldn't think so."

So after they ordered, Elise settled for looking out the plate-glass window at the gray clouds and the passing crowds of people, phones attached to their ears and none of them caring much for the cabs and cars that failed to prevent them from jaywalking. Henri settled for looking at his wife, trying to see beyond the surface—which today was heavily made up and dressed to kill—and remember the woman he'd married. His third marriage, to Laverne DiGrasso, had already soured when he began to fool around with Elise; she was just so refreshing for him after having been trapped in a loveless state for far too long. Elise had reawakened him, not just sexually but creatively, too, as he had remarkably reversed the declining fortunes of his discount Looking Great Inc. in the late nineties. A new decade, a new attitude, that's all you need, or so Elise claimed to take credit for. Of course not everything was rosy after they'd married, Elise had adjustment problems when it came to dealing with the rich and the powerful, they didn't "take" to her initially and that only frustrated her more. So, very much in love with her and very much not wanting to have to meet a fifth Mrs. P,

Henri helped mold her, shape her, bring her the kind of acceptance she'd only dreamed about. For years they went smoothly through their lives until, well, what had happened? The student became the master. Winning the lottery, good God of all things, Elise had become someone entirely different, that once insecure girl now swallowed whole by the shallow woman he saw on the opposite side of his table.

These thoughts continued as they ate, the tension severing his meat better than any serrated knife could. At last, he could stand it no more, and when he chewed the last of his meal and gulped the last of his whiskey, he threw his fork down on the plate. The sudden sound startled his starlet, and she peered steely eyes at him.

"What was that for?"

"I'm tired, Elise."

"So take a nap."

"No, I'm tired of this. What are we doing?"

"Lunching, dear."

"No, we're currently sharing a table but somehow lunching alone. You know, I believe we had the best of intentions with this trip, Elise, but as the days slip by, so too does any chance of our reconciling. On Saturday—three days from now—we will be reaching a milestone—a first for me, I might add—our tenth anniversary and I for one was looking forward to it. We're away from the troubles we had back in New York, we came looking for a fresh start. So how about it, Elise, share your thoughts with me. The trip began so well, an enchanting flight, our first day's dalliance in our suite, the promise of a new start, it was there, and now—silence pervades us?"

"Henri, please—don't make a scene," she said, looking around the restaurant for justification of her statement. Not even their waiter was nearby to care.

"Elise, it's three in the afternoon, the restaurant is nearly empty because everyone returned to work and no one is seated near us anyway. So I hardly call this making a scene."

"Oh, Henri, you're reading too much into this. So I'm quiet, I'm thinking . . . yes, about you and me and this trip, what it was supposed to mean—what it does mean. I suppose I'm a bit anxious, we've got so much riding on just one day, I wonder if that pressure for it to be perfect will destroy us even before we reach it. Henri, please tell me what you're planning, at least the location. It's nearly eating me away inside."

He shook his head, even managed a smile. How nice to know she was looking forward to their escapist weekend. No phones, no other people, no interruptions or intrusions. Just he and she and the magical night he'd been planning since they first envisioned this night a couple months ago. It was after an unusually fierce night of lovemaking and wine-drinking (not necessarily in that order) when he had looked right at Elise and said, "I wish we had more nights like this, I wish we could go back to that time when a fire crackled between us."

"Do you want me to wear my secretary's outfit?" she had suggestively asked.

Now the magic was gone, replaced by an innate petulance. Henri refused to spill his guts about their special night.

"Then I will sit here and pout until you tell me."

"Elise, darling, as long as I know my secrecy and that alone is what's got you upset, I can live with this . . . silence. Knowing that in a few days all will be revealed, well, you'll have forgotten all about the pouting and you'll be feeling like . . . a Queen."

"Henri, have you rented out Buckingham Palace?"

"Hardly," he said, and then ran a zipper across his lips in mock silence. Apparently she took that seriously, as she once again closed down the lines of communication. Henri sat there, trying to figure this woman out, what made her tick and what brought on these shifts of mood so suddenly. Was that it? Was she afraid of aging, afraid that he would turn her in for a younger model?

Words formed on his lips and he wondered if by speaking them he was opening up a can of worms. To hell with it, push had come to shove.

"Elise, do you regret not having children?"

She nearly sputtered her wine. "Shit, Henri, what are you talking about? Where on earth did that come from?"

"I was just thinking, it's a shame we never had any children."

"*I* never had," she said. "*You* did."

"Yes, with Theresa—but Michel is leading his own life and doesn't wish to associate with me or his mother."

"That's because *Michael*—that's his name, not that affected Michel—is a Vegas dancer, and if you had any sense you'd reconcile with him. You make people want to be pushed away. Though at least you do have something in common—he does like his make-up." She laughed at her tasteless joke. She was the only one laughing.

Henri sat there, steaming, his face red and ready to boil.

Elise continued on. "Really, Henri, could you imagine us with children? Like that could have saved us from reaching this point in our marriage."

Here poor Henri was, a good sport and a good chap, trying to have a mature conversation on the matter of marriage and motherhood and the reasons why they had drifted apart and the reasons why they had gone on this Godforsaken trip and all Elise could do is drink most of a bottle of wine herself and insult the only offspring it seemed Henri would ever have. This woman, maybe there was no saving her, she was so cold and callous and . . . and . . .

". . . That's it, Elise. You're so fucking rich, you pay the bill. Me, I'm leaving—for New York. Happy Anniversary—not."

With that, Henri threw down his napkin and stormed from

the restaurant, leaving Elise sitting alone and blushing, not that anyone could tell with all that make-up she'd plastered on her face. Bet Michel could give her some pointers.

Todd turned away from Brandy with obvious disgust. She looked horrible. But she was grinning too, and when Todd looked back, so was he.

"It works, it works, I'm hideous," Brandy said, jumping for joy in front of the mirror which played back her disfigurement.

Quite something to celebrate, huh? Actually, if the disguise worked, they would indeed have a reason to crack open the champagne. One masterful con, masterfully executed. They hoped.

"Let's test it out," Todd said.

He went and knocked on the adjoining door, heard Birdie grumbling from the other room. He was watching TV and try-ing not to think about the daily call he was required to make to Marta.

"What is it—" His words failed him, and in their place came a piercing scream. He fell back against the doorframe, Todd helping to catch him before he injured himself on the way to the floor. He was pointing at Brandy and his face was still a mix of horror and shock, spittle dripping from his lips.

Brandy's face had two big scars, one on her left cheek, another on her forehead. It quite looked like the stitches were still in them, as though the healing process was still, well, processing. Again she clapped, pleased with Birdie's knee-jerk response. Daddy was such a fool, didn't he know how talented his daughter was, just not with Cambridge and Shakespeare and his Ten Bitchiest Women. She could have had a real future in make-up, making people look as beautiful as possible, or just the reverse. Hollywood paid big money for such talent.

"What . . . what happened?"

"Well," Todd began, "it appears that Miss Charity Willow, model extraordinaire for all the top women's magazines—*Cosmo,* right, Charity? (this with a wink)—was off on vacation and ran low on her agency-approved make-up and ran to the local store and picked up some Looking Great brands. The chemicals ate away at her skin, until she had to have two separate skin grafts, which haven't quite taken yet—as you can see by the stitches still in her face. Really, it was a dreadful accident."

"Sounds almost plausible, doesn't it, Birdie?" said the newly-christened Charity Willow.

"God—you look terrible, it's amazing."

"Glad you think so, Birdie," Todd said. "Charity and I are off to see Daddy Bigbucks to get you your money—and then it's goodbye to this happy little threesome. I know you'll miss it, so will I. Char?"

"I'll be real sad."

Birdie hated sarcasm. "Just get me my money. One hundred thousand dollars and I'll consider us even. Okay, *Todd?* That's all I'm in it for, enough to keep Marta off my back. Anything else that's going on, I'm no part of. Now, speaking of my Marta, if you'll excuse me. Oh how I hate these international calls, they cost so much."

Hoping Birdie's pathetic personality wasn't contagious, Todd closed the door on him and then helped Brandy with the finishing touches. He took a couple shots from the digital camera he'd purchased with Birdie's money this morning while Brandy was off buying her supplies. Nice that they were staying in the heart of London's West End, where live theater meant shops for live theater needs. A nearby computer shop had been kind enough to print out hard copies of both the before and after photos. The former featured a bikini-clad Brandy posing on the bed (for a hotel holiday excursion catalog, they'd decided). The latter, developed not fifteen minutes earlier, showed Brandy as she looked now. As a finishing touch, Brandy applied thick gauze bandages to her face to cover her disfigurement. Then, with a quick kiss that held the promise of much more, they headed off to the sixth floor, where Henri Procopio had booked his suite.

They'd called first, asked for the Mrs. She wasn't around, good thing.

They took the stairs, careful to not run into anyone who might look questionably at Todd, he back in his business suit, or Brandy, bandaged so much that someone might just ring for the police. Once on their desired floor they waited for a chambermaid to turn the corner and then Todd confidently knocked on the door—while Brandy waited in the stairwell, peering at the action from that safe distance. Procopio answered the door quickly.

"What do you want—oh, if it isn't Mr. Booker. I'd nearly forgotten about you this week. Thought you'd gone for good. What is it now?"

"I think perhaps you should invite me in, don't want any neighboring guests to hear how bad your products are, might cause a stir, something could leak to the press."

Henri opened the door wider, a heavy sigh escaping his lips. "This hasn't been the best of days, kid. I told you before, I don't have time for your silly little boy's game."

"Sir, if you please," Todd said. An elderly couple had just stepped out of the room next door, gave Todd and Henri a silent acknowledgment.

Henri stepped away from the door, said, "I won't bow down to this kind of blatant blackmailing."

Todd entered the room, leaving the door slightly ajar. He distracted Procopio by displaying those "before" photographs at him. Henri examined them, smiled at the woman's obvious beauty. Todd ran a narrative as he displayed each photo, these were outtakes from the photo shoot down in the Bahamas last summer, yes, very nice, Henri agreed with the perspective of a man who had been around beautiful women all his life. Then Todd produced the after pictures, which got the right reaction out of the cosmetic king. He shuddered, turned away, thrusting them back at Todd.

"Unfortunate—but certainly my products did not cause such . . . horrific damage."

"How can you be sure?" Todd said.

Henri walked to the far end of the room, where he poured himself a whiskey. He didn't offer one to Todd. Todd decided not to take offense, just waited while the man drank. When he'd swallowed down the last of the whiskey, Henri said, "I'll give you credit, Mr. Booker, those photographs are very good. Very good fakes." He paused. "However, a deal's a deal and I'm a man of my word, you hand over those photos—though I'm not naive enough to think these are the only ones—and I'll write you a check for one hundred thousand dollars. This is what you want me to do, correct? Write that check."

Todd was nodding; he had to remind himself to stay cool. "But, sir, you said if I produced the model—Miss Charity Willow herself—you'd pay me two hundred fifty thousand. Well . . . allow me." That was Brandy's cue to walk in the door, and she did, shyly, meekly, not at all like a confident beautiful swimsuit model would do; nope, she was indulging a once-upon-a-time wish to be an actress.

"Come here, young woman," Henri said.

Brandy looked to Todd, who nodded his approval, before approaching the older man.

"Take off those bandages," he instructed.

Brandy removed the tape from the side of her face, taking the gauze with her. Henri's face reeled in disgust at the unsightly scars.

"How much did this cost you, my dear?"

"Oh, untold amounts, sir. I've lost every modeling gig I've been put up for."

Henri smiled. "No, no, I mean for the make-up and the bandages and I assume, this lovely bikini you're wearing in this photograph."

Todd's heart began to pound, there was some kind of bait and switch going on. He needed to do something. A bluff had been called. He stepped forward, standing between Henri and Brandy. "That's no way to treat this stricken woman, Mr. Procopio, surely you have some level of compassion for what she's been through, for the loss of not just her profession but her self-esteem."

"Kid, let me tell you something—you're not getting anything from me. One hundred thou, two-hundred fifty, heck, a dime. Whatever you were expecting just ain't gonna happen. And I'll tell you why. Because you—and she—though very talented and very determined and awfully clever, have messed up just one little point in this whole . . . uh, scheme. And that, my boy, has become your downfall." Henri was grinning now, and the grin washed over Todd like a heat wave. He'd begun to sweat. "This has been one crappy week, I'd been wondering when the fun would begin. You've managed to salvage part of my vacation, I'll give you that. The entertainment value alone almost has me writing you a check."

Todd began to smile.

"Almost."

There went the smile, dimples fading into the sunset. "I don't understand, sir. If I release these photos to the press . . ."

"They'll laugh in your face, just as I have. Look at the photo, Mr. Booker—Miss Willow, and tell me if you see anything familiar."

Both of them peered closely at the photograph, trying to see whatever it was that Henri had seen, and both of them came up empty. Todd looked away, pissed that they'd come so close and that now Henri was calling their bluff. He reminded himself, stay strong, stay focused . . . and so his eyes focused, all right, right at the Procopios' bed, more accurately, at the bedspread.

"Oh, shit," Todd said aloud. He couldn't help the rare burst of profanity. He wandered over to the bed, bent down and examined the pattern. It was the same exact spread as the one from their room. And as such, the same one in the photograph.

There was little else to say.

"Goodbye, Mr. Booker. Miss Willow. I'm assuming you'll be checking out of the Savoy momentarily. Can't exactly afford it now, can you?"

And that, as they say, was that. Todd put the photographs of Brandy back in his pocket as Procopio threw them out. Defeated, they were forced to return to their own room, because Brandy couldn't exactly go out in public appearing as she did now. Todd slammed the door closed, the reverberation echoing down the hallway. Fuck if he cared.

Now, our Todd is normally a very even-tempered guy, not easily defeated. But this time, oh boy, was he ever mad. Brandy stayed clear of him as he attacked the only thing that came to mind: the goddamned bed, lifting the mattress and throwing it to the floor, ripping off the sheets and throwing the pillows clear across the room, and then came the bedspread, oh that, he couldn't care less how much it cost, he went at that thing with a vengeance, until nothing remained but shreds of fabric and downy balls of fluffy insides that rained down on the carpet like snow. Then, when he'd finished, breathing heavily and looking a ruffled mess in his suit, he announced that he needed a g.d. drink. The words sputtering from his lips were nothing for a Literature major to hear.

Just then the adjoining door opened and Birdie stuck his

head in their room.

"Got my money?"

Elise Procopio sat in the American Bar at the Savoy, nursing her martini while a man with Manilow's voice played Sinatra tunes on the piano. Not a good mix; good thing the bartender knew what he was doing. She wasn't really all that thirsty, not that that had ever stopped her from downing a shot of booze. No, something was nagging at her insides and churning up all the liquor and food (in that order) that she'd consumed at lunch. Actually, she knew what was bothering her; she'd pushed Henri too far and he was threatening to end this trip today, if not sooner, and return to New York. Presumably, he had meant without her. That couldn't happen, there was no way she could allow Henri to return home, certainly not in this mood. He might do something foolish and . . . what, impulsively sell the company, just as he'd been threatening to do for months? So preoccupied with her problem was she, she failed to see the dimpled young man who joined her at her table until he'd already sat down.

Her eyes widened with surprise.

"You," she said.

She didn't know his name, he'd insisted on that detail and good thing, considering what she'd hired him to do.

"You," he said in return, this conversation sounding familiar.

"But we're not supposed to be meeting now—or did I get that detail wrong?"

"Oh, uh . . . no, I just needed a drink and I was passing by. Pretty stupid of me . . . but they make the best martini in town."

"Sshh," Elise said. Really, what kind of a professional was he? Well, a cute one . . . "Actually, I'm glad I've run into you and yes, aren't the martinis divine? Look, I need to change our appointment, tonight is no longer viable. I have plans. I don't know when is better, I need to check his schedule first. But definitely sometime tomorrow, I'll have your deposit for you."

The man nodded, slowly sipping at his newly served martini. He'd gotten control of himself, composure leading to assurance.

"Check your e-mail. Until then . . ." Elise tossed down a twenty-pound note. "You can leave the tip."

"Uh, sure. Until we meet again."

"Yes, and then you can give me a tip, maybe the rest of it, too."

With a flirtatious wave, Elise retreated from the bar and hastily made her way back up to her suite. New resolve had found its way into her soul—surprised it could find one—and so she was determined that Henri was going nowhere.

Henri certainly looked like he was going somewhere, since he was packing up his suitcase. He was dressed in his bathrobe and looked cleanly showered, something he always did before he traveled. Ten years of marriage had taught her the patterns of his life.

"Oh, Henri, please . . . please don't go."

"Elise, there's nothing you can say that will change my mind."

Shit. Drastic times called for drastic measures. "Then how about it's something I do instead?"

And with such a proclamation, Elise stripped down to her nothingness. Swaggered her way over to Henri, and planted a big wet smootchy kind of kiss smack on the lips. She grinded her hips against his, usually a tease, this time more like a promise. She smiled up at him, saw that his eyes had flickered with life; not the only thing, she noticed. She undid the belt on his silk robe, slipped the robe off and then, imagining that cutey-patooty from the bar, she hoisted herself onto her hirsute husband.

"Oh, Henri, don't go."

Henri didn't go. Instead, he came, and much to Elise's surprise, not for a while.

CHAPTER FIFTEEN

Wednesday night carried with it a forecast for heavy rains sweeping down from the north, but anyone with a brain could have made that prediction. The skies were dark gray, the streets were wet, people's umbrellas were flailing in the wind, and cars and cabs were furiously swishing away falling water with fast-moving wipers. Clive, killer for hire, watching the meteorologist make rather obvious predictions on the BBC, was amazed at what some folks did to earn a living. Enough musing, he was off to keep his appointment with the faceless stranger who would at last give him the deposit required to kill her husband. Why did she have to pick such a crappy location, and by crappy, he meant outdoors.

The Marble Arch, at the northeastern edge of Hyde Park. Her e-mail, which she had sent to Todd's laptop, which Clive had intercepted during his short possession of it, had been meant for Todd but, really, if you think about it, really for Clive. Clive of course, upon seeing the message, took that as proof that Todd was indeed moving in on his turf, that he had in fact killed Timberlake and that he could not be underestimated. Maybe that charming con routine was his front. If so, Clive found his stupid routine convincing. Still, Clive could prove that he was the man Timberlake had in mind, he had the credits—and more importantly—the revolver that was meant to put the bullet in Monsieur Procopio. Clive just had to convince the woman paying for the deed that he was the right man for the job; the only man. He would accomplish that in a matter of time, Clive thought, as he'd grabbed a cab and departed from his comfortable surroundings of Vauxhall. It was a long trip through Central London, along Grosvenor Place and up traffic-laden Park Lane. Finally, they reached the Marble Arch and Clive hopped out and attempted to shield himself from the rain by tossing up the collar of his overcoat, a black London Fog. Umbrellas were for sissies.

He crossed the street against traffic, foregoing the complex system of underground subways that had been built to help pedestrians negotiate this circuitous circus of roads. He found protective covering under the giant arch, as ornate as it was ostentatious at the edge of Oxford Street. And then he set about waiting. He was about fifteen minutes early for their designated nine o'clock meeting, and as time clicked ever closer to the clock's twenty-first hour, Clive had to admit to feeling a bit smug. Timberlake's life had been cut short, and so too had his network to these pleasant little jobs that kept Clive from being a legitimate contributing member of society; not that he thought his lot in life was unremarkable. Rather he provided a service many people didn't have the guts to perform themselves. And in this modern age, chief among the qualities you needed to survive was guts. Even with Todd's interfering ways, the bloke had been helpful in his own right, mucking things up so much that he lost possession of the one thing that allowed him to keep his edge.

Bringing the laptop hadn't brought Larry the high praise he'd originally thought. Clive knew now he owed the big lug an even bigger apology, his rare moment of fast-thinking in grab-bing the computer had provided Clive the one missing link in this whole process. He needed to reconsider his impression of Larry. Here was someone with raw potential, he just needed some direction, some shaping. Unlike Bobo, who needed . . .

what? A hole in the head. He'd get what was coming to him, maybe worse, all that stood in the way of that was time. And only a successful operation might spare him his fate. Bobo, who had seen fit to keep certain vital information from him. So until he could deal effectively with the once-trusted boob, Clive waited for this mystery woman, she who seemed to like to meet in London's parks. He'd seen her previous message to Todd about meeting in St. James's Park, near the palace. Maybe it was just her way of playing tourist; killing two birds with one stone, so to speak.

The rain wasn't letting up.

The time was passing by.

Clive's impatience was increasing. Where the hell was this woman? He prided himself on his punctuality, on his professionalism, but also on his privacy. Standing under the Marble Arch as a way of escaping the rain, that made sense, except if someone was watching and saw that Clive hadn't moved in nearly a half hour. Shelter was one thing, but loitering constituted a challenge to suspicious eyes. He'd waited this long because it was possible she was lost beneath the streets in that concrete maze. Still, too much time had passed and it was clear something had happened and she couldn't make it. Clive left, finally, out of fear of bringing attention to his behavior, and he left not at all happy. Rather the opposite, his hand twitching, frustration escalating over the lack of victim in which to lash out at. That itch, knowing he was so close. What saved his temper from rising any further was the ringing of his mobile phone.

"Yeah."

"It's Larry."

"This had better be important."

"I found Bobo."

Perfect, just what he needed—good news. And a victim for

his raging temper. "Where is he?"

"You won't believe it, he's been clever that one . . ."

"Larry. Where."

Not a question, a command.

"He took her to the girl's own flat."

Clive asked for the address and placed it into his short-term memory bank. Then he waited for a cab, couldn't find one in the rain and decided where he was going wasn't terribly far from the Marble Arch. Down Oxford Street he went, walking north up Gloucester Place and into the residential neighborhood of Marylebone. He was drenched by the time he arrived in front of the building, looking up at the windows for any sign of life. Nothing, no lights appeared to be on, not in any of the flats, including the top floor. To be sure his memory—or Larry—hadn't failed him, Clive checked the call box near the front door, Flat 4, Simon.

He stole a quick glance around, but no one was about, not close to ten o'clock on a rainy Wednesday night. There were drunken sounds coming from the Hobgoblin pub down the street, but the blokes inside were probably starting to worry about last orders and not paying attention to strangers on the street. So Clive picked the lock easily enough, and then made his way up the stairs in the darkness of the hallway. He approached the top floor, pressed his ear to the door and listened . . . and heard nothing. Could they be out, maybe part of the party at the pub? Or asleep? Clive fiddled with the simple lock, heard the click and allowed himself into Beth Simon's flat. He waited a moment for his eyes to adjust to the darkness, then slowly removed his revolver from the small of his back, screwing on the silencer next. He felt his way to the bedroom, peered in. A small glow from the mews behind the building cast enough light to see two forms beneath the covers. He could hear Bobo's intrusive snores, muffled from the covers.

"Well, Bobo's been getting himself some," he murmured to himself. "Good, nothing like one last time. Hope it was good . . . considering."

And then he aimed the gun and pulled the trigger once, then a second time. Two quick spits, the sound seemingly harmless in the quiet night. And then he got the hell out of there, a clean kill. The twitch in his hand was suddenly, efficiently gone.

The night had started with such promise, appeared to be going bust when a phone call went and salvaged both the night and his mood. Oh, there was nothing like a job well done to get his own juices flowing, and so he returned to his flat, hoping Fiona was waiting for him. She was, and she proved enough of a distraction for him until the next morning, when he knew he had to get his ass over to the Savoy and figure out why the hell his client hadn't showed herself.

"You won't be long, will you, dear?"

"Not terribly, no."

Henri gazed back lovingly at his wife, who was still spread beneath the blankets of their king-sized bed, a place from which she hadn't moved all night. Well, she'd moved; Henri thought the earth moved with her. It had been a spectacular night, probably one of the best they'd ever shared and now as Henri prepared to leave for his appointment, he felt renewed, determined that this weekend would quell any remaining doubts about their marriage.

"There are several details to take care of—and Althea being in New York, she can't see to them all. Besides, this isn't business, this is pleasure. It's love and our anniversary and who better to plan the most spectacular celebration for a deserving wife—his secretary? Well, yes, but with a little help from her adoring husband."

Henri bent over, kissed her, and then straightened his tie in anticipation of leaving.

"What will you do while I'm gone?" he asked her.

"Oh, I was thinking of spoiling myself, getting a facial."

"Like they could improve upon perfection," he said, one last overdone compliment after a night of them.

A cab took him a short distance through the heart of Piccadilly Circus and on to Mayfair, one of London's swankiest neighborhoods, to a side street off the famous Berkeley Square. Henri paid the fare, tipped generously in this golden sunlight of a new day, still deliriously satisfied as he gazed about for that infamously chirping nightingale. Instead, he was faced down by a pear-shaped woman who waited for him at the entrance of a beautiful set of homes, dubbed the Mayfair Mansions. She waved as he approached.

"Mr. Procopio?"

"Yes, Mrs. Timberlake, good morning."

"Call me Clara, please," she said, extending her hand so as to connect hers with his. They shook. "Thank you for taking the time to meet with me, though I must say your secretary has been like a general in securing these plans. Like she's preparing for battle. Anyway, I'm sorry for the delay in meeting with you this week, and that the showing of the property has to be so close to when you wanted to book the place for. But I had a bit of a . . . setback. A funeral."

"Oh, I'm sorry," Henri said, "I hope it wasn't someone close."

Clara hung her head, as though remembering the good times. "My husband, Vance, shot last Friday while showing one of his properties. Well, shall we go look at this one?"

"Oh, that's . . . terrible, Mrs. Timberlake, just awful." He stole a look at the red-brick and bay window façade of the Mayfair Mansions. Did that kind of thing happen often? Murder while showing a property? "Really, I suppose we could forego the tour, I'll write you a check now and be done with it. From the outside, it looks just perfect."

"Nonsense, Mr. Procopio, we're here, we might as well take a look-see. Besides, there's nothing I can do now for Vance, I need to look after myself and I find that business keeps my mind occupied. So cliché I realize, but what are clichés but overused truths?"

"Very well," Henri said.

Digging for a set of keys in her purse, Clara Timberlake opened the door and guided Henri inside, all the while explaining that this particular address contained four duplexes, the one she had to offer right here on the first floor. "It has a back entrance through the kitchen, so any help you require—caterers and such—can go through there. That's what makes this particular property so ideal for your purposes. You can sneak in any surprise you may want." Bypassing the communal hallway, she approached the front door to the apartment and unlocked the door, guiding her client inside. They were met first by a hollowed out hallway with high ceilings, a crystal chandelier hanging down that, once lit, illuminated shadows upon walls that spoke stories of luxury. Straight ahead was a grand, sweeping staircase made of marble, and Henri smiled, imagining Elise in a slinky gown making her way down it, like a princess looking for that other glass slipper. To their left was a graciously decorated sunken living room, its expansive windows adorned with thick burgundy drapes and lace curtains, the furniture and paintings all speaking Elise's language: money, money, money. Again, Henri flashed pictures in his mind of his lovely wife, lounging on the sofa while flipping through a magazine, a servant handing her her treasured martini.

"I'll take it," he said.

"Oh, but you haven't seen the best part, yet," Clara said. "The boudoir." This with a French accent, for effect.

"The what?"

"The bedroom, Mr. Procopio, come, let me show you."

And so they wound their way up that gleaming marble staircase, entered a bedroom that looked out over the quiet square. It was massive, the room, the bed, even in the bathroom a sunken porcelain tub that could easily be the scene of some wonderful things between a man and his wife. Yes, Henri was nodding enthusiastically, knowing he had found the perfect setting for his special night, he'd have to give Althea a bonus for searching out such a fine address.

When finally they'd returned to the hallway, Henri was taking out his checkbook and signing over a huge sum of money for what was just a two-day rental, Saturday and Sunday. Clara tucked the check into her purse and thanked Henri for his business.

"I hope everything works out for you, sir," she said.

"Yes, thank you. And to you, nothing but a bright future."

"The brightest," she said.

They parted on the front steps, strangers an hour ago, now conspirators in the grandest celebration of love ever expressed. Oh, Elise was going to die when she saw this place. Henri was in such a good mood, he walked in the glorious sunshine back to the Savoy; it wasn't every day you were blessed with such nice weather during a London winter.

To his disappointment, Elise had gone out. Why had she asked if his appointment would take long if she was planning on being out, too? How long did facials take, he wondered? He hoped she would return soon. What pleasures he had to share with her.

So he settled back, ordered a sandwich from room service, hungry now after that bit of exercise—he'd gotten a lot the last twenty-four hours or so. He contemplated how quickly life can change, on a dime he thought the poor people claimed, how well everything was suddenly going. Elise and he were back on

227

track, and that stupid con artist and his admittedly beautiful con-ette, they were history, hopefully long gone from their undeserving room at the Savoy.

Well, nope, they hadn't left yet. And the situation hadn't improved much.

"You have one last chance, Todd—get me my money or we take a visit to the police."

"Calm down, Birdie."

Donald Birdie seemed to have aged another ten years overnight, that's what Todd guessed, contemplating the idea that if maybe they waited a couple more days he might just wither away a few more decades and die. Not that he wished the man ill health—or ill death—he just wanted the jittery jinx out of their juxtaposed lives. He'd been nothing but a thorn in Todd's side from the moment he'd arrived, showing up at Todd's flat before he'd even had the chance, stumbling upon a dying Timberlake and running after calling the cops. How'd he managed all that anyway, and how'd he know where Todd was going in the first place? These were still unanswered questions, and from the fact that Birdie was tired and angry and holding a gun on him at this precise moment, perhaps there was another time to inquire.

"I promise, Birdie, this plan can't miss."

"That's what you said about the last one."

"Well, things go awry sometimes—unexpectedly. I would think you'd understand that, and if you don't, maybe we could ask Vance Timberlake. Oops, sorry, can't."

With a burst of nervous energy, Birdie thrust the gun out. "Don't mention that man to me, his death is still a horrible image, one I'll take to my own dying day."

Todd nodded. "Sure, sure, but it just helps prove a point."

"Yeah, well, I'm tired of your points. I'm tired of this city and their awful food and I'm tired of you. I want to go home and get a real bacon cheeseburger. Get me my money so I can get out of here. Marta's getting suspicious that I'm not living up to my end of our agreement. Last night she was fishing for details, it sounded as though she was losing faith in my ability to get the job done. She even said maybe she should come to New York and goose me—but I convinced her I'd be home in two days, don't go to such expense. Do you realize the disaster it would mean for all of us if Marta came to New York and no one was around to meet her at the bus station?"

"Is that like the tree falling in the woods riddle?" Todd asked, trying to imagine Marta Birdie and her swaddling furs stepping off Greyhound at Port Authority.

The gun in Birdie's hand wavered.

"Whoa, whoa, Birdie, I can understand your anxiousness, this trip hasn't exactly gone as planned for me, either. We were thisclose to getting Beth back, thisclose to getting the cash out of Procopio, and now I'm thisclose to getting the cash out of the aforementioned Procopio's Mrs." That was the latest plan, complete with a scheduled meeting where he would pick up the desired deposit. "So if you'd stop waving that gun at me and let me get to my appointment, the sooner I'm back—and this time with actual cash."

"How much?"

"That I don't know."

"If you made the deal, Todd, how come you don't know how much the deal is worth?" Birdie asked, standing firm.

Oh, it's complicated, Todd said, saying that this particular detail had not been arranged between Todd and Elise, nope, but between Elise and Timberlake, or maybe with Clive himself. But now Clive was out of the picture, he had no idea where or when they were meeting, where or when the hit was supposed to go down. Thank goodness he'd run into Elise at the bar downstairs; like she'd have been anywhere else.

"This is some bloody mess, huh?" Birdie said. "Oh, if Marta ever finds out, I think she'll divorce me anyway."

"Trust me, she won't find out. Lighten up, Birdie, you'd think worry was your middle name . . ."

"It's Umberto."

"What?"

"My middle name. My mother was Italian, so I took her father's name. And my confirmation name is Michael. Donald Umberto Michael Birdie."

Todd thought about that. Laughed inwardly. "Great, Birdie, just great. Now, if you'll excuse me . . ."

"Not until Brandy returns, Todd," Birdie said.

"What?"

"I need some kind of leverage. You could just disappear on me, and so could Brandy and then where would I be, without my money and still having to deal with my meddlesome Marta. The money, Todd, that's the only reason I haven't already turned you into the police yet, because I need to have that money."

"Birdie, you have my computer, and here—you can have my passport, how about that? Just don't make me late for my appointment or else we'll never get our money. Brandy's down having a facial, her skin was a bit raw from all those cosmetics, there's no telling when she'll be back. And, look, it's already one-thirty and depending on traffic it could take me more than a half hour to get where I'm going, assuming the cabbie knows where it is. Because I sure as hell don't."

Birdie gave in, though he took the passport anyway. "You should have been a lawyer."

Todd would normally consider that an insult, but today the comment meant he'd won this particular battle with Birdie. "D-day," he said, tapping his watch.

"I'll be happier when it's M-day. As in money."

"Yeah, Birdie, I got that," Todd said, and then patted Birdie on the cheek with a promise to return. Then he was off, silently praying that today would bring about an end to this muddled mess. Or at least have one thing go his way. Please. Todd didn't know if he could stand another thing going wrong at this point. It would be a simple exchange: Elise gives him the cash deposit for doing away with her husband, he walks away with the money, and everyone but Elise is happy. Birdie gets his money, hopefully Todd gets whatever is leftover, and most importantly, no one will be shooting at Henri Procopio. Henri may not have fallen for Todd's scheme, but he didn't wish the man dead. He was a nice man, garrulous and slightly goofy, Todd thought to himself, wondering where that untapped emotion had come from.

The meeting place was the same as last night's, or so had said Elise's morning e-mail. He'd logged on at ten in the morning, not expecting to see the message but there it was. *Meet me at two o'clock underneath the Marble Arch, same as we'd intended for last night. Better weather anyway. Oh, and don't be late. That bastard's going to get exactly what's coming to him and I for one cannot wait.*

As the cab snaked its way through mid-day traffic, Todd wondered what had set Elise Procopio off? Last he'd seen, a horny Elise had been headed back to her hotel suite, and now less than twenty-four hours later she was newly resolved to go through with her assassination plot. What had transpired during those lapsed hours? Todd was about to find out, that and a few other things. Getting to the Marble Arch was complicated, as Todd found out from the get go when the cabbie asked him which corner. Todd didn't understand the question then, but he did once they arrived at the busiest intersection he'd even encountered—Oxford Street and Edgeware Road and Park Lane all converged with Bayswater Road and it was amazing that the cars knew which way to go, wrong side of the road and all. The Arch was distinctive in the center of all the action, Todd just wasn't certain how to get there.

"Use the pedestrian subway," the cabbie said, pointing it out.

Which meant an underground passageway. Todd did, checking the posted map at the start of his descent. My God, he thought, there are fourteen exits to this subway, each of them going a different way and who knew which way was the right one? He found directions to Marble Arch Island, exit 10. Fine, he headed down the concrete steps and through the underground maze, past a skinny homeless man with two well-fed dogs and emerging into a sunken courtyard. There were toilets on his right, just in case you got so lost you could drop in for a handy pee. He turned left, went up the stairs and through a park (to Grandmother's house we'll go, he whistled) and down another subway until at last—geez, should he have left bread crumbs?—he emerged into the square where stood the Arch. Elise was already waiting, sitting on a park bench near the arch with a big olive-green canvas bag from Harrods at her feet. Todd smiled, imagining the bag weighed down with cash. His for the taking. Greenbacks, even if the money did have the Queen's face rather than Washington or Lincoln or whichever president had landed himself on one of the big bills. He was forced to remind himself that a large portion of the money was going to Birdie.

When Elise saw Todd approaching, she waved, as though this were just another innocent rendezvous, like the time a few days ago when they'd met at Buckingham Palace. Only this time the kiss she gave him was more passionate, conjured from some inner place of hers that needed the release. Pretense for anyone who might be watching, but honest emotion summoned from her needy core. Todd tried to pull away, but Elise was holding on tight, tongue slipping in and her hands caressing, uh, all of him.

"Whoa, whoa," he said, at last breaking free.

"Oh, I could take you right here and now, sink into those cute dimples. Maybe when all this is done, we can have our own little celebration, I give you the balance of the money and you give me . . . a bonus. A big one."

What the hell was going on? She wanted to bed the man who she thought was going to kill her husband? Talk about kinky. He guessed she was preparing herself for the life of a rich and widowed woman, trying out any boy toy who happened to be around. The pool boy, the garden boy, the killer boy? Pick your poison. And all of this happening while around them traffic swirled and pedestrians walked and double-decker buses cruised by and cabs honked, life moving in its circular fashion.

"Before we attract any attention, I think we should conclude our transaction." Todd paused for effect. "The money."

"Oh, you're all business today, aren't you? Can't you see that I'm upset and that I need comforting?"

"I don't think I'm the right person for it. And I suppose under the circumstances, neither is your husband."

"My husband—do you know what that bastard has done to me? He puts on this great pretense that he wants to renew our love, to the point last night where I imagined maybe it was possible that he truly meant it. He makes love to me, over and over again, like he's never done before and then this morning . . . this morning, I find this, under the bed."

Todd looked at what Elise had in her hand and had to stifle a laugh. Because it was a photograph of Brandy—the "before" picture of course—and she's there in her bikini, spread out over a bedspread that could easily have been from any hotel room. Elise naturally had assumed the bedspread was the one from her room. Todd nodded sympathetically, though inwardly he was pleased as punch, yup, he'd slid that photograph under the bed deliberately. Procopio didn't ante up the cash yesterday, well, why not a little marital strife. He never imagined it would be used as fuel for Elise's desires to see her husband offed.

"The bastard's cheating on me. So . . . so he . . . he has to die. Here," Elise said, thrusting the bag at Todd.

He looked inside it and grinned wildly, there could easily be half a million pounds in this bag, and, jokingly, he imagined it weighed that much. But then, the joke was on him, really, as a man stepped out from the behind the arch, and in a very distinctive, polite, upper crust sort of British voice, said, "I'll take that."

That rare London sunshine, it happened to catch the gleam of a rather large revolver.

CHAPTER SIXTEEN

Events were reaching a dangerous crescendo and by Thursday's end one unlucky person wrapped up with this concentric conspiracy would end up doing a fine imitation of a corpse. It began, though, with one lucky person in the grips of one of the most pleasurable experiences imaginable. No, haven't we had enough of that already? We're talking facial massage, deep and penetrating and cleansing, the kind of spoiled treatment that would peel years off anyone, not that our luscious Brandy had any such problems. But, as she'd explained to Todd early in the morning, she could still picture the horrible make-up and scars plastered on her face, and even though she'd done her best at removing them, there was nothing like a professional cleansing.

So that's where Brandy was, cucumber slices on her eyes instead of dressed up for some little tea sandwich, and slathered all over her skin was a moisturizing cream that she swore was going to make her skin feel sixteen again. Maybe eighteen, she thought, just to keep things legal. On the CD system Enya was playing, those melodious chants of hers, they were as soothing as the facial, returning Brandy to a time and place well before any of this had started, before her grandfather's death, before Daddy's shipping her off to Cambridge, before the wonderful Todd had entered her, uh, life. No, this deep moisturizing returned her to the time when she was studying for cosmetology school and she and her classmate had given each other facials and toe massages. In other words, returned her to when she'd truly been happy, perhaps for the only time in her life. How easily she had given it up for Cambridge, for the promise of Daddy's riches, how the second she was airborne regret had flooded her system as quickly as the wine had. She realized now she'd have done anything to escape her humdrum life, and in fact, she had. She'd run away from school to pursue . . . what? A con man, albeit a charming one, and in a week when she should have been analyzing Lady Macbeth's motives, she'd been finding excitement by, among other things, staring down the barrel of a gun. Someone should be analyzing her, she thought, and then laughed aloud.

"Ah, Miss Alexander, I see my powers are working, worry lines around the eyes replaced by laugh lines around the lips," spoke Natasha, a dark-haired beauty with a short-cropped haircut who had to have the most magical fingers in London, heck, maybe the world. That's how relaxed Brandy felt, so much so that when finally she did leave the spa, she imagined herself without a care in the world.

Funny how these feelings don't last.

The facial over, it was just after one-thirty when she saw Todd crossing through the lobby, his stride determined and purposeful. She tossed him an imaginary kiss, wished him luck. Let this plan work, let us get rid of Birdie first, then we can concentrate on the problem of one Clive Remington. And as though the mere thought of him conjured him into existence, there was Clive, right on Todd's tail. Brandy would recognize that bastard anywhere. Her face drained of all blood, the fresh coating of nourishing creams powerless against such a drop in circulation.

Shit. Shit. And shit.

What to do, what to do? Oh, and what to do? She heard the ping of the elevator and rushed onto it, pressing for the second floor. An elderly couple joined her, pressing one. The older man said no, it's two and his wife replied, are you sure? Brandy was tapping her feet in frustration, especially after neither of them got out at one. Damn this ground floor invention of the Europeans.

"Oh, it's two," the man said, finally finding his key.

Brandy pushed past them, running down the hall and throwing open the door to her room. She banged on Birdie's door; she banged again and had to wait a second for him to appear.

"Bird . . ."

"Sshh, I'm on the phone with Marta. Come on," he said, returning to the receiver. "No, housekeeping. Yes, they are persistent . . . what? No, I haven't met a woman here. Marta, that's crazy, that's . . . well, yes, I did cheat on you with my secretary but I've learned my lesson and . . . oh, no, please don't . . . you mustn't . . ."

He put the phone down without saying goodbye.

"What happened?" Brandy asked.

"She hung up on me—oh, and she's coming to New York."

"Birdie, you're not *in* New York."

He tossed her a look that said he'd been hanging around Todd too long.

"Well, we can't worry about Marta now. Come on, put your shoes on, we've got to go. Todd's in trouble, I just saw that jerk Clive and he's following Todd to his meeting with Elise. Hurry— and bring that gun. Maybe for once it'll be useful. And leave your shakiness behind this time."

Next on the day's agenda was Larry, and he had to admit his latest assignment gave him the willies.

"Go back to that Beth woman's flat and clean up the mess I left behind."

That's what Clive had requested this morning, just before leaving for his stakeout at the Savoy. Don't disappoint me either, he'd added, the threat more than implied, it was implicit. Also, one he'd have no trouble keeping either. Larry wanted to wait until the cover of darkness but Clive said they couldn't wait that long, who knew how fast the smell would permeate down the stairs and start knocking on the doors of the other flats. Just go, mate, be a good chap. And don't leave Bobo's cab in front of the building, either, there should be no evidence left behind.

Larry approached the building, walked up the steps and picked the lock exactly like Clive had shown him. It took a few turns and clicks, and he hoped no one from the local pub down the corner was watching. He just wasn't as skilled as . . .

"Ooh, it worked," Larry said.

The man had untapped talents.

As though following in Clive's footsteps from the night before, he wound his way up the stairs, until he was standing before the door to the top-floor flat. Gulping deeply, his heart heavy with sorrow over Bobo's demise but knowing he had to continue or meet a similar fate, he turned the knob on that door; Clive had been right, it was open.

The first thing he did was sniff the air; nothing, not flowers or an air freshener or food that had been left out on the counter, and certainly not the odor of decaying flesh. It had only been sixteen hours or so since the shooting, maybe that kind of smell took longer to form. What did he know? Larry made his way to the bedroom, where daylight was filtering in through the window. Turning his eyes to the bed, he saw the two bullet holes that went right through the thin pink comforter. Had it always been pink, or was that blood-stained? He approached the bed with trepidation, wondering if he was supposed to fit both bodies into the cab that was parked out front, and how he might manage that feat. He pulled back the cover with a quick flourish, though kept his eyes closed as he did so. Finally, he opened them.

"Oh geez, oh God . . ."

Larry's legs gave out and he crashed to the floor, his big lumbering body making a helluva racket throughout the building.

Finally, back to the Marble Arch, where a twosome had become a threesome.

"Who the hell are you?"

The new arrival laughed. "You Americans, not very polite, are you? Really, Todd, the kind of people you associate with, I'd have thought I'd taught you better these past few days. Ah well, sometimes the student never rises above his station in life."

"Fuck off, Clive," Todd said.

"My point exactly," he said, with a wave of his revolver. "Now, I believe I requested that you hand over that awfully weighty bag to me. Yes, that's it, little lady, you can do it."

"You haven't answered my question," Elise Procopio said, her eyes darting from Todd to Clive, Clive to Todd, and occasionally down at the tempting contents within the bag. And a few times at the gun, which though surreptitiously hidden within the man's sleeve, was somehow more of a presence than any of them. It had power over people, that gleaming gun did.

"Fine, the lady wants to know who I am. Todd—do you want to do the honors or shall I?"

"Elise, don't listen to a word he has to say," Todd said.

Her eyes dug into Todd's. "You've never used my name before. *Todd.*"

Todd wondered if this is what was called a misstep.

"I guess since names are being exchanged, allow me. My name is Clive Remington, and I believe it's my services you wished to engage. Todd here, for some reason I've yet to uncover, has been trying to muscle his way into my bad graces, and steal from me my livelihood."

"I don't get it," Elise said. "What's going on?"

"Todd's been pulling a scam on you—no doubt trying to get his hands on that bag of cold cash. What's the matter, Todd, didn't get enough from the hubby with your ridiculous blackmail plan?"

"Wait, you know my husband?" she asked Todd.

Todd was saying nothing, he was too busy furiously thinking of something to say, something that would, what? Make all of this plausible? Make Elise hand over the money to him? Make Clive disappear? At the moment, none of that seemed possible.

"That's what he's doing in London, attempting to con your husband out of a cool half million—of course, he owes it to me for a little outstanding bit of business of our own. Though I will admit his failure has forced me to increase the amount. You remember, I'm sure, don't you, Todd? The price of doing business with me?"

Todd nodded. Beth, poor Beth, who'd been missing for days now. The lone innocent caught up in a game with lots of guilty people, three of them gathered here near the edge of Hyde Park under a splendiferous blue sky, while birds flew overhead and tourists flocked to the green lawns and drying footpaths. Idyllic if you looked at the picture correctly.

"So if you say he's only in this for money and was never intending to . . . oh my God, you . . . you . . . weasel," she said to Todd. Anger flared from her nostrils, an angered bull getting ready to attack. Anyone wearing red?

"A weasel?" Todd said, not able to hold his laugh. "We've got a woman here who wants to hire someone to kill her husband and we've got the killer here, too, trying to collect his deposit, and the best you can come up with is to call me a weasel? That's rich, Mrs. P, but of course, you know all about rich, don't you? Got all the money in the world, and still you play the lottery, even win, for God's sake—a fortune. Some folks have all the luck."

"Yes, Todd, some people do," Clive said, the barrel of the gun sneaking further from his sleeve. "And someone's luck has just run out. Mrs. P, as you so elegantly referred to her, she only called you a weasel. I've got one far worse—dead."

Todd felt sweat on his brow and on his upper lip, the latter which was also trembling a tad. Can't blame him, what with the size of that gun and the closeness of it to his heart. His mind was reeling with the possibility that every misguided move in his misguided life had boiled down to this one, definitive and final breath-ending moment, the odd jobs and the distant family, the quest for approval from any father figure he might find, the cons and the desire to retire early. Oh, he was going to retire early, all right, right to an early grave.

"Yeah, shoot the bastard," Elise said.

"A lovely sentiment," Clive said. "Trouble is, though, shooting him here might attract too much of the wrong type of attention. So I suggest we all go for a walk, find someplace private. And then Mrs. P, you and I can at last discuss the business that has eluded us this entire week, ever since Timberlake's unfortunate and inopportune death. And without Todd's interfering ways."

"Sounds like a plan," Elise said.

Prodded by the gun, Todd stepped forward, entering the pedestrian subway once again, still clueless about how he was going to get out of this one. It did occur to him to cast some suspicion on Clive's motives here, that maybe he wasn't who he said he was and then realized he'd already spilled the beans about that. Nope, all week long he'd been trying to keep these two apart and from sealing their hellish plot, and in the end what happened? He brought them together himself, like a deadly dating service. Great, just fucking great. This was his worst week ever, maybe even his last week ever.

They were coming back into the light of day, one possible exit reading "Hyde Park," the other "Bayswater Road," Todd imagining the old days when King Henry VIII would use these grounds for hunting foxes. No doubt a fox or two had escaped somehow, perhaps even survived to tell the tale? Todd knew this was his only chance, and so with the element of surprise—and guts—on his side, he quickly turned around and with a fast kick knocked the gun out of Clive's hand. He yelled out in surprise and Elise screamed, just as Todd, in a fit of desperation, reached for the bag of money. Elise tugged back and then the bag turned over and bundles of quid tumbled to the dirty underground walkway with a thud. Damn, Todd thought, they were all wrapped in rubber bands, when in his mind he saw thousands of pounds creating a blurry whirlwind in the air. So much for that distraction.

He needed to escape, forget the money, damn it, and as he tried to run off, he felt a hand grab at him. Clive's. Todd kicked back but missed and this time Clive didn't, his fist connecting with Todd's jaw, hurtling him onto the hard, dirty ground. At least Clive hadn't recovered the gun . . . yet. Todd, trying to scamper away, saw a blur of a person out of the corner of his eye, saw that same shape tackle Clive to the ground, pounding his head on the concrete floor of the subway. Ouch, Todd thought. Yeah, Todd thought.

"Run, Todd, run," he heard, the unmistakable voice of Brandy.

Where had she come from? No doubt from one of these fourteen different entrances to this impossible maze of a subway. No, there was no way he was leaving her.

"Dammit, run, you saved me the first time, I'm saving you this time."

Todd felt a hand clasp his, swung around, saw Birdie. Saw

Birdie's gun, too. "Let's go, Todd, you blew it. No more chances."

"No, no . . ."

But Birdie had command and Todd, in his weakened, exhausted, sore-jaw state, was helpless. Especially with the second gun in as many minutes being waved right in his face. He hated guns, he never used them, and here he was caught between the barrels of two of them. As Birdie quickly led him away from the scene of the crime, he saw Elise Procopio furiously trying to gather up her cash, sticking bundles back into the bag, into her purse, and the pockets of her jacket, anyplace her desperate self could find. He also saw Brandy land a hard kick, then a second, to Clive's crotch, heard him howl in absolute pain. More a kick for womankind than an effort at saving Todd's ass. As Todd and Birdie turned a corner and headed for one of the exits, Todd screamed out, "Brandy, we'll meet back up later . . ." Where, where could they meet that Clive wouldn't be able to find them? The Savoy was out, so was Beth's place. ". . . the shower, Brandy, meet me in the shower."

That comment, echoing through the underground chamber, got more than a few looks from passersby who were intensely interested in the scuffle taking place in the subway's corridors. Police sirens were ringing in the distance, and Todd, running with Birdie in an attempt to find any exit, didn't matter which one, was reminded of his first day in London, running then and running now from the approaching sirens of the Metropolitan Police. Thanks again to the intrusive presence of Birdie.

"Geez, where are we, Birdie?"

They were standing at a crossroads underground, a number of exits to choose from.

"Even the Scarecrow only had two choices," Birdie said.

"Come on," Todd said, running like the Wizard was the only one who could help them. At last they emerged onto the far edge of the arch and quickly infiltrated the ranks of the bustling number of pedestrians along Oxford Street. Birdie hailed a cab, and the two of them piled in, both trying to catch their breath.

"Where to, mates?" the cabbie asked.

"The Savoy," Todd said.

"Sorry, change of plans," Birdie said. "Heathrow, and make it fast."

"Heathrow? Are you out of your mind, Birdie, I can't leave now."

"Too bad."

"I . . . I don't have my passport . . . shit, I gave it to you. Brandy, what about her?"

"Brandy can take care of herself, as she so ably proved just now. As for you and her, let's be honest, Todd, a woman like that is not going to hang onto you for long, she's had to have been in this for the money too. She wants her cut, why else play along with that lame scheme of yours? Forget Brandy, she's probably already forgotten you. Oh, and yes, I do have the passports, yours and mine," he said, and as to prove his point, he waved the two blue passports in the air, tucking them back into his coat pocket for safekeeping. "A precautionary measure. In case you screwed things up and we needed a fast escape I brought them with me."

"But we're not done, I haven't . . ."

"What? Finished your job? Yes you have, Todd, but you failed at it." Birdie jabbed the gun into Todd's side. "You've had three chances and you've blown them all. It's my turn now. We return to New York where you can raid some secret account which I'm convinced you have. Hell, you can roll pennies until your fingers bleed, but either I get my money or you and I go visit the police, what's it going to be?"

Todd considered his options, realized he had none. Unless . . .

"Birdie, do you know what I've inadvertently set off just

now—back at the Marble Arch, do you have any idea what was transpiring?"

"No, and I don't care."

"Henri Procopio is going to be killed," Todd said, his voice a whisper now so the cabbie didn't hear him. "His wife's been plotting to kill him, that's the reason for their trip, and Timberlake was the go-between—he hired the killer for her before someone killed him. Clive is that killer. The hit is going to go down sometime this weekend." He paused. "I need to stop it."

"Todd, you can't even pull off a simple scam, how do you expect to stop a professional killer? Besides, that's Procopio's marital problems, I've got my own."

"What are you talking about?"

"When we return to New York, Marta will be waiting for us."

Todd shivered, not sure which he was more afraid of, the police, Clive, or Marta.

Two hours later, Clive Remington was sitting in his flat with a pint in his hand and an ice-pack on his balls, which were swollen from the swift kicks that Brandy chick had given him. So it was good that Fiona was previously engaged tonight; he wasn't up for, well, being up. In review, the day had been a mixed bag. On the one hand, Todd Gleason had slipped through his fingers again, Todd whom he wanted nothing more than to put out of his—and Clive's—misery. But that would have to wait, because Clive was at least—and at last—gainfully employed. He and Elise Procopio had exchanged e-mail addresses before they had separated, before the police had arrived and found nothing but a few loose pound notes scattered among the trash. Watching the BBC news later, Clive was pleased to see the incident in the subway got about five seconds; a lover's disagreement was how witnesses described it. Clive was thankful no guns had gone off, that would have been harder to explain, would have garnered at least another five seconds on the broadcast.

He was contemplating a second pint when the phone rang. He grabbed it, barked out an unusually impolite, "What?"

"Mr. Remington, good evening. I believe you and I need to have a little talk."

He tried to pin a face to the voice, came up empty. "Who is this?"

"I know who you are, and what you are."

"Hey babe, I think you've got the wrong number."

"Oh no, I've got the right number. And I've got yours. Think hard, you'll guess who I am and what I want. No games and everyone goes home happy."

Ice filled his veins. He knew who this was, and also knew this was a complication he did not need right now. This day, if another had existed with such flips and flops, he hadn't lived it. "Very well. We can meet. Near the Vauxhall Bridge, you know the Riverside Walk? Right, just off Nine Elms. One hour?"

"Don't be late, that's not the kind of place a lady should be hanging out alone."

"Some lady."

Clive rang off and got dressed again, this time wearing loose fitting pants that allowed him plenty of room for his swollen parts, and for the gun which was itching to be used. He had reached the end of the road, the gravy train had stopped.

Detective Inspector Albert Brury of the Metropolitan Police had already retired for the night, he'd dressed in his sleep clothes and brushed his teeth, even felt for his prostate because having turned fifty he was all worried about cancer and other things which might end a man's life prematurely. As he settled beneath the covers, he was thankful for this thing called sleep, giving the body and mind a rest, particularly when it was frustrated by inactivity during the day. He had no further leads on Vance Timberlake's murder, nearly a week old now. Sometimes he hated his job, when it proved too difficult, and that's what he was thinking about when his eyes closed, when . . .

"Jesus, who's calling at this hour?"

. . . the phone rang. Once, twice.

This couldn't be good. The kind of late night calls that instilled fear in a father's heart. He wished Fiona were home, to make him a cup of coffee and to ease his mind. Late night calls were always bad and not having his daughter home, well, that just added to his concerns. As a cop, too, he knew this was bad news. Albert Brury threw back the covers, not even having had the chance to warm him up in the coolness of his room. He went to the kitchen and picked up the receiver on the fourth ring.

"Brury, what have we got?"

"A floater, sir."

He stared up at the clock, it was only after eleven. Usually the bodies didn't turn up until morning, those nice criminals waiting until the late hours to off their victims, allowing the cops the chance to sleep peacefully through the night. Not so the case tonight, and Brury found himself getting dressed and then hailing a cab.

The Thames, a body of water that had for centuries kept London afloat as a major port city, today used for shipping and for boat cruises for tourists, and of course as the dumping ground for victims of foul play. A floater, that could mean an accident or a suicide, sure, but Brury was a cop with too many years of experience to believe such was the case tonight. Nope, this was murder.

The cab he'd grabbed crossed the Vauxhall Bridge, wound its way around the Albert Embankment as Brury searched for signs of police activity. He found them waiting by the historic Riverside Walk, just a hundred yards or so from the recently constructed St. George's Wharf apartments. That's where Brury got out, a Metropolitan Police car flashing its lights like a beacon in the murky night. After such a pleasant day, this return to bad weather wasn't what Brury wanted, nor was this gloomy visit expected at the close of such a day.

"What have we got, and why have I been called?"

"Woman, gunshot to the head, execution-style. Lying amidst the rocks down there, found a half-hour ago, only slightly wet. Might have been drying in the sun all day, eh? Some blokes from a nearby pub came to the edge of the walk for a pissing contest, see if any of them could hit the river from here. Not bloody likely, especially since after what they saw in the moonlight found their little peckers doing a pretty good turtle imitation. Thought it might be a log. Weren't no log, sir."

"Indeed not," Brury said. He needed to find his way down to the rocky shoreline, found a slipway that provided access, and with a flashlight guiding his way, walked underneath the Vauxhall Bridge and at last came upon the body that had been recently covered by a blanket. He removed the cover and shined the beam on the face, recoiling in sudden, unexpected horror.

"Oh, oh . . . oh my God."

"What's that, Brury? You know the woman?"

Albert Brury hung his head and sighed, fighting back rare tears as he stared down at the latest victim of what the press had dubbed the "daddysgirl" murder. Make that plural now. And then Brury popped a Tums and wondered just what the hell was going on.

★ ★ ★ ★ ★

PART THREE
A NEW YORK MINUTE

★ ★ ★ ★ ★

CHAPTER SEVENTEEN

Ah, New York. Land of opportunity, land of chances and choices, where anything was possible at any hour, this the city rumored never to sleep. Boy, did Todd Gleason need his beloved city to live up to that reputation now. The Virgin Atlantic flight touched down at JFK at eleven o'clock Thursday evening, four o'clock in the morning London time, Todd's body timetable in a state of flux, he didn't know if he was coming or going or flying in place. Birdie, at his side the entire flight, couldn't have cared less about the time; he had more important details to consider, namely, getting back to his dump of a hotel before mad Marta arrived.

"If I didn't know better, Birdie, I'd say you're petrified of your wife," Todd had said during the meal portion of the flight, when they had had a couple drinks and were beyond caring about the events they'd left behind in London.

"You've seen her, sure, back during your scam in my little town of Tuckerville, but you've never incurred her wrath. Makes that Clive guy seem like an altar boy. She doesn't carry a gun the size of Big Ben, okay, but that voice of hers could stop a baby in his tracks. I don't envy any man who crosses her, I should know. I'm one of them, desperately trying to win her back." He sighed. "My God, what an odyssey this has been. Maybe I've had Marta's specter hanging over me this entire trip—but at least, for a while, I've been free of her actual presence. That's something, huh?"

"Birdie, I'm proud of you. If this trip has taught you nothing else, it's at least given you an appreciation of the world beyond Tuckerville, which is what that damned lottery win was supposed to enable you to do in the first place. Why you remained in Dullsville USA, I'll never understand. And your devotion to Marta, if only she knew what lengths you've gone to in an effort to keep her as your wife."

"And taking me to the cleaners if I couldn't hold onto her."

"Everyone needs a bit of motivation."

Now, the plane had landed and everyone was deplaning—a terrible word coined by the airlines to indicate the aircraft hadn't plunged into the ocean between destinations. Todd and Birdie were able to skip baggage claim since neither of them had their bags with them. Customs was a breeze, too, both of them with nothing to declare except a bottle of champagne that Birdie had bought on the plane. He thought it might be good to have one thing, otherwise customs might raise an eyebrow at their sudden reentry to their country. And that was that, the formalities of the flight over, Birdie forced Todd into a cab and they breezed along the Van Wyck and the Grand Central, traffic at a minimum at this hour. At last they crossed over the Triborough and slid onto the FDR. Todd couldn't help but smile, feeling normal again, driving on the proper side of the road and seeing those familiar sights, the Empire State Building and the Chrysler Building, the bums who littered the streets. Dorothy was right, there's no place like home.

They were nearing the 96th Street exit. Blocks from home, he thought. "Where are we going, anyway, my apartment?" Todd asked.

"Back to the hotel I was staying at when you decided to run off to London."

"No one forced you to follow me."

Birdie laughed. "Yeah, right."

"Oh, right, Marta again."

Marta. We've been hearing a lot about her, which means the buildup to such a woman could only lead to great disappointment, uh, right? Todd was convinced he'd be meeting a pussycat, the sweetest little old lady who had years ago charmed Birdie into a marriage designed to last forever, a communion of souls who would never know riches beyond the love that they shared. And then they'd hit the lottery and life had gone to hell in a handbasket; shame what money did for some folks.

"So, Birdie, this entire time we've been in London, paying for last-minute flights and staying in luxurious hotels and splurging on facials . . ."

"Facials?"

"Uh, never mind. Anyway, you've also kept your room at your New York hotel? Man, you've been bitching about nothing but money spent since you first pointed that gun at me in Cambridge, and here you are, splurging on hotel rooms we don't need. Marta's going to have a lot to complain about. Sure, London's expensive, but New York is no slouch when it comes to gouging the wallet."

"Don't I know it—but Todd, I need your assurance, Marta can never know we were out of the country. She . . . she just wouldn't understand."

"Birdie, may I remind you—you are no longer in any position to tell me what to do. It's not like you could have brought Timberlake's gun with you. In this day and age, the authorities tend to frown upon firearms on airplanes. Good that you tossed it before we reached Heathrow, might have caused us innumerable amounts of trouble. And so, without that weapon making a dent in my side, really, you're powerless."

"So why are you still cooperating with me, Todd?"

Good question, he thought.

"Good question," he said.

"I'll leave your conscience to answer it sometime."

"Ouch," Todd said.

They arrived at their destination, a seedy-looking hotel located on West Forty-Seventh Street and Eighth Avenue, not exactly the Savoy.

"Not exactly the Savoy," Todd said, mirroring his thoughts.

"Marta is the great doubter in life, doesn't believe the lottery association is going to live up to their promise of yearly payments, so she placed me on the strictest budget. That's why . . . well, you know, the Savoy was out of my price range. That's why, in addition to paying me back what you stole from me, you'll be paying all the expenses from this past week, Brandy's facial and all."

"I'm sure we can work out some equitable solution," Todd said, who allowed Birdie to pay for the forty-five dollar (plus tolls and tip) trip from JFK to mid-Manhattan. He hadn't exactly been given proper notice about changing his pounds back into dollars.

"I'm adding up those receipts, Todd. Don't think I won't."

"What's mine is yours, Birdie."

Birdie had no response to that one, since at the moment that meant a whole lot of nothing. He just wanted to climb his way to that third floor room and grab some sleep, probably his last bit of peace before the arrival of Hurricane Marta. He and Todd both clomped against the bare stairs, bypassing the clerk who was busy with a pint of what looked like the cheapest whiskey around, and arrived at last at their latest destination. The door was made of cheap wood and was chipped in each corner, the knob dangling. A bare light fixture flickered dangerously.

"Nice digs," Todd remarked.

"Shut up, Todd," Birdie said, opening the door and attempting to turn on the overhead light. The light was already on, and somebody was home.

"No, you shut up, Donald, unless of course you care to offer an excuse as to where you've been all night."

Looks like Marta had beat them to New York.

Marta Alverton Birdie, she had changed a lot since Todd had last seen her back in tiny little Tuckerville, when he'd pounced all over her insecurities about having won all that cash. She'd been wearing a drab dress and her hair had been in curlers and no make-up had made her a sight for even sore eyes. Now, though, sitting in this den of iniquity the management dared to call a hotel—really, the room was a shoebox with a bed—she was dressed as she envisioned society dames to look like. First of all, lots of rouge on her cheeks and stiletto heels on her thick feet, and in between, a garish red dress and big hoop earrings and covering it all, a fur coat. Didn't she know New York had cleaned up its act, the hookers were no longer walking Disney Square . . . uh, Times Square?

Birdie tried to embrace his long-suffering wife, but she was having none of it. She waved him off like a bad odor and focused her doubting eyes on Todd.

"Yeah, I remember you," she said, he feeling like a piece of meat the way she examined him. Beef or chicken, he wasn't sure which. "You were so charming and so full of bravado, look at you now—actually, you still look kind of yummy. But that's where my sympathy ends. Where's the cash, kid?"

Todd looked at Birdie, who stepped forward (as much as he could in these tight quarters). "I don't have the money—yet, dear."

"You told me a week ago you'd found him, surely he's been able to scrape a few dollars together to get himself out of a jail sentence. What's taking so long?"

If she only knew.

"Well, Mrs. Birdie—may I call you Marta?"

"No."

Okay. "Mrs. Birdie, your husband did track me down, noble soldier that he is, but I managed to give him the slip. He's been chasing me all over this city ever since, and tonight, well, I thought I had finally rid myself of him," Todd said, his mouth running like Beth Simon on a good day. "He's persistent, Birdie is, I'll give him that, and just as I was hailing a cab to get me—and my money—out of the country, he jumped me, right there on the sidewalk. By now I expected to be in London—have you been there? Lovely time of year to go, not that I'll ever get to experience it, the glitter and the lights, the pageantry and the royalty . . ."

"Can it, kid. You can't snow me—again."

Marta Birdie rose from the bed, her knees cracking—arthritis, she said—went over to the far wall, where Todd was surprised to see a phone. No need to use the pay phone in the lobby; it probably didn't work anyway. Why didn't these rich folks have cell phones? I mean, really, *everyone* had one these days, the homeless probably. This room came with all the modern conveniences, no wonder the roaches loved it. She picked up the receiver. "Nine-one-one, right? That'll have the cops here in no time, right?"

Todd wanted to tell her if she screamed out the window of this joint they'd probably be here even sooner. But the last sight he wanted to see was the blaring lights of New York's Finest coming by for a friendly visit. He exchanged a worried look with Birdie, who shrugged.

"Out of my hands, Todd."

"Todd? I thought his name was Richard Booker—oh, silly me, you used an alias. So, Todd, you got a last name? Sure you do, you can't have a first name and not have a last name, unless you're Cher or Madonna, though I seem to recall hearing hers once, you know, before she married that British guy. What's his name?"

"Gleason."

"No, I don't think so."

"No, no, Marta, Gleason is Todd's last name."

"Oh." She seemed momentarily thrown by the fast curves of the conversation. "So, what's it going to be Mr. Todd Gleason, the money or the monkeys?"

The monkeys? He loved the way she talked, so colorful. "Uh, the money, of course."

"Where is it?"

"Where do you think? Under my mattress at home? Your husband would have found it, now, wouldn't he?" Todd shot Birdie a look; he'd trashed Todd's apartment.

Flanked by the lady in the mink and her sniveling husband, trapped in this dreary hotel room, his body floating somewhere in between time zones, he felt bone tired and when that happened he couldn't help it, he became even more of a smart mouth. Silence would have been the better part of valor in this case.

"Don't get snippy with me, kid, I still remember the cops' phone number."

So Todd, mostly in an effort to buy time, promised that they could have their money but not until the morning, they needed to wait until then for the banks to open, so why doesn't everyone get some shut-eye? Marta, who'd been waiting all day for her husband, seemed to think that was a good enough solution, she could use some sleep.

"Birdie, stay awake and keep an eye on him."

"Are we all going to stay here—in this tiny room?" Todd asked.

"You got a better idea?" Marta asked. "I'm not spending my money on some fancy hotel room, that's just a big waste. You're sleeping, what the heck does it matter what the room looks like?"

Todd had once felt that Birdie's concerns about staying at the Savoy were unwarranted. Marta's statement took the "un" out of the word.

Todd though was still thinking quick enough to come up with a better place than the West Side Dump Hotel. "My apartment, we'll need to stop there anyway tomorrow morning, so I can get the appropriate information. Taking out such a large sum of money, the bank's going to want some verification. And besides, my place is large enough to sleep several, there's the bed and a pull-out sofa, really, we'll all be much more comfortable. Birdie, you've given the place the once-over, don't you agree?"

"Shut up, Todd," Birdie said.

And so it went that Marta, Birdie, and Todd traveled in a cab that Thursday late night, all the way to the Upper East Side, Todd's neighborhood hangout that, after the week he'd spent in London, looked comforting and foreign at the same time. The same restaurants and bars, the same dry cleaners and shops, all of which he now felt he'd outgrown. Traffic had been spare and the lights on Madison Avenue were perfectly synchronized and they made it up to East Eighty-Eighth Street within fifteen minutes.

Todd popped open the door with his keys, expecting a mess to greet him, since its last visitor had been an angry Birdie, who, according to Andy, had tossed the place something good. When he flicked the light on in the living room, what he saw made his jaw drop. First of all, the place looked immaculate. Second of all, a person stirred from the sofa, looked up when she saw the three of them standing in surprise at her presence.

"Let me guess, that woman with you two is Marta. Hi, Marta,

I've heard a lot about you, I'm Brandy."

From the East Side of Manhattan to the East End of London, the story continues. The black cab pulled into a parking spot right in front of the pleasant-looking house. They had arrived at the Isle of Dogs, a place she had only seen on that television show *EastEnders* with the catchy theme song. She used to watch it on PBS before moving to London and being able to watch it on the BBC. They knocked once on the door, waited patiently by sneaking in a kiss. Then the door opened and a couple lost in the outskirts of their sixties stared at them.

"Uncle Clyde, Aunt Bonnie, this is Beth Simon, and she's the woman I love."

Both Bonnie and Clyde had seen better days, their clothes not exactly the latest trends and Clyde wore a leg brace and a pair of crutches kept him from falling. When they attempted to smile, it was clear their teeth hadn't seen a dentist in a good long while. But Beth wasn't much to smile about anyway, not that Bobo noticed, he was too busy displaying the woman who had changed his life to the people who had done their best to raise him.

"It's nice to meet you—love your names," said Beth.

"Ooh, ain't you sweet to say such, dear, come in and have a cuppa," Aunt Bonnie said, escorting Beth from the front doorstep and into a small kitchen that was overly decorated with knick-knacks, mugs and salt and pepper shakers and trinkets from trips they had taken, brown weathered postcards pinned to an old corkboard.

Clyde and Bobo stayed behind a bit, because Clyde had something he wanted to say to his impressionable nephew.

"You get her pregnant?"

"No, no, it's nothing like that. She's saving herself—well, for me."

"Suppose when you don't have the looks, virtue's not a bad thing to cling to," Uncle Clyde said. "Nice of you to bring the cab back, though. Might be getting my brace off next week, can't wait to get back on the road, your Aunt Bonnie's driving me to drink. Not that I need an excuse, ha."

Bobo thought there was an insult to Beth lost in all those words, but he was only catching about every fifth word now anyway. He dropped his search for the insult as they entered the kitchen and were handed steaming mugs of tea.

"Blimey, that," Uncle Clyde said. "Fancy a bitter?"

"I could be convinced."

Bobo and Clyde grabbed tall cans of Boddington's from the fridge, Bonnie and Beth had tea, Bonnie wanting to know all about this grand romance of theirs, where did they meet, how long ago, all the intimate details. Both Beth and Bobo exchanged looks that said neither one of them had bothered to come up with a good cover story. Couldn't exactly cop to the truth, met her when I kidnapped her, fell in love with her when she rescued me from being killed by my boss. When the silence threatened to expose whatever lie they came up with, Beth quickly said, "Oh, we met in a bookstore, right along the Charing Cross Road. Our hands touched when we both reached for the same book."

That was it, the extent of her wordage. She smiled briefly at Bobo, who returned it. "Oh, how romantic, what book?" Aunt Bonnie said.

"*Huck Finn,*" Bobo said, stars in his eyes as he said those wonderful words.

"Fuck Huck, what's going on here?"

Oops, the impromptu party was suddenly interrupted, as the four of them turned around and saw the doorway to the kitchen filled up with the huge presence of our friend Larry. Bobo lunged at his recent partner, but it was like hitting a brick wall.

Bobo fell to the floor in a dizzying daze. Clyde stood to help his nephew, demanding an explanation. These two were the best of friends, what had happened to cause such a rift? His eyes fell on Beth. Her, she had to have something to do with all this. Virtuous my ass.

"Bo, what'd you go and attack me for?"

"Because, I know why you're here."

"No, no you don't. I'm here to say I'm sorry."

Bobo excused himself and dragged Larry back outside to the creaky porch.

"How'd you know to find me here?" Bobo asked.

"Clive sent me to Beth's flat, you know—to dispose of the bodies. He thought a watery grave was the best idea, you believe that, dropping you into the Thames in broad daylight. So I go there, and when I find he'd only managed to kill the pillows, I headed back out and, well, the cab was gone."

"Oh, right, we took that, didn't we? Well, it's not Clive's livery service now, is it? It's my uncle's and he's been wondering about those fares I was supposed to pick up. Clive never even handed us money for petrol. But good for you, Larry, picking up on a clue like that, piecing it together and it bringing you here. But now I wanna know why it is you've come here?" Bobo asked. "You still on the job for Clive?"

Larry shook his head. "He's obsessed, he is. Can't focus on what he's supposed to be doing because that Todd guy keeps mucking it up. No, I'm done cleaning up his messes for him, not worth the price. Your life. My life. Anyway, that's why I'm here, I've come to warn you."

"Like you did that first time, telling me Clive wanted to talk to me. Nice bit of warning you did then. He tried to kill me, kill Beth, too, and it's only because she's a lot smarter than all of us put together that we managed to escape his bullets. No one heard a thing, we barely heard the spit of bullets from the silencer."

"So how did you keep from being shot?"

"Simple, we were hiding in the closet. Beth was worried after your visit. Said she didn't trust Clive, and why should she, he was holding her captive, after all. Er, rather, making me hold her hostage but it's the same thing, Clive was pulling the strings as always. Time for me to take control. So Beth, she comes up with this idea to record some snoring noises and we put the tape player under the bed, stuffed the covers to make it look like two bodies were there. She read about that technique in a book; see, Larry, she loves books and she loves me, why I don't know, we just clicked and that's good enough for me. And Clive, that bastard, he clicked away, too, his gun pulling off two quick shots, not even hesitated did he. Afterwards we sat there, trying to figure out our next move. I brought her here, she's going to stay while I . . ." He let his voice trail off.

"What, Bo? What are you going to do?"

"I'm going to do to Clive what Clive tried to do to me," he said, and then with a wicked grin said, "Wanna help?"

CHAPTER EIGHTEEN

Mornings, the promise of a new day and the chance at a new life, all boiled down to the time when the sun rose and the world awakened. For Todd Gleason, he knew this one morning was tantamount to as fresh a start as possible, considering if he didn't come up with either cash or a clever plan, he might be looking at an inconvenient prison sentence. The only sign of hope he had was this vision of loveliness that lay beside him, Brandy Alexander, that miraculous woman of women, the last person he'd expected to find sitting inside his New York apartment. On the long plane ride back to New York he had imagined her back in Cambridge, she waiting in the shower for her knight out of shining armor.

Wondering how Brandy got back to New York so quickly? So was Todd. It happened like this: While Todd and Birdie waited for the next Virgin flight, Brandy just took the next possible flight, which happened to be on Kuwaiti Airlines. But how did she know that's where they were going? Because Brandy was there when Birdie learned Marta was coming to New York, so she pieced two and two together and came up with four, as in Birdie and Marta, Todd and herself. To Marta they had explained Brandy as Todd's current girlfriend, who sometimes shared his apartment, a logical and legitimate cover story. Truth was, she'd followed one of Todd's neighbors into the building, then found her way to the fire escape and pried apart the cardboard which Andy had arranged to cover the broken window. It was just a simple case of resourcefulness.

So with all those questions answered, the foursome had retired to sleep, Marta summing up the whole thing by generously saying, "We've waited this long to get our money back, what's another few hours?" True, it had been nearly two in the morning when the lights were turned out, another hour before Todd and Brandy managed to fall to their pillows with the expectation of sleep. Really, if this was imprisonment, Todd was loving the conjugal visits privilege.

The arrival of sunshine seemingly moments after his eyes had closed reminded Todd, though, that not everywhere were there sunny skies ahead. In London, clouds were brewing and murder hovered beneath them, and if he didn't figure out a way to rid himself of the married Birdies, Henri Procopio would die. And over there Clive and Elise had a five-hour head start.

"I've got no choice," Todd confessed to Brandy, as he removed himself from the tangle of covers. "I've got to arrange some money somehow; problem is, all that I have is currently tied up in investments, there's no way I can produce one hundred thousand dollars by day's end."

Just then that proverbial light bulb went on over Brandy's head. "Investments, you say? Oh, Todd, you've just given me the most spectacular idea. And it's right up your alley."

Taking her into his arms, he asked, "Who will we be conning this time?"

"Why, none other than Daddy Tight-ass himself," she said. "Mr. Thomas Marquand Alexander the second."

"What happened to the third?"

"He named her Brandy—won't he be sorry now."

Todd wasn't finished making fun of the guy's name. "Marquand?"

"As a woman, I was deemed ineligible for the family name. Can you imagine, only the men in the family can have the name, some sort of chauvinistic thing my grandfather's grandfather insisted upon. Stupid thing is, it was the maiden name of one of my relatives—a woman. Men are idiots."

"Well, at least you're not bitter," Todd stated. "So, what's your plan?"

Brandy was about to explain when the bedroom door burst open and in walked Birdie, no longer intimidating without his gun, just a middle-aged guy with bad morning hair.

"Don't you knock?" Brandy said, gathering bundles of sheets to cover herself.

He ignored her. "Rise and shine, my favorite conniving couple, it's payback time. The banks open in an hour." His eyes zeroed in on the two of them, saw the spark of a con in their eyes. He frowned. "Oh no. What are you two plotting now?"

"Brandy here's got a way for us to get our hands on some money."

"Big money," Brandy said. "By day's end, Birdie, you and the Mrs. will be headed back to Podunk USA to live out your dreams in perpetual boring togetherness."

"Oh, great," Birdie replied, his voice flatter than a pancake.

Sometimes getting what you wanted had its drawbacks.

Then, not one to be left out, Marta entered the bedroom and her mouthed dropped at the scene before her, Brandy in bed, Todd covered but naked at her side, Birdie standing so close he could conduct them.

"What the heck's going on in here?"

"The three of us are hatching a plan, Marta," her husband said.

"Donald!"

"Not that . . ."

Brandy shut him up, and for the third time in as many minutes, began to explain how she aimed to get the money back. Marta threw up her hands in protest, saying she wasn't going to be privy to any sort of criminal conspiracy, "and Donald, neither are you."

Todd interrupted. "Mrs. Birdie, it's that or you go home empty-handed because I haven't got the money. See, nothing on me," Todd said, standing as though to empty his pockets, forgetting momentarily he didn't have any pockets, or pants for that matter. Marta immediately looked away; well, not immediately.

"Goodness, the things a person is exposed to in the big city," she said, regaining her usual and less-than-sunny demeanor. "I don't want to know details, I just expect my money—today."

"Deal," Brandy said.

"Deal," Birdie said.

Todd, tossing Brandy a look that said, "Are you sure this will work?", finally agreed and said, "Deal."

"Daddy, Daddy, is that you?"

"Princess? Of course it's me, who else would be answering my cell phone. Honey, I'm in the car, one of millions stuck at the entrance of the Holland Tunnel, frustrated as hell and trying to get to work. Not that this is any different, but Fridays seem to produce so much more traffic." He paused to catch his breath, this spurt of words seemingly without punctuation. "You had better have a very good reason for calling me now, I'm just not in the mood for any games."

Brandy stifled a laugh and then like an actress preparing herself for her role, she focused on her opening line and said, "Daddy, I've been kidnapped."

"WHAT?"

"You heard me, Daddy."

"Is this some kind of joke? They have kidnappers in Cambridge, England? Not likely. Come on, Brandy, what's this all about? Is it because I'm late with your allowance? Are you mad about that e-mail I sent you? But don't worry, two more weeks and I'll have my resources freed up again, believe me, it will all be worth it. Now go back to class and study hard. Make the Marquand Alexander family proud, okay? That's it, be a good daddy's girl."

Brandy stuck her finger down her throat. Marquand indeed.

Ooh, that grated at her worse than a dentist's drill to her teeth, especially considering Todd and Birdie were listening in on the extension in the next room. (Marta had volunteered to search out breakfast while they pulled the first phase of their scam.) Brandy could see them though the doorway, both with faces of disgust. She could translate: How could you put up with that kind of baby talk? Brandy might be a babe, but no baby.

"Daddy, I . . . ow, stop that, I . . . don't touch me . . ."

"Brandy?" Doubt creeping into her father's voice.

"Sorry, Pops, sweet Brandy's indisposed at the moment. My partner has a low boiling point and the fact that you don't believe your own daughter makes me wonder what kind of lame-ass father you are, taking a chance that my partner might, well, do terrible things to her if we don't get our way—our money." This was Todd, taking up the performance that had been quickly rehearsed. Birdie didn't have the guts to fake being the kidnapper. He was playing the silent role of the silent partner with the low boiling point.

"Who the hell is this, I demand to know," insisted Thomas Marquand Alexander II. "Oh, oh shit, I'm about to enter the tunnel and we're going to get . . ."

"Cut off," Todd said to a dial tone. "Shit."

"Now what?" Birdie said.

"We call him back. I imagine Daddy Alexander is sweating bullets while creeping his way through the tunnel. A Friday morning at this hour, it could take him a good twenty minutes to reach Manhattan. What do you think, Brandy, he buying it?"

"Daddy's a great doubter—like Marta Birdie—but even more he hates to part with his money. Truthfully, I don't know what he's going to do, this is a good test. Whom does he love more, his bank account or his only daughter? To date it's been a toss up."

Birdie was shaking his head. "What do you want to be rich for, Todd, look at where it leads? Even my Marta has changed since we won the lottery; she used to protest against people who wear fur coats, now she owns three of them and defends her decision by saying the animals were already dead and the coats were already on the racks. Really, it's no way to go through life, and I for one wish we'd never won the damn money."

"Then why are you making us go through with this?" Todd asked.

"Because, whatever defective gene of yours made you steal from me, Todd, I'm hoping this will teach you a valuable lesson in life."

"Okay, okay," Brandy said. "Hate to interrupt this character-defining moment, but, well, it's making me sick. Like the end of a *Brady Bunch* episode. Birdie, when Marta gets back from the store with breakfast, I want you to distract her. Todd, you have your cell phone, right? Okay, Birdie, you've got the number and we'll keep in touch that way. It's better if Daddy needs to call us, he do it on a less traceable line."

Wow, Todd was impressed, she was good at this.

Brandy checked her watch, said, "We'll give him five more minutes and then we'll try him again from this phone. Then Todd and I will be off."

"Wait, how do I know I can trust you to return with the money?"

Todd patted Birdie on the cheek. "Maybe your little speech about life lessons has taught me a thing or two. Or not. You'll have to have faith, Birdie. Okay, Brandy, dial Pops back up."

She pressed redial and in seconds the phone on the other end was ringing, ringing again, Todd hoping it didn't go into voice-mail, when, "Yes, Brandy, Brandy, please let that be you."

"Bad news, Pops, Brandy's a bit tied up at the moment, she can't come to the phone."

"Oh my God, what have you done with my baby? She's my only child, I'd give the world for her, anything, just don't harm her."

"The world isn't necessary, just . . . half a million dollars."

"Half . . . how much?"

Todd could see the man's face tuning red, spittle splattering against the cell phone.

"Are you going to quibble over a few measly bucks in exchange for your daughter's life? Nice father, good thing you didn't have more kids whose lives you could ruin. Be glad she's not listening to this, never know what kind of permanent emotional damage you could do, Pops."

Brandy was on the other extension.

"But . . . how? Why? Why are you doing this? What has Brandy done to deserve this?"

Whoops, they hadn't anticipated such a spate of questions, hoped he'd just become putty in their hands. Todd, his mind racing, was trying to figure out exactly the right thing to say, the most plausible explanation and . . . oh, oh yes. Todd stole a look at his daddy's girl and knew just what to say.

How perfect was that?

"Listen, Pops, Brandy's gotten herself into a bit of trouble."

"Trouble?"

"You know, mixed up with the wrong crowd."

"Wrong crowd? In Cambridge?"

"We're not in fucking Cambridge, Pops."

"Don't call me that . . . Where are you?"

"At the moment, New York."

"New York? How is that possible? I spoke with Brandy just a couple days ago, she was back in Cambridge just as we'd arranged. She'd come home for her grandfather's funeral and . . . and well, while I never actually saw her get on the plane, the car service we arranged said they got her to the airport with no delay. Wait, I spoke with her, told her I had to delay her allowance . . . still . . . how could she be back in New York? I don't believe you."

Man, this guy had some nerve. "Listen, you ever hear of airplanes? They fly all over the world now, going from London to New York ain't such a big thing." That was true, it seemed, since Todd's body remained uncertain of the time zone it was in. "Look, you want proof, check the London newspapers, look for a story about the murder of a local landlord, think you'll be familiar with the catch phrase they're using for the case."

"Murder? Oh my God, what are you talking about? This is crazy. Brandy can't be involved in something like that, it's just not possible . . ."

"I told you, check out the papers. I'll give you a hint—the press is calling it the daddysgirl murder. That name sound familiar? I'll call you back in one hour's time and we can discuss the next step, sir. You know, getting us the cash." And then before Pops could sputter a response, Todd disconnected the call.

"That was brilliant, Todd, brilliant, really, stroke of genius," Birdie said. "I couldn't have come up with that, not so quickly."

"That's the thing about cons, Birdie, you've gotta be fast on your feet for them to work."

"Well, then, after the disastrous week you've had, it's nice to see you finally being up to speed."

"That hurts, Birdie, that really hurts."

"Okay, you two, what's next?" Brandy asked.

Just then the door to the apartment opened and in walked Marta with a bag full of groceries and complaining about the prices of New York grocery stores.

"Breakfast," Todd responded. "It's the most important meal of the day, they say. Give you energy for whatever the day holds. And I think we'll need all our energy and wits about us."

After Vance Timberlake's murder, Detective Inspector Albert Brury was thankful for one thing: easy identification of the body. There was the fact of his blood-splattered wallet, the fact his widow quickly connected said wallet with said body. Poor Clara Timberlake, suddenly reduced from a duo to a solo act, no kids to watch over her while she grew old. Of course, she wouldn't be growing old anymore, nope. Because the body by the river was the one and only widow herself, Clara Timberlake. Brury's first thought was, who would officially identify her? His second thought was, who would mourn for her? Turned out, Brury himself would fulfill those two roles.

"Poor woman," he'd repeatedly said.

Again, he had no real suspects, but at least this time he had a more promising lead. Just as Mr. Timberlake died while meeting with the mysterious Richard Booker, Mrs. Timberlake herself had recently shown a property, too, and not only had a search of her office provided him with the address of the house in Mayfair, it also gave him the present location of the man she had rented the place to. A Mr. Henri Procopio, currently staying at the Savoy.

Which is why, having just left the late Timberlake home in South Kensington, Brury found himself in the heart of theatre-land, traveling along the Strand to the ritzy hotel that catered to those visitors seeking discretion and luxury and privacy. Brury couldn't make any promises on that last one. The cab dropped him off in the hotel's circular drive, the doorman nodding to him as he went through the revolving door. He approached the reception desk without hesitation.

"May I help you, sir?" a clerk asked.

"Yes, I'd like to inquire if a Mr. Henri Procopio is registered here."

"I'm sorry, sir, we don't give out information on our guests."

Brury nodded. "Of course. I suppose, though, you can make an exception for the police." He discreetly showed his badge before replacing it in his pocket. Hotels hated any kind of police activity, it was bad for their bookings. "Detective Inspector Albert Brury, and it's important."

"You may use the house phone, sir, if you like. Only the manager can give out the gentleman's room number."

"That won't be necessary, thank you for the confirmation."

Brury wandered over to the house phone, where an operator connected him with Procopio's room. The call was a quick one, Brury introduced himself and asked that the two of them have a quiet talk somewhere. The man was blustery and confused, what would he know about any police matter in London, but then Brury had insisted and before long Procopio was agreeing to meet with him. He gave Brury the room number, and Brury made haste to the lift, which quickly escorted him to the sixth floor.

A man of medium height with black bristles for hair (and not much of it) was waiting with the door open.

"Inspector Brury? May I see some identification?"

"Of course," Brury stated.

He'd expected as much, and wasn't insulted. This wasn't a very trusting world they lived in. Where landlords could be killed in their own properties, no telling what could happen in a hotel. He produced his badge, which Procopio stared at for longer than the desk clerk downstairs had. Finally, Henri nodded, stepped aside to admit Brury, pointing to a chair in his suite.

"We can talk here, my wife is out shopping. It's our anniversary tomorrow and we've got a big night planned tomorrow, she needed to find the perfect outfit. I'm sure you understand, a decent family man like yourself."

"My wife died several years ago, but yes, I have a daughter and can appreciate the finer things in life to celebrate," he said, digging into his pocket for his trusty roll of Tums. He popped one of the tablets, offered one to Procopio. He declined. "Mr. Procopio, I'll get right to the point of my visit. It's tragic, honestly. You see, a woman was murdered last night, her body found along the banks of the Thames down in Vauxhall and I have reason to believe that in the days before her death she met with you."

Henri's mouth dropped open, and his body followed suit, falling to the edge of the sofa. "I have to admit, Inspector Brury, I don't even know what you just said, not being familiar enough with the city. But I suppose that's irrelevant, considering that wherever you mentioned, it's where you found a body. Excuse my ignorance, but how is it I can help you?"

"The woman's name was Clara Timberlake, does that name ring a bell with you?"

"Certainly, yes, but . . . we only met yesterday morning, she showed me a property that I'm renting this weekend. I've already paid my deposit, she's given me the key and . . . goodness, what does this do now to my plans? Oh my, that's so insensitive of me, thinking of myself at such a time, she seemed like such a nice woman. But other than speaking with her once on the phone and meeting her that one time in person, I never knew the woman. And I had absolutely nothing to do with her . . . murder . . . did you say?"

Brury nodded. "Yes, murder, and I suppose as a visitor to

our city, there's no way you could have any involvement. Still, I wonder if you'd indulge me a few more questions. You see, her death has complicated an already puzzling case. Just last week—a week ago today, in fact—Mrs. Timberlake's husband died . . ."

"Oh, of course, she mentioned that to me when she was showing me the property, apologizing for the delay in her being available, can you imagine? Apologizing for having had to attend your better half's funeral? Oh my, first the husband dies and now the wife is . . . killed, when your number is up, there's nothing you can do, I suppose."

"They were both murdered, sir. Mr. Timberlake was shot as well."

"Oh my."

"It appears they both angered some nefarious person, the same some nefarious person I have reason to believe. Tell me, Mr. Procopio, and I realize what a long shot this is, but do you know a man by the name of Richard Booker?"

Procopio's face seemed to noticeably pale. "Booker, you say?"

"Yes, it's another name I found in the log book back at Mr. Timberlake's office. This Booker was supposed to rent a flat from Mr. Timberlake last week and never showed, never even called Mrs. Timberlake to cancel the booking. The very flat where Timberlake was found dead. An odd coincidence, and coincidence is not something I believe in."

"No, coincidence usually means a hidden connection, doesn't it?" Henri said.

"So, do you know this Mr. Booker? Richard Booker, sorry, I do not have a description available. Just his name, and an ordinary and unmemorable one it is. Still, I was hopeful the name might strike a chord with you."

Henri quickly said, "No, I'm sorry, I thought there was . . . no, Inspector, the name means nothing to me. Would you care for a drink?"

"No thank you, but don't let me stop you."

"Certainly not, I think I need one," Henri said.

Henri made his way to the bar, poured himself two fingers of whiskey, Brury noticing he downed nearly half the contents in one gulp. Then he turned back to Brury and said, "I'm sorry, all this talk of murder, I suppose it's made my legs a bit rubbery. I can't even watch television what with the kind of gratuitous violence they show nowadays. Tell me, Inspector, however did my name pop up in association with this Booker fellow?"

Brury hesitated, making a mental note, and then said, "I'm following up all possible leads, and quite simply stumbled across your name in Mrs. Timberlake's date book. The property listed in Mayfair, am I to assume that's where I can reach you this weekend if I need anything further?"

"Well, if the property is still available, considering . . ."

"Mr. Procopio, at the moment I have no reason to suspect the property in Mayfair has anything to do with Mrs. Timberlake's murder, it's just one of many she and her husband used to book on behalf of clients—renting to both tourists and businesspeople alike. So, no, I'm not going to impound the property, or stop you and your wife from celebrating your anniversary in grand style. A husband and wife of nearly thirty years died within a week of each other, no, I'd like to know I was helpful toward another husband-and-wife team. Happy Anniversary, Mr. Procopio."

"That's it?"

"Yes, Mr. Procopio, unless you can think of another matter between us?"

He shook his head, "No, sorry I couldn't be more helpful."

Brury handed over his card, said, "Yes, well, if anything further comes to mind, something she might have said or done, perhaps a phone call she received or made? A clue toward identifying our mysterious Mr. Booker? I'd be grateful if you'd ring me. The Timberlakes, they were fine, upstanding citizens and I don't like it when the criminal element decides the world can do without their type. It's one thing when the crooks kill the crooks, weeding out the weaker ones in some kind of Darwinian efficiency, shall we say. Of course, that leaves me searching for what is no doubt a diabolical, dangerous criminal, and who knows what he's capable of."

As Brury left the Savoy, he forewent a cab and headed down to the Victoria Embankment, where he walked along the Thames, thinking about that nasty thing called coincidence. If thirty years of police work had taught Brury anything, it was that there's no such thing as coincidence, and that every man has something to hide from the police, no matter how small. It was human nature, it was instinct. And instinct was telling Brury that Procopio had been lying about not knowing Richard Booker. Was Procopio himself Booker, renting a different property from the wife after killing the husband? But why? What hidden motive could Henri Procopio possibly possess?

Chapter Nineteen

While they waited for Brandy's father to come up with the ransom money, they needed to decide two things: where the drop-off would take place, and who exactly was going to pick it up. Couldn't exactly be Brandy herself; he'd never hand over the cash to his supposedly kidnapped daughter. And it couldn't be Todd either; Alexander would later be able to identify him to the authorities. Yes, officers, that's him, with the flush bank account and dimples. The Birdies were out of the equation as well; the two of them were firm about staying out of this portion of what was transpiring. They just wanted their money and would then be out of Todd's life for good.

"And you out of ours," Birdie said.

"Hey, I was already gone from it," Todd reminded him.

Well, breakfast was cleared up and that's when Todd made the follow-up call to Brandy's father, who was now out of the Tunnel and finally entrenched behind his desk at Bernstein, Gilbert & Young, no doubt waiting for the call. Todd had said he'd call back in an hour, but he let an additional fifteen minutes pass just because he thought Brandy's Pops was a total jerk and the added stress aided their scheme. When he did call, Alexander answered on the first ring and before a hello or before he gave Todd a chance to talk—really, not very polite of him—he just said, "Fine, I'll do whatever you want. Just don't hurt my Brandy, she's all I've got. Look, I managed to find everything about that murder from a Google search. The story is all over the papers there, the *Daily Mail,* the *Standard.* You've already killed two people, you don't need to add a third to your growing list, do you?"

Todd looked at Brandy and mouthed, "Two?" Then, into the phone he said, "Uh, Pops, we'll be in touch about the where and when of the drop-off point. But be assured if we don't have the money today, your daughter becomes that third victim you fear so much. Later, man." He hung up.

"Third victim?" Todd asked aloud.

Brandy had a second question. "Who was the second?"

Birdie was curious too; Marta was busying herself by drying the dishes and humming loudly so as not to listen to any part of this.

"Excellent questions." Todd looked at Birdie and said, "If Henri Procopio is dead, it's on your conscience, Birdie. If I hadn't been dragged out of the country, I could have saved him. But that's all going to have to wait, isn't it? Come on, Brandy, we've got some details to take care of. Birdie, I assume you'll be remaining back here with your wife?"

"Yes, he will be," Marta said, walking in, wringing a dishtowel around her fingers. "And don't pull any funny stuff, we know enough about you, Todd Gleason, to put you away for life, maybe longer."

That Marta, she sure was a charmer.

Thrilled to be away from that malcontent Marta Birdie and her simpering spouse, Todd and Brandy made their way out into the Friday sunshine of the Big Apple. Really, New York was looking positively tropical compared to the damp and dreary London weather they'd witnessed.

"So, now what, Todd? What's the plan?"

"Well, first I want to find out what your father was talking about, because obviously there was a new twist in the case while we were flying back over the Atlantic. Like a lawyer in court, you should never ask a question you don't already know the answer to. We need to be as informed as possible. And then we need to figure out who's going to pick up the money, because it sure can't be either of us, right? Well, wait a minute . . . of course."

"Of course what?"

Todd leaned over and kissed her. "You've done it before, why not again? Do you wish to play master cosmetician again, my beautiful con-ette?"

A smile brightened her already flushed face. She was thrilled at the opportunity to practice her art and innate passion once again, glad too she didn't have to defile her own beautiful face to do it. Because following his request, Todd had volunteered himself.

"Tell me what you're thinking?" she asked, and Todd, as he always did when it came to Brandy, slipped her the info. Her smile never wavered, nor her confidence at pulling it off.

So with a solid plan in motion, Todd and Brandy got busy. Onto the 6 train at 86th and Lex, they took it to 59th and Lex, transferred to an approaching N train and got off at 49th Street, where they headed into the heart of the Theatre District. There they found a store along Eighth Avenue that sold all sorts of disguises, make-up supplies, and costumes. They also found a newsstand that carried international papers; Todd picked up the *Evening Standard* and didn't need to look beyond the front page for the story that had freaked Mr. Thomas Marquand Alexander. That's how Todd and Brandy learned about the murder of Clara Timberlake.

"Well, whoever killed the Mrs. most probably killed the Mr.," Brandy said.

"Which eliminates our Birdie, and also knocks out any leverage we might have had over him."

"Beneath it all, Birdie's sweet. I never believed he was capable of pulling the trigger, Todd."

"So then who did?"

"Probably someone who had nothing to do with us," Brandy said. "Timberlake, he was into some bad shit, maybe it had nothing to do with you and Clive and the Procopios."

Todd said nothing, busy concentrating on his thoughts.

"What is it?"

"I think Clive killed the Mrs.—but he definitely did not kill Timberlake. I was the one who told him about Timberlake's death, that was no acting job on his part. He was totally surprised. I remember him lashing out when he learned the truth." Feeling his cheek, Todd gazed back at the newspaper article, as though between the lines of type were a hidden truth.

"Hey, you two," the store clerk said from behind his counter, "either buy it or put it down, I'm not running a library here."

"Come on, Todd, we can't worry about the Timberlake murders, they have nothing to do with us, at least not directly. We've got some work to do," she said, patting the bag of supplies from the costume shop.

But Todd paid for the newspaper; he'd only scanned the article and wanted to absorb the details when he had more time. For now, Brandy was right, time was precious and not just for their kidnapping ploy. Something more important loomed. Since Clara Timberlake was the second victim, that meant only one thing. The hit on Henri Procopio was still on the calendar.

Back out onto the streets of New York's West Side, Brandy asked, "You got any suggestion where I can transform you into the master kidnapper? And don't say back to your apartment. Those Birdies have all but worn me out."

"And I thought they were growing on you."

"Like moss."

Todd did have an idea, and this time hailed a cab that took them across town, from the neighborhood where life was lived upon the wicked stage to Sutton Place, a land of money and wealth and great river views, specifically to the home of one Andy Simon. Just as Andy had keys to Todd's place, Todd had keys to Andy's, and what better place to wait for the ransom than in one of the city's more exclusive enclaves. The doorman, a Yankees fan who was always crowing about their twenty-six championships, knew Todd was a baseball fan. A Mets fan, the doorman would say with derision.

"Two months, thirteen days to opening day," the doorman said.

Todd, who had no doubt that tomorrow the guy would be spouting "Two months, twelve days," just laughed, and in seconds he and Brandy had boarded an available elevator and practically flown up to Andy's twentieth-floor apartment. Todd unlocked the door, smiling.

"What's put you in such a good mood?" Brandy asked him.

"I want you to meet someone."

"Who? This Andy guy? You said he was at work."

"Not Andy. Toad's here."

"Oh, God, not the frog."

Todd flipped on the lights, then made his way over to the dining-room table, where his familiar-looking frog tank was thankfully intact. Toad was floating silently on the bottom of the tank when Todd rapped his knuckles against the side of the glass. Toad immediately reacted to the company, his legs stretching outward until he broke the surface of the water. His big eyes stared up at Todd, as though he knew exactly who had come to visit him and wasn't it about time, where ya been, ya big lug. Todd lifted the cover, and scooped Toad into his hand, bringing him over to the sofa. There he held the dripping frog in his open palm, encouraged Brandy to say hello.

"Not exactly a lap dog, is he?" she said.

"Oh, come on, say hi to Toad."

Todd was petting the frog's backside, its skin forever smooth from the water. Brandy reached out a finger as well and Toad hopped off Todd's hand, onto his lap.

"He can sense your hesitation."

"That's okay, I don't want to touch him, won't he give me warts?"

"Maybe you should kiss him, he'll turn into a prince."

"Maybe I've already met a prince," she said.

Todd admitted that comments like that could distract him from the business at hand, and maybe they should hop to it. He replaced Toad into his watery home, fed him a few granules of food, which Toad happily lapped up. Todd's hand momentarily rested on the plastic covering of the tank.

"I don't get it, Todd."

"What?"

"The frog. You and the frog. It's not like you can claim him on your taxes, so what's the deal?"

"Oh, I know, it's silly."

"No, it's not silly, you're obviously very taken with him. And he with you, I could tell he recognized you. Which is weird. But . . . nice, I guess. I just . . . well, why frogs?"

"We've shared a lot, Bran, these last few days. I think I can trust you . . ."

"Todd, it's just a frog, there can't be much baggage there."

Todd leaped onto the topic. "Short version? The day before my father skipped out on us, he took me fishing. I was five and oblivious to things like parents who weren't there for you, didn't know what words like betrayal meant. Maybe he already knew he was leaving, wanted to leave me with a good memory. Whatever. I didn't catch any fish that day, but I did find a frog. I brought him home and my father helped me make a home for him. Suddenly my father was gone, and in its place—that stupid frog. He got me through a tough time. Ever since then I've had a soft spot for our amphibian friends."

"Something tells me there's more to this story."

Todd found himself watching Toad happily swim around before answering. "Yeah, the long version—which we don't have time for."

Which reminded them that they were running out of hours in this day, the noon hour approaching and only three hours remaining until the banks closed. Brandy's father, they hoped, was busy putting together the money, and in preparation for the drop-off, Todd became putty in Brandy's hand. Like that hadn't already happened before.

She worked diligently for nearly an hour, sculpting and molding and gluing, transforming Todd until even his mother wouldn't recognize him, that's what Brandy said proudly. Todd kept silent on that comment about his mother not recognizing him without the disguise. He pushed all such poisonous and distracting thoughts from his mind, and instead proclaimed Brandy a genius once again. He stared at himself in the mirror, at the fuzzy graying beard which now covered his cheeks and chin, the thick black glasses that hung from the bridge of a nose that had been slightly enlarged and made slightly crooked. His hair had been slicked back, some gray had been added as well, aging Todd by twenty years.

"My sugar daddy," Brandy proclaimed.

"Real funny. Let's call Pops, see what kind of progress he's made," Todd said, walking from the bathroom which had been their lab to the dining room, where the frog continued to happily swim. Todd peered into the glass and Toad peered right back, big eyes blinking. "Seems confused, like he doesn't recognize me. That's a good sign." Todd dialed from his cell phone the number of Mr. Alexander's cell phone, and he answered on the first ring.

"Yes, this is Thomas Alexander."

"I should hope so. Do you have the money?"

"Yes, I do. It wasn't easy, you know, bells go off in bank managers' minds when you withdraw the kind of sums we're talking about . . ."

"Mr. Alexander, I'm not concerned with your problems, unless of course they pertain to getting your daughter back."

"How do I even know she's still alive?"

"Hey, I'm a man of my word. But here . . ."

Todd handed the phone to Brandy, who grabbed at it. "Daddy, I'm . . . I'm okay . . . for now," she said, conjuring up a sense of fear from deep inside her devious mind. "Just give them the money, please, please, I can't stand this captivity. It's . . . torture, the kind of things they're threatening to do to me . . . oh, Daddy . . . it's only money . . ."

Brandy handed back the phone and Todd listened to her father's desperate pleas. "Sorry, she's gone for now, in the grip of my associate. Now, about the drop-off, you know the park by the United Nations? I'll be waiting on one of the park benches facing the East River, uh . . . reading the newspaper. You'll recognize the paper, I'm sure."

"But wait . . ."

"One hour, Mr. Alexander, and come alone. If I don't phone my associate the moment the transaction is completed—and every five minutes until I'm back safe—he will do things to your precious Brandy that not even your worst fears could imagine. Oh, and what were you thinking, naming your daughter Brandy? Brandy Alexander? She's not a party favor, man. Still, when all this is over, you're going to need a drink, that's for sure." Then he pressed "end" on his cell phone.

"You're wicked, Todd Gleason."

He took Brandy in his arms and said, "Just think, in a matter of hours we'll be rid of the Birdies, once and for all, and we will have made a tidy profit, too, huh? We split what's left after

Birdie gets his cut, and then . . .." Todd's voice faded, his face taking on a sudden, worried expression. Brandy asked him what was wrong and he said, "I was just thinking about kids and their parents, wondering what this con will do to your relationship with your father? I mean, if he ever found out the truth."

"He won't, and besides, it would probably improve our relationship. You heard him, Todd, he's moved heaven and earth to come up with the cash to save me from my tormentors. Just as he said he would. Makes me realize that maybe he does love me, that he sees me more than just a person he can try and shape and manipulate with threats of withholding money from me. I never knew how far he would go for me—you know, if I really was in trouble. Now I know; and it's only cost him half a million dollars. Heck, therapy would have cost more."

"And in the process?"

"For me? That's easy. No more Cambridge, no more studies. I can play it to the hilt. I wasn't just interested in being a make-up artist, I've acted too. Look at me, I'm too traumatized to return." She feigned a faint, and then she giggled. "And I have enough money to make a fresh start."

Andy Simon was sitting behind his desk reading the stock reports after a morning fraught with phone calls from clients asking for this and asking for that, both of which boiled down to money, everyone wanted to make money and then even more money and then they wanted to retire and read magazines poolside. Could you blame them? He'd thought of retirement often, too, but that was a direct result of playing nursemaid to millionaires and resident investor for friends like Todd. Though now he was thinking about lunch and that's when his telephone rang.

"Andy Simon, let's make some money."

"Andy . . . ?"

"Beth . . . my God, Beth, is that really you?"

"It's me, yeah."

"You . . . you sound . . . ?"

"What, Andy?"

"Quiet."

His saying that produced even more quiet, to the point where Andy feared that whatever had been happening in London, it had changed his sister in a very profound way. His chatterbox of a sister, suddenly reduced to short, clipped, inexpressive sentences. Hey, truth be told, not a bad benefit to a terrible situation.

"Where are you? Are you safe?"

"Yes, I'm in hiding if you can believe such a thing, but yes, I'm free from . . . from those beastly men who took me hostage. Bonnie and Clyde are taking very good care of me, feeding me fish and chips and bangers and mash and keeping me company."

Bonnie and Clyde? Andy didn't want to know.

"Where's Todd?" That he definitely wanted to know.

"I wish I knew, Andy. I haven't seen or heard from Todd in days, not since he left my flat . . . oh, when was it, Sunday night, I guess."

"I could kill him for dragging you into . . . this."

"Andy, I don't think even Todd understood what he'd gotten himself caught up in."

"Which is what, exactly?"

"It has something to do with some landlord's murder and a guy named Clive. I think he's the killer, because I met him and he's got a real nasty temper. Todd got on his bad side, that's for sure, and I was the bait. But I've escaped."

"That's good to hear, Beth. Stay safe. I'm going to send Todd another e-mail; he hasn't checked it in two days, I'm beginning to fear the worst. And if what you say is true and Todd's made an enemy of some . . . did you say killer? Well, Todd's smart but he's no match for someone like that. You know, a pro. Todd's a rank amateur. Thanks for calling me, Beth, to tell me you're okay."

"Oh, there's one other thing, Andy."

"What's that?"

"I've fallen in love."

What?

"What?"

"You heard me, oh, but I should go, I don't like the idea of running up Bonnie and Clyde's phone bill with this international call, they refused to take my money, said I'm practically family . . . so we'll talk again and I'll explain in more detail. Goodbye, Andy."

"Um, okay, bye, Beth."

Andy replaced the receiver, confounded by the phone call. In the span of five days his sister had been kidnapped and fallen in love. That was more excitement than she'd had in decades. How had she the time to meet Mr. Right when she'd run afoul of Mr. Wrong? Then the phone rang again, this time an inhouse call.

"Simon, get in here," came the voice of his boss.

Andy knew what side his bread was buttered on, he got up from his desk, tossing on his suit jacket and making haste down the long corridor, past all the other stockbrokers who were busy on the phones, oblivious to the things around them. Money had a way of keeping turks young and old focused. Mr. Alexander's secretary was out to lunch so Todd knocked on the door, stepped inside when the voice behind it told him to.

"Sir, something I can do for you?"

"Yes. You're . . . you're a smart guy, Simon, one of my smartest. Good on the phone, good on your feet, too." The man paused, then said, desperation in his voice, "I need your help."

"Help with what, sir?" Andy asked, taking in his boss's ap-

pearance. He looked haggard, his usual put-together self looking more than a bit disheveled. Truth was, he thought his boss
had been acting strange all morning, in and out of the office, on
the phone, unavailable for advice or consultation. Sitting behind
his desk, typing away furiously on his computer, ordering his
secretary to find him newspapers. Now it seemed Andy was
about to learn what it all meant. It was nice to be trusted.

Situated on his boss's expansive and expensive cherrywood
desk was a silver-metal case, not his usual black briefcase. Andy
had the sense that something was very wrong. Then Thomas
Alexander began putting on his overcoat, told Andy to fetch his.
"You're coming with me."

"Where, sir?"

"To run an errand, I'll explain on the way."

"And my role, sir, in this errand?"

"Oh, that's easy, Simon. You're my back-up."

"Don't you need back-up?"

"Ideally, yeah, a second set of eyes would be nice. But we're
not exactly strong on manpower, Brandy. Besides, I'm not sure
how other kidnappings work, but I'll hazard a guess that usually
the victim doesn't assist in the pick-up of the ransom. I think
your father's running so scared he won't do anything to mess
this up. Also, we haven't exactly given him much time to do
anything except get his hands on the money. Even if he'd had
time to call the police, I doubt very much he'd want to involve
them. That would mean the press would get wind of it and
everything would be blown out of extortion, uh, proportion."
He paused. "I'll be fine; you wait here at Andy's and I'll be
back shortly."

Brandy agreed, and so sending him off with a kiss that sent
him practically floating back to ground level, Todd was all set
for his biggest con yet; his biggest payoff yet. He used the service

exit, so the doorman didn't see him. Todd one, doorman nothing. That would raise an eyebrow or two, enter the building with
a hot blonde and a couple hours later leave looking twenty
years older. Heck, if she was doing her job right, he should look
twenty years younger. So Todd emerged onto the sidewalk,
slipped on his sunglasses and headed for the U.N., the *Evening
Standard* newspaper he'd bought in Times Square firmly tucked
under his arm. There were plenty of benches available, since it
was windy by the water and a workday to boot; plus it was
winter, so Todd wasn't exactly competing with sunbathers and
the casual weekend strollers. Just a couple of elderly folk, a
woman with a yappy little dog, a group of tourists with cameras,
everyone ignoring everyone else, the great New York way of life.
Todd unfolded the paper and, since he had a few minutes before
Alexander was supposed to arrive, he read in full the article on
Clara Timberlake's murder. Found along the banks of the
Thames, not even an hour after her shooting death. Police were
convinced her death was related to that of her husband, shot
and killed a week before. Different caliber of gun from the one
which had killed her husband, that much the press had been
able to learn. Everyone was still baffled, police included, about
what the daddysgirl message on Timberlake's neck meant and
how it related to the Mrs. being offed. Detective Inspector Albert Brury was said to have a lead on a suspect, but at this time
was unable to give out many details. But he was convinced that
the same person had killed both Timberlakes.

Todd hoped the inspector was wrong. He hoped Clive was
guilty of one of the murders, but heck, let him hang for both of
them.

Just then a man settled down on the same bench as Todd,
placing a metal briefcase down between them. Todd, still holding the paper close to his face, slowly turned his head. From the
description Brandy had given him, he knew for certain this

distinguished-looking gentleman was the aptly-named Thomas Marquand Alexander II. Old money had a certain look. Fear had a certain smell. This guy evoked both.

"Relax, Pops, you don't want to attract any attention now, do you?"

"Where's Brandy?"

"She's safe, don't worry. As long as the money's there, no harm will come to her. But if even a single measly dollar is lacking, you'll get body parts in the mail until you've paid in full. Consider her fingers the first invoice—though that's not a guarantee."

"It's all there, you bastard. Now call your associate and tell him to release her."

"Not so fast, Pops. Open the briefcase."

"You're a little old to be calling me Pops, aren't you?"

Good point, Todd thought. And good make-up job. "Just open it," Todd said, his voice low, his emotion high.

With shaking hands, Thomas Alexander unlatched the briefcase and lifted the metal lid. Todd stole a glance, noted that indeed the briefcase was filled with bundles and bundles (and more bundles!) of cash. He was quickly reminded of his last such experience with a huge stash of cash, just yesterday in London with Elise Procopio. That had gone horribly wrong, and this, well, so far so good. He instructed Alexander to close the lid, Todd gazing about for any sign of curious activity. Nothing out of the ordinary, just that yappy dog down the promenade.

Todd set down the newspaper on top of the briefcase, looked at Mr. Alexander squarely and said, "A pleasure doing business with you."

"Who are you?" Mr. Alexander suddenly asked.

If only he knew, oh if only he knew. "Don't ask questions, Pop . . . Mr. Alexander. I'm going to leave now—and take my goody-bag with me. You will remain on this bench for the next fifteen minutes and await my phone call. If anything happens to me before I am reunited with my associate, you will never again see your daughter—alive or dead. No body, no closure. You believe me when I say that, don't you, *Pops?* Just nod, don't say another word."

Todd's hand grasped the handle of the briefcase and then he stood. His heart was beating fast, knowing that this was the most dangerous part of the entire con. The money was in his hands and if Alexander had pulled a fast one on him, this was the moment of truth. But Todd walked away with the confidence of a con man, his own fears buried below the surface. He kept walking, through the park and past the security guards at the U.N. and up a few blocks until he was once again outside Andy Simon's building. He called up to Brandy, told her to meet him in front of a pub on Second Avenue named Jameson's. He waited for her to arrive, and then once she had, they grabbed a cab and headed back to Todd's Upper East Side apartment. Along the way he gave his cell phone to Brandy.

"Call Pops, tell him you're safe."

And that's when Todd at last breathed a sigh of relief, glad that one of his cons this week had worked. Still, though, he knew the game was far from over. He'd overcome one obstacle, but a major one still stood in his way, several time zones away. That's where a killer still lurked, where an assassin waited in place.

CHAPTER TWENTY

Thomas Marquand Alexander II, Wall Street big shot and all-around Mr. Money Bags, cried when he heard his daughter say that she was fine, free from the evil clutches of her faceless kidnappers. Todd could hear the sobbing through the phone, could hear the horn of a freighter as it made its way up the East River. Which meant Pops had done as instructed, remained behind on the bench in the U.N. park. So they were in the clear.

"I need to see you, my precious little girl."

"Okay, Daddy," Brandy said, mocking tears herself.

"Where are you?"

"They . . . they let me off in the middle of Times Square. I'm . . . I'm going to check into a nearby hotel and get cleaned up, then I'll come see you. Oh, Daddy, thank you so much, you're my hero, I'll see you soon."

She hung up the phone and leaned in and gave Todd a quick kiss.

"I need to see him. Daddy's not as young as he used to be, who knows what I've done to his heart."

"Well, at least you found out he has one."

Brandy smiled at Todd. "At least I'm off the hook, and he doesn't suspect a thing. He thinks we shouldn't tell a soul what's been happening, we certainly don't need to worry my mother. I agree. It's time now to put this all behind us and reap the benefits."

"Not a bad day's pay," Todd had to admit.

The cab had pulled up in front of Todd's building. He paid the near ten-dollar fare, tossed in a couple bucks tip, and then with briefcase clutched in his hand, he and Brandy returned to his apartment. Marta and Donald Birdie were lounging on his sofa watching a steady diet of nutrition-starved talk shows, including *Jerry Springer,* whose topic today was fitting from a certain perspective: Men Who Slept with Their Girlfriends' Fathers.

"Well, I screwed him over, does that count?" Todd remarked as he grabbed the remote and shut off the television.

He placed the briefcase on the coffee table and opened it up, his cohorts gathering around the table as though this were some ritual, the counting of the spoils. Inside the heavy case were stacked all those marvelous bundles of money, cash, greenbacks, the kind of stuff from which dreams were made. For Todd this was a master coup, the achievement of his goal, even if he did have to share a fair portion of it. He counted out one hundred thousand dollars and handed it over to Birdie.

"Well, I don't believe it, Todd. A con man who is better than his word."

"That hardly qualifies him for sainthood," Marta said, taking possession of the money by rudely grabbing it from her husband's sweaty hands.

"Now, I reckon that completes our little transaction, right, Birdie?"

Birdie looked once at his wife, who nodded her approval. "Yes, it does, Todd. And while I won't say it's been a pleasure doing business with you, it sure has been . . . interesting. But the quiet world of Tuckerville awaits us, our old life. So, if you'll excuse us, my wife and I are going to leave this apartment and leave New York and certainly leave your life. Brandy, it's been a pleasure knowing you. Can't imagine what you see in this man, though, he'll only lead you down a crooked path. And speaking of paths, Todd, may ours never cross again."

Todd, despite the obvious insult, shook the man's hand. "I quite agree."

Marta Birdie wrapped herself up in her fur coat and Birdie himself helped her with it. So dutiful, Todd almost felt sorry for the poor man. He had the potential to stick up for himself and take charge; he'd been a man of action in London and now that reality had intruded, he was back to being afraid of a woman—admittedly Todd found her scary, too. And so with less fanfare than when he entered Todd's life, Birdie departed, having gotten back his money and a little bit extra for good measure.

"One question, Birdie," Todd said, as Birdie looked back at him from the hallway. There was an expression on Birdie's face, as though now that he was returning to the simple life with Marta securely back at his side, he suddenly envied Todd, his life and his world. "How'd you find me, you know, in London? You never did tell me."

"The address in South Kensington, I found it on a scrap piece of paper when I was searching your apartment. Wasn't hard to find."

"Yeah, but . . . how'd you know I was going to London—that day. You couldn't have been that good a guesser."

This time Birdie grinned. "The car service, they called while I was digging through your file cabinet. Left a message on the machine saying they were coming a half hour sooner because of the traffic. I waited for them and pretended to be you, they took me right to the Virgin drop-off."

"Clever, Birdie, very clever."

"Thanks, Todd." Birdie seemed pleased at the compliment.

"Have a good life, Birdie," Todd said, remorse temporarily washing over him.

Without looking back, Birdie ran after Marta, who was

demanding he follow closer behind. She wasn't letting him out of her sight again, that's for sure, not even for a minute, that's what she said as their voices drifted off. Once they were gone, Todd made sure to lock the door.

"So, Miss Brandy Alexander, how do you feel?"

She was grinning. "Horny. Todd, look at all this money . . . I . . . I feel like celebrating," she said, wrapping herself up in his arms. "I feel like peeling away that beard and that horrible fake nose, peeling off a few more layers, too. Don't the victors usually roll around in the money?"

"That's as pleasing an image as I could come up with, Brandy . . ."

"Why do I sense there's a but coming?"

"Getting this money? It's only step one—getting rid of the Birdies. But . . ."

"See, there's that but."

"It's unavoidable. I can't sit idly back while I know over in London some man is about to be offed by his wife—or rather, by the guy his wife has hired."

"But Henri Procopio's life—or death—doesn't have anything to do with you, Todd," she said. "With us."

Todd shook his head. "Sorry, I think it does. Maybe not when I planned this whole scheme, but now it does. You see, I think Elise was getting ready to call off the hit until a . . . a complication revealed itself to her. Elise found out ol' Henri's been having an affair—except it's not true." Todd proceeded to tell Brandy what he'd learned during the exchange at the Marble Arch yesterday, the photograph of Brandy herself in her bikini, lying on the bed. "The before picture, of course. I deliberately placed the photo under the bed when I was checking out the bedspread. I know, it was stupid of me, but after Procopio foiled our scam, well, I wanted some kind of retribution. Elise found it and she was so furious she couldn't wait to meet up with me—or the me who she thought was the killer. So now, not only is she angrier with her husband, she's also connected with Clive. Courtesy of me. You saw him leave the Savoy right after me—he followed me and here we are. I'm to blame, so I've got to stop it."

"By going back to London? That's insane. You may not have enough time, anyway, the hit could already have gone down." Brandy looked at her watch. "Or it could be happening now, it's Friday night in London, we don't even know when Elise was planning the hit, do we? If it will make you feel better, why not call Procopio and warn him?"

"Oh sure, just call him up and tell him his wife's hired a killer to do away with him, and oh, yes, by the way, this is the man who just a couple days ago tried to con you out of a quarter million dollars. He'll never believe it, Brandy. He'll think it's another scam, that I'm really not looking out for him. No, I've got no choice but to go back. To stop it. Elise mentioned the timing needed to be perfect—Saturday night, the actual night of their anniversary."

"Todd, you're hopeless. A con man with a conscience." She kissed his lips, his neck, began unbuttoning his shirt. "Surely we have time for a quick celebration."

"What about Daddy? Isn't he expecting you soon?"

"He can wait. I can't."

Damn but she was persuasive. Well, maybe they could kill two birds with one stone. Or some other phrase that didn't seem so violent.

He said he'd hop in the shower and remove his fake disguise, she was welcome to join him . . . for a while. But then, really, he had to get to JFK and get the first flight out. She kissed him again, deeply, soulfully, told him she'd be right in. Todd undressed and stepped beneath the hot spray, thankful for the strong water pressure. Like tiny needles that turned his skin red. The steam in the bathroom circled above the fan in misty whorls. He waited, and he waited further still, until he started to grow concerned. Was she already rolling around in the money, without him? The image had a particular effect on him. He poked his face out from behind the shower curtain, said, "Brandy, come on, I'm ready."

No response.

"Huh."

He stepped out of the shower and wrapped a towel around his waist and opened the door.

"Brandy?"

His voice echoed in what, to him, seemed like an awfully quiet apartment.

He padded his way to the bedroom, which was empty. So was the living room, and so was . . .

"Oh shit."

. . . the coffee table.

The briefcase with the money, it was gone. Also gone? Brandy herself.

Todd stood in the center of his apartment, his mind trying to absorb this latest blow. Couldn't be, she couldn't have . . . not after the week they'd shared, not after . . . Christ, had she pulled her own scam on him? How could he have been so trusting . . . thinking, of course, not with his brain.

The ringing of the telephone jarred Todd from these horrible thoughts about Brandy, about her . . . deception, her betrayal. Or was that her, calling to apologize for running out? She'd only gone to see Daddy, she'd meet up with him later. He could hope. Todd ran to answer it.

"Hello?"

"It's Birdie, I'm sorry, I had to call. Marta's in the bathroom down the hall. You know, at that horrible hotel on the West Side."

"Birdie, I thought we'd concluded . . ."

"Shut up, I only have a second before she gets back. Todd, she's going to turn you in, that's all she talked about in the cab ride back. No names, just a simple anonymous call to the police. I'm sorry, we had a deal and I intended to honor it. Just as you honored yours. But, Marta, it's impossible to get her to change her mind."

Shit, this was all he needed.

"Try, Birdie, like you've never tried before. If I go down, you go down. Marta will learn about the entire week in London, Vance Timberlake's shooting, Beth Simon's kidnapping, criminal conspiracy, fraud, you name it. You may not be guilty of it all, but you're certainly not so innocent. You'll go away for far longer than me."

"Please, Todd, don't do this to me. I'm no longer involved."

"Then stick up for yourself, Birdie."

"But, Todd . . ."

"Birdie, it's time to channel that fear of Marta, make it work to your advantage. Reverse the power, be firm with her. You can do it, remember how unflappable you were in London. Confronting Clive with the gun, rescuing us from his clutches. If you won't do it for me, and you don't do it for yourself—though God knows you should—then do it for Henri Procopio, whose life depends on what happens in the next twenty-four hours."

"You're going back to London, aren't you?"

"If you give me the chance to escape, yes, I have to."

There was momentary silence, as though Birdie had lost, in addition to his manhood, his voice. Then he finally said, "No promises, Todd. My suggestion to you? Get out of town fast . . . Marta . . ." A noticeable increase in falsetto to his voice. "Oh, no, I was just talking with the front desk, that's all. No, Marta, no . . ."

Todd replaced the receiver and hung his head. So much for sticking up for himself. Having gotten used to having a team of conspirators, Todd was suddenly on his own and if he knew what was best for him, he'd get the hell out of town. Before Marta Birdie had the cops banging down his door.

Wasn't this how this whole ridiculous thing started, Todd thought? Him running from his apartment, from the demons of his past?

He did make one more phone call before he left.

Friday night and central London was abuzz with life. Kids and adults alike thronged the busy section of Leicester Square and Piccadilly Circus, restaurants and pubs and coffee shops and arcades and music stores doing a brisk business while inside all the West End theatres comedies and musicals entertained thousands more, them to soon join the thousands already taking advantage of the beautiful night in this unpredictable city. It was getting on toward ten o'clock and for Elise and Henri Procopio, they were just two more people who were out for a night's stroll. They had just finished dinner at a fabulous Indian restaurant on Charing Cross and were now entering Leicester Square.

"Reminds me of Times Square," Elise said.

"Yes, but it's more concentrated here, it's thriving really, Elise. Look at all these kids, at all this untapped potential. Maybe it's time for Looking Great Cosmetics to beef up its international sales division, get the marketing geniuses to target these British kids, who as far as I'm concerned, look like they have money to spare. Market the Youth America line here— gotta change the name to something snappy. It's all about appearances anyway, and girls today love make-up even more, it identifies who they are, how they wish the world to view them. How about it, Elise, can't you just see a Looking Great advertisement positioned next to all these movie posters?"

Elise patted her husband's arm. "It's a nice pipe dream, Henri, but that's all it is. For you, at least. Darling, all you've been talking about for months is selling the company. You said you'd done all you could with the products and with the market. You've said you want out, so as to spend more time with me. Retirement, remember?"

"Yes. But somedays I just have to wonder if I'm making the right decision."

"Let's worry about that next week, when we return to New York," Elise said. "Until then, let's just enjoy our anniversary week. A couple more hours, Henri, it will be Saturday, our magical day will finally have arrived. Imagine, ten whole years."

Henri pulled her closer, nuzzled her neck. "I know a way we could get the celebration started early."

Elise feigned a laugh while pulling away from her husband. "No, no Henri, we agreed, no fooling around tonight, it's going to be a repeat of ten years ago. I wouldn't even let you see me after midnight and the same is true tonight. I'll be using the other bedroom in our suite."

"Such a traditional girl, my Elise. Still traditional, underneath all that haute couture and New York attitude and good fortune," Henri said. "I suppose you're right, we should each stick to our plan. So tomorrow, we move into our . . . private residence for our final night together. At least, here in London."

Wherever the hell that "private residence" is. Elise had tried six ways to Tuesday to get Henri to reveal the whereabouts of their weekend love nest and each time she tried Henri either told her she had to wait or just simply ignored the bait she offered; she was fishing alone. She was running out of time to find out; what was she going to do, call a halt to Henri's special night because she needed to notify his killer where they were? Damn, why did Henri pick now to be so evasive, usually he wore his heart on his sleeve. Nothing left to hide, no emotions, no secrets. It's why his business had been failing so recently.

Recently my ass, Elise thought. She'd saved that company from certain bankruptcy eight years ago when she came up with the idea of the new line of cosmetics—Youth America, it was called. Specially designed packaging to appeal to the younger set, hot new names for their favorite colors, a sexy advertising campaign that suddenly had the company's stock soaring and its investors pleased as punch. Did Elise get the credit? Did Elise get to work on the account? No, no wife of Henri Procopio's was going to work, especially not for his own company, why not contribute time and money to some noble and notable charity, that's a good girl. For someone who had made a fortune on what women like, Henri Procopio had no idea what women were like, not this woman anyway.

For too long Elise had swallowed her pride and her ambition, knowing one day she would regain them, and something more too, Henri's company. And then what does he do, announce that he wants to sell the business—*if* he can find a buyer to pay his ridiculous price. He'd over-inflated the worth of Looking Great to the point that even his investors were getting cold feet, bailing out by selling out. Stock prices had tumbled, Henri's quoted buying price hadn't, out of a sense of pride or maybe just stupidity. It was obvious to Elise, Henri had overstayed his welcome in the company he had built from nothing. But now his investors no longer had confidence in him. If only they knew the truth behind the brains behind the Youth America line, Henri would have been gone years ago. Really, Elise deserved total credit, that much she knew. A little slip of a comment to Henri one night at dinner a couple years into their marriage: "You should appeal more to the youth market, there's a certain granny feel to your ads and your products. Move with the times, Henri, or get left behind." Henri the next day acting as though he'd dreamed it, oh how Elise had vented to Mimi Ledbetter that one day.

"Too bad you couldn't do away with the aging goat," Mimi had said back in her drinking days, when cocktails at five meant five after or five of any hour. She was so sloshed by the end of that supposed "high tea," Elise doubted she'd remember even her response, "Oh, right, and end up in jail. Nice plan, Mimi. They always suspect the wife."

"Dear heart, you don't do the deed, you hire something to do it."

"And where would a society woman like myself find such a . . . low life."

"Oh Elise, do I have to teach you everything? Nothing mixes better with wealth and high society than the criminal element. They go hand in hand."

Last fall's unexpected windfall, that glorious lottery win which had enabled Elise to do as she pleased, that had changed everything. No longer did she have to rely on Henri's wealth. No longer did she need to worry about that pesky police question: motive. How could they think her a gold digger when she had her own pot of gold?

Henri's voice intruded on her thoughts. "Elise, what are you thinking?"

"Oh, just what a glorious night tomorrow will be. The start of a whole new life."

"That was the idea."

By now they had returned to the Savoy, where Henri announced that he was tired and was going to bed. Elise wanted to catch up on the news, maybe have a little nightcap. So, there they were, standing in the middle of the lobby amidst prying eyes, and that's when Henri gave Elise a deep kiss, one that would linger and last, not just in their minds but in the minds of any possible witness.

"Goodnight, Elise," Henri said when finally the kiss ended. "I love you."

"I love you too, Henri," Elise said, her voice only slightly louder than his. Really, it reverberated in the gilt-laden lobby and was music to the ears of all who were around them. The crowd broke out into spontaneous applause at this tender display of true love. Henri, red-faced, retired for the night, and Elise, bowing for her audience, retreated at last to the bar. She ordered a double martini, "as dirty as you can make it."

Once she was served, she ran the olive around the rim of her mouth, taking away the taste of Henri's lips, themselves still tasting of whiskey and curry. She gazed about the darkened room, her eyes focusing on a lone gentleman at the table in the corner. He was eating peanuts and scratching at his chest and staring right at her. Elise, checking around for anyone who might be checking her out, decided it was safe enough to risk. She made her way to the table and with drink still in hand, grinned down at the man she knew as Clive.

"Is this seat taken?"

"Please," Clive said. "How pleasing to have such charming company. So, do you have information for me? Where will I find you and the love of your life tomorrow night?"

"I still don't know, Clive."

"I don't like this, Mrs. P. This is not my usual way of operating. It's dangerous to get so specific about . . . how you want things done. Part of the enjoyment of my job is the creativity I bring to it, also the spontaneity. Why are we waiting until exactly ten o'clock?"

"Because I don't want to be sitting around all night wondering when it's going to happen."

"And why exactly does it have to be tomorrow night?"

"What better night to play the grieving widow than on my anniversary?"

"Right, another grand performance, like the one we just witnessed back in the lobby."

"You saw that?"

Clive smiled daggers. "Who do you think started the applause?"

Elise leaned in closer, frightened suddenly of this man across from her. He was calculating, manipulative. But he also looked like any person you'd walk by on the street, not think twice about. He wasn't gorgeous and that wimpy goatee did little for his looks. For looks, she'd take that Todd any day. But Todd wasn't the man she'd thought he was and she wasn't one for betrayal. Thankfully, Clive was a man of action, not only would he take care of Henri (for a price) he'd also promised to take care of Todd, too (that one was free). The thought of what he did for a living excited her. He was enigmatic, scary.

"You've been following us?"

"All day."

"Wow, you're good. Never suspected a thing."

"That's what you're paying me for."

"So then you'll be following us tomorrow, too."

"You leave me no choice, you've failed in your efforts to give me advance info."

"Just so you don't fail me, Mr. Clive Remington, or whatever your name really is. I know none of you criminals use your real names. Hiding from society, hiding from yourselves."

"Thanks for the insight, saves me a visit to the shrink," he said. "Oh, I won't fail—in either mission."

"Any sign of . . . you know."

"Todd? Don't worry about him; if he shows up to spoil the party, Henri won't be the only corpse. And trust me. It will be my distinct pleasure to kill Todd Gleason."

Ten o'clock Friday night, New York time. Andy Simon returned home to his apartment, drained from what had turned out to be an exhausting day. From the moment he'd left the office with Thomas Alexander, Andy had been constantly on the go, occasionally reporting in to his boss on his progress. You see, he'd watched the entire exchange down at the United Nations between Alexander and the bearded gentleman, couldn't get close enough without arousing suspicion. But once the two men had concluded their business, Andy had stepped up his role, shadowing the man with the briefcase.

It sure blew his mind to see the blonde woman emerge from Andy's own building, hook up with the bearded man and get into a cab with him, kissing him. Andy had hailed his own cab and told the driver to follow that other one.

"Don't worry if you get lost, I think I know where we're headed."

"You're the boss."

Turned out, Andy was right on the money, as he watched the bearded man and the blonde woman go into a building Andy knew well. After all, he'd rescued Toad from the top-floor apartment last week after it had been burglarized.

"What are you up to, Todd?" Andy had wondered. "Why are you back in New York and working alongside the boss's lovely daughter?" Brandy. He'd seen the photo on his boss's desk, he couldn't help but notice it whenever he got called in.

He watched from the corner coffee shop the series of activities from the building. An older couple, the woman wearing a fur coat that looked like it was made from rats, the man chasing after her fast-moving body, they came out first. They left about twenty minutes after Todd and the blonde had shown up. Then came Brandy, about fifteen minutes later, she carrying the metal briefcase. Then, forty-five minutes later came Todd, he looking less than pleased, almost frantic. He'd gone to the corner and hailed a cab, making Andy have to rush out of the coffee shop and grab the next, again with the instructions, "Follow that cab, and don't lose him." Andy hadn't a clue where they were headed, not at first.

Once they left Manhattan and drove on past LaGuardia, Andy was convinced Todd was headed to JFK.

"Which airline?" Andy's cabbie asked him.

"How should I know?" Really, didn't this guy know what following meant?

They pulled to Terminal One, in front of the Virgin Atlantic signs. Andy told his cabbie to pull over before reaching the same place, got out in front of Kuwaiti Air and hid behind a large van which was illegally parked. Andy saw Todd glance around, checking for . . . what? Was he expecting company?

Andy watched as Todd bought a ticket. Okay, that meant this trip was unscheduled.

It was at the security check where Andy lost Todd, since he couldn't go through to the gate without a ticket. The guards might have a problem with Andy if he claimed he only wanted to follow some guy. So instead he hung around the terminal, keeping an eye out for either the horrible couple or, more likely, Brandy. None of them showed up, not as far as Andy saw, and at last he gave up the ghost. Todd's flight had just taken off, he noted on the monitor.

During this entire sequence, Andy had regularly checked in with his boss. No, he hadn't learned anything, no, sorry, nothing, and finally, while in the cab ride back to his apartment, Andy's cell phone rang for the last time that night.

"Anything, Simon?"

"Nothing, sir. I lost the man, somewhere in the streets of the Village. You know how tiny those streets are, how quickly you can lose sight of someone."

"Thank you, Simon, I knew I could trust you. Brandy is safe and secure, out of the clutches of that evil man. She's going to stay in New York for a couple days until she decides what she's going to do with her life, the entire Cambridge kidnapping has spooked her into returning to the States. That disappoints me, but I suppose all that matters is her safety, her happiness."

"Good to hear, sir. I'll see you Monday morning."

"Oh, and Simon?"

"Sir?"

"Discretion has its own rewards."

Andy had smiled at that one. "Indeed, sir."

Now back home, Andy cracked open a bottle of Sierra Nevada pale ale and was tossing the cap away when he saw an unfamiliar-looking bag in the trash. He pulled it out, examined it. From a costume store in Times Square. He threw it back into the trash and settled at his table, where he stared through the glass of the tank at that damned frog named Toad.

"So, you saw your Daddy today—did you even recognize him with that disguise?"

Toad ignored Andy, like always.

So Andy didn't feed him.

Andy took a long pull on his beer. "Todd Gleason, what the hell is going on? And what does my boss's daughter have to do with this? Though I'll give you credit, my man, blonde and built like she is, nice work." But silently Andy wondered why Brandy had ditched Todd—presumably taking the money with her. She hooked up with Daddy to assure him she was fine, but meanwhile Andy knew she'd never been in any danger. They just needed cash, and knew just who to get it from. But for what purpose? And where was Brandy now? Were they meeting up back in London? And then what? How had they even met? Way too many questions had Andy more confused than ever.

He went over to his computer, logged on and sent Todd an e-mail, hoping the fool would be checking his messages soon. The fool, that was right on the money this time. He'd obviously gotten himself mixed up in something worse than usual, something that had gone horribly awry. And sure, he was concerned about his friend. But Andy wondered if he could use any of this to his advantage.

CHAPTER TWENTY-ONE

"How'd you do?"

"Horrible, as always. Why I waste my money on these things I'll never know. Spent twenty bucks and won back a whole two bucks."

"Oh, not good odds."

He'd been working against the odds all week.

Todd had needed a release, and also a sense of normalcy, so he had bought a bunch of instant lottery tickets and spent a good portion of the flight back overseas scratching away at the squares of silver foil to discover the potential hidden treasures these damn tickets held. Why was he so tempted by the lottery? Well, like most addictions, they held empty promises of a quick fix. He never gambled when he was working a scam, figuring he didn't need the distraction, or a false sense of hope during a time when he otherwise felt secure and confident. Now, on board yet another plane and this one sorely lacking one Brandy Alexander—or anyone else remotely as visually interesting— sitting beside him, he was glad for the distraction afforded by the lottery tickets. He'd paced himself, and so by the time all was said and done, the meal, the movies, the mini bottles of Merlot, they were in landing mode as Todd scratched away at his last and final ticket. Nope, no big win there.

The flight attendant looked at him with sheepish eyes and then asked if he wanted to toss them in the trash bag she was holding. Final preparations before landing.

"It's where they belong, I suppose."

"Better luck next time."

"Let's hope so," Todd said, not meaning the stupid lottery tickets at all. He buckled himself back up, put up his tray table like a good little flyboy. Outside the rain was falling hard—like cats and dogs went the expression, Todd visualizing the scene with one of the damn animals getting caught in the powerful engines, causing the plane to plummet to the Earth. Not such a bad way to go, quick and fiery, and with the way his luck had been going, a probable scenario that would remove from him any sense of responsibility he felt toward stopping Elise—or rather Clive—from killing Henri Procopio. No such bad luck happened, the plane landed just fine and the captain welcomed them to London's Heathrow airport, local time eight thirty-seven in the morning.

"We hope to see you again on a future Virgin Atlantic flight," the captain added, the comment seemingly directed at Todd, who thought he heard laughter coming from the cockpit. Was he going crazy? No, he was just tired, beyond tired really, exhausted and ready to sleep the languid sleep of Rip Van Winkle. Fat chance of that, Todd told himself. He had too much to accomplish, and in too little time.

Thirty minutes later, after having cleared the immigration desk with a raised eyebrow but nonetheless a fast stamp of his passport from the inspection agent, he was hurtling his way back toward central London, this time foregoing the expense of a cab and taking the Heathrow Express to Paddington Station. His eyes kept closing and he needed something to distract him from falling asleep. His eyes fell on a fellow passenger who was immersed in the day's latest news, courtesy of a crisp new edition of the *Daily Mail*. There was some headline about a crippling earthquake in India, another about a fire that devastated a home in South Kensington, another highlighting the latest scandal involving some former member of Parliament.

Finally they arrived in London, site of atrocities such as fires and scandals. From Paddington, Todd took the Tube back to the Savoy, the last known whereabouts of his clothes, his computer, his con. In his haste, Birdie had never checked out. Fortunately Todd still had his room card key and so he went quickly through the lobby, up the lift and at the second floor, hopped out. Like magic, the card worked and the little green light was lit and Todd was once again in the lap of luxury, the room clean and neat, almost as though it hadn't been slept in for a night or two. He dropped to the bed, listening to the silence, grateful for it. He gave himself fifteen minutes to crash, then, fearing a long sleep might win out over quick action, he threw himself into a hot shower and emerged ready to fight the good fight.

"Okay, Clive, I'm not afraid of you," he said with a wavering voice.

Being back in this room, Todd was flooded with remembrances of Brandy, of their scam in the making and of their love in the making too (more of those memories, really). He shook it off, though, knowing he couldn't lose focus. Brandy didn't matter, not now, hell, not anymore. Stop Clive from killing Henri, save Beth from the evil clutches of Clive's associates, that's what mattered. Was there ever a simpler plan? How about leaping over tall buildings in a single bound, that might qualify.

Todd actually had a plan, however foolish it might be. First, he grabbed his laptop, plugged it in and logged onto the Internet. It had been days since he'd had the opportunity to check his e-mail and indeed, popular guy that he was, he had new messages. Three of them from Andy; Todd read them quickly, hoping for news of Beth's release, that would be nice, remove the guilt as well as one of his missions. But no, the latest missive was from last night and Andy seemed madder than ever, why

311

hadn't he heard from Todd, what was the status of Beth's kidnapping, what the hell is going on over there? Unfortunately, that's all there was (so maybe he's not *that* popular), there were no messages from "daddysgirl" to "frogman" and for a moment Todd considered sending one to his charming, albeit conniving con-ette. No, forget about Brandy, she'd showed her true colors, money over . . . over what, exactly? She'd known Todd for barely a week, money her entire life, why not choose what you were more familiar with? Still, he had to admit that Brandy's sudden flight from his life had hurt. In all of this, the only person he hadn't been conning was her.

An idea, formed from betrayal and completed by bitterness, washed over him. Suddenly he was logging onto Brandy's Internet provider, putting in her e-mail address—daddysgirl. Next, though, he needed a password and he searched his mind for the perfect code for Brandy. He tried Cosmogirl, he tried Cambridgegirl, he tried Shakespearegirl, thinking she may have kept things simple, linked by things she hated. None of them worked and he was in danger of being tossed off; one last try, come on, come on, think, think . . . and then there it was, a brainstorm and sudden success. Because he typed in "Marquand." The family's old world name. The one she'd not been worthy of. You had to learn something when you slept with someone, it wasn't all just noises and climaxes and nodding off into the comfort of your pillow and someone's tender embrace. You had that pillow, make talk.

Turns out, she had mail, but Todd didn't care who she was communicating with. No, Todd checked for her address book, found her father's e-mail address. What he typed was quick, fast, and very much to the point. *Look no further than your beloved daughter for the truth behind the kidnapping.* Todd read over those cryptic yet damaging words, considered deleting it before his nerve won out. And then he pressed send, and the message went out over cyberspace, itself a betrayal born of betrayal. Then he logged off.

"I hope I know what I'm doing," Todd said to no one but himself.

No one answered.

Time to get a move on.

Todd hopped back onto the elevator, this time heading further up. He was going to see Henri Procopio; didn't it make sense to warn the man? Maybe that was all that was required of Todd, tell the cosmetics king what he'd uncovered. And what if he ran into Elise? That thought stopped him cold halfway down the corridor. Todd retreated to the stairwell, the same place Brandy had hid while Todd had put the first phase of their con on Henri; now he was staking out the room, waiting for some kind of life to emerge. At least that way he'd know he wasn't too late. It took nearly a half hour of (im)patience, but finally Henri himself left his room, his overcoat over his arm and a large umbrella in his other hand.

"Yes, dear, about an hour. And don't even attempt to follow me, surprises are not meant for spoiling," he said before closing the door.

Well, that answered that, Henri was alive and alone, and Elise was inside. Todd left his hideaway and started after Henri, who had already pressed for the elevator. The doors pinged open and Henri stepped in, Todd following close behind. They weren't alone, four other folks were with them, some nodding and one actually saying, "Good morning," violating that unwritten rule about talking in elevators. Henri hadn't yet noticed Todd, so Todd cleared his throat loudly, causing everyone to look at him. He shrugged.

"Frog in my throat," he offered up as an excuse.

Henri's eyes flashed with recognition, but he said nothing. Words were unnecessary.

It was an agonizing ride down six floors. At last the doors opened, almost like a breath of oxygen as the people spilled out, Todd hurried up until he was right at Henri's side.

"Go away, Mr. Booker."

"Please, Mr. Procopio, I need to speak with you. It's a matter of life and death."

"Oh, is Miss . . . Willow not feeling well? Bad reaction to stage make-up? Shame, really."

"No, she has nothing . . . forget her. Mr. Procopio, it's about your wife."

That stopped him in his tracks, right there in the midst of a busy Saturday morning at the bustling lobby of the Savoy. "Look, I don't know what kind of game you're playing, but do not bring my wife into this. You tried—valiantly, I might add—to con me out of a small fortune, well, a fortune in your world maybe, and since that hasn't worked you've obviously come up with something new. Save it, Mr. Booker—and if you continue with this harassment, I will hesitate no longer and call the police. They're already looking for you, you are aware of that?"

Todd's face lost all color; man he hated mention of the cops. They bugged him.

"What are you talking about?" he asked.

"I had a visit from a certain Inspector Brury of the Metropolitan Police, just yesterday, as a matter of fact. About the terrible deaths of a husband and wife, their names which escape me at the moment. Local property owners from what I understand. I'm sure you could provide me with their names, right? Because you're wanted in connection with their deaths—or should I say murders? Unless of course there are two Richard Bookers running around the wrong side of London's law, which I doubt very highly. Coincidence has its place in fiction, my boy, not in real life."

"What did you tell Brury?"

"Oh, you're familiar with him? Newspaper reports catching your interest, perhaps? I understand a good conman must stay in touch—and one step ahead of the law. Sometimes I think the press helps the criminals more than they do the public. And no, for some reason I didn't tell the detective about our unfortunate situation, why I don't know, perhaps a moment of sympathy for your plight? Or maybe the usual case of not wanting to get involved. The poor man, Brury—eats Tums like they're candy, investigating murder must wreak havoc on the man's stomach—I suppose I could have helped alleviate that condition."

"Look, Mr. Procopio, this isn't the right place to discuss all this, in public. Can we meet somewhere? It's vital . . ."

"My boy, today is my wedding anniversary and that means all my meetings will be with my wife and my wife alone. Besides, knowing what I know about you, there's no way in hell I'd meet you anywhere. Good day, Mr. Booker, and good luck. If I see you once more, I will phone that inspector and you will spend what I'm sure will be an uncomfortable stint behind bars. Pretty boys have their appeal, no?"

Procopio turned on his heel, but Todd grabbed his wrist, preventing him from moving forward. Todd had no choice but to conjure honesty. It felt weird. He whispered, "Your wife is trying to kill you."

Henri, red-faced and about to boil over, jerked free from Todd's hold. "This is one sick game you're playing, Mr. Booker, and a pathetic attempt to blackmail me. This is a special day for my wife and myself, how dare you taint it with such . . . vile suspicion. How low will people sink for the almighty dollar? I think I'm looking the answer in the face. Now, I have an appointment to keep. As for you, I suggest you leave this hotel, leave London, and we'll forget any and all mention of this. Goodbye."

"Mr. P . . ."

Todd's pleas fell on suddenly deaf ears as Procopio exited the hotel. Todd felt helpless, but somehow determined still. He wasn't going to give up. No, he'd just have to try another tactic. What that other tactic was, well, beats him. He retreated back upstairs, was unlocking his door when he felt a shadow envelop him. He turned quickly and his mouth dropped. This was one more complication he did not need. You see, a gun was pointed directly at him.

"Open the door," said Larry, Clive's hulking beast of an associate.

Todd did as instructed, at first. Then, turning tables on the man, Todd immediately tried to close the door on Larry by thrusting his body against it. Larry had managed to insert his foot and the door slammed against it. He howled in pain but the foot didn't move. Then the door was pushed open with such force that Todd found his body hurtling through the air, thrown down to the floor. He was panting as he stared up at the lug, who was busy slamming the door behind him.

"I could kill you," Larry said.

"Yeah, but you won't," Todd said, hoping that was the truth at least.

"That's right, mate. Because Clive wants that pleasure all his own. Now pack your stuff, it's time to check out of this place, enough of the good life for you. Actually, enough of any kind of life for you."

Despite the gun in his face, there was an unexpected bright spot to this current predicament. Being forced to check out of the Savoy, a delightful surprise awaited Todd at the reception desk. Todd's bags were at his feet, Larry standing behind him with his hand in his pocket, no question what he was holding, when he announced to the clerk on duty that he had to unexpectedly leave the hotel. The clerk said that was fine, let me check on the bill. Exactly what Todd had been dreading, but then came reason to laugh.

"Mr. Birdie, shall I leave everything on the credit card you gave me?" the young clerk asked, showing Todd an itemized accounting of his stay.

Over five thousand dollars, including drinks, meals, and Brandy's facial. "Yes, that will be fine," Todd said, silently adding a "sorry, Birdie," who would surely endure considerable wrath from Marta when the credit card statement arrived. Too bad, considering Marta wanted to turn Todd in, the least he could do was stick her with the bill. Todd scribbled a signature on the slip and then he was off. Rather, they were off, 'cause Larry was still hovering dangerously close. Through the revolving doors they went and into the waiting cab.

"Where's your friend, what's his name, Dodo?"

"Bobo," Larry said.

"Is he joining us?"

"No."

"Is he still keeping watch over Beth Simon? Tell me, please, is she all right?"

"You ask too many questions, mate, questions I'm not supposed to answer."

"Why not?"

"See, now that's another question. Just shut your trap and let's go. Oh, and by the way, you'll have to do the driving."

"Excuse me?"

"Well I can't drive and keep my gun on you," he explained. "So you'll have to drive us to our destination."

"But you guys drive on the wrong side of the road."

"Only if you don't follow the signs will you be on the wrong side," Larry said, laughing at his own joke.

"How about if I make a promise to you, no funny stuff, I'll sit back and enjoy the ride."

"Like you didn't pull anything up in that hotel room? Sorry, I know better than to trust the likes of you. Now get in, and watch the road."

"I don't even know where we're going."

"Oh, to Clive's."

Great. With any luck (which he was sorely lacking in, remember those lottery tickets?), Todd would get them killed in a car crash before they reached their dreaded destination. With no choice, Todd got in behind the wheel, immediately a sense of disorientation overtaking him. Sitting on the right side of the car, this just felt unnatural. He started the cab, positioned his feet, said a mental prayer and then joined the traffic on the busy Strand. Adding to the misery? The rainy downpour hadn't let up all day.

It was a wild ride, to say the least. Driving on the left was difficult enough when the road was straight, but entering the traffic circle at Trafalgar Square was a near nightmare, scaring off tourists and Londoners alike as Todd turned the wheel this way and that, almost going down the wrong way and colliding with another cab. Lots of shouts, lots of horns, even Larry tried to block out one particular incident involving a courier on a bicycle, that near-crash a sure sign that Todd wasn't doing a bang-up job on his first-ever English road test. But finally, after a few other close calls and careful turns of the wheel past the very busy Victoria Rail Station, Todd got control of the cab and they cruised along the busy but wide Vauxhall Bridge Road. From there it was much smoother sailing, that's how Todd classified it, chancing a look out the cab window as they crossed over the murky Thames. In the end, they made it to Vauxhall in one piece, Larry instructing Todd where to park. Safely back on the sidewalk, Todd's legs felt like rubber. Larry wasn't much better off. Still, the crook was in control, pushed Todd along, the gun prodding from behind. Todd didn't need encouragement, he was happy just to escape the drenching rain.

"Could we stop for a pint, I think my nerves need it," Todd suggested.

"No."

Really, what kind of Londoner was Larry, refusing a quick stopover at the local pub? But they skipped the Frog and the Firkin, and instead climbed up the stairs to the top floor. Larry pushed Todd inside, despite the fact that Todd wasn't quite ready for his reintroduction to his friend Clive Remington. Yet the flat was quiet—no Clive, no Fiona, no marathon sexcapades—just Larry and Todd and the furniture. Something smelled wrong, and not just the odors permeating from the pub.

"What the hell's going on?" Todd asked.

"I said no questions," Larry said, who then took out his mobile phone and quickly dialed a number. "Yeah, it's me. Yup, I've got him and no, he's not going anywhere."

Elise Procopio was wearing a blindfold.

"Henri, really, this is so unnecessary."

"No, it is part of my surprise, and you'll do well to play along, Mrs. Procopio of Ten Years."

Yes, their anniversary had finally arrived, and all the months of talking about having achieved ten full years together, the weeks of planning and the tumultuous days just passed that had led up to this moment, there was no way Henri Procopio was going to allow anything to go wrong at the last minute. The weather? As far as he could tell, the rain was the only wet blanket on the whole day. What could he do, it wasn't his fault this was London and it was January. The rain played a steady beat on the roof of the car, danced on the streets.

They were traveling in a sleek black limousine, its darkened windows keeping them immersed in their own world, just as

Henri wanted it. No intrusions, not today. Arriving in front of the rented house in Mayfair, Henri helped Elise out of the limo, guiding her up the stairs, warning her when she needed to lift her feet.

"Maybe you should have brought along a seeing-eye dog, dear."

"Very funny, Elise. I'm glad to see you have a good sense of humor about my little indulgences. Sorry that the blindfold is necessary, but otherwise you'd see the outside world, and that's a no-no on this day. Relax, my love, all in good time and your eyes will feast again, and believe me, it will have been well worth the wait."

Henri unlocked the front door, then picked up Elise, who laughed in surprise, chastising him at the same time to put her down, he couldn't handle the weight, laughing again while her husband carried her over the threshold of their London version of Paradise. When they entered the hallway, Henri set her down and then closed the door, flipping the lock behind him.

"May I take off the blindfold?" Elise asked.

Henri gave a quick survey of their whereabouts and then told her yes, she could see again. And what an image she was rewarded with, the flickering glow of candlelight—hundreds of candles that had been placed throughout the first floor, in the hallway and into the living room, the latter room blazing with seductive, alluring flame. Another burst of light wound its way up the marble staircase, candelabras positioned on the edge of each stair, like guards posted at sentry. And sprinkled all over the stairs and marble floor were rose petals, red and vibrant, a virtual carpet of flowers that, combined with the candlelight gave off shimmering crimson images that reflected off the walls, against themselves.

"Ta-da," Henri said, with a proud, indulgent flourish.

"Oh, Henri, it's . . . beautiful, remarkable . . ." Elise said, gazing about, trying to peek out the window but seeing only vague shapes through the lace curtains. "Where are we?"

"Where we are is of no concern to you, other than in a magical land that exists only in this dimension, one far away from the world beyond that locked door. Come, be my Elise in Wonderland, won't you?"

Taking her hand, Henri escorted her into the brocade-draped living room, where he set her down upon the settee, her fabulous legs outstretched, making her look like a queen. A bottle of Dom Perignon was cooling in a wine bucket just on the other side of the plush red sofa. Henri opened it with a romantic, yet erotic flourish, the cork shooting high into the air, the sparkling liquid bubbling over the bottle. Henri filled two crystal flutes, handed the first to his wife.

"To a day—and night—filled with nothing but surprise piled upon surprise." He clinked his glass with hers and drank.

Elise, she hesitated a moment, and then she drank, not just a sip but the entire glass and then held it out for more. Ten o'clock couldn't arrive soon enough.

"Oh my love, we must pace ourselves today, it's going to be a long night, one of the longest of your life. You'll wish it to never end."

That's how the Procopios began the celebration of their anniversary.

The time of the cork popping? Two-twenty in the afternoon.

There were more corks to go off, more explosions to come in the ensuing night.

CHAPTER TWENTY-TWO

Two hours had passed since his capture and Todd was growing weary of waiting . . . but waiting for what? That's what his mind kept asking, since that's the only place his questions were allowed. Larry had continually refused to provide any insight into why Todd had been brought here, other than so that Clive could kill him. Did he want info first, what was the holdout? Couldn't we at least get this over with, the waiting was agony. Todd, working on little sleep and more than a bit jet-lagged and feeling little energy, too, since he'd forgotten to eat as well, started to nod off from the boredom of waiting to be killed. A slap to his cheek awakened him fast, and he feared Clive had at last arrived. Something he thought defined "mixed blessing" rather well.

But no, it was just Larry trying to keep Todd conscious.

"How's it going to look, Clive comes in and sees you asleep in the chair, not much of a challenge for him, is it? You'd be dead inside a minute."

"Yes, we wouldn't want to prolong my death with that nasty torture stuff, would we?"

Larry's hearty laughter rocked the walls of the flat.

Todd took that sound to heart. "Nice to be appreciated, Clive doesn't think much of my humor."

"Well, Clive and I are different people. Don't exactly see eye to eye on everything."

Well, wasn't that Todd's first inkling that maybe not everything was as it seemed here. Like someone had opened a door a crack, all Todd had to do was push hard. "Come on, Larry, tell me, what's this really about? I promise, I won't tell Clive that you told me, it'll be our little secret. We'll leave the telling just between us, what do you say, will you tell me what's really going on?"

"I'll tell you to shut up, you're giving me a headache."

They waited in silence for another twenty minutes, time a-wasting and Todd a-needing to figure something out, and fast. But what? He was nothing against a beast of a man who took up more space on this earth than any human should be allowed to. At last, though, his patience was rewarded when the door buzzed. Gave Todd some sense of hope. First, had it been Clive, he doubted he'd have announced himself. And whoever else it might be, hopefully there'd be a pick-up in the level of conversation. A loser on both counts was our Todd, because it wasn't Clive but rather Bobo. He quickly turned his attention to his latest kidnap victim and quipped, "Well, look who it is, the prodigal con."

"The what?" Larry asked.

"You know, if you read once in awhile you'd have a vocabulary," Bobo said before turning his attention to Todd. He sat down opposite Todd on the sofa and clasped his hands. "Todd Gleason, I'm so glad we've caught up with you again. Larry and I, we have a proposition for you."

"Fuck you," Todd said. There, take that.

"I'll give Clive credit where credit's due, at least he's polite. You, Todd, you need to be nice to me—to us—and if you are, you just might survive past this day."

"My survival is only part of it. Where's Beth Simon?"

"She's . . . fine," Bobo said, and Todd thought he detected a faint glimmer of a smile crease the lips of this psycho-in-training. "Don't worry about her."

"For now," Larry added, an attempt at a threat.

Bobo shot him a look that clearly said, "Shut up." Todd was busy calculating the subtext of this conversation, still came up empty. Were these guys friends, associates, conspirators with their own plan?

"Now, back to my proposition."

"Oh, please, I'm on the edge of my seat," Todd said, crossing his legs. Might as well get comfortable.

"You got guts, I'll give you that, Todd. Which makes you the ideal person for this particular job. You see, Larry and I have decided what we want out of this . . . life. We are both looking for a new line of employment, or at least a new boss. But no one just up and leaves Clive's employ . . . unless it's in a pine box, if you get my drift."

Todd nodded and waited for more. This was getting interesting.

"When you boil it down, Todd, it's either us or him, and Larry and I are not willing to be the sacrificial lambs in Clive's meadow."

His metaphor was one step removed from mixed. But Todd let that go and said, "That would require . . ."

"Killing Clive, yes, you're smart, probably smarter than me. Except now."

This was like seeing through binoculars, Todd thought. "I see it all up close now. You want me to kill Clive for you—and in effect, take the fall, too. Giving you and Larry a clean escape."

"See, I was right, much smarter."

"Except I won't do it. Killing is not my bag, you know? I just like money, that's all."

"Come on, we all know you killed Timberlake."

"I didn't . . . I don't know who did . . ."

"Whatever you want to say and believe, it really is water under the dam. It's either kill or be killed, that's your choice."

That didn't sound like much of a choice. "Care to elaborate?"

"Clive called Larry this morning from his stakeout at the Savoy—and I'm sure you know why he was there. But who does he see come shooting through the lobby? One Todd Gleason, elusive pain in the ass. Now, Clive's on assignment and can't be distracted from that, not today certainly, so he asked Larry to fill in for him, take Todd hostage and bring him back to his flat. He promised that he would deal with you later, and Clive's got a way of keeping his promises, I'm sure you know. But now, what you don't know is that Larry—and myself—are tired of taking orders from Clive. His gainful employment has gone bust with Timberlake's murder—which he blames you for—and so this week has seen his usual calm face begin to weaken, crumble, pick your metaphor."

Todd preferred to. "You think the Procopio hit is Clive's swan song?"

"Ooh, so you do know what's going down. Is it Clive's retirement? Perhaps. He's got enough money, he doesn't need to do this anymore. Except he likes it, he feeds off it like some sort of sexual release. He might just go underground for a while, resurface later. Larry and I, we're not so keen on the 'life' anymore, and besides, we don't want to take the chance that Clive's cleaning house."

"Clara Timberlake," Todd said. "He killed her—that's what's got you two running so scared. He was worried what she might know, what she could tell the police."

"Sounds reasonable," Bobo said. "Clive also believes he's already successfully disposed of one of the two of us."

"Well, since he called Larry this morning, my lucky guess lands on you, Bobo. He thinks you're dead. Any reason why that would be the case?"

"Because he took a shot at me; me and Beth."

Todd jumped up from the chair. "Beth?"

"She's fine, we both escaped. I told you, put Beth Simon out of your mind, none of this concerns her any longer," Bobo said. "Now, back to the issue at hand. Larry's a good friend of mine, we've known each other since our prison days—yes, big deal, it happens—and after he was released I took good care of him, got him a job—this job, of all things. So when he learned that Clive had tried to kill me, well, Larry's good on loyalty, to his friends, not to the job. We both agreed we needed a clean break from Clive and, well, we've already established how one does that, right? So here's what we're going to do, Todd. Larry and I are going to leave you here all by yourself, and when Clive returns later, he'll see you and he'll kill you."

Larry jumped in then. "Unless you kill him first."

"If you're going to leave, what assurance do you have that I'm going to stay, too?" Todd asked, fearing the answer even before he spoke the question aloud.

"Oh, we're going to tie you to that chair—tie the chair down, too, just so you can't move. In fact, the only thing you'll be able to move, and only slightly—will be your hand. Now, which hand do you shoot with?"

"I don't shoot."

"Tell Timberlake that."

Todd shook his head. "I told you, I didn't kill him. I don't do guns."

"You've had a policy change."

Larry removed from the small of his back a shiny little pistol, handed it to Todd. With reluctance, Todd found himself reaching out for it, the metal cold to the touch. Like touching evil.

"See, that's not so bad."

"I could shoot you both now—and escape."

Bobo extracted a gun of his own and said, "No, you won't. Remember, I'm much more familiar with how they work than you. Take one shot and you'll be leaking blood on this floor faster than a steak cooked rare. Larry, tie him up—and good."

Larry was loyal, all right, and prepared. He already had the rope inside the flat, and he proceeded to wrap it around Todd's torso and his legs, securing him to the chair. Then secured the chair in place, too, by tying the rope around the pipes from the heating unit at the base of the window. The whole process took a whopping five minutes.

"Wow, were you a boy scout?" Todd asked.

"It's good that you can keep your sense of humor, Todd, you're going to need it. Who knows when Clive will return, but he most assuredly will. We won't be returning, so you'll be all alone until he comes home to roost. You'll have just a short window of opportunity to get a shot off, and you better make it a good one."

"Because you'll only get one," Larry said.

Todd didn't have to ask why.

Bobo and Larry packed up their stuff, cleared out of the flat with a simple wave and a smile. Not even a thank you, ungrateful lugs. Todd couldn't return either the wave or the smile. His left hand held the gun and he was able to point it toward the door, little else. Larry the Scout hadn't left him much maneuvering room.

"Great," Todd said to the empty flat. Maybe he should have just crashed the cab when he had the chance. "Now what?"

With nothing else to do, Todd's eyes began to gaze about the flat. It was something to pass the time. In the corner of the room something caught his attention. Though the light was fading, he guessed the metal object was a safe. Unopened, tucked out of the way. Hmm, Todd thought. What secrets do you hold? He supposed he had a lot of time of wonder.

Todd looked at the clock on the wall; it was five-twenty in the afternoon.

The ticking sound was like a steady taunt.

"Henri, I've never been so spoiled, my goodness, the expense you've gone to."

"Nothing is too extravagant for you, dear."

They had just finished a spell on the impromptu dance floor, in which a hired violinist had played an assortment of lovely classical music. Music that filled the great hall with life, with Henri's laughter and with Elise's radiant smile as they swirled and twirled, dancing to both the music in their ears and the music that filtered its way to their hearts, for the moment shutting out whatever other feelings might be there. For thirty minutes they had indulged themselves in such splendor, really, it was sinful how much decadence a person could insert into one magnificent day.

Just then another of the help Henri had hired, a waitress from the catering company, entered the hall and announced cocktails and hors d'oeuvres. As the Procopios ceased dancing, Elise stole a look at the waitress, knowing she must be filled with such envy. What an unfortunate-looking girl, buckteeth, thick glasses, she'd be waiting for her prince for a long time. Elise, her prince was here—for now.

"My lady," Henri said, escorting his wife back inside the living room, where apple martinis on a tray were awaiting their consumption.

"Oh, Henri, you certainly think of everything."

Everything included a tray of Beluga caviar, foie gras, liver pate.

He fed her, he held her drink as she sipped it, he would have peeled a grape had he ordered them, all the while kneeling before her. A loyal subject before his royal queen. The young girl looked on, he happily noticed. He leaned in and stole a kiss from his wife, tasting the vodka from her martini, smiling at her as though that kiss had sealed their fates forever.

"Henri, this week . . ."

"Sshh, there'll be no talk of anything beyond these walls. No, my love, tonight is about you, about me, about us in a world created only for us, by us. The violinist, the caterer, they are our only links to the outside—and they have to use the servants' entrance, ha ha. No, there'll be no one passing through this alternate universe of ours. Luxury is a way of life here, love powers all that surrounds us."

"Oh, Henri, how devastatingly romantic you are."

"Just you wait, my love."

"Can you give me a hint?"

"No, my dear, this entire week has been about mystery and about surprise, I'm sorry but I must keep it up the night long."

"Lucky me if you can."

Henri smiled devilishly at his wife. "Oh, you're a bad girl, aren't you? Yes, our romance will blossom later with a passionate moment of lovemaking, we will share our bodies in the ultimate expression of love. Just you wait, Elise Procopio, the surprises continue."

Time now, six-fifteen.

Detective Inspector Albert Brury had chewed through three rolls of Tums and still his stomach juices were bothering him, not a good sign. He arrived home at seven o'clock that Saturday evening, absolutely drained of energy, spent from yet another fruitless day of investigating. He had been called out at seven o'clock in the morning and had spent the last twelve uninterrupted hours with fire investigators, with the press, with his superiors, some of whom had answers, some of whom had questions, some of whom demanded a solution to the Timberlake case. You do the math.

Not a good day.

Brury was surprised to see a light on inside his South Kensington home. He couldn't remember the last time Fiona had been at home on a weekend, and here she was, two nights in a row staying in. She was situated in front of the television watching *Coronation Street,* her fingers caught in the strawberry-blonde locks of her hair. Which to Brury meant only one thing, she was worried about something.

"Hello, Fi," Brury said, hanging up his coat. "Fancy a drink?"

"No thank you, Daddy."

"Suit yourself."

Brury bypassed the living room and headed directly for the kitchen, thankful there was a can of Carling's brew with his name on it. He'd considered stopping at the Hansom Cab, the pub near the station house, fancying a pint and a bit of conversation that didn't have to do with crime and then decided he could do without conversation altogether. He poured the beer into his favorite tall glass, taking comfort in the small things in life that meant so much. He settled at the kitchen table and took a healthy pull from the glass. Grabbed for the bag of Walkers crisps, too, and began munching. Even though outside it was damp and cold and rainy and the fog was beginning to roll in, the cold lager felt like a godsend as it slid down his throat. A perfect complement to the cheese-and-onion-flavored crisps. He didn't realize that his eyes were closed, so he missed the fact that Fiona had joined him.

"Oh, Fi, hi."

"I've decided to take you up on that drink offer," she said, pouring herself a glass of white wine. She sat down across from him, her face sullen.

"You want to talk about it?" Brury asked her.

"I was going to ask you the same thing," she said. "How 'bout that, father and daughter on the same wavelength. Quick, call the press."

Brury's stomach grumbled in protest. "Oh, please don't."

"Rotten day, eh?"

"Had better, will have worse, I'm sure. It's just . . . this Timberlake case, it's downright puzzling, I'll admit to that one. Just when I thought I had a lead yesterday, it dried up, and my only suspect, this ever-elusive Richard Booker, slipped through my fingers. And then . . . I'm sorry, Fi, we were going to talk about what's troubling you."

Fiona drank down her wine. "Oh, the romantic wails of a twentysomething mean nothing in light of what you're facing— real life-and-death matters."

"For the moment, I would treasure knowing a bit about my daughter's, uh, love life. Certainly take my mind off the Timberlakes."

Fiona Brury needed no more persuading, and she launched into a discourse on why all men were pigs, all they wanted was sex—sorry, Daddy, she said, I am twenty-two—and Brury nodded because he'd once been twenty-two and wanting . . . that . . . and who else were you going to do . . . that . . . with than some woman who also had a father somewhere. She'd met this bloke—Clive, who when Brury had met briefly had given Brury the willies—at a pub, she'd been there with some friends and he'd started talking to her. He was charismatic, his own man, self-employed and slightly dangerous. He had sex appeal, and Fiona found that hard to resist.

"But lately, Daddy, I've been thinking he's . . . not what he seems. Or maybe he's more than he seems. I think he scares me."

"Then I think it's clear you shouldn't see him again. You know I don't like to interfere in your personal life, not unless you ask for it—which I'm assuming you're doing now. Fi, when he came to pick you up the other day I got a bad vibe from him. Found him completely unsuitable for you, despite his polite demeanor. It was overly polite, if you ask me. Downright fake. Just remind him your father is a police officer, that'll even up the score, he'll be scared of you."

"Oh, that's the thing, that's when he changed."

Brury's ears perked up, his investigative skills once again alive. "What exactly does that mean? Fiona?"

Fiona squirmed in her chair, just as she'd done as a child when she'd brought home a note from her teacher. Some characteristics you never outgrow.

"Fiona Ramona Brury, I want you to tell me what this Clive fellow did."

"He broke into someone's home—and he made me stand watch so he didn't get caught."

Brury didn't react the way she might have expected, a big blowup that would get his stomach going again. No, Fiona was in trouble and she was confessing her sins and he needed to be a father first, a detective second. Still, there was no reason both men couldn't get more details, and so he asked her to explain what had happened. And that's what Fiona did, she told him everything, how Clive had picked the lock, spent about a half hour inside the home. The important detail, though, was the fact that, a couple days later, Clive had told Fiona to go away, he was busy and didn't need her inexperience getting in the way.

"Inexperience? What did he mean by that, Fi?"

"He said that when we left that home, I'd left the door open and that's how the owner knew someone had been there. I guess she knew he'd been there—Clive himself. Oh, Daddy, he was furious with me."

"And that's why you've been hiding out here, twirling your already curly hair?"

She smiled. "Yes."

"Okay, Fi, I appreciate your honesty here, and believe me,

nothing is going to happen to you, it's this Clive fellow who's at fault. I'm glad you're away from him. But I need to know, I need to report the break-in and see about helping the folks whose house he burgled. Do you think you could find it again?"

Fiona nodded. "Oh, yes, it's nearby."

Once again Brury's instinctive hackles were raised. "How nearby?"

"Onslow Square, real nice home it was."

Was being the operative word, Brury thought. "Fi, do you know why I was wrested from my bed so early this morning—on a Saturday? It was because a fire had broken out at a home on a nearby street. You may have even heard the sirens. Now, fires aren't my concern usually, but this had a particular connection to the case I'm working on. Remember the one where the husband was shot dead inside the flat he managed, and a week later the wife found shot, as well, after having been fished out of the Thames? Vance and Clara Timberlake lived in South Kensington, in a very nice home on Onslow Square."

"Oh, Daddy, what have I done?"

"You, nothing, darling," Brury said, drinking his Carling. "Clive, perhaps a great deal."

Brury finished off his beer and Fiona her wine, and then he asked her to accompany him on a short trip. They both donned their coats and umbrellas and battling against the rain and the wind, they walked along the busy Old Brompton Road until reaching the picturesque—even in this weather—Onslow Square. A short walk down, Brury pointed to what was once that "very nice home," now with its white facade blackened from fire and smoke.

"Oh, Daddy."

"The inside is worse, totaled actually. It's as though someone is systematically trying to wipe out any existence of the Timberlakes—their lives, their home, the very notion of their existence.

I need to know, Fi, is this the home you and Clive broke into?"

Fiona nodded, her tears indistinguishable from the rain which splattered her face.

Brury's mind was racing.

"Where can I find this Clive fellow?"

"I'll take you there."

"No, Fi, I don't want you further involved. Just tell me where, and then I want you to go straight home and lock the door, don't let anyone in, especially not Clive." He paused. "This Clive, does he go by any other name?"

Fiona gazed at her father with empty eyes. "No, why?"

"What about the name Richard Booker, does that mean anything to you?"

"Never heard of him."

"Okay, thanks, Fi. Now, that bloke's address?"

She gave him instructions for an address in Vauxhall and he grabbed the first cab he saw, commandeering it for official police business. The cabbie, glad to do his part in keeping London safe, drove like a madman through the wet, glistening streets, along the Chelsea Embankment and Grosvenor Road until crossing the Vauxhall Bridge. A few minutes was all it took, Brury feeling like he'd just overpaid for a ride on a roller coaster.

"Good 'nuf, guvner?" the cabbie asked.

"Yes, thanks," he said, happily stepping out of the cab.

Brury was standing before the Frog and the Firkin pub, the address of it corresponding with the information Fiona had supplied. He circled around the building, found the entrance to the flats and realized he was stymied. No key, no search warrant. Well, that's what probable cause was for, he was on the trail of a suspected killer. Next thing he knew he was kicking in the door, the force behind it surprising himself. To hell with Tums, the better fix for an upset stomach was to release those bottled up endorphins. Brury went racing up the steps and

334

without any announcement, kicked down the door to the top floor flat.

With his gun raised, he entered the flat.

And just what did he see? A gun staring right back at him.

The time was eight-thirty and the clock was still very much ticking.

CHAPTER TWENTY-THREE

Clive Remington's fingers tingled and his blood ran fast, his adrenaline at peak power. Yes, this was the feeling which even he agreed was better than sex, the anticipation before the kill, the explosion of the gun like a climax, and as we know already about Clive, he likes to withhold that moment for as long as possible. So today he had been savoring the seduction, waiting for just the right moment for his release. His trusty revolver fit snugly in the jacket pocket of his London Fog overcoat, the perfect guise on this day of downpours. Tonight he'd even gone so far as to use an umbrella, there was no taking a chance at messing with the gun's well-oiled mechanics.

He was positioned across from the Mayfair Mansions. Elise Procopio may have failed in uncovering the secret location for her anniversary celebration, but that only meant Clive needed to step up to the challenge. He might just charge Elise a bit more for the trouble; really, following Henri around all day hadn't been easy, especially on these short, curving streets of Mayfair when one cab successfully pursuing another was chancy at best. But it had worked, and once he knew the where, he could relax, concentrate more on the who, what, and when. He couldn't care less about the why, and he knew the how. A simple shot, at ten o'clock she'd demanded, the timing had to be ideal. We'll see.

He'd watched as the limousine poured out the supposedly

happy couple. He'd watched as the catering van pulled up, the two women using the back servants' entrance to load in plates of food, wine, champagne, dinnerware and crystal, to the point where Clive had to wonder if the Procopios were expecting more than just themselves; was Henri hosting a dinner party? That worried Clive; Elise had assured him this was definitely a party for two. Which it turned out was the case, no one else showed up. Unless you counted the damned violinist.

"Bloody sod, he's thought of everything," Clive remarked.

Still, under cover of night at last and with the fog beginning to roll in off Green Park, the wet sidewalks giving off a shimmering glow underneath the streetlamps, Clive was eager to get the job done. Surely the caterers were nearly finished with their duties. He needed them gone, there need not be any witnesses— other than Elise, the cold-blooded little bitch. Clive rubbed himself at the thought of what was soon to happen; maybe he'd need to have his way with Elise, make the entire robbery thing look legit. That would serve her right.

Clive was glad for the rain, it kept foot traffic to a minimum. Nothing aroused suspicion like a man who'd been hanging around scoping out a particular house all day. Now, though, Clive saw a gentleman heading down the street, so he himself started walking, hiding along the passageway to the servants' entrance. When the man turned down that same mews, Clive's mind began to race. Who was he? What did he want?

As the man approached the rear door, Clive reached out and grabbed him, bringing his gun down hard on the stranger's head. Knocking the man unconscious. It was only then, as the man crumbled to the ground, that Clive saw just what role he could play at the anniversary celebration of Henri and Elise Procopio.

"Good Lord," Clive said appropriately, a smile lighting his face.

The time was eight forty-five.

Todd was sitting in the dark when the door opened and light spilled in from the hallway. First he saw the shadow of the gun, then the gun itself, shadowed itself by the figure holding it. His finger itched against the trigger, but his palm was sweaty, making it difficult to maintain his hold on his own gun. Shit, he thought, goodbye cruel world.

"Don't shoot," he suddenly heard, an unfamiliar voice. Now who?

"I don't think I could if I wanted to," Todd replied.

The new arrival flicked on the overhead light and Todd's eyes squinted in the sudden brightness. When his pupils readjusted, he found himself staring at a fifty-ish man, gray hair, slightly rumpled and slightly overweight. He looked harmless enough. Appearances, though, could be deceiving, and he did have that gun pointing straight at him. What was it with the guns this week? They really didn't come into play in his choice of profession, his usually simple lottery cons. Still, he was thankful this man was not Clive. Todd released the gun, watched it fall harmlessly to the carpeted floor.

"Who are you?" Todd asked him.

"I think I'm in the position to ask the questions," the man replied.

No argument there. "Okay."

The older man approached him without a measure of concern. Todd was, after all, tied up, not even a danger to himself.

"Mr. Booker, I presume?"

Well, you could have knocked Todd over with a feather. Who was this man and how did he know . . . and then Todd knew the answer to both questions.

"Inspector Brury," Todd said.

"Very good, lad. I see you've finally found new accommodations after those arranged by Mr. Timberlake went belly up, though I can hardly think it's in an ideal neighborhood," Brury said, pointing to the fact that Todd was tied to the chair. "Not the Savoy, eh? But still better than Timberlake's current home. You want to tell me all about it?"

"I didn't kill Timberlake. Please, Inspector, can you untie me?"

"Not yet, I rather like having such a captive audience."

"Funny," Todd said. "But we don't have time for jokes, sir, there's somewhere I need to be . . . it's . . ." What? He was in the hands of the police, and they believed he was responsible for a couple of murders, was he now going to say he needed to stop a murder? He didn't even know where the hit was to take place and he'd all but run out of time.

"Come on, Mr. Booker, you were saying something?"

"I've forgotten."

"Where's Clive?" Brury asked.

"I don't know," Todd replied, honestly. "He's expected back—later."

"And you were going to shoot him? You're not exactly positioned well for maximum effect."

"No kidding."

"Mr. Booker, I've got nearly thirty years of police experience under my belt, dealing with crimes and criminals and some of the nastiest people you'd ever want to meet. It's a career where I've been very successful, honed to perfection by both experience and a natural instinct. Do you know what those instincts are telling me now?"

Todd shook his head.

"It's telling me I'm hardly in the company of a killer."

Todd stared at Brury, looking for any sign of trickery, or sarcasm, he was usually good at seeing either of those qualities. Nope, the inspector looked sincere, and worse, he looked like maybe he could be . . . trusted? Gosh, did Todd just think such a thought about this man, he who represented law enforcement and who was probably someone's father? As if to confirm his words, Brury stood up and untied the rope from Todd's body.

"Now that you're more comfortable, Mr. Booker—can I call you Richard?—"

Todd nodded, sure, anything but Todd Gleason.

"—good, now, why don't you tell me exactly what's going on, *Richard.*"

Why did everyone insist on speaking his name with italics? "I'd love to, *Inspector,* but right now . . . there's something more pressing I need to . . ."

"That's the second time you've mentioned your need to be elsewhere. Now, I'm one for being punctual for appointments but even you have to admit, Booker, that the investigation into a double murder, as well as a case of arson, takes precedence over anything else."

"Not if it's trying to prevent another killing," Todd blurted out.

The man blanched. "Excuse me, lad, what did you say? Who's going to die, and how do you know? Clive, isn't it, the two of you have cooked up some scheme and at the last minute he betrayed you, tied you up until he could finish with whatever he's plotting. Right?"

"Not exactly—look, Inspector, I'll tell you everything you need to know—later. But for now . . ."

"Yes, I know, that pressing appointment. Look, Booker, we're not leaving here until you give me something to go on."

"There's this man, an American here on vacation . . . holiday, whatever you want to call it, he's here celebrating his wedding anniversary tonight, only he doesn't know that his life is in danger, that Clive is going to end it."

"Henri Procopio," Brury said.

Todd's eyes widened with obvious surprise. This guy was good, he knew about Richard Booker, he knew about Henri Procopio, he even knew about Clive and how dangerous he was. But did he know how it was all tied together?

"How much else do you know?" Todd asked. "Do you know where the Procopios have gone, surely they've checked out of the Savoy by now. That was the plan, I recall. To celebrate at some fancy—and private—place."

"We'll compare notes in the cab. Between the two of us, I think we can figure out where they've gone and whether we're too late. Oh, and no funny stuff or you'll spend the rest of your life behind bars, that's a promise you can bet I'll keep."

Todd raised his hands, virtually turning himself in. "Best behavior."

Another cab, the same horrible rainy night. Todd was glad not to be behind the steering wheel this time, even if it meant he was sharing space in the back seat with a police officer. Who would have thunk it, he teaming up with the law to stop a murder from happening; or would they just be cleaning up the mess after Henri Procopio's death?

He hoped they weren't too late.

The time now was ten minutes after nine.

In the grand dining room, beneath a chandelier that housed soft warm glows, Elise and Henri Procopio sat at opposite ends of the table, more than satisfied. This was style, very much an old money kind of way of dining, and Elise had loved every minute of it. The serving girl, that poor unfortunate girl who could only dream of such a life, she bringing out course after course, salad with a champagne vinaigrette, succulent lobster with dripping butter sauce and filet mignon so tender they barely needed a knife to cut it. And wine, white first, then red, perfect vintages that had Elise's head swimming on top of the champagne and martinis she'd consumed. Now, as that serving girl—really, she was the only ugly thing about the whole décor—was busy removing the last of the plates, Henri rose from his chair, made his way down to Elise's end of the table, and held out his hand.

"My love, will you join me?"

"Where?"

"Please, indulge me."

She had so far, and it had been a perfectly marvelous experience. Maybe it was the wine, maybe the candlelight or the soft romantic music which was piped through a stereo system that had speakers hooked up to each room, but Elise had found herself being swallowed up by the mood, as though nothing beyond these walls existed. With her hand clasped gently in Henri's, he led her to the marble staircase that was covered in a glorious carpet of rose petals. Henri took a step upwards, and then said, "Come with me, more pleasures await."

Henri began the long climb upstairs, Elise at his side, her silver gown brushing against the stairs and the rose petals swirling beneath her. Just as they neared the top, Henri turned to her, knelt down in courtly fashion to help her with that last step. Elise, though, she either tripped on her gown or slipped on the silky rose petals—the booze maybe?—but she began to lose her balance and she cried out quickly, her sense of self-preservation strong. Henri's mouth opened in surprise and his hand instinctively reached out and latched onto hers, pulling her up that final step and avoiding what could have been a terrifying accident. She could have fallen, she could have died.

"Oh, Henri, Henri," Elise said, lying atop her husband at the top of the stairs, breathing heavily, the full implication of what had almost happened hitting her. "Oh, you saved me, my dear, sweet, wonderful Henri." Her body was trembling as Henri got her back to her feet, and he guided her along the final few steps to their destination.

Her face was white as a ghost, Henri's not much better.

Inside the luxury-laden bathroom, this room like the others lit by candlelight, was a sunken porcelain tub. Already filled with hot water and foamy bubbles, here was the perfect relaxant after a fulfilling meal, perhaps a good way to calm her down too after her almost nasty fall.

"You do think of everything, don't you," Elise said.

Henri helped her with her gown; that is, helped her out of her gown, revealing beneath it her slim, well-toned body, those supple breasts and pink nipples, jutting forth out of excitement or just plain fear from before, but prominent and wanting to be touched and caressed. Henri helped her into the tub. She "oohed" over the warmth of the water as it soaked her skin, penetrating deep into her aches and pains.

"Henri, aren't you joining me?" she asked.

"Oh yes, one moment," he said, retreating to the accompanying bedroom, where he brought forth a silver tray, on it two more flutes and one more bottle of champagne. He poured her a glass and handed it to her, her arm covered with bubbles and her face covered with a smile. Then Henri himself disrobed, and in seconds had plunged into the water. Elise and he clinked glasses in one more toast.

"This is the perfect ending to a perfect night," she said.

"Oh, the surprises aren't nearly completed, my Elise," Henri said, pulling her into his arms, feeling her body tight against his. Exciting him.

"So I can tell," Elise remarked with a throaty laugh.

"No, that's not the surprise I meant, you wicked woman."

Still, you take advantage of certain situations, and so there in the tub, while the water splashed around them and the bubbles disintegrated into the air, Henri and Elise Procopio made love, a fierce coupling, no doubt intensified after her near brush with death. When finally he released himself, Elise was in the throes of a climax all her own, and one she wasn't faking, oh no. What had gotten into Henri this week, his passion was absolutely limitless, almost as much as his bank account. Elise imagined herself living like this for years to come, surrounded by luxuries beyond her wildest dreams, Henri inside her, making her feel like the queen she knew she was.

That's when her eyes popped open, and she realized that the fantasy was just that. That life was on a collision course all its own, one she had completely set in motion.

"Oh, Elise, I love you so," Henri said, taking her in his arms. "And I'm going to prove it, because now that we've shared . . . well, the honeymoon, we're going to go backwards in time and relive the ceremony. The pièce de résistance, Elise, you won't believe it, but I have hired a minister and we're going to renew our vows—tonight."

Elise found she couldn't say anything, her throat too clogged with other, more conflicting emotions. So they'd each hired someone, but for altogether different reasons.

The time now? Nine-fifty.

Brury spent much of the time in the cab on his mobile phone. He'd called the office, asked one of the desk sergeants to check his file on the Timberlake murders. What he was looking for was an address he'd made a note of, the place Clara Timberlake had shown to Henri Procopio. As Brury explained, he'd taken down both the Savoy and this location in Mayfair, that much he knew, because had he not found Procopio at one place, surely he'd be at the other location. The sergeant found the address, Mayfair Mansions. A quick call to the Savoy confirmed that the Procopios had indeed checked out this afternoon. So the cabby had firm instructions on where to go. They hopped out at Berkeley Square, a block away from where the Procopios were staying— and presumably, Clive was lurking.

"Remember, Booker, this is a police investigation, I don't need any further interference from you," Brury warned Todd. "You've come this far only because I needed you to fill in some blanks. You've filled in the background, it's time for me to complete the picture. The wife put a hit out on her husband, you stumbled upon it and have been running from the hired killer all week. For now I'm buying this whole scenario, only because it sounds too crazy for you to have invented it all in the cab ride. But I'll want many more details later. Bollocks, I should have dropped you off at the station house and had you held there."

"We don't have time for that—and I'm not running, Brury."

"You're also not coming inside."

"But I'm the one who knows what Clive looks like."

"I know what he looks like, lad, don't you think my eyes took a good picture of the man who's been dating my daughter?"

"Your daughter . . . Fiona?"

Brury didn't want to discuss this now, he just told Todd to stay back. Brury withdrew his gun, keeping it carefully concealed. Together, they inched their way down the street, their eyes peeled for any suspicious activity. Other than their own. The only thing they noticed was the white catering van. Brury moved forward, walking up the steps to the front entrance, peering inside the window. Just a common hallway that serviced all the flats. He studied the names on the buzzer, Easton, Murphy, none of which meant anything. Those folks could be anywhere, renting out their flats during the off-season or they could just be out for a night on the town. In the flat to the right, not a light was on, but to the left came a glow of light through the lace curtains. Someone was home, and something

345

was going on in there. Brury wondered if he should ring the bell, this was official police business, after all. Maybe that would stop the hit from going down, just taking the simple approach. No heroics.

While Brury was busy playing it by the book, Todd slipped away from the front entrance, making his way down the foggy mews. He was drenched from the rain, hoped his squeaking shoes weren't loud enough to give himself away. Just then the door opened, and a woman emerged carrying a box marked "Pish Posh Caterers." Todd crept into the corner to avoid being seen; it worked, the woman just walked right past him. Todd seized the opportunity, entering the building through the back door. He found himself inside a large kitchen, where a second woman was packing up the last of the supplies but certainly taking her time doing so. Poor thing, she wasn't much to look at, Todd thought, trying to refocus on the problem at hand. Still, her calm manner told him at least nothing terrible had happened here; probably Clive wouldn't make a move until the caterers had left.

Was Clive even here yet?

And then the door to the kitchen opened and a man stepped inside. Todd drew back into the nearby pantry, happily gone unseen. But he'd certainly seen enough. The other man was Clive all right, and he was dressed . . . oh gee, that was sure to gain him the trust of whoever had let him in. Clever man.

Clive addressed the caterer. "The happy couple are getting dressed, so I have a spare moment. Is there any food left, I haven't eaten all day."

"Oh, I'm sorry, Reverend, everything's packed up."

"Yes, well, I suppose my job shouldn't take too long."

Todd was floored, and not just by Clive's ungodly imperson-ation of a minister. He waited as Clive retreated into the other room and then emerged from the musty pantry, quietly approaching the caterer. She still hadn't observed him. He grabbed her from behind, his hand covering her mouth. She struggled, trying to let out a scream and failing miserably. He dragged her into the pantry and closed the door, for privacy.

"Todd!" the woman said.

"Hello, Brandy," he said. "Nice disguise, another true masterpiece. Those buckteeth look very convincing. But you know, sometimes you should make an effort to hide those very obvious curves of your body, they're almost as memorable as your pretty face."

"Leave it to you to remember all the details," she said.

"You want to tell me what the hell you're doing here? Have you been in on this from the beginning? Who are you working for? Clive? Elise?" His mind reeled, how was that possible? Thankfully, it wasn't.

"No, no, God no," Brandy said, trying to kiss her way back into Todd's good graces. For the moment it wasn't working. "I . . . I felt bad, Todd, ditching you like I did. When all you'd been was good to me, trusting, helping me get out from under Daddy's cheap clutches. But there I was after my happy reunion with Daddy, en route to some beautiful Caribbean island when I remembered the plight of the Procopios. I couldn't go, not knowing what I knew. The money I had, it suddenly felt like blood money. We were supposed to use the money to get rid of the Birdies, sure, but it was also to stop Clive. Besides, I also knew you'd come back to London and try to stop it; I wanted to be part of the action. So I hopped the first flight, and when I arrived here I kinduv bribed the girl who was supposed to cater."

"Why should I believe you?"

"Maybe this will convince you of my intentions," she said. She kissed him, a big, wet, long, passionate, knock-your-socks-off kind of kiss, and when at last they parted, Brandy said,

"That kind of passion, Todd, you can't fake."

"Well, isn't that nice?"

That wasn't Todd's voice, and it wasn't Brandy's either. Nope, the door was open and good Ol' Clive was standing before them, watching this tender exchange between the two people who had been the bane of his existence all week. He had his gun outstretched, really he looked quite oddly juxtaposed with his minister's collar and that big-ass revolver.

"Say your prayers," Clive said, funny guy that he was.

"Yes, prayers . . . and vows, too. Huh, Reverend?"

Todd watched as Clive's expression faltered, because a new voice had entered the fray. Another person had entered the kitchen. Clive stuffed the gun quickly back into his pocket. Then he turned and smiled at the sudden appearance of his able host, one Henri Procopio. The man was dressed in a smashing tuxedo, so crisp and elegant.

"Who were you talking to?" Henri asked.

Clive opened the door to the pantry more fully, revealing the con man and the caterer, still locked in a tight embrace, less out of passion and more out of survival.

"I realized you needed witnesses—for the ceremony," Clive said, not very convincingly. "Well, come on, you two, we need your help. I managed, Mr. Procopio, to persuade this lovely caterer and her, uh, boyfriend who just came by to pick her up, that they could act as your witnesses . . ."

Henri wasn't buying it. He might not have recognized Brandy/Charity under yet another of her disguises, but he sure as hell knew the boyfriend, one Richard Booker. "What the hell's going on here? That man," Henri said, pointing, "is nothing but a two-bit con and . . . oh, of course, hello Miss Willow, I see you've recovered from your scars. Though now it looks like you need a capable dentist. As for you, Reverend, I don't quite understand what's going on, but all I know is I've paid good money . . ."

"Shut up. Now," Clive said, removing the gun from his pocket and pointing it at Henri. "There's not going to be a wedding. Very possibly, though, a funeral. Come on, all of you, let's retire to the living room, not a very apt name, though, huh?"

The revolver was big enough to intimidate them all, and Todd, Brandy, and Henri formed a frightened little conga line out of the kitchen and through the dining room. When they made their way into the foyer, Todd was thinking, Brury, where the hell are you and why haven't you called for back-up yet? His thoughts were interrupted by a new voice to the mix, the only other voice it could have been. Elise Procopio, who called out to her husband from the top of the stairs. Everyone turned and looked up, Clive, Henri, Brandy, Todd. There stood Elise in a lovely white wedding dress, the flickering candlelight casting an aura of light around her, creating an angel-like vision. A veil covered her face, but she lifted it and even from this distance Todd could see confusion . . . horror cross her lovely face. Her eyes fell upon Clive. Henri had been gazing at Elise, but then he too looked at Clive. Clive raised his gun and pointed it at Henri.

"Oh, no . . . Elise . . ." Henri said, as though he'd just then figured the whole thing out.

"Freeze!"

The sound of this one-man cavalry shattered the quiet of the night, and what happened next, well, only slow motion could do it justice.

Brury had at last appeared and was pointing his gun at Clive. Clive turned toward Brury and pulled the trigger. Brury did the same, while somehow diving out of the way. The bullet missed Brury, who crashed to the floor. As for Clive, the bullet from Brury's gun caught him in the shoulder and he reeled back- wards. Taking advantage of Clive's weakened state, Todd lunged for the killer, while Brandy grabbed at Henri and shoved him out of the way. Elise, she watched from the top of the stairs at the violence that was transpiring below her, all of it happening because of her.

"Bloody bastard," Clive yelled as Todd landed on top of him. Todd got off a good slap across Clive's face, then punched him real good. But Clive kneed Todd, missing the groin but getting his stomach, causing Todd to lose his advantage as he doubled over in pain. Clive recovered quickly, and with blood pouring from his shoulder wound but his grip still strong on his gun, aimed it at Todd. Just then an explosive burst from a gun set off further screams and Clive recoiled again, this time hit in the thigh and thrown against the stairs, his blood mixing with the rose petals, turning them a darker shade of crimson. Damn if that Brury wasn't a good shot.

But Clive wasn't down for the count, no, he got up from the stairs, slightly dizzy from the loss of blood and searing pain shooting through his body. Not even attempting to aim, he shot off two bullets in quick succession and he heard one blood-curdling scream, really just an awful sound, the kind of sound which could haunt nightmares for years. That was followed by a crashing and a tumbling that seemed to go on forever. And everyone turned to watch helplessly as Elise Procopio rolled down the marble stairs, rose petals flying high into the air, sprinkling the image of death with a remarkable vision of beauty. She landed at the base of the stairs face up, and there in the center of her chest was a blossoming pool of blood forever staining the white wedding dress she wore. Clive's bullet had hit probably the one person he hadn't wanted to hit, the person with the checkbook.

"ELISE!" Henri yelled out, running now to her side. He grabbed her, cradled her.

Todd and Brandy stood over them, watching this last terrible scene, knowing there was nothing further that could be done for Elise Procopio.

There was nothing further to do—at the moment—about Clive Remington either. In the drama of Elise's fall, Clive had managed to slip away, leaving a bloody trail behind him. Brury ran after him, the two of them disappearing into the foggy night. He fruitlessly returned minutes later, while Elise still lay at the base of the stairs and Henri sat on the sofa in the living room, Brandy trying her best to comfort him. Todd, waiting on the doorstep, looked at Brury.

The inspector shook his head. "He got away."

The time was ten-thirty.

Ninety minutes to a new day and good thing, this one had sucked.

Still, though, Todd knew there was much about this horrible mess that remained unfinished.

CHAPTER TWENTY-FOUR

What a mess.

Elise Procopio was pronounced dead at the scene of her own fantasy wedding. Henri Procopio was taken to the hospital and treated for shock, so was the real minister who was scheduled to perform the canceled nuptials, he found lying in the back alley with a big bump on his head but otherwise okay. Credit Clive with not killing the clergy; maybe he had hopes for himself in the afterlife? Brandy and Todd were escorted to the Kensington police station, where they were questioned for hours by Albert Brury, who had fortunately found a spare pack of Tums in his desk drawer. Out came the truth; well, most of it. Todd admitted to finding Timberlake's body but ran because he was scared; he really was only looking to book the flat. He copped to calling the police, taking that particular fall for Birdie, whose role in all of this remained undisclosed. Why had Todd come to London, Brury wanted to know, and that's when Brandy jumped in, saying they had recently broken up because she was studying in Cambridge and didn't want to carry on a long-distance relationship and Todd followed her, trying to prove he could live here and be with her. Todd did tell Brury about being taken hostage by two of Clive's thugs, Bobo and Larry (sorry, no last names known), that they'd left him to die at Clive's hands, why not turn those bastards in? He gave good descriptions of them. As for Clive, the way Todd told it, the man was afraid Todd was trying to hone in on his territory, that Timberlake was getting ready to end his business relationship with Clive. So no doubt Clive killed Timberlake, and then in trying to cover his tracks, realized Clara Timberlake knew all about her husband's sideline jobs. So she had had to die, and then their home had been torched, both acts performed by Clive, who was desperately trying to destroy all evidence of the contract killings he'd been hired to perform. Of course, Todd had no evidence of any of this, it was pure speculation. And he still didn't know who had killed Vance Timberlake.

"Bloody hell," Brury said, "and I was convinced all along that the Timberlakes were so innocent, my God, what was happening just blocks away from my own home? Makes me want to remove Fiona from such a bad element, keep her safe."

In the end, Todd and Brandy were released—pending further investigation.

"It depends on what Mr. Procopio has to say."

So with that lingering detail hanging over their heads, Todd and Brandy left the police station. Time was nearly six in the morning, Sunday, and even though Clive was still out there somewhere, he had two bullet wounds in him and as a result they felt safe enough. They walked the waking streets of London, still wet after the incessant rains of the day before, but there was a new scent in the air and perhaps even the sun might shine today. The fog was lifting, literally and figuratively. Brandy grabbed Todd's hand, happy to be back at his side.

"So, now what, Todd?"

"Well, there's still the issue of my friend Beth Simon. Bobo and Larry—they've still got her hostage and I still need to figure out a way to free her. Though I suspect they'll release her once they read the morning papers and learn about what happened at the Mayfair Mansions last night. That's my hope, anyway. Bobo seemed a bit defensive when I asked him about Beth. I think he kind of likes her."

"Very strange, the whole thing. But you, Todd, you're such a good man, you risked so much to save Henri Procopio and you did," she said. "When this is all over, I think we should both go to that Caribbean island I almost went to, you and I can celebrate our freedom from the things that haunt us. There I can show you how much I appreciate all you've done for me. Beth may be a hostage still, but I'm not, no longer. Remember, we've got Daddy's money."

Todd looked away, not able to face Brandy.

"What's wrong?"

"You're going to hate me, Brandy, because I'm going to spoil that admittedly perfect scenario with an awful bit of truth. After what you did, the way you ran off back in New York, taking the money with you and leaving no explanation, well, I felt so . . . betrayed. I turned you in, Brandy—to your father. I sent him an e-mail—from your address no less—telling him the entire kidnapping was a scam, and that you'd organized it."

"You did what!"

"I'm sorry, Brandy . . . it's just . . . you left, you left with all the money. I was left with . . . with nothing except the threat of being hunted down by the police—no thanks to Marta Birdie. How did you expect me to respond? It was impulsive, stupid, but . . ."

"Oh, Todd, what have you done to me? Daddy will insist on having the money back, insist I go back to Cambridge—or worse, keep me close, stuck under his overprotective thumb. This is worse than prison, it's a death sentence."

They had been walking without knowing where they were headed, through Hyde Park, that's all they knew. Turned out, they found themselves at the edge of the park, back at the Marble Arch, where they had last separated in London. Beneath the busy intersection was that crazy maze of exits. Brandy, in tears, said she wanted to use the bathroom to fix herself up, and so Todd patiently waited for her in that concrete courtyard. Wondering what she was thinking, what she was going to do. Could she forgive him his betrayal? He'd forgiven her, right? Sounded lame and desperate even as he thought it. He waited, and he waited some more. Ten minutes elapsed and there was no Brandy. Todd waited another five, saw no one either enter or leave the ladies' toilet, and so he ventured inside.

It was empty.

Brandy was gone, she'd somehow given him the slip. Todd wasn't completely surprised and wondered if in a way he'd let her go, that he knew it was over from the moment he'd spilled the truth. She could have escaped from any number of these exits, be headed in any direction. Probably to that Caribbean island, with four hundred thousand dollars of her father's money. She might as well have a bit of fun before the shit hit the fan. Good luck, Brandy, it's been fun, it's been real, and it's been real fun. She had the money, now, and Todd, what did he have? He had come to London to get his hands on a mere one hundred thou, had managed to get five hundred thou by returning to New York, and then he'd lost it all. With costs, he was deep in the red instead, the entire scam an absolute disaster. There was nothing left to do, nowhere to go.

Where he ended up that morning was Beth Simon's flat in Marylebone. He still had her spare key and he needed sleep, maybe sleep for days on end. He unlocked the door and was surprised to see that he wasn't alone. For a fleeting second he gave out hope that he'd be greeted by Brandy. No such luck, there was ugly Beth Simon, sitting on her sofa with a book, and at her side was none other than Bobo, who was listening to her voice go on and on, a big smile lighting up his face.

"Todd!" Beth said, dropping the book. "Oh my God, I thought you'd disappeared for good, look at you, you look terrible, come on, sit down, can I get you something to eat or drink or . . . what's been going on? Can you believe it, Bobo tells me it's all over, that I'm safe and thankfully so are you, oh, Todd, guess what? I've fallen in love, I know, I can hardly believe it, Andy's got his doubts but so what, he doesn't run my life . . ."

Todd's mind was reeling and he was trying to absorb everything he'd just heard, which was quite a lot (how nice that this experience hadn't changed Beth Simon), she was still that chatterbox who had such a zest for life. And apparently a zest for Bobo, Bobo who through eye contact was trying to convey a message to Todd. Don't turn me in. Well, not to Beth, he wouldn't, but the police? Too late. Maybe he could work out a deal with Brury, for Beth's sake. Still, Bobo aside, there were a couple important points made in that torrent of words, and Todd was trying to sort through them.

"Wait, Beth, did you say Clive was no longer a problem?"

It was Bobo who nodded. "He's not the only one who can follow folks without being seen."

Todd nodded as he felt a bit of unsettled tension lift away. But that still left a tremendous amount more. "Beth, what's this about Andy? When did you talk to him?"

"Oh, a couple days ago—Friday I guess it was, told him about Bobo and me, he's skeptical but happy for me, that's our Andy, one big skeptic."

Since Friday? How could Andy have known she was safe? Dread fell over Todd like the proverbial ton of bricks. "Oh, shit," Todd said, thinking Andy was a lot more than a skeptic, he was one big fat liar, probably better than Todd would ever be. A stockbroker looking out for other people's interests—and interest. Right, and Richard Booker is my real name. Andy was not just a liar, was it he who was the bigger con man? Todd turned right around and headed out of the flat.

"Where's he going?" Bobo asked.

"Good question. Todd, what's going on? Todd you just got

here, you need rest and food and oh, what's that boy doing now? To think, once there wasn't anything I wouldn't have done for him. Bobo, do you think we should go after him? Oh, never mind . . . *Bobo* . . . BOBO!"

At least some people had found happiness.

As for Todd, he didn't hear that Bobo had stopped Beth from talking. He didn't hear her giggles, her eager squeals. Todd's mind was reeling, and all he could hear were his feet, running, running once again and one last time down the hardened pavements of the London streets.

Todd arrived back in New York Monday afternoon; it had taken him that long to get back his passport from Inspector Brury and hop, yes, another flight. Twenty-four agonizing hours had passed, giving Todd ample time to worry about Andy Simon. Meanwhile, the newspapers, here like in London, were filled with photos and articles and gossip about the death of Elise Procopio, some of the details right on the money but none confirmed by any of the people involved. Henri Procopio was in seclusion, his whereabouts unknown, according to a company spokesman. But the article did have a big benefit for Henri Procopio, the stock for Looking Great Cosmetics had soared at the opening of the market. Sympathy? Perhaps, or maybe greedy investors knowing this was the time to take advantage of a company's very public profile. As they say, there's no such thing as bad publicity.

Todd tossed the papers aside and grabbed a cab at JFK and headed directly for Andy Simon's office at Bernstein, Gilbert & Young down in the financial district. Was he expected? No, but I'm a friend, Todd told the security guard in the lobby, I've just arrived from London and I'm supposed to be staying at Andy's place, see I've even got my bags. Maybe it was the luggage that did it, or the truthful details about Andy's life that Todd was more than forthcoming with, but the guard handed over a visitor's pass and Todd was soon hurtling up to the sixteenth floor. When he arrived at the reception area, he asked the woman behind the desk to please ring Andy Simon.

"Oh, I'm sorry, he's not come back from lunch. If you'd like to have a seat, Mr. . . ."

"Gleason. Todd Gleason. I'm an old friend of his." This Todd said through gritted teeth. Old friend? Try former friend. Not back from lunch, my ass, it was nearly five in the afternoon. But Todd figured he'd give it a few minutes, what more did he have to lose but time, so he took up a position on the sofa next to a preserved woman of indeterminate age who was biting her once manicured nails. He tossed her a sympathetic smile, his dimples causing the woman to gaze back in acknowledgment. She couldn't smile, not with all the work she'd had done.

"You look like you're waiting to see the executioner," he said.

"Oh, no, once I get my hands on the weasel, I'll be playing the executioner."

"You're not waiting for Andy Simon, are you?"

She flashed him a look. "Not anymore, the bastard. I've been waiting three hours and he's still at lunch. My ass, he is."

Just then a set of wooden doors opened and a distinguished-looking—and familiar-looking—gentleman with silver hair approached the reception area. Todd squirmed in his seat, afraid he'd suddenly been exposed. But the man ignored Todd and said, "Mrs. Ledbetter, I'm Thomas Marquand Alexander, one of the senior partners. Sorry for the delay, it's been one of those crazy days in the market and I've been locked up in meetings all day. I'm sorry for this confusion about Mr. Simon, I can't for the life of me understand where he is. He's usually so reliable. Will you come back and tell me what's wrong?"

"Thank you, yes, and please, call me Mimi. As for what's wrong," Mrs. Ledbetter said as she got to her feet, "is that that snake stole a fortune from me, those Looking Great stocks paid off huge today and . . ."

Mr. Alexander stopped her and said, "Did you say Looking Great . . . ?"

And then those thick wooden doors closed and Todd was shut off from anything more revealing. Todd sat in the reception area in absolute shock, trying to absorb exactly what'd he'd just heard. So many ideas were swirling in his mind, but one of them did pop to the surface, and in seconds Todd was racing out of the building, hailing a cab, directing the driver to Sutton Place.

"Traffic's bad," the cabbie announced.

"Yeah, when isn't it," Todd said angrily. Why did he always get the drivers with attitude? If you didn't want to deal with New York traffic, what the fuck were you doing driving a cab?

Twenty minutes later he was being let off in front of Andy's building, where he just waved a hello to the doorman who'd been on duty the other day.

"No, no, don't announce me, it's a surprise," Todd said, thinking oh boy, was it ever.

"But Mr. Gleason . . ."

Todd arrived at his desired floor and used his key to enter the apartment and . . .

"Shit, shit, shit."

He was getting tired of empty apartments. With sudden fear, Todd made his way over to the frog tank, tapping his fingertips against the side. Toad sprung to life and Todd, for a brief moment, felt comforted by the fact that at least some things were still the same. Todd went to feed his pet, since there was no telling when last he'd been treated to some nourishment. That's where Todd found the note, in a simple white envelope marked "Todd" in a familiar scrawl, one he'd known since college, when the two guys had been part of an inseparable trio, back when trust between friends was a given.

TODD: By now you've probably learned the truth. Sorry, my friend. All that talk about early retirement, I suppose it got to me. That daily chase for the next big payoff, it was wearing thin and so I decided to take advantage of a certain situation. You've had your fun since college, not working and somehow still making a living, while I've been working my ass off with no end in sight, and little reward. So I decided to reward myself. I couldn't really see you retiring anyway, Todd, not from the cons, you live for them. So consider this a license to continue your life as you've been living it, pros, cons, and all. And know this, you're a hell of a teacher, see how much I learned? Though I'm still trying to figure out what you were doing conning my boss, I'll think about that one while I sip Mai Tais on some sunny beach. Don't despair, my friend, there's always the lottery, hey, you never know? All you need is a dollar and a dream, so they say. ANDY.

"Fuck," Todd said, tossing down the letter.

He didn't even need to check his offshore account to know it was empty, completely drained of everything he'd been working for. He'd entrusted it to Andy, who for years had helped exponentially increase it, seemingly doing it for the good of their friendship, for the good of Todd. Ha.

As Brandy might have said, "Now what?" only this time Todd was asking it of his good friend Toad, perhaps the only living creature he could depend on.

Because Todd Gleason was now and suddenly flat broke. He was not going back to temping for a living, Lucille and her employment agency were no longer an off-duty option. This past week, defeating a killer, outsmarting him and saving the day, well, Todd had joined the big leagues.

So what he needed, and needed fast, was one last con. The biggest.

Fortunately for Todd, the idea had already occurred to him.

He had a call to make, a job to secure.

A week, that's how long he'd needed to wait.

But that next Monday morning, Todd dressed in his best suit, looking very much the corporate raider that he wasn't. But he had to look the part of the eager shark to pull off what he hoped was going to be the biggest payoff of his young life. For the past week he'd been living hand to fist, comfortably settled back into his apartment, Toad at his side again. He hadn't the money for lottery tickets and so he'd been just plain bored, reading the newspapers at the library and keeping current with all the news of the world, London, New York, the financial papers, anything. Now, that very long week was over, and Todd was ready.

He hopped the subway, because it was fast and it was cheap, and before long he was standing before a glass and chrome skyscraper in the heart of Times Square. With the crowds of workers heading for their offices, Todd just looked like one of the bunch. Except he had a slight gleam in his eye, while all those others looked like drones, ready for another week of corporate nothingness. He watched as everyone took out their cardkeys and passed through the turnstiles, where two guards were standing, um, guard.

One of them said to Todd, "Can I help you, sir?"

"Oh, yes, I'm temping here, sorry, I wasn't sure just what to do."

"Yes, we need to call upstairs and confirm your assignment," the man said, wearing a uniform that proved he worked for the building's management company. "Who were you scheduled to work for?"

So Todd told him, stating it had been arranged by Street Help Temporary Services, and after everything had been confirmed and Todd was hurtling up his way to the twenty-ninth floor, he said a silent thank you to Lucille, who never failed to get him the type of assignment he wanted. She'd been confused the other day, though, and had said of his request, "You usually want the financial companies, what's with your sudden interest in the fashion biz?"

"Oh, I'm expanding my horizons," he'd told her.

In the elevator, he took one last look at this neatly dressed self and thought, hey, I'm looking great.

And then the doors opened up to the corporate offices of Looking Great Cosmetics.

The reception area was beautifully decorated, shimmering glass tables and black metal chairs, very modern. Todd announced himself to the receptionist, who fortunately didn't know that he was the man who was supposed to be temping there. Instead, he just said, "Yes, I'm Mr. Richard Booker of Brury Investigations, I'm here to see Mr. Procopio." The sweet receptionist punched in numbers with elongated fingernails— pink, with black and white swirls on them—all the while smiling back at Todd. She spoke into the phone and a frown crossed her pretty face.

"Mr. Procopio's secretary says she knows nothing about your appointment."

"Tell her it was arranged personally with Mr. Procopio, and that she should announce Mr. Richard Booker. The man will see me."

"Okay . . ." she said, suddenly doubting his story. Not that he'd told much of one.

Still, he was getting antsy, and he was worried too about the person he was supposed to check in with about his temp gig. He had no intention of clacking away all day at a computer, no, he had more pressing business. At least, he hoped he did. He wiped a bit of sweat from his forehead, hoped his newly surfacing nervousness wasn't too visible. Last thing he needed was for security to come and escort him out . . .

Just then a set of glass doors opened and there stood an imposing woman of six feet. She could have been the female equivalent of our friend Larry back there in London.

"Come with me, Mr. Booker," she said, her voice stern.

Todd was led down a corridor and escorted into an office marked "Henri Procopio."

"Have a seat."

The wait lasted only five minutes and Todd didn't mind. The surroundings were nice and it gave him time to pull together his thoughts. So far, so good, he'd gotten through many gauntlets. Then Henri Procopio, dapperly dressed in a dark blue suit—not black, Todd noted—entered his office, his style fast and breezy, as though he'd been running a marathon. He was smiling, which was surprising, and he was affable in his greeting, not at all what Todd had been expecting.

"Sorry, sorry, business meetings and such, they do go on. My new creative director had so many ideas, it took nearly two hours to cover them, we've been here since seven this morning ironing out our new plans. But that's what happens in the big bad business world, and sometimes that early start enables you to beat the competition," he said, taking a seat behind his desk. He laced his fingers and then Todd found the man staring right back at him. "Well, Mr. Booker, I admire your guts in coming here."

"Sir?"

"I could have you arrested, you know. That scam you pulled on me in London, it almost succeeded."

"Yes, sir. Desperate times and all."

"Indeed," he said. "But I'm not going to call the cops, no I'm going to shake your hand."

And he did, his grip firm. Todd's face revealed his confusion.

363

"Yes, I suppose this isn't exactly going the way you'd scripted it."

"Sir?"

"My nice guy routine, you didn't expect it. Still, I'm sure you've come here to convince me to part with some of my money, though for the life of me I can't imagine what you've thought up this time. Something better than Miss Willow's spurious injuries. So, come on, out with it, I'm a busy man these days. It's exciting to be back on top."

Henri's forceful, take-charge nature was putting Todd on the defensive, and that wasn't the position he wanted to be in. But it was now or never, and so Todd cleared his throat. "Mr. Procopio, your dearly departed wife was willing to pay a man one million pounds—nearly two million dollars—to end your life. She very nearly succeeded. So what I'm looking for, it's not based on some con or by trying to deceive you. You're too smart to fall for anything like that, I learned that lesson in London. No, I'll be absolutely honest, thanks to me and what I stumbled upon across the pond, you weren't killed, and in fact the whole experience has turned out very well for you. Looking Great's stocks rose, your public image is huge—and sympathetic to your plight—really, I suspect you've had quite the windfall since you went on what you thought was a vacation."

"Yes, I'll admit that my cash flow problem has reversed itself. In fact, I'd been planning to sell my company and retire, only no one would meet my high standards—or high price. Perhaps that was my subconscious not wanting me to sell, who knows. But just last week, a consortium of men approached me with a bid for my company—it was worth a lot more suddenly, more than the original price I was asking. I upped the price even more, but it proved too rich for their blood and one of their banks pulled out. But I would have turned them down anyway, and you want to know why? Because I'd been given a new lease on life, and I realized the last thing I wanted was to leave behind all I had built. Elise had been dragging me down for years. Now . . . ?" He actually smiled.

"Indeed, just my point, you've come out of this smelling like rose petals . . ."

Henri frowned at that one. "Get to the point, son."

"I think you owe me a reward—for saving your life."

"Hah, that's a good one. And how much do you think is fair?"

"Well, like I said, your wife was willing to pay two million to have you killed, so saving your life ought to be worth at least half of that amount, don't you think?"

"You want me to write you a check for one million dollars?"

"Well, actually I prefer a wire transfer—to this account." He handed over a slip of paper on which were written a series of numbers. He considered them his lottery numbers.

"Bollocks, as they say in England. You must be out of your mind."

"Hardly, sir. And I think in the end you'll give it to me."

"And why is that?"

"Do we really need to get into that, Mr. P?" This was good, now Todd had just turned the tables and he had Procopio on the defensive. "You see, Henri—may I call you Henri? Good— I've had some time this past week to think about everything that happened in London and one thing still sticks in my craw. When I told you about what Elise had been plotting—in the lobby of the Savoy, you recall?—you told me that the police had already been to see you and that you could have turned me in then. You knew they were looking for Richard Booker—for murder, no less. Why didn't you tell them about me, I wondered? Surely you had nothing to fear from the police, you were just an innocent bystander, on vacation with his wife, plotting . . . uh, sorry, planning the most romantic night imaginable to celebrate your anniversary."

"What's your point, kid?"

"Well, since only you and I are privy to that little detail, I suspect we're the only ones who know the truth behind the entire trip. That all along you were planning to kill your wife."

Henri froze in place as those words hovered in the air between them. Todd watched carefully for any movement, any twitch, any hint of body language that might reveal the thoughts inside the aging man's fuzzy dome.

"That's a load of hogwash, my boy—imaginative, I'll give you that. But rubbish."

"Is it? Remember, sir, I had done my research on you and Elise before undertaking my con and if I learned one thing, it was how much Elise's lottery win had bothered you. Created quite a stir in the press, that even your wife had lost confidence in your financial stability. In your ability to keep her in the lifestyle she'd become very accustomed to. So did the Street, your investors, perhaps the public? She'd become a sudden liability, Henri, threatening your livelihood, all you'd built, as you've said. So you planned the most magnificent celebration possible and draped yourself over her all week for anyone to see. Ask anyone, they would have said you doted on her, loved her with every fiber of your being. A good one, sir. Quite a good con."

Henri said nothing during this exchange and his face betrayed nothing, confirmed nothing. Todd figured it was his turn to speak again.

"One million dollars, sir, or I go to the press and reveal what I know. Remember, I'm one of those insiders in the case, directly involved. Consider what this revelation might do to your new-found reputation, to your renewed sense of commitment, not to mention the continuing good health of your great company. Everyone likes a success story, but what they enjoy even more is the downfall of the rich and famous."

Henri drummed his fingers against his desk.

"Well?" Todd asked.

Just then the office door opened, and Todd swung around, fearing that the man had called for security, or the cops. Instead, who stood before him now, well, let's just say Todd's mouth could have vacuumed the carpet.

"Give him the money, Henri, and let's be done with him."

"Do you think that's wise?" Henri asked her.

"It's all he cares about, the money," said Brandy Alexander, looking great in her sharply cut business suit, a royal blue which worked well with her luscious and lustrous blonde hair. "Hello, Todd—and yes, Henri knows Richard Booker is not your real name. We had a lot to talk about when we left London, didn't we dear?"

"Dear?" Todd asked.

"Todd," Henri said, "meet my new creative director."

"Not just that, but after a decent interval, the fifth Mrs. Henri Procopio, and thank God for that. I'm so tired of being Brandy Alexander, really, what the hell was my father thinking giving me a name like that. Serves him right, his misfortunes."

"But . . . Brandy, are you sure? I mean . . ."

Todd turned back to Henri, who was beaming brightly over the new babe in his life. Todd hadn't gotten the girl, but that's not what he'd been in this for. Meeting her on the plane had been pure accident. As Brandy said, the money was the game. So stay focused. "One million dollars, Henri, and all this—the company, the girl, it's all yours. You win the big jackpot."

Henri paused before picking up the phone and calling his bank. He barked orders into the receiver until he was speaking with the manager of the bank, and then instructed the man to wire "one million dollars"—Todd liked the sound of that—into an account and proceeded to read the series of numbers off Todd's slip of paper. The bank manager didn't question anything, that's what having power meant. Henri at last set the receiver down and gazed over at Todd. Henri's expression wasn't kindly, no one liked to lose that much money so quickly. Still, Todd was grinning the entire time, a wire transfer was like cash; it would be at his disposal today.

"A pleasure doing business with you, sir." Todd stood, shook the man's hand, and then congratulated him on the new lady in his life. "She's a peach, you take very good care of her. And Brandy, don't let the money spoil you, don't become an Elise."

"She's forbidden to play the lottery," Henri said.

Todd gave Henri a conspirator's smile, and then made his way out of the office, heading down the corridor with more than a bounce in his step. He found Brandy chasing after him, calling his name. He turned and faced her, unable to find any suitable words. He'd gotten what he'd always wanted, so had she, he supposed. And then he asked her, "Are you happy?"

"Yes, I am now. Daddy was furious with me, said my little stunt cost him a big deal, he lost out on this takeover bid, one of the bankers from where he'd gotten the ransom money called his other investors, feared Daddy was in some kind of trouble, maybe they shouldn't be throwing their money in with his. Todd, Daddy was trying to buy Looking Great—he was planning to buy it—for me, as my reward for getting through Cambridge."

Todd grinned. "You beat him to it, didn't you? Didn't need no degree in Shakespeare."

"Todd, that's not proper English," Brandy said.

"Bloody hell, who cares."

"Hey, Todd, I've got a question, something that's been bugging me since I got back."

"What's that?"

"Who killed Vance Timberlake?"

"I suppose that's one for Inspector Brury to answer. Me, I've had my fill of murder plots. The idea of a wife trying to kill her husband, that's enough for me."

Brandy leaned in and kissed Todd on the lips, a goodbye kiss.

"We had some good times together, Brandy, but you know what we never did do?"

"What's that?"

"We never did join the mile-high club."

Brandy laughed at him. "Speak for yourself," she said. "Goodbye, Todd Gleason, take care of yourself, and take care of Toad, too. He okay?"

"That stupid frog?" Todd said with a grin. "Yeah, he's the only one I know who truly knows how to keep a secret."

EPILOGUE

"So endeth this chronicle," Mark Twain wrote at the end of *The Adventures of Tom Sawyer,* himself unwilling at that time to reveal any more of the lives of the people he'd written about. "Most of the characters that perform in this book still live, and are prosperous and happy," Twain continued. "Some day it may seem worthwhile to take up the story of the younger ones again, and see what sort of men and women they turned out to be; therefore it will be wisest not to reveal any of that part of their lives at present."

Bollocks, as any Londoner might say, don't you want to know what happened next?

In London . . .

Larry, whose full name was Lawrence Lassister and who had done time in prison for assault and battery, gave up his life of crime on that fateful Saturday night in January, and that following Monday morning applied for a license to be an official cab driver in London. He'd had lots of practice driving the tricky streets, and his only concern was fitting inside the front part of the cab. He still feared the cops might come after him for his connection in the events leading up to the Mayfair Murder, which is what the local press had dubbed the case. But they never did.

Bobo, whose full name was Beauregard Bolotov, hence Bobo—got a job at Waterstone's Bookstore on Charing Cross

Road but still lived on the Isle of Dogs with Bonnie and Clyde, at least until the June wedding. Then he and Beth, who still worked for that British publisher as an editor, would live together at her flat in Marylebone. He did receive a visit from Inspector Brury after his fingerprints were lifted at Clive's Vauxhall flat. There were no charges brought, no evidence of any wrongdoing. He'd moved onto reading *The Prince and the Pauper.*

Beth Simon still talked a lot. But mostly they were someone else's words. Her favorite activity was reading books aloud to Bobo, it gave them a distraction from what they were both thinking about, that magical wedding night when all would be bliss. She was thinking of changing jobs to record audio books. Beth didn't hear from Todd again, not that she expected to, but she did receive a postcard from Andy. He said he'd be in touch some day, maybe he'd drop in for the wedding.

Detective Inspector Albert Brury went to the doctor and got proper medication for his stomach ailment and was told to cut back on stress. Like that was possible, a job like his. But the job did have one benefit, satisfaction when the right thing happened to end a case. He'd been at work a few days after the Mayfair Murder—how he hated the press and their labels, first daddys-girl and now this—when his phone rang, saying they had a floater. This one was genuine, pulled out of the Thames by a dockworker. The victim had two bullet holes, one in the shoulder and another in his thigh. Both shots fired from Brury's own gun, so ballistic tests had proved. That's not what had killed him though, an autopsy revealed. No, his throat had been crushed. Brury was currently heading a task force investigating all of Clive's reputed jobs, courtesy of a safe that had been found inside Clive's flat. The safe matched one that Vance Timberlake had owned, and when Brury had gotten it open, he'd discovered all sorts of interesting information. The most telling: a gun with Clara Timberlake's fingerprints on it, the caliber a direct match with the gun that had killed her husband. Brury had shaken his head over that one, wondering if any marriage was truly sacred. Couldn't people just divorce?

Clive Remington was buried in a pauper's grave and as far as anyone knew, the fortune he'd amassed as a professional hit man sat lonely and ignored in some bank account, collecting piles of interest. That was one piece of information that went with him to his grave.

Fiona Brury was told by her father that she had to get her act together, no more wasting away her life. She had applied to Cambridge University, and was admitted after her interview. One of the fellows was quoted as saying she looks "like a walking statue, perfectly sculpted." When she arrived at school, Fiona made instant friends with a homely-looking girl named Jennifer Most and passed her Shakespeare course with an A. She went punting with a guy named Liam, who favored blondes.

In New York . . .

Thomas Marquand Alexander II wanted nothing to do with his daughter, how could she have treated him so horribly after all he'd done for her? His wife, whose name was Candy, knew nothing of the fake kidnapping and so Thomas was forced to endure family dinners with Brandy his wife insisted upon hosting. When it was announced that Brandy would be marrying Henri Procopio, Thomas fell to the floor. He'd had a heart attack, but the prognosis was good and he returned to Bernstein, Gilbert & Young without further incident. Though the buyout of Looking Great Cosmetics hadn't happened, he'd been rewarded with a full partnership for his insight into the complex world of the stock market.

Henri Procopio maintained his position as the chairman of Looking Great Cosmetics, and now flush with cash and a healthy business reputation, he was busy expanding his company's reach. Currently there were plans to launch Looking Great's "Youth America" line in England—albeit with the clever new name "English Youth"—and Henri himself had promised to be in the center of Leicester Square for the unveiling of the new billboard which would announce his company's arrival on the British Isles. He made sure that Althea booked him anywhere but at the Savoy. Beautiful place, but too many memories.

Brandy Alexander took like a fish (frog?) to water as the head of the new creative division of Looking Great. She had drive, she had personality, and she was something nice to look at. She'd never forget Todd Gleason, though, not the way he'd showed her that life was meant to be lived to the fullest and you had to search out your dreams no matter what, even if that required taking drastic measures to break free of the constraints of your parents. Her engagement to Henri Procopio catapulted her into New York society, and she was taken under the wing of one Mimi Ledbetter, who knew anyone and everyone and who had recovered nicely from losing her own fortune.

Donald Birdie actually found his spine and once he'd returned to Tuckerville he gave Marta an ultimatum. She either stopped bossing him around or he'd divorce her, ha, how do you like that? You can either live happily with me and all the money, or by yourself and half. Marta liked the idea of living with all the money and since then had rejoined her charitable works in her small town, including protesting against people who wore fur coats. She only wore hers when alone, usually to bed. Donald never did call the cops on Todd, even after he'd received that bill from London. He figured he owed Todd Gleason a break. Look what the damn con man had done for him, after all. He'd given him something back, and not just money.

Somewhere other than London or New York . . .

Andy Simon made off with millions of dollars, money he'd made on the surge in Looking Great's stock. He'd invested his client's money, that same Miss Mimi Ledbetter, and then used the money from Todd's offshore account to finance his own purchase of the stock. When on that Monday morning the stock price soared thanks to the press over Elise Procopio's death, Andy sold at a high price and steered his incredible profits into a bank account of his own, one also controlled offshore. He realized the time to get out was then, and so on that fateful day he claimed to leave for lunch, and like a delinquent father going out for cigarettes, he never returned to the gainful employment of Bernstein, Gilbert, Young & Alexander. Andy was currently living on some remote part of the world, tan and relaxed and sipping on those Mai Tais he'd dreamed of.

Todd Gleason. Ah, what became of our friend Todd? He sublet his apartment in New York, set up a new bank account all on his own—he'd once been involved in the financial world, he still had some contacts that could help him. Currently his million-dollar windfall was earning interest each and every day. He was last seen hopping a schooner out of the Florida Keys, with his laptop and one suitcase and a small plastic aquarium that carried with him his pet frog. That big frog tank was too bulky, and besides, Todd had destroyed it after removing the false bottom from it and extracting the only set of papers he deemed too important to lock in some dumb file cabinet or even a bank's safe deposit box. A driver's license, credit cards, social security card, birth certificate, and most importantly, a passport. A whole new identity, or maybe a return to a previous one?

Toad had always kept good watch over him, no one would have suspected to look in the frog tank for clues on Todd's mysterious life. And now those treasured papers would enable Todd to continue to live this chosen, nomadic life of his. Gone were thoughts about Clive and Fiona, about Beth and Bobo and Larry, Birdie and Marta, Henri and Elise, Inspector Brury and the doomed Timberlakes. Even the fictional Richard Booker, whose investment schemes seemed to be a thing of the past, was relegated to history. The only person he couldn't forget was one lovely Brandy Alexander, she wasn't so easy to put out of his mind. They had shared too much, themselves, their minds and bodies, their hearts, their lust and zest for life and each other and the grand adventures they schemed together. Todd reminded himself next time he was on a plane—which he hoped was a long way away—to talk to the person next to him. You never knew who you'd meet.

For now, he hopped that tiny boat and with sun beaming high above him—no fog here—the shimmering blue water stretched endlessly before him. Todd readied himself for his next adventure, wherever that might be. Andy was right about one thing, he could hardly retire from what had become his way of life, it was second nature. For now, though, he just wanted to disappear for a while.

When he arrived at his port of call, he had to hand over his passport.

"Anything to declare?"

"One frog," Todd said, holding up the portable frog tank, where Toad was happily swimming.

"Welcome to Paradise, Mister . . ."

The name spoken by the customs official wasn't Gleason. You didn't actually think Todd Gleason was his real name, did you? What kind of con man do you think he is?

ABOUT THE AUTHOR

Joseph Pittman is the author of three previous novels: *Legend's End, When the World Was Small,* and *Tilting at Windmills,* which was an alternate selection of the Literary Guild and Doubleday Book Club. His novels have been translated into several languages. *London Frog* is his first venture into crime fiction; he's at work on the next caper featuring Todd Gleason.